PUFFIN BOOKS

YOUNG SAMURAI

THE WAY OF THE DRAGON

Praise for *Young Samurai: The Way of the Warrior*:

'A fantastic adventure that floors the reader on page one and keeps them there until the end. The pace is furious and the martial arts detail authentic' – Eoin Colfer, author of the bestselling Artemis Fowl series

'Bradford comes out swinging in this fast-paced adventure . . . and produces an adventure novel to rank among the genre's best. This book earns the literary equivalent of a black belt' – *Publishers Weekly*

'I promise you will hold your breath until the end . . . this is a super novel' – *First News*

'The story brims with energy, suspense and thrilling, if violent, action' – *Books for Keeps*

'This is a very fast-paced book, with tons of action . . . the book keeps things moving right along with no dull moments' – *School Library Journal*

'A cutting-edge James Bond thriller, Oriental style' – *Japan Times*

Praise for *Young Samurai: The Way of the Sword*:

'Fierce fiction . . . captivating for young readers' – *Daily Telegraph*

'Addictive' – *Evening Standard*

Chris Bradford likes to fly through the air. He has thrown himself over Victoria Falls on a bungee cord, out of an airplane in New Zealand and off a French mountain on a paraglider, but he has always managed to land safely – something he learnt from his martial arts . . .

Chris joined a judo club aged seven where his love of throwing people over his shoulder, punching the air and bowing lots started. Since those early years, he has trained in karate, kickboxing, samurai swordsmanship and has earned his black belt in *taijutsu*, the secret fighting art of the ninja.

Before writing the Young Samurai series, Chris was a professional musician and songwriter. He's even performed to HRH Queen Elizabeth II (but he suspects she found his band a bit noisy).

Chris lives in a village on the South Downs with his wife, Sarah, and two cats called Tigger and Rhubarb.

To discover more about Chris go to *www.youngsamurai.com*

Books by Chris Bradford

The Young Samurai series (in reading order)
THE WAY OF THE WARRIOR
THE WAY OF THE SWORD
THE WAY OF THE DRAGON

Published exclusively for World Book Day 2010
THE WAY OF FIRE

YOUNG SAMURAI

THE WAY OF THE DRAGON

CHRIS BRADFORD

PUFFIN

PUFFIN BOOKS

Published by the Penguin Group
Penguin Books Ltd, 80 Strand, London WC2R ORL, England
Penguin Group (USA) Inc., 375 Hudson Street, New York, New York 10014, USA
Penguin Group (Canada), 90 Eglinton Avenue East, Suite 700, Toronto, Ontario, Canada M4P 2Y3
(a division of Pearson Penguin Canada Inc.)
Penguin Ireland, 25 St Stephen's Green, Dublin 2, Ireland (a division of Penguin Books Ltd)
Penguin Group (Australia), 250 Camberwell Road, Camberwell, Victoria 3124, Australia
(a division of Pearson Australia Group Pty Ltd)
Penguin Books India Pvt Ltd, 11 Community Centre, Panchsheel Park, New Delhi – 110 017, India
Penguin Group (NZ), 67 Apollo Drive, Rosedale, North Shore 0632, New Zealand
(a division of Pearson New Zealand Ltd)
Penguin Books (South Africa) (Pty) Ltd, 24 Sturdee Avenue, Rosebank, Johannesburg 2196, South Africa

Penguin Books Ltd, Registered Offices: 80 Strand, London WC2R ORL, England

puffinbooks.com

First published 2010
2

Text copyright © Chris Bradford, 2010
Cover illustration copyright © Paul Young, 2010
Map copyright © Robert Nelmes, 2008
All rights reserved

The moral right of the author has been asserted

Set in 11.5/15.5pt Monotype Bembo by Palimpsest Book Production Limited,
Grangemouth, Stirlingshire
Made and printed in England by Clays Ltd, St Ives plc

Except in the United States of America, this book is sold subject to the condition that it shall not, by
way of trade or otherwise, be lent, resold, hired out, or otherwise circulated without the publisher's
prior consent in any form of binding or cover other than that in which it is published and without a
similar condition including this condition being imposed on the subsequent purchaser

British Library Cataloguing in Publication Data
A CIP catalogue record for this book is available from the British Library

ISBN: 978-0-141-32432-6

Disclaimer: *Young Samurai: The Way of the Dragon* is a work of fiction, and while based on real
historical figures, events and locations, the book does not profess to be accurate in this regard.
Young Samurai: The Way of the Dragon is more an echo of the times than a re-enactment of history.

Warning: Do not attempt any of the techniques described within this book without the
supervision of a qualified martial arts instructor. These can be highly dangerous moves and
result in fatal injuries. The author and publisher take no responsibility for any
injuries resulting from attempting these techniques.

www.greenpenguin.co.uk

Penguin Books is committed to a sustainable future
for our business, our readers and our planet.
The book in your hands is made from paper
certified by the Forest Stewardship Council.

For Sarah, my wife

CONTENTS

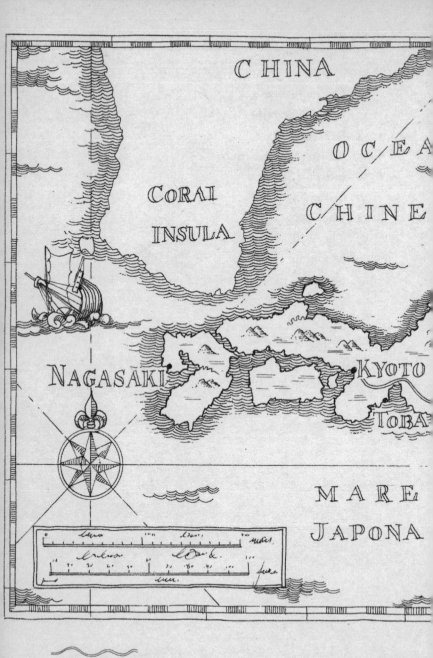

CHINA

OCEA

CORAI

CHINE

INSULA

NAGASAKI

KYOTO

TOBA

MARE

JAPONA

TOKAIDO ROAD

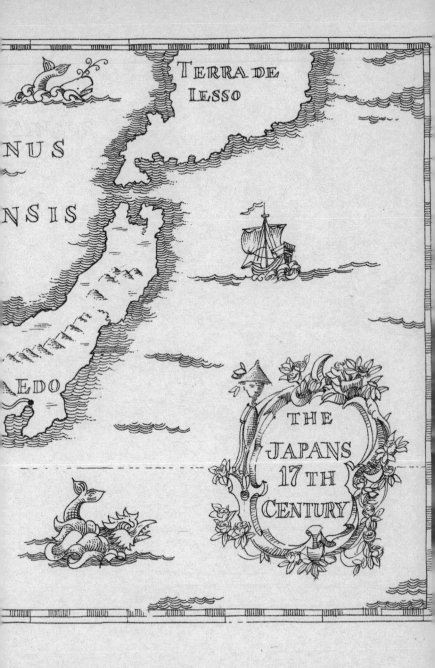

TERRA DE
IESSO

NUS

NSIS

EDO

THE
JAPANS
17 TH
CENTURY

PROLOGUE
THE ASSASSIN

Japan, June 1613

Silent as a shadow, the assassin flitted from roof to roof.

Hidden by the darkness of night, the ninja crossed the moat, scaled the inner bailey wall and infiltrated deep into the castle grounds. His objective, the main tower, was a formidable keep of eight floors that sat at the heart of the supposedly impregnable castle.

Evading the samurai guards on the outer walls had been a simple matter. Lethargic due to the hot, airless night, they were more concerned about their own discomfort than the safety of their *daimyo* lord within the tower. Besides, their very belief that the castle was impenetrable meant the guards were lax in their duty – who would even attempt to break into such a fortress?

For the assassin, the hardest part would be getting inside the keep. The *daimyo*'s personal bodyguard wouldn't be so negligent and the ninja had come as close as he could by traversing the roofs of the outer buildings. He now had to cross open ground to the solid stone base of the tower.

The ninja dropped from the roof and skirted the edge of a courtyard, using the plum and *sakura* cherry trees for cover. Passing silently through a tea garden with an oval pond, he made his way to the central well house. The assassin ducked inside as he heard a samurai patrol approach.

When the way was clear, the ninja darted across to the keep and like a black-skinned gecko effortlessly scaled the steep slope of its immense base. Swiftly reaching the fourth floor, he slipped in through an open window.

Once inside, the assassin knew exactly where he was going. Padding down the darkened corridor, he passed several *shoji* doors then bore right, making for a wooden staircase. He was about to ascend when a guard suddenly appeared at the top of the stairs.

Like smoke, the ninja sank back into the shadows, his all-black *shinobi shozoku* clothing rendering him virtually invisible. Quietly, he drew a *tantō* knife in readiness to slit the man's throat.

Oblivious to his proximity to death, the guard came down the stairs and walked straight past. The assassin allowed the man to live, having no wish to draw attention to his presence within the keep. As soon as the guard rounded the corner, the ninja resheathed his blade and climbed the stairs to the upper corridor.

Through the thin paper *shoji* before him, he could see the halos of two candles glowing in the gloom. Sliding open the door a notch, he put a single eye to the crack. A man knelt before an altar deep in prayer. There were no samurai present.

The assassin crept inside.

When he was within striking distance, the ninja reached

into a pouch on his belt and removed a rectangular object wrapped in black oilskin. He placed it on the floor beside the worshipping man and gave a brief bow.

'About time,' growled the man.

Without turning round, the man picked up the package and unwrapped it to reveal a worn leatherbound book.

'The *rutter*!' he breathed, caressing its cover, then opening its pages to examine the sea charts, ocean reports and meticulous logging of tides, compass bearings and star constellations. 'Now we possess what is rightfully ours. To think, the fortune of the world is in my hands. The secrets of the oceans laid bare for our nation to command the trade routes. It's our divine right to rule the seas.'

The man placed the logbook on the altar. 'And what of the boy?' he asked, his back to the ninja still. 'Is he dead?'

'No.'

'Why not? My instructions were explicit.'

'As you know, the samurai Masamoto has been training the boy in the Way of the Warrior,' explained the ninja. 'The boy is now highly skilled and has proven somewhat . . . resilient.'

'Resilient? Are you telling me a mere boy has defeated the great Dokugan Ryu?'

Dragon Eye's single emerald-green eye flared in annoyance at the man's mockery. He contemplated snapping the man's neck there and then, but he had yet to receive payment for retrieving the *rutter*. Such pleasures would have to wait.

'I employed you because you were the best. The most ruthless,' continued the man. 'Am I mistaken in my judgement, Dragon Eye? Why haven't you killed him?'

'Because you may still need him.'

The man turned round, his face cast in shadow.

'What could I possibly want with Jack Fletcher?'

'The *rutter* is encrypted. Only the boy knows the code.'

'How do *you* know that?' demanded the man, a note of alarm registering in his voice. 'Have you been trying to break the cipher yourself?'

'Of course,' revealed the ninja. 'After the mistake of acquiring the Portuguese dictionary, I thought it wise to check the contents before delivery.'

'Did you have any success?' asked the man.

'Not entirely. The unfamiliar combination of Portuguese and English made the task somewhat more complex than anticipated.'

'No matter. It's of little consequence,' said the man, evidently pleased that the knowledge remained secret from the ninja. 'There's a Franciscan monk in the dungeons, a mathematician and fluent in both the languages. The mere promise of freedom should secure his decoding services.'

'And what about the *gaijin* boy?' asked Dragon Eye.

'Once the code's broken, complete your mission,' ordered the man, turning to kneel before the altar once more. 'Kill him.'

1

THE CRUTCH

Jack's blood pounded in his ears. His heart raced. His lungs burnt for oxygen. But he couldn't stop now.

He tore headlong through the bamboo forest, ducking and weaving between the maze of thick stems that stretched like bony fingers into a vast canopy of olive-green leaves.

'Where's he gone?' came a shout from behind.

Jack didn't stop running, despite his protesting muscles. He would not give up the pursuit.

Ever since Jack's fateful arrival in Japan, when his boat, the *Alexandria*, had been shipwrecked then attacked by ninja, the assassin Dragon Eye had been the bane of his life. The ninja had murdered his father then followed Jack across Japan, hunting him down until finally stealing his father's *rutter*.

Jack was now intent on finding the ninja and getting the logbook back.

'We've lost him!' declared a second voice in disbelief.

Jack slowed his pace and frantically looked around. His friends were right. The man they were chasing had vanished into the thicket.

Yamato and Akiko caught up with Jack. Akiko was forced

to sit down and rest. She still wasn't fully recovered from her recent poisoning and the chase had taken its toll on her. The usual white glow of her complexion had dulled and dark shadows ringed her half-moon eyes.

Jack felt a pang of guilt. Even though Akiko didn't blame him, he was the reason for her condition. In an attempt to protect the *rutter*, Jack had hidden it in the castle of *daimyo* Takatomi, the lord of Kyoto Province. It had seemed the safest place. He now knew different. Dragon Eye had broken in, Akiko had almost died trying to defend Jack, and *daimyo* Takatomi's life had been put in danger.

'How could he have got away?' demanded Yamato, leaning upon his *bō* staff and catching his breath. 'He was crippled!'

'He must have tricked us,' said Jack, turning on the spot, his eyes scouring the forest for any sign of disturbance. 'Or else he's doubled back.'

Jack knew his friend was as determined in his pursuit as he was. Four years ago, Dragon Eye had assassinated Yamato's older brother, Tenno.

'I can't believe he stole Akiko's pearl!' exclaimed Yamato, kicking out in fury at a nearby bamboo. He yowled in pain as his foot collided with its rock-hard stem.

Akiko sighed and rolled her eyes at her cousin's characteristic hotheadedness. 'Don't worry,' she said, tying her hair back, several long black strands having come loose during the pursuit, 'there are plenty more where that came from.'

'That's not the point. He took the pearl, but didn't give us any information in return.'

Jack agreed with Yamato. This had been the whole purpose of their mission into the foothills of the Iga mountains. Shamefully dismissed from samurai school for jeopardizing *daimyo* Takatomi's safety, they'd been sent to Akiko's mother in Toba until a final decision was made as to their fate. On the way, though, their samurai guide, Kuma-san, had dislocated his shoulder in a fall from his horse. They'd been forced to stop over in Kameyama while he recovered. It was during this time they'd learnt from a passing merchant that a crippled man called Orochi had been bragging about knowing the infamous Dragon Eye. The village of Kabuto, where Orochi supposedly lived, was not that far, so the three of them had set off to find him.

Jack hoped that by finding Orochi they might discover where Dragon Eye's lair was. They could then inform Yamato's father, Masamoto Takeshi, of the murdering ninja's location, and maybe retrieve his father's *rutter* too. This, he prayed, would redeem him and his friends in the eyes of the legendary swordsman and they would be allowed back to the *Niten Ichi Ryū* to continue their training as samurai.

Kabuto turned out to be little more than a scattering of farmhouses built on a crossroads, with a decrepit roadside inn that served the few travellers who made their way from the main Tokaido Road to the castle town of Ueno.

It was in the bar that they found Orochi.

As Jack and the others entered, the bar went quiet. Jack's appearance often caused quite a stir, especially outside Kyoto where foreigners were rarely seen. His thick straw-blond hair and sky-blue eyes fascinated the black-haired, dark-eyed Japanese. The problem was, despite being only fourteen years old, Jack's height and strength now exceeded many of the smaller Japanese men and they tended to react with suspicion or fear, especially since Jack dressed and acted like a samurai warrior.

Jack glanced around. The bar appeared to be more gambling den than rest stop. Low tables, sticky with spilt *saké*, were the subject of several dice and card games. A mix of merchants, wandering samurai and farmers eyed the newcomers warily. When Akiko entered, there was a low murmur of manly approval and Jack noticed that, aside from a small nervous serving girl in one corner, there were no women.

The three of them made their way over to the counter, the eyes of every customer following them.

'Excuse me?' asked Yamato of the proprietor, a compact barrel of a man with meat slabs for hands. 'Do you know where we can find Orochi-san?'

The man grunted and gave a single nod of his head towards the far corner of the bar. In a darkened recess lit by a single candle sat a hunched man, a wooden crutch propped up behind him.

'May we talk with you a moment?' asked Yamato as they approached.

'Depends on who's buying,' wheezed the man, looking them up and down and clearly wondering what a spiky-haired boy of samurai status was doing with a pretty girl and a foreigner in such a disreputable bar.

'I guess we are,' replied Yamato, bowing in acknowledgement.

'Then you're welcome to join me. Even the *gaijin*.'

Jack ignored the insulting term for a foreigner. This man was their only lead and they needed him on their side. Besides, it could only work to their advantage if Orochi wasn't aware that Jack spoke fluent Japanese.

The man raised a deformed-looking left hand at the proprietor and asked for *saké*. With the drink ordered and Orochi having apparently accepted his three guests, conversation and gaming resumed throughout the bar.

Jack, Akiko and Yamato sat cross-legged on the opposite side of the low table, while the serving girl delivered a large flask of *saké* and a single small cup. She took payment from Yamato, then left.

'I must apologize for my terrible table manners,' Orochi wheezed genially to Akiko, indicating his dirty right leg resting upon a cushion, the sole of his foot in full view. 'I don't mean to insult you, but I've been crippled from birth, you see.'

'It's not a problem,' she replied, pouring Orochi his drink, as was the custom if a woman was present.

Picking up the cup with his good hand, Orochi knocked it back in one go. Akiko refilled it.

'We'd like some information,' began Akiko, keeping her voice low as Orochi reached for his *saké* again, 'about Dokugan Ryu's whereabouts.'

Orochi's hand faltered at the mention of Dragon Eye's name, but then he took the cup and downed its contents.

'This *saké*'s horrible!' he complained, coughing loudly and thumping his chest. 'To get the stuff *you're* after, though, costs a lot more.'

He gave Yamato a meaningful look, while Akiko poured him another cup. Yamato understood the implication and nodded to Akiko. She removed a large milky-white pearl from the sleeve of her kimono and placed it on the table before Orochi.

'That should *more* than cover your costs,' Yamato stated.

The man's dark eyes gleamed at the sight of the pearl, then darted around the room to check no one was paying them attention. Satisfied, Orochi's mouth broke into a smile as crooked as his hand.

He reached for the pearl.

Yamato grabbed hold of the man's wrist.

'I usually pay on delivery of an order,' observed Yamato.

'Of course,' agreed Orochi, withdrawing his hand. Then, in a low voice, he whispered, 'If I were you, I'd visit the village of –'

A bell tinkled as the entrance *shoji* slid open and two new customers came in. Orochi stopped speaking and waited for them to be seated at the counter. Jack noticed one of the men had a little finger missing as he beckoned to the proprietor to place his order.

'You were saying?' prompted Yamato.

For a moment Orochi appeared distracted, but his attention quickly returned to the pearl.

'Yes . . . would you excuse me? The call of nature,' he said, reaching for his crutch. 'Takes me a little while to get there, so when I feel the need I have to go. I'm sure you understand.'

As Orochi rose to his feet, he fell against the table, knocking over the *saké* flask and spilling its contents across the surface.

'This weakness in my leg is insufferable,' he mumbled, by way of an apology. 'I'll be back in a moment. Girl, clear this up!'

Bent double, Orochi hobbled over to the back door. The serving girl hurried to their table and began to clear up the mess. As she did so, Jack noticed something was missing.

'Where's the pearl?'

They looked on the floor and then, with a dread realization, stared at one another. Orochi had stolen it!

The three of them ran out of the back door.

Orochi was nowhere to be seen. Then Akiko caught a glimpse of a figure entering the bamboo forest, which backed on to the inn. Surprisingly nimble, Orochi had disappeared into its depths before any of them managed to reach the forest edge. They plunged in after him and gave chase . . . until the thief vanished into the thicket.

'Did you hear that?' said Akiko, interrupting Jack's search for Orochi.

'Hear what?' asked Jack.

'Shhh, listen!'

They all fell silent.

There was the gentle wash of noise, like a wave upon the shore, as the leaves rustled high in the canopy. This peaceful sound was punctuated by the occasional creak of bamboo stems rubbing against one another, but there was nothing out of the ordinary to Jack's ears.

'Can't you hear it?' she insisted, before whispering, 'Hold your breath.'

Mouths closed, they all looked at one another.

Someone could *still* be heard breathing.

The sensitivity training Sensei Kano, their blind *bōjutsu* master at samurai school, had taught them paid off once again.

Jack immediately pinpointed the source of the sound and crept towards it.

Suddenly Orochi exploded from the thicket, barely five paces ahead of Jack. He'd been hiding beside them all along.

'Come back!' shouted Jack, his cry disturbing a bird high up in the canopy.

'Go on!' Akiko urged, too weary to give chase. 'I'll look after the bags.'

Yamato threw down his knapsack and hurried after Jack, who was already racing after Orochi. Then the man ducked down again into the thicket.

Jack kept going. He wouldn't be fooled this time. As he hit the spot where Orochi disappeared, his feet went from under him and he tumbled head over heels down a steep slope.

Rolling back on to his feet at the bottom, he found himself on a forest track. A few moments later, Yamato joined him. Forewarned of the danger by Jack's cry, he'd managed to avoid falling down the slope himself.

'Which way did he go?' asked Yamato.

'I don't know. I was too busy working out which way was up!' Jack replied irritably, brushing dead leaves from his hair.

'Right, you head that way and I'll go in the opposite direction,' Yamato commanded. 'Shout if you find him.'

Yamato sprinted off.

Jack was about to do the same, when he heard the sound of snapping bamboo. He spun round.

'I know you're there,' said Jack.

Orochi got unsteadily to his feet with the help of his crutch and emerged from the undergrowth.

'Ah! You understand Japanese. That's good.'

He gave Jack a pitiful bow and hobbled towards him.

'You wouldn't hurt a cripple, would you?' he pleaded, his misshapen right hand outstretched in surrender.

'You're not lame!' exclaimed Jack, studying the man carefully. 'Wasn't it your left hand that was deformed before?'

Orochi smiled his crooked smile.

'True. But I had you all fooled, didn't I?' he replied as he straightened his leg, stood to his full height and unclasped his twisted hand.

With lightning speed, he pulled apart the shaft of his wooden crutch, revealing a jagged steel spike.

Orochi drove the deadly weapon at Jack's chest.

BLOW DART

Only Jack's samurai training prevented him getting skewered.

He twisted his body sideways, the spike passing within a hair's breadth of his heart. Without hesitating, Jack whipped the knife-edge of his right hand straight into his attacker's neck.

Choking on the blow to his windpipe, Orochi staggered backwards against the bamboo. As he fought for breath, Jack went to finish him. But Orochi lashed out again with the spike and forced Jack into a tightly knit grove of bamboo stems. Confident of victory, Orochi launched the sharp end of the spike directly between Jack's eyes.

Hemmed in on either side by bamboo, Jack had nowhere to go but down. He dropped to his knees. There was a sickening crunch as the metal spike pierced the bamboo stem where his head had just been.

Orochi swore in frustration, his weapon now stuck. Jack punched him hard in the stomach. Orochi grunted but refused to let go. Jack then grabbed the back of Orochi's ankle in one hand and rammed his shoulder into the man's gut, sweeping him off his feet.

Orochi crashed to the ground, winded and dazed.

Jack seized the opportunity to put the man into an arm-lock, but he hadn't counted on Orochi still holding on to his weapon. Jerked free of the stem, the man was now swinging it towards Jack's ribs. Jack blocked the strike but was knocked aside. In an instant Orochi was on top of him.

'No escape this time, *gaijin*!' spat Orochi, raising his weapon for the fatal blow.

As the spike plunged towards his head, Jack scrabbled at the earth to get away. His fingers came across a loose piece of bamboo and he snatched it up to protect his face.

The point pierced the stem, stopping just short of his right eyeball.

Orochi yelled in fury and pushed down on the spike. Jack's arms shook as he kept the deadly tip away. Orochi leant his full weight to the task but Jack was stronger, and when Orochi had fully committed Jack twisted sideways, wrenching the spike out of Orochi's hand and causing him to fall forward face first into the earth.

Throwing the spike deep into the thicket, Jack then pounced on Orochi before he could recover. He dropped his knee on to the man's shoulder, twisting Orochi's left arm into a lock.

Orochi was pinned.

He fought to get free, but Jack applied pressure to the man's elbow joint. Orochi screamed in pain and immediately ceased moving.

'Stop! Please! You'll break my arm!' he pleaded, spitting earth from his mouth.

'Don't struggle then,' replied Jack, before calling for Yamato, his shout disturbing a large unseen bird in the canopy.

Orochi attempted to escape, but Jack put on the lock again. Hard. Orochi whimpered and lay still.

'Are you going to kill me?' he moaned.

'No, I'm not going to kill you,' replied Jack. 'I just want to know where Dragon Eye is. Then I'll let you go.'

'Telling you *that* is more than my life's worth,' the man spat. His eyes glanced nervously around as if he expected the ninja to appear at the very mention of his name.

'Your life's not worth much so far as I can tell,' Jack retorted. 'Besides, the pearl you stole should more than make up for it. In fact, I think you should return it until you tell me what I need to know.'

Jack leant harder into the lock. Orochi cried out and, to Jack's surprise, the small white pearl fell from his mouth.

'You can have this back once you tell me where Dragon Eye is,' said Jack, tucking the gem into his *obi*.

'What if I don't tell you?'

'We'll kill you.'

'But you said –'

'No, what I said was, I'm not going to kill you. But I can't promise the same for my Japanese friends. As true-born samurai, they'd see it as their duty to rid the world of your sort.'

Orochi swallowed, understanding the truth behind Jack's words. They both knew that the samurai dealt out justice and, as a convicted thief and liar, Orochi would receive little mercy.

'Let me go and I'll tell you. I give you my word,' promised Orochi reluctantly. 'But you're walking into your own grave.'

Jack released him, glad that his ruse had worked. He knew

16

full well that neither Yamato nor Akiko had the authority to kill a man for such a petty crime. 'So, tell me, where can I find Dragon Eye?

Orochi sat up and massaged his arm. 'Where did you learn to fight like that?'

'The *Niten Ichi Ryū* in Kyoto.'

'You're one of Masamoto Takeshi's students!' he exclaimed in wide-eyed wonder. 'I'd heard rumours he'd adopted a *gaijin* boy, but I never dreamt the great Masamoto would train him to become a samurai –'

'Stop wasting my time. Where's Dragon Eye?'

'You must have a death wish, young samurai, to go seeking that devil!' breathed Orochi, shaking his head in disbelief. 'Last I heard, his ninja clan had settled on the west side of the Iga mountain range, close to the village of Shindo. Visit the Dragon Temple there and ask for –'

Orochi stopped speaking. His mouth opened and closed like a fish out of water, but no sound emerged. His eyes went glassy, his gaze unfocused. Then he slumped to one side, twitching twice before lying dead still.

'I warned you, Orochi!' said Jack, taking a cautious step towards the prone figure. 'No more tricks.'

Wary of the man, Jack picked up a piece of bamboo and prodded Orochi with the tip. He got no reaction. Then he noticed a tiny dart sticking out of the man's neck.

A blow dart, poisoned to kill.

Such a weapon could only mean . . . Jack spun round, bringing the bamboo stem up to defend himself.

But he couldn't see any ninja.

That didn't necessarily mean there was none. Ninja were

trained in the art of stealth. There could be one, or a hundred assassins, hiding among the thicket.

Jack tightened his grip on the bamboo. How he wished Masamoto hadn't confiscated his samurai swords as part of his suspension from school. If there was ever a time Jack needed a blade, this was it.

Jack listened hard for the slightest indication of an approaching assassin, but he could only hear the swish of leaves high up in the canopy and the creaking of bamboo. He retreated back into the tightly knit grove of stems for cover. As he did, there was a tiny *phut* sound and a thin dart struck the bamboo directly in front of his face.

Jack hunched down lower. Peering between the stems, he desperately searched for the source of the poisoned darts. But the attacker was too well hidden.

Hearing the sound of another bird taking flight, he glanced up and this time saw two dark-green shapes. Dressed in green *shinobi shozoku*, the ninja blended perfectly with their surroundings as they leapt cat-like between the uppermost stems of the forest to get a better fix on Jack.

Gripping the bamboo with their legs, the two ninja raised their blowpipes and fired.

3

THE THIRD NINJA

Jack bolted from his hiding place as the darts struck the bamboo grove on either side of him.

Keeping his head low, he weaved in between the stems. He heard several more darts pierce the bamboo as he fled.

But he didn't look back.

He hit the forest track and ran for his life.

Eventually he slowed down, checking the canopy above and behind him. It was difficult to tell but it appeared he'd given the two ninja the slip. Jack hurried back in the direction of the village, worried that Akiko might also be in danger.

Out of nowhere, a ninja dropped like a panther in front of him.

Jack held up his improvised bamboo sword and prepared to defend himself.

The ninja calmly raised his hands.

But not in surrender. Both palms were armed with metal claws. The ninja's *shuko* were used to aid climbing, but also proved lethal weapons, their four curved spikes capable of ripping through flesh and lacerating any enemy.

Jack didn't wait. He struck first.

The ninja didn't even flinch as the stem cut down towards his head.

Then inexplicably Jack's arms came to an abrupt halt.

Glancing up, Jack saw that his improvised sword had collided with an overhanging bamboo stem. A long weapon was useless in such confined surroundings.

The ninja hissed and, in the blink of an eye, he swiped with his claws, catching both of Jack's outstretched arms. Jack grimaced as eight bloody lines were scored into his skin, forcing him to drop the piece of bamboo.

Ignoring the pain, Jack front-kicked the assassin in the chest.

The ninja, not expecting such a powerful and rapid kick from a mere boy, was thrown backwards into a clump of bamboo. Jack followed up with a jumping side-kick, but the ninja leapt above it and shot up the bamboo stem like a monkey.

Jack, recalling his own days as a rigging monkey on-board the *Alexandria*, grabbed hold of the bamboo as if it were a mast and clambered after the ninja. He pursued the assassin high into the canopy, astounding the ninja with his unexpected agility and confidence at climbing. The ninja fled.

Jack jumped from stem to stem after him.

At this height, the bamboo was green and flexible and Jack swayed towards his enemy. He caught him hard in the gut with a front kick. The ninja lost his grip under the force of the blow, crying out as he tumbled through the leaves to the ground far below.

The ninja lay motionless, sprawled in the thicket, one leg

twisted at an impossible angle, and Jack breathed a sigh of relief.

He began to drop back down, when the second ninja suddenly emerged out of the foliage below him, brandishing a sword. Jack heard a sharp crack as the ninja sliced through the stem he was holding on to.

Jack plummeted towards the earth, the wind whistling past his ears. His hands grabbed blindly for anything to break his fall. Somehow he caught hold of another stem, but this bamboo was young and bent under his weight. He continued to fall. The bamboo finally gave way and snapped. Gravity took hold and Jack dropped like a stone for the last five metres.

The impact knocked all the breath out of him.

As he lay there dazed, he heard something land close by.

Glancing behind, he saw the green ninja stalking him, his *shuko* claws primed to strike and rip the skin from his back. Jack crawled on all fours, desperate to get away. The ninja crouched winding up to strike.

Jack pulled himself to his feet and stumbled into the thicket, but he knew he had little chance of survival. His fate was sealed as a third ninja dropped down in front of him and blocked his escape.

This ninja wore a black *shinobi shozoku*.

For a moment, no one moved.

Then the black ninja kicked Jack in the chest, throwing him backwards. At the same time a *shuriken* knife plunged into a bamboo stem right where Jack had just been standing.

Before Jack could register what had happened, the black ninja attacked him again. This time sweeping him off his feet.

He landed hard upon the ground only to see the green ninja above him, in mid-strike, his *shuko* claws swiping through thin air instead of gouging deep into Jack's back.

The green ninja hissed in frustration, then glared in furious amazement at the black ninja. He struck with his claws, but the black ninja blocked and countered with a lightning spear-hand thrust to the throat. The green ninja gagged and staggered backwards. He went on the attack again, swiping with his *shuko*, but the black ninja stood his ground, calmly drew a *tantō* and sliced a cruel line across the green ninja's chest. Staring down in shock as blood soaked his chest, the green ninja backed away, then fled in panic into the thicket.

The black ninja turned on Jack, blade in hand.

Jack stared up in terror.

'Jack!' came a cry.

The black ninja didn't hesitate.

Flicking the blood from the blade, the ninja leapt up a bamboo stem, disappeared into the canopy and was gone.

Moments later, Yamato burst through the thicket to find Jack lying on the ground, his arms bloodied and his face a curious combination of fear and disbelief.

'Are you all right?' demanded Yamato, his *bō* staff raised to fight. 'I found Orochi dead. What happened?'

'We were attacked by ninja and they killed him,' replied Jack, grimacing as he inspected his wounds. Though the score marks weren't deep, they were painful. 'Then they came after me, but . . . but I was saved by another ninja.'

'Saved? Are you sure you haven't fallen on your head?' said Yamato, helping him to his feet. 'The ninja are our sworn enemy.'

'I'm sure of it. Twice this ninja stopped the other one killing me.'

'Well, I've never heard of a guardian ninja!' laughed Yamato. 'Whatever the reason, you should be grateful.'

'Yes. But what *is* the reason?'

'Who knows, but we'd better get back to Akiko if ninja are around.'

'First, let's search this ninja,' replied Jack, going over to the prone body of the fallen assassin.

'But what about Akiko?'

'It won't take long. Besides, she can handle herself.' They both knew this to be true, though Jack didn't want to admit that she was still weak from her poisoning and therefore vulnerable. He would have to work quickly.

'What are you looking for?' asked Yamato.

'I don't know,' answered Jack, rifling through the man's garments. 'A clue of some sort.'

Yamato looked around uneasily, worried the other ninja would come back. Jack beckoned him over.

'Look at this.' Jack held up the man's hand. 'A finger's missing.' He pulled off the cowl to reveal the ninja's face. A thin stream of blood ran out of the corner of the man's mouth.

'So what?' said Yamato.

'Don't you recognize him? He was one of the customers who entered the bar after us. No wonder Orochi ran. He must have known they were after him.'

Jack continued to search the ninja. He found a length of hooked climbing rope attached to the back of his belt, five *shuriken* stars, some *tetsu bishi* spikes in a pouch and an *inro* case containing several pills and some unidentifiable powder. On the man's hip was a *tantō*.

Jack unsheathed the knife, cursing as the blade cut into his thumb.

'Careful, Jack!' said Yamato. 'It could be poisoned.'

'Thanks for the warning,' replied Jack grimly, sucking the blood from his wound.

The blade gleamed maliciously in the forest light. A series of *kanji* characters could be seen etched into the steel.

'What does that say?' asked Jack, whose knowledge of *kanji* was still limited despite Akiko's daily tuition.

'Kunitome!' growled the ninja who had come to. He seized Jack by the throat. 'It's the name of the maker of the blade.'

Jack gasped for air, the fierce grip of the ninja crushing his windpipe. Too shocked by the man's unexpected revival, Jack forgot all his training and futilely tugged at the man's hand.

Yamato rushed forward and kicked the ninja in the ribs, but the assassin refused to let go. Jack's face turned bright red, his eyes bulging. Yamato lifted his *bō* staff and struck the ninja's broken leg. Writhing in agony, the ninja released Jack and Yamato quickly dragged his friend beyond the assassin's reach.

'A samurai stealing,' the ninja spat, in between pained gasps. 'How dishonourable!'

'We weren't stealing. We were looking for clues,' croaked Jack, getting unsteadily to his feet. 'I needed to know who you were and where Dragon Eye is.'

The ninja gave a throaty laugh and more blood bubbled from his lips.

'We should turn him in, Jack. Take him to Ueno Castle,' suggested Yamato, uneasy with interrogating a ninja. It was as dangerous as taunting a wounded lion. 'They'll get the truth from him.'

'No,' Jack countered. 'But maybe he'd be willing to tell us about Dragon Eye in exchange for his life?'

'No samurai can command my life,' replied the ninja, removing a dark round bead from the *inro* on his belt.

Popping it into his mouth, he bit down hard on the poison pill and his lips started to foam.

'You'll never find Dokugan Ryu, young samurai,' he croaked with his last breath. 'But he'll find you . . .'

4

THE DEMON BLADE

'THAT was a stupid idea!' exclaimed Yamato, ignoring the *sencha* offered to him by Akiko. 'Once again you almost got yourself killed!'

'But now we know where Dragon Eye's camp is,' Jack protested. 'It's near Shindo. That's less than half a day's journey from here. We can't give up now.'

Jack looked to Akiko for support. She finished sipping her tea and was about to speak, but Yamato broke in.

'All you have is the name of a village and a temple. Do you think we'll simply drop in and find Dokugan Ryu and his ninja clan enjoying afternoon tea? Anyway, Orochi was a thief and probably lying. It's a miracle we got Akiko's pearl back.'

'But this lead's got to be worth chasing,' insisted Jack. 'It was fate when we bumped into that tea merchant. We were *meant* to find Orochi. The fact that ninja attacked us and Orochi got killed is proof we're on the right path.'

'No! We're already in enough trouble with my father as it is. I can't risk it again. He would never forgive me. And then we'll *never* return to the *Niten Ichi Ryū*!'

Yamato ended the conversation by turning his back on Jack. He stared out across the ravine from their tea house to the rocky heights opposite. Located on a ridge beside the Tokaido Road, the Kameyama tea house commanded a spectacular view and attracted numerous visitors from Kyoto. Following the glorious summer day, the tea house was packed with travellers watching the sun set over the rugged beauty of the mountains.

Jack moodily toyed with the dead ninja's *tantō*, its gleaming steel marked only by a patch of dry blood where Jack had cut his thumb the day before. After the ninja had committed suicide with the poison pill, Jack had decided to keep the blade. Besides, it was the only weapon he now possessed since their suspension from the *Niten Ichi Ryū*.

He didn't blame Masamoto for his decision. He realized now that he'd been foolish to try and hide the existence of his father's *rutter* from the one man who could truly protect him from Dragon Eye. But Jack had thought he'd been protecting his guardian Masamoto by keeping it secret. Jack's father had made him swear not to tell anyone of the logbook's existence; had entrusted him with the code that kept its information safe from prying eyes. It had been his responsibility to ensure the *rutter* never fell into the wrong hands. At the time Jack hadn't known whom to trust with such a valuable and sought-after possession, so he hadn't told anyone. And that was why he'd hidden it in *daimyo* Takatomi's castle.

The *rutter* was also his last link to his father and his only chance of a secure future. He'd had to do all he could to protect it. If one day he ever did reach the port of Nagasaki, his experience as a rigging monkey and his ability as a navigator would hopefully gain him passage on-board a ship bound for England where Jess, his little sister, was still waiting for his return.

Or at least he hoped she was. Without a family in England, her future was as uncertain as his. But with the *rutter* he could look after both of them as the respected pilot of a ship, just like his father had been before Dragon Eye murdered him in cold blood.

The deadly steel of the *tantō* seemed to throb in Jack's hand at the very thought of Dragon Eye garrotting his father. Revenge flashed through his mind. Everything Jack held dear to him had been taken by that ninja – his father, the *rutter* and almost Akiko's life too.

When Jack and his father had set out with the Dutch crew of the *Alexandria* from England four years ago, they had dreamt of discovering new lands, making their fortune and returning home heroes. Not for one moment had Jack thought he would end up alone, in a dangerous foreign land, training to be a samurai warrior.

But now he wouldn't even be doing that.

'Where did you get that knife?' demanded the owner of the tea house, breaking Jack's thoughts as the old man cleared away their cups of *sencha*.

'We found it . . . in a forest,' Jack replied, the question taking him by surprise.

The proprietor's beady eyes studied him with an unsettling intensity. He clearly didn't believe Jack.

'Do you know what that is?' the old man enquired, his gaze not leaving Jack's face, almost as if he was unwilling to look back down at the knife.

'It's a *tantō* . . .'

'Yes, but not just any *tantō* . . .' The proprietor drew closer and spoke under his breath, not with reverence, but with fear. 'That knife was forged by the swordsmith Kunitome-san.'

'We know,' interjected Yamato, annoyed by the owner's prying. 'It says so on the blade.'

'You know! Yet you still keep it?'

'Why not?' asked Jack, baffled by the owner's strange behaviour.

'Surely you've heard that Kunitome-san's swords are evil. They're not the weapons of a virtuous samurai,' he explained, looking at Yamato. 'Kunitome-san's work is infamous round these parts. He resides but ten *ri* west of here in the village of Shindo.'

At the mention of the village's name, Jack glanced over at Akiko and Yamato. Both their faces registered the same astonishment he felt. This was too much of a coincidence.

'Kunitome-san is a violent man and possesses an ill-balanced mind, some say verging on madness,' confided the proprietor. 'These traits are said to pass into his blades. Such a weapon as yours hungers for blood, impels their owner to commit murder!'

Jack gazed down at the *tantō*. It looked like any other knife, but then he recalled the throb of revenge it triggered in him when he thought of his father's death.

'We appreciate your concern,' said Akiko, a wry smile on her lips, 'but we're too old to believe in such superstitions. You can't scare us.'

'I'm not trying to scare you. I'm trying to warn you.'

The proprietor put down his tray.

'If you would allow me to tell you a story, then you might understand.'

29

Akiko politely acknowledged his request with a nod of her head and the old man knelt beside them.

'Kunitome-san is a student of the greatest swordsmith to have ever lived, Shizu-san of the Soshu School of Sword-making. Several years ago, Kunitome-san challenged his master to see who could make the finer sword. They both worked at their forges day and night. Eventually Kunitome-san produced a magnificent weapon he called *Juuchi Yosamu*, Ten Thousand Cold Nights. Shizu-san also completed his, which he named *Yawaraka-Te*, Tender Hands. With both swords finished, they agreed to test the results.

'The contest was for each to suspend their blades in a small creek with the cutting edge facing the current. A local monk was asked to preside over the competition. Kunitome-san went first. His sword sliced through everything that flowed its way – dead leaves, a lotus flower, several fish, the very air that blew upon it. Impressed with his protégé's work, Shizu-san then lowered his sword into the stream and waited patiently.

'It didn't cut a thing. Not a single leaf was parted; flowers kissed the steel and floated by; fish swam right up to it; the air sang as it gently blew by the blade.'

'So Kunitome-san's was the better blade,' interrupted Yamato.

'No! The monk declared Shizu-san the winner. Kunitome-san contested the decision, for his master's sword had failed to cut anything. The monk then explained. The first sword was by all accounts a fine weapon. However, it was blood-thirsty and evil for it didn't discriminate as to who or what it cut. "It may just as well be cutting butterflies as severing heads," the monk had said. Shizu-san's sword, on the other

30

hand, was by far the finer of the two for it didn't needlessly cut that which was innocent and undeserving of death. The spirit in his sword demonstrated a benevolent power worthy of a true samurai.

'Because of this, it's believed that a Kunitome blade, once drawn, must draw blood before it can be returned to its *saya*, even to the point of forcing its wielder to wound himself or commit suicide.'

Jack glanced down at his healing thumb, then at the *tantō* with his blood still stained upon the steel. Perhaps there was some truth in the old man's warning.

'Mark my words, that *tantō* is a demon blade. It's cursed and will breed bloodlust in those who carry it.'

'Old man, are you serving or gossiping?' demanded a samurai who sat impatiently at a table on the other side of the tea house.

'My apologies,' replied the proprietor, bowing. 'I will be with you right now.'

He got up and retrieved his tray.

'My advice is to lose that *tantō* in the forest you found it in.'

The proprietor then bowed and left the three of them to ponder his words. They all gazed at the blade, its awakened spirit seeming to draw them in as if they were caught in a whirlpool.

'What did I tell you?' said Jack excitedly, breaking the spell. 'It's fate. We have to go to Shindo. The *tantō* comes from the same village that Orochi mentioned. This must mean the ninja came from around there too.'

'Didn't you hear anything the man just said?' asked Yamato,

his dark brown eyes wide in disbelief at Jack's jubilant reaction to the news. 'That knife is cursed.'

'Surely you don't believe that?' dismissed Jack, though he wasn't quite as certain as his bravado made out.

'Yet you believe in fate; that we should go to Shindo.'

'Yes, but this is different,' Jack argued, cautiously sheathing the *tantō* and slipping it into the *obi* around his waist. 'The knife's superstition. This is a clear sign we must follow our destiny. We must follow the Way of the Dragon – find where the ninja hides. Isn't that right, Akiko?'

Akiko was flattening the folds of her ivory-coloured silk kimono and appeared to be thinking very carefully before answering. Jack had used the very words she'd whispered to him after she'd awoken from her poisoning. Jack just hoped Akiko would still be on his side, despite the obvious danger of such a venture.

'I think we should go,' agreed Akiko. 'Masamoto-sama made clear to us that we *have* to tell him any information we know about Dokugan Ryu. That includes anything we find out about him too. Imagine if we could give Masamoto-sama the location of the ninja's headquarters. We may even get back Jack's *rutter*.'

'Why are you suddenly so keen on pursuing this ninja, Akiko?' Yamato demanded, turning on his cousin. 'You almost died the last time we agreed to help Jack.'

'More reason for me to want to find the ninja. Besides, weren't *you* the one who suggested we should try and trap him in the first place? It was your golden opportunity to get revenge on Dragon Eye for your brother's murder, a chance to restore the family honour.'

'Yes . . .' spluttered Yamato, 'but . . . that was before my father found out and dismissed us. He would never forgive me if we tried to capture Dragon Eye ourselves.'

'We're not attempting to capture him,' appeased Akiko. 'We simply need to locate his camp and tell your father.'

'I still think it's a bad idea. What about the mysterious black ninja who saved Jack? That makes no sense.' Yamato stared gravely at the two of them. 'Have either of you thought that the reason we're discovering these clues is that Dragon Eye wants us to find him? That he's leading us into a trap?'

There was a moment of uncomfortable silence as the possible truth sank in. Then Akiko dismissed the idea.

'Ninja don't just fight samurai. They fight one another too. The black ninja was probably from a rival clan and the green ninja out of their territory. Yamato, you probably turned up just in time to save Jack's life.'

Yamato looked unconvinced.

'If we don't go, what else are we going to do?' implored Jack. 'With his dislocated shoulder, Kuma-san said he won't be fit to travel to Toba for at least another day or so.'

'He's right,' agreed Akiko. 'If we take the horses, we could get to Shindo and back in a day. Jack can ride with me. Kuma-san wouldn't question us about visiting a nearby temple.'

Yamato remained tight-lipped, turning his attention to the glorious sunset instead. A stillness settled over the tea house as the sun clipped the top of a mountain peak. Golden rays of light fingered into an indigo-blue sky that hung like a silken kimono above the hazy range of mountain ridges and darkening valleys.

As the light began to fade, Jack made one last plea.

'This is our one and only opportunity to find Dragon Eye before he finds us again.'

'But he has no reason to return. He's got your *rutter*,' countered Yamato.

'The logbook is encrypted. Only I know how to decipher it,' Jack revealed. 'Once Dragon Eye realizes this, he *will* be back.'

Jack knew the ninja was enlisting the help of a Chinese cryptologist, but he doubted the man could easily break a code written in such an unfamiliar language. It would take time. The question was: how long?

Dragon Eye might lose patience and decide to break Jack instead.

5

MOTHER LOVE

'I've a very bad feeling about this place,' muttered Yamato, his right hand anxiously clasping the shaft of his *bō* staff.

Shindo's only road was deserted. Dust swirled in lonely eddies and disappeared between a row of rundown shacks that appeared as if they'd been dumped from the sky then forgotten. Though the day was warm and sunny, heat and light seemed to shun the village and the interiors of every abode remained dark and uninviting.

'It's a ghost town,' said Jack, a chill running down his spine as they tethered their two horses and entered the lifeless village.

'Not quite,' whispered Akiko. 'We're being watched.'

Jack and Yamato exchanged nervous glances.

'By whom?' Yamato asked.

'That little girl for one,' replied Akiko, nodding towards a thatched hut on their right.

Hidden in darkness, a small dirty face with wide fearful eyes peeked out at them, then disappeared. Akiko headed over to the shack, looking back over her shoulder when Jack and Yamato failed to follow.

'Come on, you two. I think you can handle a little girl, can't you?'

Shamed by their lack of nerve, they both hurried after her.

Akiko peered into the darkness beyond the doorway, then called, 'Hello? Excuse me?'

Inside, they could hear a rattling wheeze of breath like a dying dog's. Suddenly a man's hollow-cheeked face appeared at the door.

'Leave us be,' he snapped. 'We've nothing to give you.'

The little girl they'd seen earlier was now hiding behind the man's legs, her eyes fixated on Jack's blond hair. Jack smiled at her.

'We're sorry to disturb you, but we don't want anything,' explained Akiko.

'Where is everyone?' Yamato asked.

'They left. You should too.'

The man began to push the flimsy door of his hut closed.

'But we've come to find Kunitome-san,' Jack insisted.

The man stared at Jack as if noticing his presence for the first time. His face remained blank, the strange sight of a foreigner clearly nothing compared to the horrors he'd already witnessed.

The man snorted.

'That devil! He's dead!'

'What? When did that happen?' Jack asked. 'Who killed him?'

The man sighed, the burden of conversation seeming to drain him.

'He committed suicide. By his own sword,' spat the man.

'He's the reason this village is dead. That swordmaker was a blessing and a curse for Shindo. His skill drew people here from far and wide and we villagers welcomed the money they brought. But his art in devilry, forging evil blades, attracted the worst sort. Now he's gone, no one comes. But his spirit remains. It casts a dark shadow over Shindo. You should leave. This place is bad karma.'

'So why haven't you left?' Yamato enquired, putting his hand against the door as the man tried to close it.

'We would, but do you hear that?' said the man, referring to the rattling wheeze. 'That's my sick mother. She refuses to die. And until she passes away, we're stuck in this death trap. Now goodbye.'

With that, he shut the door in their faces.

They looked at one another, astounded at the man's story.

'Seems we've come to the end of the trail,' said Yamato, the relief in his voice apparent. 'No point in hanging around, we'd better head back before Kuma-san notices we're gone.'

'No,' said Jack, walking in the opposite direction to Yamato. 'We've still got to find the Dragon Temple that Orochi talked about. Look, that must be it.'

The village road ended in a large, eerie temple that sat upon an earthen mound, its red and green paint faded and peeling. Tiles were missing from the roof and two carved dragon finials had fallen from its corners to lie rotting on the ground. The main door to the temple was open and about as tempting as a tomb.

'You're not going in there, are you?' said Yamato, appealing to Akiko for support. 'It looks as if it's going to fall down at any moment!'

Akiko smiled apologetically, then followed Jack up the worn stone steps.

Inside, as if all light had been sucked out, the temple appeared an ominous cave of darkness and shadows. Where the smell of incense should have been, only the stink of decay hung in the air.

Jack stepped across the threshold and peered into the gloom.

He almost cried out at the sight of two gargantuan warriors on either side of him, their muscles rippling, their faces contorted. One, who was baring his teeth, wielded a huge thunderbolt club. The other, his mouth tightly shut, swung an immense sword.

Jack stumbled into Akiko.

'They're just *Niō*,' she laughed. 'Temple guardians.'

'They're terrifying!' exclaimed Jack, gathering his wits at the sight of the gigantic wooden statues.

He followed Akiko warily inside and over to the central altar where a number of smaller effigies encircled a dust-ridden Buddha. 'What are the warrior statues guarding?'

'The Buddha, of course. The right statue is Agyō. He symbolizes violence. The statue on the left with the sword is Ungyō. He depicts strength,' Akiko explained, then pointed to their faces. 'Do you see the first one has his mouth open and the other has his closed? They form the sounds "ah" and "un", the first and last characters of the Buddhist language. Together they encompass all knowledge.'

'History lesson over,' Yamato butted in. 'There's no one here. This is a complete waste of time. Now that Kunitome-san's committed suicide, we've hit a dead end. We'll never find Dragon Eye, so let's go.'

As Yamato turned to leave, there was a shuffling noise behind the Buddha.

'The swordmaker didn't commit suicide!' rasped a figure in the darkness.

They all spun round to defend themselves. An old hunched woman, dressed in a ragged cowl and robe, hobbled towards them through the shadows.

'Our apologies,' said Akiko, startled. 'We didn't mean to disturb your prayers.'

'Prayers!' she croaked. 'I long since abandoned my faith in Buddha. I was sleeping until you rats scurried in.'

'We were just going,' explained Yamato, taking a step away from the foul-looking woman, her face veiled by the lice-ridden cowl.

But Jack remained where he was. 'What did you just say about Kunitome-san?'

'You're not from here, are you, boy?' the hag spat. She sniffed the air, then seemed to gag on the smell. 'You're *gaijin*!'

Jack ignored the insult. 'Did you say the swordmaker did *not* commit suicide?'

'No. He didn't.'

'Then what happened?'

The old woman stretched forth a bony hand, its skin dead as a corpse. She remained silent, but the message was clear. Akiko reached inside the folds of her kimono, pulled out a small string of coins, removed one and dropped it into the woman's waiting palm. The hag snatched her prizeaway.

'He didn't commit suicide, but he *was* killed by his own sword.'

'What do you mean?' asked Jack.

'Kunitome-san had been commissioned to make a special sword for a very special client,' she explained, letting her fingers run down the splintered edge of an effigy's carved wooden blade. 'The sword was called *Kuro Kumo*, Black Cloud, on account that it was finished on the night of a great storm. It was his finest sword yet, sharper and deadlier than any blade in existence. It turned out to be the last sword he ever made.'

The hag shuffled closer to Jack.

'That night the client came and demanded a cutting test to prove the quality of the blade. Kunitome-san arranged for four criminals to be bound over a sand mound. Black Cloud went through all four bodies like a ripe plum cleft in two. You should have heard their screams.'

She extended a talon of a finger and ran it across Jack's neck. He shuddered at her touch.

'The client was so impressed he beheaded Kunitome-san there and then with his own creation.'

'Why did he do that?' asked Jack, swallowing back his revulsion.

'He wanted to ensure Kunitome-san never made another blade that could defeat Black Cloud. But when Kunitome-san was murdered, a fragment of his maddened soul entered the sword. As if possessed, the storm then raged all night long, ripping the heart out of the village, ravaging all the crops, destroying the temple. Little was left standing by the morning.'

'Who was the client?' asked Akiko.

The old woman looked up, and though Jack couldn't see her face within the cowl, he swore she was smiling.

'Dokugan Ryu, of course. The one you seek.'

The hag leant forward and whispered into Jack's ear, 'You wish to know where he is?'

'Yes,' breathed Jack.

The old woman put out her skeletal hand again. Akiko dropped another coin into the grimy palm.

'Where is he?' demanded Jack, impatient for the answer.

She beckoned Jack closer, then croaked, 'Behind you!'

All three of them spun round to be confronted by a huge green eye.

The old woman cackled at their gasps of shock. But the eye only belonged to a large dragon carving hanging over the doorway, its head turned to one side, its forked tongue flicking out of its red-painted mouth.

'Very funny,' snarled Yamato, lowering his guard. 'There's no one there.'

'Oh . . . but there is,' corrected the woman. 'Dokugan Ryu will always be behind you, sneaking up on you like a poisonous shadow.'

'Let's go,' Yamato insisted. 'This witch is mad.'

Jack had to agree and turned to leave.

'But it would help if you knew who Dokugan Ryu really is, wouldn't it?' whispered the old hag.

Jack stopped in his tracks.

'Don't you want to know?' she taunted, her palm already outstretched, fingers beckoning like an upturned crab.

Jack looked to Akiko. Yamato shook his head in dismay

as Akiko begrudgingly handed over another coin.

'You're very eager for knowledge, young ones. And I won't disappoint,' the hag cackled, slipping the coin into her filthy robes. 'Dokugan Ryu is the exiled samurai lord, Hattori Tatsuo.'

'That's ridiculous!' scoffed Yamato. 'That warlord was killed in the Great Battle of Nakasendo.'

'Listen, you little rat!' she hissed, cutting him off. 'You paid for a story and I *will* tell it. Hattori Tatsuo was born in Yamagata Castle in the summer of the Year of the Snake. As a child his eye became infected with the smallpox. He pulled the diseased organ out of his skull himself!'

Akiko recoiled at the thought.

'Because of his missing eye, his own mother considered him unfit to be the future head of the Hattori family, so began favouring his younger brother as heir. She even poisoned Tatsuo during dinner once, but miraculously he survived, though somewhat maddened and his eye now green as jade.'

Yamato was shaking his head in disbelief and signing to Jack that the woman was crazy.

'Tatsuo then killed his own brother in order to ensure his rise to power. When he was barely sixteen, he went on his first raid with his father. His father was killed during a skirmish, some say by Tatsuo himself. Tatsuo was now head of the family. But not satisfied with this, he set his eye upon becoming the *daimyo* of northern Japan. First, though, he sought revenge for his mother's betrayal.'

'How?' breathed Akiko, but not really wanting to know the answer.

'How else? By gouging out *both* her eyes!' screeched the hag.

42

'That's enough!' ordered Yamato, seeing Akiko wince at the horrific image the woman had conjured. 'None of this nonsense explains how Tatsuo supposedly ended up a ninja.'

The old hag, tutting, wagged a bony finger at Yamato.

'Such impatience! There is more. Much more. On the battlefield, Tatsuo gained a fearsome reputation as a ruthless warrior. Soon he became *daimyo* of all northern Honshu. During his campaigns, he'd borne a son. So he now desired all of Japan for his heir. Tatsuo's army crushed all those before him –'

'Until they were defeated at Nakasendo,' interjected Yamato.

'Yes, you're quite right. The battle raged many days and nights. But only the combined forces of the southern and central lords, *daimyo* Hasegawa, Takatomi and Kamakura, defeated the great Tatsuo.' She spat on the floor. 'Kamakura, that traitorous samurai, had switched sides and sealed Tatsuo's fate. His army was slaughtered, his son cut down defending him before his very eye, by one of *daimyo* Takatomi's bodyguards. Yet, despite all this, Tatsuo fought to the bitter end.'

'But I've already told you, Hattori Tatsuo was killed in battle,' Yamato stated. 'It's impossible for him to be Dragon Eye.'

'No, Tatsuo survived. He escaped into the Iga mountains. Hunted down, he was forced into hiding. But fortune was on his side at last. A ninja clan took him in, where he studied their secret arts and became the man he is today. Dokugan Ryu, the most feared ninja to have ever lived.'

The old woman sounded almost proud at the idea.

'But how do you know all this?' demanded Jack. 'No one else seems to know his identity.'

'No one's ever asked *me* before,' replied the old woman, pulling back her hood to reveal a gruesomely scarred face . . . with two empty eye sockets.

6
UEKIYA'S GARDEN

Jack touched the arrow buried in the *sakura* tree.

His fingers lightly brushed the weathered flights and the sensation sent a chill through his body despite the sticky summer heat. He couldn't quite believe it was still there, piercing the bark of the cherry blossom tree like a needle in the eye. Its target had been Dragon Eye, but he had escaped, as always.

'Masamoto-sama commanded me not to remove it.'

Jack spun round in surprise to find Uekiya, the old gardener, tending an immaculate rose bush. The withered man blended in like an ancient tree. He was as much a part of the garden as he was of Jack's fond memories of Toba, the little port where he'd first arrived in Japan.

Although the reason for Jack's return was dishonourable, the welcome by Hiroko, Akiko's mother, had been warm and reflected the care she'd given Jack during his first six months in Japan.

After their disturbing encounter with the blind hag, Jack, Akiko and Yamato had hurriedly left Shindo and the next day departed on the final leg of their journey to Toba. The going had been slow due to Kuma-san's injury and was made even more arduous by the stifling heat. Upon their arrival, Hiroko had provided much needed refreshments and organized for the bath to be filled so they could wash away the dirt of the trip. While Yamato took the first *ofuro* and Akiko caught up with her mother's news, Jack had sought the cool shade of the garden to recover.

The old man smiled a toothy grin, obviously pleased to see Jack once more in his garden.

'Did Masamoto-sama give a reason for leaving it?' Jack asked, letting go of the arrow.

'It's to remind us never to lower our guard.'

Uekiya's smile faded as he gently cut a blood-red flower from the bush and presented it to Jack. 'And this rose bush I planted to remind me of Chiro.'

Jack could no longer meet the gardener's gaze. He recalled the night when Dragon Eye had initially attempted to steal the *rutter* from him. It had been the first time Jack had witnessed Akiko's fighting skills, which after two years of training at the *Niten Ichi Ryū* had now been honed to a fine art. Chiro, however, wasn't a warrior. She was Hiroko's maid and had been killed in the attack, while the samurai guard, Taka-san, had been seriously injured defending the home.

It had been a great relief for Jack upon returning to Toba to find Taka-san fully recovered, the only indication of his injury a vicious scar across his belly, which he bore with some pride. But the guilt of Chiro's death still remained.

'Welcome home, Jack-kun,' Uekiya added, forcing a smile back on his face as he continued to prune the rose bush.

'Thank you,' Jack replied, settling down beneath the cool shade of the *sakura* tree. 'After such a long time in Kyoto, it is almost like returning home. I'd forgotten how beautiful your garden was.'

'How can that be?' said the old man, his brow furrowing in puzzlement. 'You've been carrying a piece of it with you ever since you left.'

'You mean my *bonsai*?' asked Jack, referring to the miniature cherry blossom tree he'd been given by the gardener the day he'd departed for samurai school.

'Of course, it's grown from the very tree you sit beneath. It's not dead, is it?'

'No,' said Jack quickly, 'but it does need some attention after the long journey.'

As he had no idea how long he would be staying in Toba, he'd brought the tree back with him in its original carrying case, along with all his other possessions.

'Let me do it,' said Uekiya, putting down his pruning knife. 'Though if the truth be known, I never expected to see it alive again. *Bonsai* are very difficult to grow. Perhaps you do have a little Japanese in you, after all.'

With a wry smile upon his wrinkled face, the old gardener bowed and walked across the little wooden bridge that spanned a pond dotted with pink water lilies. He weaved his way along the pebbled path towards the house, leaving Jack alone to his thoughts.

Jack had spent many happy hours beneath this *sakura* tree. At first recovering from the broken arm he'd sustained escaping the ninja attack on the *Alexandria*; then studying his father's *rutter*; and, most enjoyable of all, being instructed by Akiko in her language and customs. Sitting there now, it was like finding sanctuary again.

But it *wasn't* like returning home.

England was his home. Though after nearly four years, two of which had been at sea, it had become a distant memory. The only things tying him to his native land were his heart, his little sister Jess, his father's *rutter* – now stolen – and a scrap of paper he'd found tucked within it.

Jack opened the *inro* carrying case attached to his *obi* and carefully took out the fragile paper. It was a drawing given to his father by Jess before they'd left for the Japans. As had become habit, his fingers traced the outlines of his dead father, his sister in her summer smock holding hands with his own stick-thin body, and lastly his mother with her angel wings. Wiping a tear from his eye, Jack said a little prayer for Jess. Having only an old, ailing neighbour to rely on for his sister's welfare, he feared for her future without a family. Jack *had* to find his way back to England.

Yet he was trapped by circumstance. Adopted by Masamoto, his guardian considered himself responsible for Jack's care until he was sixteen and deemed 'of age'. Besides, any journey to the southern port of Nagasaki, where foreign trading ships docked, was fraught with danger now that *daimyo* Kamakura, the lord of Edo Province, had begun to rouse the population against Christians and foreigners.

Not only that, Jack had to contend with the constant threat to his life posed by Dragon Eye. He couldn't leave Japan without his father's *rutter*. It was rightfully his and the key to his future. He had to retrieve the logbook before the code was broken. The hunter had now become the hunted. He *had* to find Dragon Eye.

Dokugan Ryu's eyeless mother had laughed at the suggestion of seeking out her ninja son. Dragon Eye was like the wind, she said, and moved with the seasons, never settling in the same place twice. Despite the offer of another coin, she refused to reveal his location. Yamato very much doubted she knew it anyway. He believed she was making the whole story up and they'd wasted their money on worthless lies.

'Nice picture,' Yamato commented, rounding the trunk of the *sakura*, fresh from his bath. 'That the one Akiko rescued from the tree?'

'Yes, it is,' mumbled Jack, startled by his friend's sudden appearance.

He'd been so deep in thought that he hadn't noticed Yamato's approach. Jack carefully folded the parchment and slipped it back inside his *inro*. He was far more guarded with it ever since Kazuki, his arch-rival at school, had snatched the picture from his hands and thrown it into the topmost branches of a maple tree. Thankfully, Akiko had retrieved it for him, with an astounding display of agility.

'I've been thinking we should keep our training up, just in case my father decides to allow us back to school,' suggested Yamato.

Jack looked up in surprise. Clearly, the bath had not only cleansed his friend's body but his mind too. It was the most positive thing Yamato had uttered in ages. He knew his friend feared his father. Masamoto was a hard man to please since the death of his firstborn son, Tenno, and Yamato was desperate for his approval.

Perhaps there was some hope for Yamato and Akiko of going back to the *Niten Ichi Ryū*, but Jack doubted he would ever be allowed to return.

'It'll be like old times. Remember when we used to spar with our *bokken* over there?' said Yamato merrily, indicating a bare patch of training ground at the back of the house.

Jack nodded.

'And he used to thrash you!' cried a small voice.

Jack turned round to see a young boy thundering full pelt across the wooden bridge towards them.

'Jiro!' exclaimed Jack as the boy ran into his arms.

Apart from Akiko, Jiro – her brother – had been Jack's only companion in those early months following his arrival. Back then, he and Yamato hadn't been friends. Jiro was quite right. Their sparring sessions had been more an excuse for Yamato to beat him up. Yamato's harsh instruction, though, had helped Jack learn the basics of sword fighting and this had led him to be invited by Masamoto to train at the *Niten Ichi Ryū*, the One School of Two Heavens.

'You've grown,' observed Jack, measuring up the grinning brown-eyed boy.

'Big enough to carry a sword now!' Jiro replied in a defiant tone.

'Is that right?' said Jack, raising his eyebrows at Yamato. 'Think you're big enough to challenge me, do you?'

'No problem,' said Jiro, resting his fists upon his hips.

'A duel!' exclaimed Yamato in mock horror. 'There's no escape for you, Jack. I'll be the judge. Jiro, get your *bokken*.'

Thrilled at the prospect, Jiro sprinted off to get his wooden sword. It reminded Jack of his own excitement when he'd first trained in the Way of the Warrior. But the opportunity to become a samurai had given Jack more than just a thrill. It had given him hope. For with such fighting skills at his disposal, Jack had a chance of survival. Maybe even of defeating Dragon Eye.

'Yamato,' he asked, while they waited for Jiro to return, 'why were you so convinced the old woman in the Dragon Temple was lying? Isn't there a chance Hattori Tatsuo could have survived to become Dokugan Ryu?'

Yamato rolled his eyes, clearly exasperated that Jack was still pursuing the idea after three days. 'That hag was crazy. She was playing a sick joke on you. Tatsuo died in the Nakasendo War ten years ago.'

'How do you know that for sure?'

'I *know* because my father was *daimyo* Takatomi's personal bodyguard at the time. My father saw Tatsuo's beheading with his own eyes.'

Jack was momentarily stunned into silence. Before he could ask more, though, Jiro came charging out of the house, wielding his *bokken*. He fought his way in mock combat across the garden. Jack couldn't believe the old woman had made everything up. There *had* to be a grain of truth in her story. But maybe she was as convinced in her tale as Jiro was in battling his imaginary ninja.

7

THE PEARL

'Hurry up, Jack!' urged Akiko. 'The sun's about to rise.'

Akiko trotted ahead on her white stallion, the same one Jack had seen her with the morning after the *Alexandria* had been shipwrecked off the coast of Japan. It had been dawn and she'd been praying at a temple overlooking the cove where their ship lay. Jack had spotted the horse before being transfixed by the sight of a dark-haired girl, her skin white as snow. Akiko had been his first impression of Japan.

'The darned thing won't obey me,' complained Jack, struggling to stay mounted on his smaller brown mare. 'Give me a ship any time!'

He bounced along the coastal path behind her, gripping tighter to the mane and desperately trying to match the horse's rhythm. Having been a sailor, Jack had never learnt to ride. The closest experience he'd had was riding the bucking yardarm of the *Alexandria* in a storm.

'You managed to ride all the way from Kyoto to Toba,' noted Akiko.

'Yes, but I rode with Kuma-san on his horse. And look what

happened! We got thrown, he dislocated his shoulder and I bruised my backside!'

Akiko laughed at Jack's pained expression as he continued to jolt along. 'Don't worry, we're nearly there.'

They rounded a small headland and Akiko dismounted. She hurried over to Jack and helped him down.

They'd been in Toba over a month now and, thanks to a good dose of motherly care and attention, Akiko had fully recovered from her poisoning. Though their return hadn't been a matter of choice, she clearly relished being back at home and spending time with her mother and brother. In the half-light, Jack could see her face was aglow, her jet-black eyes sparkling with a newfound energy.

Jack couldn't quite say the same for himself. It was still far too early in the day. Somehow Akiko had managed to persuade him to rise before dawn and join her to watch the sunrise at Meoto Iwa, a headland a little round the coast from Toba. Yamato had sensibly decided to have a lie-in and said he would join them later for sword practice.

Jack followed Akiko down to the rocky shoreline. She seated herself upon a flat rock, crossing her legs in the lotus position in readiness for the sunrise.

Jack breathed in the salty air, the smell instantly evoking memories of his ocean-going days. He itched to be out at sea again, to feel the roll of the deck beneath his feet, to hear the snap of the sails as the wind took hold and to steer a course for home. He looked up into the lightening sky and spotted the northern star still burning in the heavens.

'What are you doing?' asked Akiko, as Jack began to turn on the spot and scan the horizon.

Jack pointed into the distance. 'That way lies England.'

Seeing the longing in his blue eyes, she smiled sadly at him.

'You'll get there one day,' she said, indicating for him to sit beside her, 'but, until then, you should enjoy the moments you have here.'

Jack looked down at Akiko. Perhaps she was right. He was so intent on returning home, he often overlooked the good things about Japan. From the calm order of samurai life to the thrill of wielding a sword, from the exquisite taste of *sushi* to the beauty of the cherry blossom, Japan offered so much more than England could ever give him. And if he did leave for home, he'd miss all his friends greatly – Yamato, Yori, Saburo and, of course, Akiko.

Returning her smile, he sat down next to her and waited for the sun.

'Here it comes,' Akiko whispered, taking a deep breath as golden rays of light fanned out across the horizon.

Out at sea, the morning sun rose between two rocky outcrops. Pitch-black against the crimson sky, their peaks were joined by a huge knotted rope, and upon the larger of the two stacks perched a miniature *torii* gateway.

'What are those?' asked Jack, awestruck at the sight.

'They're the Meoto Iwa,' replied Akiko. 'The sacred Wedded Rocks. Beautiful, aren't they? And over there is Mount Fuji.'

Jack looked to his left and could just see a conical snow-capped peak in the haze on the horizon. He could only imagine how big the mountain was for it to be visible at such a great distance. From here, though, he could cover it with his entire hand.

After the sun had risen and they had completed their

meditation, Akiko paid her respects at the nearby Shinto shrine. When Jack had first attended the *Niten Ichi Ryū*, he hadn't been able to understand the dual religious practices of the Japanese. They followed Buddhism and, at the same time, Shinto, the worship of *kami*, the spirits they believed were contained within everything living and non-living.

Back in England, Jack had been brought up as a Christian, following the Protestant not the Catholic belief system. His father had explained this was the reason Europe was involved in so many conflicts. The division in faith had set Catholic Spain and Portugal against Protestant England. Since the battle for dominance was also being fought at sea and in the New World, this meant the *rutter* had immense significance. The possession of such an accurate navigational logbook, like his father's, could tip the balance of power in favour of one country and its religion over the other.

Yet, in Japan, two religions coexisted in perfect harmony.

It was Buddhism's respectful acceptance of other faiths that had allowed Jack to come to terms with practising Buddhist rituals in samurai school, while remaining at heart a Christian.

His decision was also a matter of survival. With the growing animosity towards foreigners in Japan, Jack needed to blend in as much as possible and show his willingness to accept Japanese beliefs. He needed to prove he was samurai not only in mind and body, but in spirit too.

Jack bowed his head before the Shinto shrine and said a prayer for his father and mother in heaven and for his little sister Jess on the other side of the world, his words carried away by the gentle lapping of the waves.

★　★　★

Walking along the coastal path, Akiko and Jack guided their horses back in the direction of Toba.

'Thank you,' said Jack, feeling at peace and happy to have shared the moment alone with Akiko.

'I thought you'd like to see the ocean again,' she replied, smiling warmly.

Jack nodded. The new dawn had given him fresh perspective and time to think. He would always be a sailor. It was in his blood. But he was now samurai too.

As they climbed a small rise overlooking a crystal-clear cove, Akiko stopped, her hand going to her forehead.

'Are you all right?' asked Jack.

'I'm fine, just a little light-headed,' she replied. 'It must be the sea air.'

'Perhaps you're not fully recovered. You should sit down,' suggested Jack, tying the horses to a nearby tree, then settling beside her at the edge of the cliff.

'It's amazing you survived the poisoning in the first place,' Jack commented, recalling how Akiko had almost been killed by the ninja that Dragon Eye had sent to assassinate him, while he stole the *rutter*. The ninja had favoured a poisoned hairpin as a weapon. Akiko had been struck in the neck and she'd collapsed unconscious. By all accounts, she should have died.

This was just one of a number of unexplained skills and mysteries about Akiko. Like how she'd climbed the maple tree with such grace and agility to retrieve Jack's drawing, or how she'd survived for so long beneath the waterfall during the Circle of Three. Perhaps now was the time to ask such questions.

'When you were sick, I overheard Sensei Yamada and Sensei

Kano mentioning *dokujutsu*, the ninja art of poison. They thought someone might have trained you to resist such poisons and that's why you survived?'

Akiko picked up a small pebble and threw it over the edge, watching it tumble through the air and into the sea.

'It wasn't anything as mysterious as that,' she dismissed. 'I've always been lucky that way. Do you remember when you first met me I used to dive with the *ama* people searching for pearls? Well, I've been stung by jellyfish so many times I lost count. Once I was even bitten by a blowfish, and they're deadly. I was ill for a number of days after, but I recovered. I've just got a high tolerance to things like that.'

That seemed logical to Jack, but it didn't explain her other mysteries. 'So what about . . .'

But Akiko rose to her feet and began to undo her *obi*. Jack gawped in astonishment. A Japanese lady would never remove her *obi* in public. Then again, Akiko was not a typical Japanese girl. Being of samurai class, she shouldn't have associated with the *ama* divers in the first place. It was considered beneath her status. But, as Akiko had once explained to Jack, she loved the freedom of the ocean. It was the only place she could escape the rigid confines of Japanese life.

'Talking of the *ama*, I really need a swim,' announced Akiko.

She noticed Jack staring.

'No peeking,' she laughed, indicating for Jack to turn round, before handing him the outer layer of her kimono. Securing her undergarments tightly round her, she dived off the cliff and into the cove.

Jack rushed to the edge, but could only see the white ripples of water where she'd entered the ocean. He caught sight of a shadow swimming deep within the bay and, if Jack hadn't known better, he would have sworn it was a mermaid.

After a while, though, Akiko hadn't surfaced and he began to worry, fearing that something had happened to her. Then, just like a seal pup, her head popped up on the other side of the cove. She swam over to the inlet beach and beckoned Jack to join her. Jack untied the horses and led them down the path towards her.

By the time he got to the beach, she was almost dry and Jack passed her the kimono. Back turned, he waited patiently for her to get changed.

'You may look now.'

Jack found Akiko holding out her hand. In her palm was a large, closed oval-shaped shell.

'It's an oyster. I spotted it under a rock at the bottom of the cove,' she explained, placing it in his hand. 'Go on, see if there's a pearl inside!'

Jack took the gnarled shell and, using the ninja's *tantō* he carried, prised the shell apart. The knife slipped as it broke the seal and he pricked his finger on the blade again. Jack quickly sheathed the weapon before the cursed *tantō* did any more damage.

Akiko gave a small gasp as Jack opened up the oyster. Inside was a black shiny pearl, the colour of Akiko's eyes.

'That's a rare find,' she breathed. 'It must be one of the most perfect black pearls I've ever seen.'

Jack passed it back to Akiko.

'No,' she said, closing his palm round the precious pearl. 'It's my gift to you.'

Jack wanted to thank her, but for a moment words failed him.

'There you are!' cried the samurai guard Taka-san, riding down the beach on his horse. 'You're summoned back home immediately. Masamoto-sama's on his way.'

8

BUSHIDO

'A disgraced samurai must commit *seppuku*!' Masamoto thundered, delivering his judgement upon Jack.

He sat upon a raised dais in the reception room of Hiroko's house, his face fuming like a volcano. Even after two months, his anger at his adopted son still raged, the scarring that ran down the left-hand side of his face was inflamed and his amber eyes burnt fiercely.

Jack looked fearfully at his guardian. He'd once been told by Akiko what *seppuku* was, but his terror at Masamoto's anger had wiped it clean from his mind. All he knew was that it wasn't good. Jack glanced over to Akiko for an explanation, but she remained bowing, face down to the floor, just as Yamato was.

'*Seppuku* is ritualized suicide,' stated Masamoto, noting Jack's bewilderment. 'In the Way of the Warrior, it's considered an act of bravery for a samurai who knows he's defeated, or disgraced, to take his own life. The deed wipes away all transgressions and the samurai's reputation remains intact.'

Jack now understood. He had disgraced himself in the worst possible way for a samurai. By not telling Masamoto about his father's *rutter*, he had broken the code of *bushido*, the seven virtues a samurai strove to adhere to: Rectitude, Courage, Benevolence, Respect, Honesty, Honour and Loyalty. His dishonesty had cost him his guardian's trust and a lot more besides.

He'd also failed in his fundamental duty as a samurai to serve his lord. By hiding the *rutter* in *daimyo* Takatomi's castle, which Dragon Eye then infiltrated, he had endangered the *daimyo* himself, the very man Masamoto was employed to protect.

Without warning, Masamoto drew his *wakizashi* sword. The blade glinted in the light, hinting at its intent.

'*Seppuku* is an extremely painful and unpleasant way to die. First, you slit open your own belly . . .'

Jack trembled at the thought. He recalled the warning of Father Lucius, the Jesuit priest, now deceased, who'd once taught him Japanese: 'Step out of line and he'll cut you into eight pieces.'

Jack had stepped out of line and he was to pay the price.

All the training he'd struggled through and everything he'd strived for was to come to nothing. He would never see his sister again. He would die in Japan.

'. . . then at the moment of agony, your head is chopped off!'

'It wasn't their fault!' blurted Jack as the fate of his friends suddenly came to mind. Would they be forced to commit *seppuku* too? '*Please* don't punish them for my mistake. I swore them to secrecy and forced them to help me. I hid the *rutter* on my own. Akiko and Yamato are blameless!'

'I admire your loyalty to your friends, Jack-kun, but I've made my decision.'

'I'll leave,' begged Jack, bowing until he was prostrate on the floor. 'I won't burden you any more.'

'You can't leave,' stated Masamoto coolly. 'You're well aware that it's not safe for you to travel alone. We *both* now know that Dokugan Ryu wants you dead – and for good reason. But, more importantly, I'm your guardian and you are my responsibility until you are of age. You can't leave, since you need to return to school.'

'W-what?' stuttered Jack, raising his head to glance at Masamoto.

The samurai was actually grinning at him, the smile crinkling the scarred left-hand side of his face.

'My idea of a little joke, Jack-kun,' said Masamoto, letting out a short grunt of laughter as he resheathed his sword. 'You don't need to commit *seppuku* and I won't chop your head off. You haven't disgraced yourself enough for that.'

'But I thought I'd broken the code of *bushido*,' exclaimed Jack, not appreciating his guardian's macabre sense of humour.

'No, you did many things, but you always maintained *bushido*.'

Jack allowed himself to breathe again as Masamoto settled back on the dais. Picking up a cup of *sencha* from a nearby table, his guardian savoured the brew.

'Sensei Yamada petitioned me on your behalf and I am inclined to agree with him that your decisions, however misguided, were made with the greatest consideration and respect to me. The three of you demonstrated immense loyalty to one another in your actions and you maintained your honour in fighting a formidable foe.'

'So do you mean we're *all* going back to school?' asked Yamato timidly, bowing his head to the *tatami* mat.

'Of course you're going back!' snorted Masamoto, glancing at his son with annoyance. 'But it was important that I showed the rest of the school you'd been disciplined appropriately. What you had done cannot be condoned. You jeopardized *daimyo* Takatomi's safety so deserved to be suspended – in fact you warranted a far greater punishment.'

He stared gravely at each of them in turn to ensure their complete understanding of the severity of the matter.

'However, you also deserve recognition for what you attempted and the bravery you displayed. You were bold, daring and courageous – qualities I wish to foster in all samurai of the *Niten Ichi Ryū*. And in light of your previous service to the *daimyo* Takatomi, his lordship has graciously pardoned you all.'

He clapped loudly once and the *shoji* doors of the reception room slid open. Three of his samurai guards entered carrying weapons. They placed a tall bamboo bow and quiver of hawk-feather arrows before Akiko. Then they presented Jack and Yamato with their confiscated *daishō*, the matched pair of samurai swords that represented the social power and personal honour of a samurai.

'I reinstate your right as samurai to bear arms,' announced Masamoto, indicating for them to pick up their weapons.

Grateful for their reprieve, they all bowed.

Jack reached for his swords. He relished the cool touch of the lacquered *sayas*, the jet-black scabbards decorated only with a small golden phoenix near the hilt. The firebird was Masamoto's family *kamon* and the two swords, the *katana* and the shorter *wakizashi*, had been Masamoto's first *daishō*. Jack had been given them for winning the inter-school *Taryu-Jiai* contest and he was glad to have them back in his possession.

He drew the *katana*, enough to check the blade. Etched into the gleaming steel was a single name.

Shizu.

Jack smiled. Masamoto's *daishō* had been forged by the greatest swordsmith, Shizu-san. Jack now knew the blades were true and that they harboured the benevolent spirit of their maker – unlike the ninja's cursed *tantō* he also possessed.

'Thank you for your forgiveness, Masamoto-sama,' said Jack, bowing once more.

Masamoto nodded his head in acknowledgement and indicated with a wave of his hand that they were to leave. Standing, Jack slipped the two swords into his *obi*, where they rested comfortably against his hip. He couldn't quite believe he was returning to the *Niten Ichi Ryū*. He would be allowed to complete his training. And he would need every ounce of skill for when he faced Dragon Eye next.

At the doorway, Jack hesitated before turning back to Masamoto.

'What is it, Jack-kun?' enquired his guardian.

Jack glanced apprehensively at Yamato. Even though his friend had insisted Hattori Tatsuo was dead, there was still a remote chance he had survived as the old woman had said. And Masamoto *had* commanded them to tell him everything they knew or discovered about Dokugan Ryu. If his guardian knew who the ninja really was, he may have an idea where he was located.

'On our journey to Toba, we met an old woman who said she knew who Dragon Eye was.'

Masamoto put down his teacup and looked at Jack with sudden interest. Yamato started to shake his head, willing Jack to stop talking.

'And? Who is he?' demanded Masamoto.

'Hattori Tatsuo. The woman swore he didn't die in the Nakasendo War.'

Masamoto stared at Jack a moment longer, then began to laugh.

'That is a tale told to scare children, Jack-kun. The Old Warlord of the North coming back from the dead. I'm afraid she was teasing you. I won't deny that there were rumours Hattori Tatsuo had been sighted after the war, but I found them a little difficult to believe.'

'Why?' asked Jack.

'Because I chopped the man's head off.'

Jack nodded slowly, finally accepting the truth. The only lead he had turned out to be a dead end. Literally. He realized now all he could do was wait for Dragon Eye to come to him.

'Dokugan Ryu is no ghost,' said Masamoto, the utterance of the ninja's name making him scowl. 'Evil, despicable and ruthless, yes, but he's an assassin for hire. No more, no less. Talking of which, I've made some careful enquiries as to this *rutter* of yours.'

Jack looked up hopefully.

'I'm afraid no one has come across it, or even heard of it. The ninja himself has gone to ground. Probably in preparation for a new assignment. But considering the value of the *rutter*,

65

I'm sure it will turn up sooner rather than later. I'll let you know if I hear any more.'

'Thank you,' said Jack, bowing to hide his disappointment.

'In the meantime, you should stay alert. If Dragon Eye does fail to decipher it, he will undoubtedly be back. And you need to be ready. That is why, when we return to Kyoto next month for the opening of the Hall of the Hawk, you will have a new sensei. And I understand he is a tyrant.'

'Who is he?' asked Jack, worried the teacher might be as vindictive and bigoted as his *taijutsu* master, Sensei Kyuzo.

'Me!' Masamoto laughed. 'It's time I taught you the Two Heavens.'

9

THE HALL OF THE HAWK

'YOUNG SAMURAI!' roared Masamoto across the expanse of the *Niten Ichi Ryū*'s pebbled courtyard.

The entire school fell silent, having gathered excitedly for the opening ceremony of the *Taka-no-ma*.

Masamoto stood upon the veranda of a magnificent wooden building, accompanied by his sensei, the *daimyo* Takatomi and a Shinto priest.

Though about half the size of the *Butokuden*, the Hall of the Hawk complemented its larger brother like the two swords in a *daishō*. Constructed entirely of dark cypress wood, the hall was eight columns across and six deep with a large curved roof of pale-russet tiles. The borders of the roof were decorated with rows of ceramic roundels, each bearing the *kamon* of a crane.

'We are greatly honoured by the presence of *daimyo* Takatomi,' began Masamoto, bowing deep in respect to his lord, 'for it is he who has graciously bestowed this new training hall upon the *Niten Ichi Ryū*.'

The students clapped loudly and their *daimyo* stepped forward.

Takatomi was dressed in his finest ceremonial kimono, the family crest of a crane picked out in white and silver thread. His right hand stroked his pencil-thin moustache, while his left rested nonchalantly upon his sword and generous round belly. Jack had met with the *daimyo* before the opening ceremony to offer his formal apology for hiding the *rutter* in his castle. It had been accepted, but the warmth of friendship the *daimyo* had once extended to him was now gone. Jack knew he'd burnt that bridge and would not be invited back to Nijo Castle ever again.

'In recognition of the great service Masamoto-sama and his school have rendered me over the years, I am proud to be opening the *Taka-no-ma*. It is my hope that this hall will be a beacon of light in dark times.'

A genial man of typically good humour, the *daimyo*'s expression was uncharacteristically solemn as he nodded to the Shinto priest to begin the ceremony.

The priest, in his traditional white robe and black conical hat, made his way over to the main entrance where a temporary altar had been erected – a small square marked out by a thin-knotted rope and four green stems of bamboo. In the centre a tiered wooden shrine held a green-leafed branch from a *sakaki* tree, festooned with white paper streamers.

Jack watched with interest as the Shinto priest intoned an incantation and lit an offering of incense.

'Has the ritual begun yet?' whispered a small voice to Jack's right.

Jack looked down at his friend Yori, a boy large of heart but slight of stature. He couldn't see the proceedings from behind the taller students.

'I think so,' replied Jack. 'The priest's now scattering salt and waving a flat wooden stick at the shrine.'

'That's his *shaku*,' explained Yori eagerly. 'He's purifying the new building. He'll then make an offering to the gods and invite the *kami* spirits in.'

'What for?' asked Jack.

'We hope the *kami* will bless the hall's shrine with their energy and bring prosperity and good fortune to the new building.'

Jack watched as the priest summoned *daimyo* Takatomi over and presented him with a small evergreen sprig. The *daimyo* turned to the shrine and placed the sacred sprig on the lowest shelf of the wooden altar. Then, as was the custom, he bowed deeply two times, clapped his hands twice and bowed once more.

With the formal offering made, the Shinto priest invited the *kami* to leave the ritual site, scattering water at the entrance. There was a brief moment of silence, then the doors to the Hall of the Hawk opened.

'What did our *daimyo* mean by a beacon of light in dark times?' asked Kiku, Akiko's good friend, a petite girl with dark brown hair and hazel eyes.

'I'm not sure, but it *was* a very strange thing to say,' Akiko agreed, as they all slipped off their sandals and entered the *Taka-no-ma* to view its grand interior.

Once inside, they gathered at the edge of the training area, a beautifully polished wooden floor empty save for a stack of small tables in one corner. Upon the rear wall was a raised shrine, which the students would bow to before commencing their training. Apart from that, there appeared to be little decoration.

Until they looked up. The ceiling had been painted with a mural of a huge hawk in mid-swoop, its wings spread wide, its talons splayed. The strength and swiftness of the bird was apparent in every brushstroke. Standing beneath it, Jack realized the students were meant to be the hawk. Otherwise they would be its prey.

'Maybe the *daimyo* thinks there's going to be a war,' suggested Jack.

The previous year, Jack had overheard his school rival, Kazuki, talking about Kamakura, the *daimyo* of Edo Province, planning to wage all-out war against Christians in Japan. Since then, there had been increasing cases of persecution and a growing prejudice against foreigners, but the campaign itself had yet to amount to a full-blown crusade.

'Jack could be right,' said Yamato. 'We all know what *daimyo* are like. They're always fighting over one another's territorities.'

'But the Council of Regents have held the peace for almost ten years now,' Kiku replied. 'There's not been a war since the Battle of Nakasendo. Why should there be one now?'

'Maybe *daimyo* Takatomi was referring to the martial art we'll be taught here?' proposed Yori, his eyes wide and fearful at the talk of war.

'But what exactly are we going to be learning?' butted in Saburo, a round-faced, jovial boy with thick bushy eyebrows. 'I can't see any weapons in this *dojo*. And who's going to teach us?'

'I believe that's our new sensei,' said Akiko, indicating a tall, thin lady talking to Masamoto.

Dressed in a black kimono with a stark white *obi*, the

woman had ashen skin and colourless lips. Her eyes were the deepest brown and, despite their warmth, spoke of a great sadness. Yet the most striking aspect of her appearance was the waist-length mane of snow-white hair.

'Who is she?' asked Saburo.

'Nakamura Oiko,' breathed Kiku in awe. 'My father once talked of her. She's a great female warrior who became famous when her husband was killed during the Nakasendo War. Her hair turned white with grief overnight, but she still took over his battalion and led them to victory. She's legendary for her skill with the *naginata*.'

'*Naginata*?' queried Jack.

'It's a long wooden shaft with a curved blade on the end,' Yamato explained.

'It's a woman's weapon,' dismissed Saburo.

'Not if you're on the wrong end of it,' snapped Akiko, irritated by Saburo's remark. 'The *naginata*'s only favoured by women because it has a greater reach than a sword, allowing us to overcome a much *bigger* opponent.'

She stared meaningfully at Saburo's well-fed stomach. Saburo instinctively placed a protective hand over his belly, his mouth falling open as he tried to think of a suitable reply.

'Who's the boy next to Sensei Nakamura?' Yori asked quickly, aware the conversation was in danger of becoming an argument.

They glanced over to a good-looking boy with dark hair tied into a topknot. He appeared to be a couple of years older, but his physique was slight and he possessed the soft cultured features of a nobleman. He stood quietly beside Sensei Nakamura, seemingly at ease in his new surroundings.

'That's Takuan, her son,' said a voice from behind.

Jack turned round to see Emi, *daimyo* Takatomi's elegant daughter, a slender girl with long straight hair and a rose-petal mouth. Either side of her were her two friends, Cho and Kai, both of whom seemed transfixed by the new boy.

'Emi, how are you feeling now?' asked Jack, bowing.

The last time Jack had seen Emi she'd been unconscious after the female ninja Sasori had struck her in the neck and knocked her out.

'Fine,' she replied coolly, 'though it took over a week for the bruising to go down.'

'I'm sorry,' mumbled Jack.

'Not as sorry as my father was for having invited you into his castle.'

Jack didn't know what to say. He hadn't expected such a prickly reaction from Emi. He thought they'd become friends. Emi gave Jack an icy stare before turning on her heel and gliding away in the direction of Takuan.

'I don't think you're her favourite samurai any more,' commented Saburo in Jack's ear.

'Thanks for pointing that out,' replied Jack, irritably digging Saburo in the stomach with his elbow.

'*I'm* not the one who almost got the *daimyo*'s daughter killed!' Saburo complained, rubbing his injured belly.

'That's enough! Jack's already made his formal apology to the *daimyo*,' interrupted Yamato, seeing the shame in Jack's eyes. 'The new boy does seem to be making rather an impression, though.'

Jack looked round and saw that the girls in the hall had their attention turned towards Takuan, many whispering and

72

giggling behind their hands. Takuan, who was engaged in conversation with Emi, glanced over in their direction and spotted Akiko beside Jack. He gave her a broad smile and inclined his head, inviting Akiko to join them. Akiko returned the greeting, her face blushing at the attention.

Still smarting from Emi's harsh reception, Jack was surprised to find himself irritated by this exchange. 'He looks more poet than warrior,' commented Jack. 'What's he doing in a samurai school?'

Akiko frowned at Jack. 'I expect that he's going to train with us.'

'*Us?*' said Jack.

'Yes, he probably knows a lot more than just poetry considering his mother's reputation. We should go and welcome him.'

Jack lingered behind as Akiko, Kiku and Yori went over to greet Takuan.

'Hey, the *gaijin*'s back!' mocked a familiar voice.

Jack groaned. Of all the people he didn't want to see the first day back at the *Niten Ichi Ryū*, it was Kazuki.

His sworn enemy strode over, arrogant as ever. His head recently shaved, and wearing his jet-black kimono with its red sun *kamon* emblazoned on the back, he looked every bit the son of a man supposedly related to the Imperial Line. His dark hooded eyes glared at Jack as if offended by his very presence.

Kazuki was flanked by the core members of his so-called Scorpion Gang: Nobu, who by his huge girth appeared to harbour hopes of becoming a sumo wrestler; Goro, a tough-looking boy with deep-set eyes; and Hiroto, thin and wiry as a stick insect, with a cruel, high-pitched voice. The only one missing was Moriko, the black-toothed samurai girl, who studied at their rival school, the *Yagyu Ryū*. The gang, formed in preparation for *daimyo* Kamakura's supposed crusade, were firmly against the idea of *gaijin* settling in Japan. Since Jack was the only foreigner in the *Niten Ichi Ryū*, he was their primary target for harassment.

'We were trying to decide whether you'd been roasted, boiled or burnt alive!' said Kazuki.

Jack stared impassively back. He was determined not to give Kazuki or his gang the reaction they wanted.

'Go away, Kazuki,' said Jack. 'That's old news.'

'Is it?' Kazuki taunted. 'The last I heard, *daimyo* Kamakura was offering rewards to those who brought Christians to justice. You do realize, Yamato, that these *gaijin* are spreading an evil religion. They're trying to convert samurai to their alien beliefs in order to overthrow all the *daimyo* and rule Japan for themselves.'

'If that was the case, why would *daimyo* Takatomi convert to Christianity?' challenged Yamato, stepping between Jack and the approaching gang. 'He serves the Emperor and is no fool.'

'He doesn't realize the true extent of their plans,' replied Kazuki, lowering his voice, 'Unlike *daimyo* Kamakura who's passing a law that will banish all Christians from Japan. And good riddance to them!'

'That may be *daimyo* Kamakura's will in Edo Province, but it's not here in Kyoto,' retorted Yamato. 'Now back off!'

Kazuki took a step closer.

'I've no quarrel with you, Yamato. My issue is with the *gaijin* only. There's no need for you to be involved.'

Yamato stood his ground, eyeballing Kazuki.

'You pick a fight with Jack, you pick a fight with me too.'

10

THE MATCH

Kazuki and his gang closed ranks against Jack, Yamato and Saburo.

The Hall of the Hawk was busy with students and the confrontation passed unnoticed amid the crowd.

'Why do you always insist on protecting the *gaijin*?' demanded Kazuki.

'Because he's family,' replied Yamato.

Kazuki stared at him dumbfounded. Even Jack was taken aback by his friend's statement. Yamato had never before declared their relationship in such a binding and familiar manner.

'I remember a time when you hated him,' Kazuki spat. 'You despised your father's decision to adopt a *gaijin*. He's taking your brother's place! Can't you see he's even replaced you in your father's affections?'

'What do you mean?' retorted Yamato.

'Unless I'm mistaken, it's Jack, and not you, who's being taught the Two Heavens. He's not even samurai! How can you stand by and let a *gaijin* be taught your father's secret sword technique?'

Yamato's face went taut as he fought with his emotions.

Jack knew Kazuki had hit a raw nerve. Yamato was always struggling to gain his father's respect. His failure to enter the Circle of Three and warrant learning the Two Heavens was still a sore point for him.

'Doesn't it bother you that you're not considered good enough for the Two Heavens? And *he* is!'

Jack immediately rose to his friend's defence. 'Yamato doesn't need the Two Heavens when he could defeat any of you with his *bō*.'

'I doubt that,' said Kazuki, raising his eyebrows sceptically.

Saburo now stepped into the fray.

'Think again. Yamato's so skilful with the staff,' declared Saburo, patting his friend firmly on the shoulder, 'he could take on all of your stupid Scorpion Gang at once.'

Kazuki gave an incredulous laugh. 'Is that right?'

'You could blindfold him and he'd still win!' added Jack emphatically.

Yamato stared aghast as Jack and Saburo made their boasts.

A sly grin spread across Kazuki's face. 'Perhaps we should put your claims to the test. Are you up for some sparring, Yamato?'

'What are you suggesting?' replied Yamato cagily.

'A knockdown match. Exactly as the *gaijin* said: you, blind-folded, with your staff against me and my gang, weapons of our choice.'

'Doesn't sound fair,' stated Yamato.

'You've only got the *gaijin* to blame. It was his idea.'

'No, I mean *you* won't stand a chance.'

Kazuki nodded appreciatively. 'Now that's fighting talk. I propose a match tomorrow evening at the Enryakuji Temple on Mount Hiei.'

'I'll be there,' agreed Yamato, his face impassive.

Saburo, caught up in the heat of the moment, squared up to Nobu. 'Bring a priest. You'll need one.'

Nobu growled back but Kazuki, laughing, indicated for them to leave, and the stand-off between the two groups of boys came to an end. Yamato turned to Jack and Saburo. He grabbed them both by the lapels of their kimono.

'What have you two got me into?' he exclaimed, shaking them angrily.

'*You* agreed to the match!' spluttered Saburo.

'Yes. It would have been dishonourable to back down after all your bragging.'

'Kazuki had no right to say those things about you,' replied Jack in his defence.

'That may be the case, but I can fight my own corner.'

'It's going to be a great fight too,' enthused Saburo. 'Five against one. You'll be a legend in the school.'

'I'll be dead more like,' shot back Yamato. 'Blindfolded! What were you thinking, Jack?'

'Sorry, I got a bit carried away. But you won't lose,' Jack replied, with as much gusto as he could muster. 'With all our *chi sao* training and your extra *bō* lessons, you're by far the best in Sensei Kano's class.'

Yamato shook his head in despair. 'I'm no Sensei Kano. Against five opponents, I'll be annihilated in this match!'

'What match?' demanded a gruff voice.

Sensei Hosokawa, the school's *kenjutsu* teacher, a fierce man with a sharp stub of a beard, stood behind them, his arms crossed and his two swords tucked into his *obi*.

Yamato let go of Jack and Saburo and bowed an apology. 'Just a training match, Sensei.'

'To test Yamato's *bō* skills,' added Saburo, putting on his most innocent smile.

'Sounds intriguing,' said their teacher, eyeing the three of them suspiciously. 'But you should be getting ready for Sensei Nakamura's first class this afternoon. Don't be late!'

Sensei Hosokawa strode off and began to usher the students out of the *Taka-no-ma*.

'Sorry for getting you into this,' said Jack as they put on their sandals outside. 'I'll go and tell Kazuki the match is off.'

'NO,' replied Yamato, grabbing Jack's arm. 'Kazuki was looking for a fight. If we pull out now, I'll lose face.'

'So you're going to do it?' Saburo asked eagerly.

Yamato nodded. 'It's time *someone* taught Kazuki a lesson.'

11

HAIKU

Having returned to his tiny paper-walled bedroom in the Hall of Lions, Jack got changed out of his ceremonial kimono into his training *gi*. He neatly folded the kimono and laid it upon the *tatami*-matted floor beside his swords, *bokken* and the little *inro* carrying case containing Akiko's black pearl. The ninja *tantō* was wrapped in a cloth nearby and he slipped it beneath the kimono. It felt safer there, out of sight and out of mind.

As an afterthought, he placed the Daruma Doll on top. The single eye Jack had painted on its mischievous face two years previous stared back at him with indifference. Jack was supposed to fill in the other eye once the wish he'd made on the doll came true. But the Daruma Doll had yet to deliver on its promise. Until then, Jack thought, it would make a good talisman against the evil spirit of the Kunitome blade. Not that he believed a word the tea-house owner had said.

Hearing the other students leave their rooms, Jack got up and quickly watered his *bonsai*, which sat upon the window sill of the room's small lattice window. The little tree looked a great deal healthier since being cared for by Uekiya. Then he hurried from his room to find his friends waiting in the courtyard. Together they headed over to the *Taka-no-ma* for their first lesson with Sensei Nakamura. No one yet knew what martial art she would be teaching but, like many of his classmates, Jack had decided to bring his *bokken* just in case.

Inside the Hall of the Hawk, they were greeted by five regimented rows of tiny wooden tables laid out across the *dojo* floor. Upon each table was a bamboo writing brush, an ink block and several sheets of plain paper.

'Leave your weapons at the door,' instructed Sensei Naka-mura. Her command was softly spoken, though her voice carried clearly throughout the Hall.

She sat motionless beneath the shrine in her black kimono, her hair a billowing snowdrift down her back.

The thirty students did as they were told and Sensei Naka-mura waited patiently while everyone settled at their tables. Jack found a place between Yamato and Saburo in the third row and sat down cross-legged upon the floor. Akiko, Kiku and Yori took their places in the line in front. On the first row, Jack spotted Emi, Cho and Kai. They'd positioned themselves next to the new boy, Takuan, while Kazuki and his Scorpion Gang ensured they had the back row all to themselves.

The lesson was still a mystery to everyone, so there was a great air of expectation in the room. Jack looked around and couldn't see anything in the *dojo* that resembled a *naginata*. Without weapons, he wondered whether they might be train-ing in *taijutsu*, but Sensei Kyuzo already taught them hand-to-hand combat. The pieces of paper upon the tables hinted that they might be doing *origami*, but Zen Buddhism, meditation and the spiritual arts were Sensei Yamada's respon-sibility. With the ink and brush present, Jack feared they would be doing a written test. In spite of Akiko's private lessons in *kanji*, Jack knew he wouldn't be capable of writing at any length.

Before the sensei even spoke, the class became still as if some soundless command had been issued.

'My name is Sensei Nakamura,' she said quietly, 'and I will be teaching you *haiku*.'

The announcement provoked a mixed reaction from the class. Many of the students were disappointed, while a few looked absolutely delighted with the news.

'What's *haiku*?' whispered Jack, seeing that Yori had already picked up his brush in eager anticipation.

'Poetry,' groaned Saburo in response.

Sensei Nakamura's eyes turned upon Saburo and he fell silent under her stern gaze.

'For those unfamiliar with the form,' continued Sensei Nakamura, addressing the class, 'let me explain its main principles. *Haiku* is a short poem, usually consisting of seventeen sound syllables, in which it should be possible to deduce the season. However, these basic rules may be disregarded, for it is the spirit of *haiku* that counts above all.'

Sensei Nakamura picked up a piece of paper by her side and read slowly from it.

> *'Flying of cranes*
> *as high as the clouds –*
> *first sunrise.'*

Several of the students began a respectful round of applause at the verse and everyone else soon joined in. Sensei Nakamura gave a slight incline of the head to show her appreciation.

'*Haiku* is a keen observation of the world around you,' she lectured. 'A great *haiku* verse should pin the moment; express the timelessness of it.'

She extracted another sheet from her pile and in a voice that seemed to whisper into each individual's ear, she read:

> '*Look! A butterfly*
> *has settled on the shoulder*
> *of the great Buddha.*'

This time every student applauded.

Yori leant over in excitement to Kiku and enthused, 'Did you hear how Sensei compared the fleeting nature of a butterfly with the eternal Buddha? Suggesting there's no difference between a living being and the embodiment of life in a stone statue.'

'Yes,' agreed Kiku breathlessly. 'Magical!'

Saburo rolled his eyes at Jack. 'So, it's "Yori the Poet" now, is it?' he teased good-humouredly.

Jack laughed. They all knew Yori was the eager scholar, being the only one among them who could solve Sensei Yamada's *koan* challenges. The riddles the Zen master set each week seemed impossible, yet somehow Yori always came up with an answer.

A sharp clap of Sensei Nakamura's hands ceased the chatter.

'As I've demonstrated, *haiku* is to look closely at the world around us and our place within that world. Now I want you all to attempt your own *haiku*. Think about a moment in your life and capture it in a poem. Don't worry about form. Focus on the spirit. Try to leave yourself out of it. No thoughts. No opinions. Just let it be.'

Everybody studiously bent their heads to the desks and began preparing their ink blocks to write.

Jack did the same, but had no idea what he was supposed to write about. He stared out of the window at the afternoon sun warming the green tiles of the Buddha Hall opposite.

His concentration began to drift.

Kazuki's threats earlier that day played on his mind. The news *daimyo* Kamakura was offering rewards to hunt down Christians was worrying. While he was relatively safe under Masamoto's protection inside the *Niten Ichi Ryū*, he was now fearful that *anyone* might try to attack him, not just samurai loyal to *daimyo* Kamakura.

The situation in Japan appeared to be getting worse, but what else could he do other than let matters run their course? When he'd first been suspended from school, Jack had considered heading to Nagasaki to try and find a ship bound for England. There had seemed little point in staying if he couldn't continue his samurai training and learn the Two Heavens. Yet he knew it was foolish of him to think he could make it all the way to Nagasaki on his own, half-trained. With no food, money or weapons, he wasn't likely to survive much beyond the outskirts of Kyoto. Besides, every time he thought about leaving something held him back. After two years in Japan, he realized he'd become attached to the place. More importantly, he owed his life to Masamoto and felt duty bound to stay.

Thankfully, having been given a reprieve, his guardian would now be teaching him his legendary double sword technique. Gazing out of the window, Jack wondered how hard it would be to learn to fight with two swords. He envisaged that once he'd mastered it, he would be invincible like Masamoto himself. He would no longer have to fear for his life. Jack began to imagine fighting Dragon Eye and defeating him once and for all.

He noticed Yamato was also staring into space. No doubt he was preoccupied with the forthcoming match against Kazuki and his gang. Jack had tried to dissuade his friend, but the jibe that he didn't merit Two Heavens training had riled him. Yamato stubbornly refused to back down. He seemed determined to prove himself against all the odds.

Jack wasn't sure how long he'd sat there daydreaming, but suddenly he became aware that Sensei Nakamura was looking at him.

'Do you require some help?' she enquired.

'Sorry, Sensei,' mumbled Jack, 'but I'm not sure what I should be writing about.'

She nodded once thoughtfully.

'When a friend asks you, "What is it?", "What's the matter?" or even "What made you smile?", *haiku* is the answer to that "what?",' she explained. 'You cannot share your feelings with others unless you show the cause of those feelings. *Haiku* is about sharing the moment. Now try again.'

Jack took up his brush and pretended to write. Though he understood the principle of *haiku* a little better, his mind remained blank. Everyone else appeared to be progressing well with the task, even Saburo. He glanced over at his industrious friend, only to discover he was doodling pictures of samurai and ninja.

'This lesson's for girls,' complained Saburo.

Akiko turned round and glared at him.

'No, it's not,' she said, indignant at Saburo's prejudice. 'Most of the *famous* poets happen to be men. Not that their work is any better than a woman's, as proven by Sensei Nakamura's *haiku*.'

'What's the point in a samurai learning *haiku*?' Saburo persisted. 'We're supposed to be training to be warriors, not poets. You can't exactly fight an enemy with words.'

'Those that talk most hear least,' Sensei Nakamura observed from her position beneath the shrine. Again her command wasn't loud, but it was as forceful as if she'd shouted at them.

'Still seems pointless to me,' he muttered under his breath as he bowed and dipped his brush back in the ink block.

'He who works only with his hands is a mere labourer,' proclaimed Sensei Nakamura.

Jack almost jumped out of his skin. The teacher had drifted across the hall as silently as a ghost and was suddenly beside them.

'He who works with hands and head is a craftsman,' she continued, inspecting Saburo's sketches with weary disappointment. 'But he who works with his hands, head and heart is an artist. The same can be said of the swordsman. You may be able to use your hands, Saburo-kun, but you've yet to prove you can use your head or your heart.'

Shamed into silence, Saburo bent his head and began to write.

Jack returned to staring out of the window. He was still uninspired and any ideas he did have seemed weak or stupid to him. He watched the sun slowly make its way across the temple's roof, time seeming to stretch on and on.

Sensei Nakamura eventually brought the exercise to an end.

'Now I want you to share your *haiku* with the person next to you,' she instructed. 'See if they can experience the moment you were trying to express.'

Jack turned to Saburo, empty-handed.

'Don't worry about it,' said Saburo. 'I think you'll like mine, though.'

Saburo quietly read his poem to Jack and Jack couldn't help but snigger.

'You find the task amusing?' enquired Sensei Nakamura.

'No, Sensei,' replied Jack, trying to suppress his grin.

'Perhaps you'd like to read out your *haiku*.'

Jack looked down at his desk, embarrassed. 'I couldn't think of one.'

'You've had all afternoon, yet not managed a single word?' she said, dismayed. 'Well then, let us hear from your friend.'

Saburo looked shocked. He clearly hadn't thought they would have to read out their *haiku* to the class.

'Do I have to? It's not very good,' he excused himself.

'Let me be the judge of that,' insisted Sensei Nakamura.

Saburo reluctantly got to his feet, his paper trembling in his hand. He cleared his throat, then began:

> *'Letting out a fart —*
> *it doesn't make you laugh*
> *when you live alone.'*

There was a burst of raucous laugher from the back row. Most of the students, however, tried to hide their amusement when they saw the icy look Sensei Nakamura gave Saburo.

'Very amusing,' she noted. 'In fact, it's *so* good, I think you should write it out a thousand times.'

Immediately regretting his rebellious act, Saburo bowed and sat back down.

'I trust other attempts are more appropriate for the classroom.'

'Sensei?' invited Emi, putting her hand up. 'I think this one's good.'

'Very well, let's hear it,' agreed Sensei Nakamura, nodding. Emi passed the *haiku* back to its owner.

Takuan graciously accepted it and stood. He gave a humble bow, then in a honeyed tone read:

> *'Evening temple bell*
> *stopped in the sky*
> *by cherry blossoms.'*

There was a hushed silence as the students nodded appreciatively, then everyone started to clap.

'Very perceptive,' commended Sensei Nakamura, 'but if it had been anything less, I would have been very disappointed.'

Takuan appeared a little downhearted at his mother's damning praise. He bowed and sat down.

'We will continue next week. In the meantime, I expect everyone to have composed at least one more *haiku*.'

The students all bowed and made their way out of the *Takano-ma*, leaving the lone Saburo to write out his poem a thousand times.

'He'll be lucky to finish before bedtime,' observed Yamato as he slipped his sandals back on.

'Serves him right for being disrespectful,' Akiko declared.

'But you have to admit, it was funny,' replied Jack. 'And you can't deny he captured a moment.'

'But he didn't suggest a season!' argued Akiko.

'Does it matter what time of year you fart?' asked Yori innocently.

Jack and Yamato burst out laughing.

'Excuse us,' said a less-amused Akiko, beckoning Kiku to join her as Takuan emerged from the Hall of the Hawk. 'We must congratulate Takuan on his fine *haiku*.'

Takuan, despite already being surrounded by several other admirers, bowed at their approach. Jack saw that Akiko had opened her fan and was gently wafting herself with it while talking to Takuan.

'How can one poem make someone so popular?' exclaimed Jack.

'Don't worry,' consoled Yamato as they headed towards the Hall of Butterflies for dinner. 'I bet he can't wield a sword like you.'

12

TWO HEAVENS

'Masamoto-sama and Sensei Hosokawa are fighting!' exclaimed a student, hurrying in the direction of the Hall of the Phoenix.

Jack and Akiko, already heading that way for their first morning lesson in the Two Heavens, ran after her. As they neared the *Hō-oh-no-ma*, Masamoto's personal *dojo*, Jack could hear the clash of *katana*. Pushing his way through the students crowded round the entrance, he could see the samurai engaged in brutal combat. To his surprise, they *both* wielded two swords, their *katana* and *wakizashi* flashing through the air like steel birds of prey.

Hosokawa seemed to have the upper hand and drove Masamoto back on to the wooden dais. But Masamoto now gained a height advantage, his retreat clearly a ruse to get Hosokawa to over-commit to his attack. Masamoto retaliated with a double strike, almost cleaving in half the silk-screen painting of the flaming phoenix that hung on the rear wall. Hosokawa blocked Masamoto's *wakizashi* but was caught out by the longer blade of the *katana*. It broke past his guard, threatening to skewer him through the heart. Only a late deflection and rapid footwork saved the sword teacher. Masamoto kept up the pressure and went in for the kill.

'Did you know they once duelled for *real*?' whispered a student standing beside Jack.

The boy was familiar to Jack. Tall and handsome, with strong arms and dark eyes, Taro was known to be one of the best *kenjutsu* students in the school. But it was the bushy eyebrows that gave it away. Taro was Saburo's older brother. An accomplished samurai who commanded great respect among his peers, he was everything his younger brother wished he could be.

'Looks pretty serious to me,' said Jack, staring in disbelief as Hosokawa viciously cut down at his guardian's exposed neck.

'It *was* serious once,' Taro replied. 'While on his *musha shugyo,* Masamoto-sama challenged Sensei Hosokawa.'

'But I can't imagine Sensei Hosokawa having ever lost a fight.' Jack winced in sympathy as Masamoto cross-blocked the sword teacher's *katana* and shoulder-barged him in the chest.

'He didn't,' replied Taro.

Jack's brow wrinkled in puzzlement. 'But I was told Masamoto-sama *never* lost a single fight during his entire warrior pilgrimage.'

'You're right. Their duel lasted a day and a night without rest. Eventually a town official had to step in and stop the fight. They'd wrecked two tea houses and several market stalls in the process!'

Jack smiled at the idea. Sensei Yamada, his Zen master, had once told him Masamoto had been a fierce and independent samurai in his youth. He could just imagine the carnage these two warriors had wrought.

'Their epic duel led to a mutual respect and it was deemed a draw,' Taro explained, as Masamoto and Sensei Hosokawa stopped their fighting in the *Hō-oh-no-ma* and retreated to a safe distance. 'Sensei Hosokawa eventually persuaded Masamoto-sama to teach him the Two Heavens and they became allies, founding the *Niten Ichi Ryū* together.'

Sheathing their swords, the two samurai bowed to one another. A servant entered through a side door bearing a pot of *sencha* and two china cups. Sharing the green tea, the two samurai laughed at a private joke and toasted one another. '*Kampai!*'

'Sensei Hosokawa is possibly the only samurai who can match Masamoto-sama's skill with the sword,' whispered Taro, as if it was blasphemy to suggest such a thing. 'But, for honour's sake, they have yet to finish the duel.'

'Everything you've learned so far at the *Niten Ichi Ryū* was merely preparation for the Two Heavens,' declared Masamoto to the eight students gathered before him.

Jack was in full agreement. He felt like a novice again. Standing in the Two Heavens upper fighting stance, a wooden *katana* borne high in his right hand and a shorter wooden *wakizashi* at waist-level in his left, he struggled to keep control of his swords as he attempted the cuts Masamoto had shown them.

He struck down at the *bokken* held aloft by his training partner, Sachiko. A girl from two years above with a reputation for being lightning fast with the samurai sword, she had a sharp angular face and dark hair pulled back and secured with a red ornamental *hashi* stick.

Jack switched stance and cut down, using the *wakizashi*. He repeated the strikes, each time attempting to get faster and more accurate. However, the coordination required made his efforts appear clumsy and awkward. He was used to holding one sword in both hands, but the weight of two made his arms ache and his grip weak.

'You may ask why two swords are better than one, when all other samurai schools teach single sword techniques,' Masamoto lectured as he studied his students' form. 'Admittedly, there are situations when one sword has its advantage, but if your life is on the line, you need all your weapons to be of service. For a samurai warrior to be defeated with a sword still sheathed is a disgrace.'

After several more attempts, Jack swapped with Sachiko to hold the *bokken* aloft while she practised her double cuts. Already a year into her Two Heavens training, Sachiko was more fluid with her movements and struck the *bokken* with greater force, each hit jarring Jack's arm painfully in its socket.

There were only six other students privileged enough to be taught the technique. Immediately to his right were Akiko and Kazuki who, like Jack, had conquered the Circle of Three challenges and therefore earned the right to be taught the Two Heavens early. Jack was reassured by his own progress when he saw that Kazuki was also finding the exercise tough. The next two students, Ichiro and Osamu, were more advanced. Like Sachiko, they'd been selected from the years above for their exceptional fighting skills. Having already had some training with two swords, they were striking at one another rapidly. At the end was a girl called Mizuki, whose sword partner was Taro. They attacked one another's *bokken* with practised ease, not even breaking into a sweat.

Masamoto called a halt to the practice. 'Take up your fighting stances.'

He then went round correcting everyone's posture.

'Put strength into the nape of your neck, Sachiko-chan.'

He pushed down on Jack's shoulders. 'Keep your back straight. Don't stick out your rear.'

Masamoto looked Kazuki up and down. 'Good. A very solid stance. Everyone here needs to be thinking of their body as one, like this.'

He adjusted Akiko's grip on her leading sword. 'Your grasp is too loose; you should always hold the sword with the intention of cutting down your opponent.'

'Ichiro-kun and Osamu-kun, you're too close. Beware of *ma-ai*. Mizuki-chan, put more strength into your feet. Perfect, Taro-kun, but ensure you're employing *metsuke*.'

Masamoto noticed the confused look on Jack's face.

'*Ma-ai* is the distance between you and your opponent. *Metsuke* means "looking at a faraway mountain". You should already be familiar with this second concept, Jack-kun. I believe Sensei Kano has taught you the principles of the *Mugan Ryū*, his School of No Eyes. This is similar. It's the ability to see everything at once without focusing on one particular object. You should be aware of your opponent's sword, yet at the same time *not* be looking at it.'

Jack nodded his understanding. Sensei Kano, their blind *bōjutsu* master, had spent most of the previous year teaching

94

him not to rely on his sight during combat. This unusual skill had saved his life on two separate occasions, once against Kazuki, and the other time in a fight with Dragon Eye and his female assassin Sasori.

Eventually satisfied with his students' stances, Masamoto continued the lesson. 'Let me show you the advantage of holding a sword with just one hand.'

Masamoto drew his blade so fast, the air whistled. He stopped short of Jack's throat. Jack gave an involuntary gasp. Kazuki smirked and Jack silently cursed himself for showing weakness in front of the class.

'When you hold a *katana* with both hands, it's more difficult to move freely to your left or right and you have less reach with your blade.'

Masamoto now grasped the sword with both hands to show the difference in range. Jack breathed a quiet sigh of relief as the razor-sharp tip drew back from his Adam's apple.

'By fighting with two swords, you'll overcome the limitations of single sword fighting,' Masamoto explained, resheathing his *katana*. 'I'll demonstrate a basic Two Heavens technique with Sensei Hosokawa.'

He turned to the swordmaster, who'd been observing the lesson from the *dais*. Hosokawa bowed and stepped forward. He drew his *katana* and Masamoto unsheathed both his swords. A split second later, Hosokawa attacked, his blade arcing towards Masamoto's head. Masamoto blocked the cut with his *wakizashi*, simultaneously stepping to one side and thrusting his longer *katana* at Hosokawa's throat.

It was over in an instant. If it had been a real fight, the

swordmaster would now be choking to death on his own blood, his neck impaled by the hard steel tip of the blade.

Hosokawa retreated to a safe distance.

'As you've just seen, the Two Heavens style is uncomplicated,' Masamoto explained, resheathing his swords and bowing to Sensei Hosokawa. 'There are no flamboyant or exaggerated movements. Targeting is precise, and distance and timing are tight, with no wasted movement. I compare the Two Heavens sword style to water, fluid and pure.'

The students were now given the opportunity to try the 'parry and strike' technique themselves. Jack was paired off with Kazuki this time. He faced off against his rival. Kazuki struck with his *katana* and Jack managed to block it with the *wakizashi*, but he completely missed Kazuki's throat with his other sword.

Despite the apparent simplicity of the technique, Jack discovered the Two Heavens was like trying to pat his head and rub his stomach at the same time. It required intense concentration and coordination.

He tried again, this time focusing on his attack. The tip of his *katana* found its target, but he completely forgot about blocking. His head was almost knocked off his shoulders as Kazuki's wooden *katana* smashed into his ear.

'Careful!' exclaimed Jack, clasping his battered ear.

Kazuki shrugged unapologetically. 'You should have blocked it.'

'And *you* should have controlled your strike, Kazuki-kun,' observed Masamoto from the other end of the *dojo*.

'Yes, Sensei. Sorry, I'm not used to holding two swords,' replied Kazuki by way of an excuse. 'My apologies, Jack.'

He inclined his head respectfully to Jack. But the sly grin on his face told Jack that Kazuki was more skilled than he let on – and far from sorry.

Jack couldn't wait for this evening when Yamato would wipe that smile off his face.

13

KNOCKDOWN

'I wasn't expecting an audience!' muttered Yamato as he limbered up for the match. 'How did everyone find out?'

'I may have told a couple of friends,' admitted Saburo sheepishly.

'A couple! It's more like the entire school's here.'

A buzz of excited chatter filled the air as groups of students crowded along the edge of the central courtyard of the Enryakuji Temple. The surrounding buildings were in ruins, destroyed by the samurai general Nobunaga forty years earlier. Yet Sensei Kano still occasionally taught the students the Art of the *Bō* here. He said the temple was possessed with the spiritual strength of the *sohei* monks. Even now, a solitary monk prayed inside the broken shell of the Kompon Chu-do, keeping the Eternal Light burning as it had done for over eight hundred years. The flame could be seen flickering in the shadows, its light playing off the cracked beams and shattered stone idols of the otherwise deserted shrine.

Outside, the rays of the evening sun filtered through the trees and transformed the fractured stone courtyard into a golden arena. Kazuki and the founding members of his Scorpion Gang were gathered at the other end, eagerly awaiting the forthcoming fight. Moriko, the fifth core member, arrived with supporters from the rival samurai school, the *Yagyu Ryū*. Her bleached-white face and black arrow-straight hair gave her a devilish appearance, only added to by her blood-red lips and dark raven eyes. Yet the most disturbing thing about the girl was her teeth, painted black as tar.

Each of the gang had chosen a training weapon. Kazuki had his wooden *bokken*. Goro carried a staff. Hiroto swung a *surujin*, the weighted ends of the rope wrapped in cloth to lessen its lethal force. Nobu held a pair of *tonfa*, wooden batons with handles on the side. Moriko, though, didn't appear to have brought any weapon. But Jack knew she was devious and was probably concealing it so that Yamato wouldn't know what to expect during the match.

'Yamato, you don't have to do this,' said Jack as Kazuki approached. 'Not for my sake.'

'This isn't about *you* any more,' replied Yamato sternly. 'It's about honour and maintaining face.'

'You could get seriously hurt.'

'Wounds heal, broken bones mend, but my damaged reputation is far harder to fix. I need to restore my honour.'

'But —'

'Jack, a samurai lives and dies by his name and reputation. I'm judged differently because of my father. The fact that I'm not training in the Two Heavens is seen by everyone, including my father, as a failure. But I don't need the Two Heavens to be a great samurai. I intend to prove myself worthy of being a Masamoto.'

Jack knew how much Yamato desired his father's approval. Ever since his brother had been murdered by Dragon Eye, Yamato had been living in Tenno's shadow. Nothing he did ever seemed to match up to his older brother's achievements, at least in Masamoto's eyes. This match would be the ultimate test.

'*That* is what I'm fighting for,' stated Yamato, snatching the staff from Jack's hand.

Kazuki stopped and bowed to Yamato.

'It appears we've drawn a crowd,' he said, glancing around. 'I hope they won't be disappointed.'

'They won't,' replied Yamato. 'But you will be when I've finished with you.'

Kazuki laughed. 'If you're that confident, perhaps we should raise the stakes a little. Give us something more than honour to fight for.'

'What do you have in mind?' said Yamato guardedly.

'If you win, I promise to leave your family pet alone,' he said, glancing at Jack.

'And if I lose?'

'You leave the *gaijin* to us.'

'Agreed,' said Yamato, to Jack's utter astonishment.

'That's very courageous of you!' mocked Kazuki. 'But you do realize that win or lose, he's a lost cause. When *daimyo* Kamakura has his way, any *gaijin* found hiding in Japan will be executed or crucified.'

'That won't ever happen,' said Yamato.

'Yes, it will. You can't deny there's a change coming. Japan is entering a new age and we need a strong lord like Kamakura to lead the way.'

'He only governs Edo Province, not Japan. The Council would never allow it'

'No, but *one* day he will rule.'

Turning on his heel, Kazuki returned to his gang.

'Yamato!' exclaimed Jack, pulling him to one side. 'What were you thinking in agreeing to his bet?'

'Don't worry, I have no intention of losing.'

'But what if you do?'

'Then nothing's changed. He'll continue to harass you as before. Besides, you're the one who told me I couldn't lose.'

Jack realized he had to trust his friend. Yamato needed to focus on the fight and couldn't allow doubt to enter his mind. 'You're right. You're the best in Sensei Kano's class. They've got no chance.'

'Sorry we're late,' said Akiko, appearing slightly flushed as she hurried across the courtyard with Kiku, Yori and the new boy. 'We wanted to show Takuan the view over Kyoto.'

'It's truly magnificent,' said Takuan, bowing a formal greeting to them. He looked at Jack.

'Yes, it is,' replied Jack, giving a short but courteous nod of the head in return. He knew the exact spot they'd been to. It was where he and Akiko had shared *hatsuhinode* together, the first sunrise of the year. Foolishly, he'd always thought of the viewpoint as their little secret.

'I could even see the Imperial Palace,' Takuan enthused. 'Akiko's kindly agreed —'

'Sorry, but the contest is about to start,' Jack interrupted. 'And Yamato needs to get ready.'

'Of course, how disrespectful of me,' said Takuan, somewhat embarrassed. '*Gambatte*, Yamato.'

Yamato inclined his head in acknowledgement. Takuan took his place in the crowd beside Akiko. Emi and her friends had also arrived and went over to greet Takuan. Soon a small group of admirers had gathered round the new boy.

'You'd have thought *he* was the one fighting,' Saburo remarked, shaking his head in disbelief.

Jack focused his attention on helping Yamato, and prepared the blindfold.

As the three of them walked into the centre of the courtyard to meet with Kazuki and his gang, the students to their right suddenly parted and Masamoto appeared, accompanied by Sensei Hosokawa and Sensei Kano.

'What's my father doing *here*?' exclaimed Yamato, all the blood draining from his face.

Saburo swallowed nervously. 'Now we're in trouble.'

But Masamoto and the sensei simply made themselves comfortable on the main steps.

'Looks like he's come to watch!' said Jack.

'You must *really* be feeling the pressure now,' goaded Kazuki, seeing Yamato's confidence waver. 'Don't worry, we won't let your defeat look too easy. In fact, we'll come at you one at time to give you a fighting chance.'

'Ignore him,' whispered Jack, tying the blindfold round Yamato's eyes. 'He's lying. Just be prepared for anything.'

Yamato nodded, taking a deep breath to calm himself. His hands gripped the staff so tightly his knuckles had gone white. Jack realized his friend was struggling to maintain focus.

'You can beat anyone with a *bō*. Trust your senses,' Jack advised, repeating Sensei Kano's advice from *Chi Sao* training the previous year.

Jack and Saburo moved to the sidelines, leaving Yamato alone in the centre of the courtyard. The five members of the Scorpion Gang encircled him.

The crowd fell silent.

Five against one, with Yamato blindfolded. This would be a stunning victory. Or a swift and shameful defeat.

Goro went first.

Hearing him approach, Yamato spun to face his opponent. He was alerted to the attack by the swish through the air as Goro struck with his staff. Blocking it with his *bō*, he then whipped the other end of his staff into Goro's gut. The force of the blow bent Goro double. Yamato quickly followed up, bringing the shaft down hard across the boy's back. Goro dropped to the ground.

The crowd were momentarily stunned. No one had really expected Yamato to win even one bout. Jack breathed a sigh of relief. At least his friend had proved he wasn't an easy target. He gave Yamato a great shout of encouragement. The rest of the students soon joined in.

Nobu now approached and the students quietened down.

Yamato easily picked up the boy's heavy footsteps. Without hesitation, he swung his staff at Nobu's head. But Nobu was ready for him. He deflected the *bō* with the shaft of his right *tonfa*. He then spun the other baton into Yamato's face. Yamato reeled from the blow to his jaw. The crowd groaned.

Seizing the advantage, Nobu flipped the *tonfa* over in his right hand and brought the tip of the handle down on to Yamato's head. Despite the pain and disorientation, Yamato sensed the attack and dived out of the way. At the same time he swept his staff across the ground, catching Nobu behind both ankles.

The crowd erupted into amazed applause as Nobu was knocked off his feet. Glancing over at Masamoto, Jack saw his guardian remained impassive to his son's courageous display. Then again, the fight was far from over.

Hiroto made his move, swinging the *surujin* above his head. Yamato noticed the change in sound as Hiroto released one end of the roped weapon at his legs. He jumped into the air to avoid becoming entangled, but the rope wrapped round the shaft of his staff. Grinning, Hiroto yanked back on the *surujin*, hoping to disarm Yamato of his staff. Yamato let Hiroto pull his *bō* but guided its tip straight towards his opponent's chest. Winded by the strike, Hiroto fell to his knees.

The crowd went wild. Yamato had defeated three attackers. What had seemed an impossible challenge might now be a glorious triumph. But Jack could see his friend was tiring. This was the moment in a fight when mistakes were made.

The students began a chorus of 'Yamato! Yamato!' but this was soon stopped as Moriko went on the attack. However, the *Yagyu Ryū* students didn't stop clapping. Despite efforts to silence them, they continued to make as much noise as possible.

Jack now realized Moriko's weapon was her group of supporters. Their shouts masked her approach and Yamato was taken by surprise as she side-kicked him in the back. Yamato almost dropped where he stood. But somehow he managed to keep his footing and spun round to confront her. Grimacing with pain, Yamato tried to sense her attack above the noise of the *Yagyu Ryū* students.

Moriko went to finish him off with a roundhouse kick to the head, but Yamato began to twirl his staff until it became a blur. The whirling *bō* formed a defensive wall that Moriko couldn't penetrate. He drove her back until she was almost in the crowd. Realizing Moriko was trapped, he stopped the *bō* and thrust its tip into her midriff. With cat-like grace, Moriko leapt to one side grabbing the shaft to try to disarm him. But Yamato countered, twisting the end over and putting her into a wrist lock. Moriko was forced to the ground. She submitted under the pain.

The crowd applauded, then went quiet for the climax of the match.

Only Kazuki remained.

But Yamato was on his last legs, his breathing ragged.

The tension mounted as Kazuki calmly approached Yamato. He made no attempt to conceal his advance.

'If you want to hit me, I'm right here,' he declared.

Yamato didn't wait to be told twice. He struck for Kazuki's head. But Kazuki was simply too fast. He ducked beneath the staff, then cut down at Yamato's neck with his *bokken*.

He stopped his wooden sword short. Yamato felt the blade upon him.

'You just lost your head,' said Kazuki.

There was a moment of awed silence before the students cheered Kazuki's consummate skill. A single attack and Yamato had been defeated.

Jack ran over as Yamato removed his blindfold. Disappointment was etched in his face and a dark red bruise was forming where Nobu had hit him with the *tonfa*.

'That was very impressive, though,' added Kazuki with sincerity. 'I expected you to be knocked down first time. You may have lost the match, but you've earned my respect.'

Kazuki bowed.

Then, with a grin, he turned to Jack. 'I'm looking forward to claiming my prize.'

Kazuki strode off.

'Sorry,' said Yamato, unable to meet Jack's gaze.

'Don't be,' replied Jack. Even though Kazuki's threat now hung over him like a guillotine, he knew his friend had done his best. In fact, better than anyone would have imagined. 'You beat four of them. Everyone's talking about it.'

'But I lost,' he sighed. 'That's what they'll remember. There's no glory in coming second.'

'It's not what I'll remember,' replied Jack. 'I'll remember a friend fighting for me and for honour.'

Yamato attempted a smile, but he was inconsolable. His chance to prove his worth had slipped through his fingers. And now, as Masamoto approached, Jack saw the weight of failure hang heavy on Yamato's shoulders. Yamato dropped into a bow and awaited his father's verdict.

Masamoto studied his son, an austere expression on his face.

'Yamato-kun, you lasted far longer than I predicted. But you let Kazuki outwit you. By telling you where he was, he also knew where you would attack. That was your mistake.'

'Yes, Father,' mumbled Yamato.

Jack knew his friend was needing more than a lesson in combat. He needed to know his father accepted him whatever the outcome.

Masamoto turned to go. 'Once your talent for the *bō* translates to the *katana*, you'll be as fine a swordsman as Tenno was.'

14

YABUSAME

'*IN-YO, IN-YO, IN-YO!*' cried Sensei Yosa.

Jack saw a flash of colour as her horse thundered by, the steed snorting under the exertion. An arrow howled through the air, whizzing past Jack and shattering the square wooden target beside his head with a loud *crack*!

The students rattled their quivers to signal their delight at Sensei Yosa's extraordinary display of horsemanship and archery. Having let go of the reigns to nock, draw and shoot her arrows, she continued down the track, standing high in her saddle and guiding the horse with only her toes.

Approaching the next target at breakneck speed, she raised her bow and released her second arrow. This too hit the mark and the cedar wood exploded into several pieces.

She had only moments in which to prepare herself to draw a third and final time, her stallion galloping past the target just as she launched her final arrow. With a hard *bang*, it struck the very centre of the mark, snapping it in two.

Her students shook their quivers and applauded even louder.

Sensei Yosa turned her steed on the spot and cantered back

up the archery course. Situated in the picturesque wooded grounds of the ancient Kamigamo Shinto shrine, it was a purpose-made track with ropes down either side and three head height wooden targets in a line.

Jack and the others had been back at school just over a month when Sensei Yosa had announced that her *kyujutsu* class was competent enough to begin training in *kisha*, the art of shooting arrows from horseback. That morning they had gathered at the school's stables, bows and arrows in hand, to select five horses for the lesson. From there, they'd made their way to the northern district of Kyoto where the Kamigamo shrine was located.

Sensei Yosa drew up her horse beside the group of trainee warriors lined along the edge of the track. Taking a moment to tie back her long dark hair, she revealed a face of quite startling beauty, graced with chestnut-coloured eyes. She could have been mistaken for a royal *geisha* rather than a warrior, if it had not been for the cruel red battle scar that cut across her right cheek.

'The form of *kisha* you will be studying is called *Yabusame*,' declared Sensei Yosa, dismounting. 'It will not only sharpen your skills as an archer, but it's a ritual that pleases the gods and will encourage their blessings upon our school.'

She pointed down the track.

'Note the height of the targets. They're at the same level as the space between the peak of an enemy's helmet and their facemask. A direct hit here represents a fatal blow on the battle-field.'

Removing an arrow from the quiver attached to her right hip, she showed the class its blunt, wooden ball tip.

'When training, you'll use *jindou*, instead of the usual steel-tipped arrows. Since *Yabusame* is a ceremony dedicated to the gods, any weapon which draws blood cannot be used.'

As Sensei Yosa replaced the *jindou*, Jack leant over to Yori to whisper in his ear.

'You have a question, Jack-kun?' Sensei Yosa enquired, her eyes sharper than a hawk's.

Jack looked up, startled. He hadn't wanted to ask her in front of all the class in case he appeared stupid.

'I was wondering,' he said, sensing the eyes of the other students upon him, 'what you were shouting *In-Yo* for?'

'Good question,' said Sensei Yosa. 'It's an old samurai prayer meaning darkness and light. It focuses your samurai spirit on the target. Now, do you wish to be the first to try *Yabusame*?'

Jack shook his head. Although he'd had two years' intensive training and his archery skills were much improved, he didn't fancy his chances from the back of a horse.

'Sensei, with respect, I think I need to learn to ride first.'

'I understand,' she replied. 'Who would be willing to teach Jack how to ride like a true samurai?'

Jack glanced down the line at Akiko, giving her a hopeful smile, but the new boy, Takuan, had already come forward.

'I'd be honoured to,' he said, bowing. 'I was lead rider at the *Takeda Ryū* in Wakasa.'

'Thank you, Takuan-kun,' replied Sensei Yosa. 'Take the brown mare. She's got a good nature and should behave well.'

Takuan led the horse over to the treeline, Jack trailing a little behind.

Jack was surprised the boy had offered to help him. They'd

barely spoken since his arrival. Not that he'd made a purposeful decision to avoid Takuan. It was just that the boy was constantly surrounded by admirers.

'It's a privilege to assist you,' said Takuan, bowing formally to Jack. 'I've heard so much about you.'

'Really?' said Jack, a little taken aback.

'Yes. Akiko told me how you won the *Taryu-Jiai* against the *Yagyu Ryū*. That was true sacrifice, giving up the Jade Sword to Yamato.'

Takuan began to make adjustments to the saddle, patting the horse reassuringly.

'And Yori, he praised you to the heavens. He told me how you saved his life during the Circle of Three. You're quite some samurai for a *gaijin* . . .'

Jack tensed. For a moment he'd thought Takuan was being friendly and had begun to let his guard down. But the boy had let slip his true feelings.

'My apologies . . . I meant to say a foreigner,' said Takuan hurriedly. 'It's just where I come from *your* sort aren't particularly popular.'

'My sort?'

'Yes. Christians. We had a number of Jesuit priests try to convert everyone in our town. They were insisting we obey them and serve Jesus Christ over and above our Emperor. That didn't please our *daimyo* and his samurai. They saw it as a threat to their authority. Though I'm sure that's not your intention.'

'Why should it be?' said Jack, crossing his arms defensively. 'I'm not a Jesuit and I'm not Portuguese.'

'But I thought you were Christian. Isn't that the same thing?'

'No, I'm an English Protestant. The Jesuits are Catholic and England's at war with Portugal. We're sworn enemies. I have *no* intention of converting anyone.'

'I'm so sorry. This conversation hasn't gone at all the way I'd intended.' Takuan bowed his head low and didn't look up. 'Please accept my apologies for my ignorance.'

'You weren't to know,' said Jack.

Jack had come to understand the many intricate formalities of Japanese etiquette. Apologizing was considered a virtue in Japan. When someone said sorry and expressed true remorse, the Japanese were willing to forgive and forget.

'Thank you, Jack,' replied Takuan, smiling. He stroked the neck of the mare. 'Now would you like to mount your horse for your first lesson?'

Jack positioned himself near the saddle, putting his left foot in the stirrup and took a hold. Until now he'd always had the benefit of a guide like Kuma-san to pull him up, so he struggled to get on. The horse kept shifting round every time he attempted to mount her.

Takuan took hold of the horse's head.

'Don't use your arms to pull yourself up,' he advised. 'Use the spring of your right leg. And lift your leg high so that you don't kick the horse or hit your leg on the back of the saddle.'

Jack tried again and to his surprise got on first time.

'Excellent,' praised Takuan. 'Now make sure you're sitting squarely. Like in martial arts, it's important to find your balance.'

Jack shifted around trying to get comfortable. He felt very high and vulnerable. Ever since being thrown from Kuma-san's horse, he'd become nervous of riding.

'Relax. You're so stiff,' said Takuan. 'The horse will pick up on any tension or fear. You need to show you're in control.'

He handed Jack the reins and attached a lunge line to the bridle.

'Better. Now use both lower legs to squeeze the horse lightly. At the same time, push forward slightly in your seat. This is your cue to the horse to walk.'

Jack did as he was instructed and the mare began to move forward.

'See! There's nothing to it.'

'Thanks for your help,' said Jack. He was beginning to wish he hadn't been so distrustful of Takuan. He seemed to be genuine in his offer of friendship.

'My pleasure. We'll keep going until you get used to the rocking motion. Then I'll teach you how to stop.'

Takuan led the horse round in a circle using the lunge line.

'So how's the Two Heavens training going?'

'It's tough,' replied Jack. 'It's like juggling with knives. As soon as you get the right hand working, you forget about the left.'

Takuan nodded sympathetically. 'I wish I had the sword skills to be chosen to learn the Two Heavens. But what I don't understand is why Yamato isn't in your class?'

'He didn't get into the Circle of Three,' explained Jack. 'But he should be able to train in a couple of years or so.'

'If it was me, I'd be so frustrated. And a little embarrassed. I mean he's Masamoto's son.'

'Yamato's brilliant with a *bō*. That makes up for it.'

'And what about Akiko?' asked Takuan casually, nodding in her direction.

Akiko was mounting her steed for a first attempt at *Yabusame*.

'What about her?' said Jack, surprised at the directness of the question.

'Tell me what she's like. She's so different from all the other girls I've met.'

Akiko acknowledged them as she made her way to the head of the course. Takuan immediately bowed back. He seemed to have forgotten Jack completely and cheered Akiko on as she started down the track.

'Isn't she a natural on a horse?' said Takuan, not taking his eyes off her. 'Most impressive form.'

So this was the real reason for offering to help, thought Jack, seeing how entranced Takuan was. Takuan wasn't interested in teaching him horseriding. He was interested in finding out about Akiko.

Standing up in the saddle, Akiko attempted to nock an arrow, but she'd already passed the first target before she could take aim. As she galloped past them towards the second target, Jack's mare suddenly picked up speed and began to follow Akiko's horse.

'Takuan?' called Jack nervously, but the boy was so focused on Akiko's run he didn't appear to hear him.

Akiko successfully released her second arrow but missed. Off-balance, she tried to keep a grip astride the saddle with her thighs. She reached for another arrow. Takuan let go of the lunge line and began to clap and shout encouragement. At which point Jack's mare suddenly bolted.

The horse seemed to think it was a race and charged down the track after Akiko. Jack held on for dear life.

'*How do I stop this horse?*' he screamed, almost bouncing out of the saddle.

Takuan, suddenly aware of the problem, shouted, 'Pull back on the reins!'

In sheer panic, Jack wrenched on the reins.

The mare came to a sudden halt, flinging Jack over its head. He cartwheeled through the air before landing heavily in the dirt, a cloud of dust billowing out around him.

Jack lay there very still, the wind knocked out of him. He felt sick from the shock and ached all over, but he didn't think anything was broken. As the dust settled, Takuan and Sensei Yosa appeared by his side.

'Jack-kun, are you hurt?' asked Sensei Yosa.

'I'm . . . fine,' Jack groaned.

Takuan and Sensei Yosa gently helped Jack to his feet as the rest of the class gathered anxiously round. He saw Kazuki and his gang sniggering.

'Next time don't pull back so hard on the reins,' advised Takuan, brushing the dirt from Jack's *hakama*.

'You could have told me that before!' said Jack.

'I'm so sorry. I had no idea the mare would bolt like that.'

'Forget about it,' Jack wheezed, though he was surprised Takuan had let go of the lunge line in the first place.

Sensei Yosa ushered everyone back to the edge of the track.

'Jack-kun, I think until you're more competent riding, you should use my training horse to practise *Yabusame*,' Sensei Yosa suggested kindly. 'You'll find it far more docile.'

'Thank you, Sensei,' replied Jack, rubbing his ribs. 'But isn't your horse a little big for me?'

A few of the students looked enviously at Jack and then at Sensei Yosa's magnificent steed.

'No, not this horse,' she smiled. 'That one.'

Sensei Yosa pointed to the corner of the field where a target had been set up. Beside it was a wooden dobbin complete with saddle. The class burst into laughter, while Jack stared in dismay at the model horse.

15

BŌ RACE

'It's humiliating!' said Jack as he and the others made their way through the picturesque gardens of the Eikan-Do Temple to their *bōjutsu* class.

Up on the hillside, the spire of the *Tahoto* pagoda poked through the tree canopy like a tiered crown. The leaves surrounding it were still green, but with autumn not far off these would soon turn into a glorious blaze of red, gold, yellow and orange. Then the gardens would fill with people to experience the wonders of *momiji gari*, the maple-leaf viewing ceremony.

'I have to sit on a wooden toy, while everyone else rides around on real horses!' he protested.

'It won't be forever,' consoled Yamato.

Suppressing a grin, Saburo added, 'No, I'm sure Sensei Yosa will put some wheels on it soon.'

Yamato and Saburo convulsed with laughter.

Jack glared at them. 'Kazuki hasn't stopped taunting me about it all week. I don't need you two rubbing salt into the wound!'

'But Takuan's still helping you learn to ride, isn't he?' asked Akiko, trying to maintain a straight face herself.

'Yes,' Jack admitted, glancing ahead to where Takuan was chatting with Emi and her friends, Cho and Kai. The girls were giggling behind their hands at something he'd just said. 'But I don't altogether trust him.'

'Why not?'

'He let go of the leading rein when my horse bolted.'

'Why would he do that?' said Yamato, suddenly serious.

Jack shrugged. 'To show me up in front of the class. To prove *gaijin* can't be samurai.'

'I think you're being overly suspicious, Jack. He's been nothing but friendly and courteous towards us,' insisted Akiko. 'He actually mentioned to me how responsible he feels.'

'I'm sure he'd tell *you* anything.'

'What do you mean?' asked Akiko.

He immediately regretted his rash comment. He knew Akiko was only trying to help.

'Oh . . . nothing really,' said Jack, quickening his pace to get ahead of his friends.

Yori caught up with him.

'Are you all right?' he whispered.

Jack shook his head. 'Not really,' he confessed. 'The *Yabusame* training is making me look a fool in front of everyone.'

'Everyone's got to start somewhere,' said Yori. 'And you can't be the hero *all* the time.'

'I didn't mean it like that,' said Jack, sighing. 'But Takuan's so good at *Yabusame*. Everyone's talking about it – he's even impressed Sensei Yosa. And he seems to be spending a lot of time talking to Akiko.'

'He spends a lot of time talking to everyone,' said Yori. Studying Jack with a serious eye, he then pronounced, 'Beware the tiger that tears not only its prey but also its own heart.'

'What does *that* mean?' said Jack, utterly perplexed.

But Yori only raised his eyebrows in an all-knowing Sensei Yamada-like way and walked on.

Sensei Kano rapped his long white staff upon the ground, ending the student's *bō kata*.

'Now you've warmed up with your staffs, we'll move on to honing your balancing skills,' he announced in his booming voice.

Big as a mountain bear, with a short crop of black hair and a fuzzy beard, Sensei Kano was a formidable samurai. He strode over to a wooden jetty at the edge of the Eikan-Do's central pond. The confident manner in which he walked gave no indication he was blind. Only his eyes hinted at the truth. Misty grey and unfocused, they registered nothing. With his other senses, though, he saw everything.

He tapped the edge of the landing stage with his staff. Several small rowing boats were bobbing gently in the water.

'I want you to pair off and row these boats to the other shore and back.'

'How's that going to help with our balance?' asked Saburo.

'One of you will be rowing. The other must stand on the stern,' explained Sensei Kano. 'Change over when you reach the far bank. It's a race, but one not necessarily won by the fastest rowers. If your partner falls in, you have to row in a complete circle before continuing again. Yori-kun, can you ensure everyone observes this rule?'

The class began to pair off and clamber into the boats.

'Would you join me in my boat?' asked Takuan of Akiko, stepping in front of Jack in the line.

'I was intending to row with Kiku,' she replied, bowing her head in appreciation of the offer.

'Of course,' replied Takuan. 'But wouldn't it make more sense if Saburo partnered Kiku?'

Saburo's mouth fell open at the suggestion, while Kiku blinked in surprise.

'A big strong samurai like you would surely relish the opportunity to race with a light, fast girl like Kiku.'

Saburo stood tall, tightening the *obi* round his ample waist, trying to match up to the praise. 'Well, if you put it like that . . .'

'Excellent,' said Takuan, as if the decision had been made. 'Don't look so put out, Jack. I'd row with you, but it would be an unfair advantage.'

'What do you mean?' said Jack, taken off-guard.

'With you having been a sailor, you stand the best chance of winning,' explained Takuan, helping Akiko into a boat. 'It wouldn't be fair if the girls didn't have some male strength to even up the competition.'

'Not that Akiko needs any help,' Takuan added quickly, noticing her brow furrow slightly at his comment.

'You're certainly right about that,' said Jack, climbing into a boat with Yamato. 'It's good of you to add ballast to her boat, though! But I still don't rate your chances.'

'That sounds like a challenge,' grinned Takuan. 'See you at the finish line.'

Takuan eased his boat away from the jetty, Akiko settling in the stern.

'He's certainly got a way with words,' said Yamato, taking up the oars.

Jack nodded his agreement, watching Akiko drift by, her gentle laughter carried on the breeze. He very much hoped she wasn't being taken in by Takuan's charms.

Once everyone was lined up, the non-rowers climbed on to the rear rail of their boats. Many of the students were wobbling precariously, despite holding out their staffs for balance.

'Are you ready . . . go!' shouted Sensei Kano.

The little boats surged forward. There was a huge splash as Saburo was the first to topple into the water. He came up gasping and nearly capsized the boat as Kiku helped him back in, before picking up the oars and starting their penalty circle.

Jack quickly found his sea legs and urged Yamato to paddle harder. They eased ahead of the pack. Behind them, Jack heard another splash and glanced round to see Cho floundering in the pond. Emi was irritably telling her off, saying she should have chosen Kai instead. Kai looked like she would have appreciated swapping over, considering her partner was the heavyweight Nobu.

Akiko and Takuan were making steady progress, with Takuan being careful not to rock the boat as he rowed, though Jack knew Akiko could probably stand on one leg in a storm and still not fall over. These days her new talents seemed boundless. Then Jack spotted Kazuki and Hiroto speeding up behind them, Hiroto rowing in long, powerful strokes while Kazuki crouched on the stern, keeping his centre of gravity low and his *bō* in hand.

'Row faster!' shouted Jack. 'They're catching up.'

Yamato put his back into it. They passed the midway marker of an ornamental stone, but Hiroto proved the better oarsman and soon the two boats were drawing level with one another. All of a sudden, Jack's ribs flared with pain and he almost toppled overboard.

'That's cheating!' exclaimed Yamato, having witnessed Jack receive a jab in the back from Kazuki's staff.

'No, it's not. It's tactics,' Kazuki replied as Hiroto brought their boat alongside. 'This is a *bōjutsu* class after all. And don't forget our agreement!'

Kazuki thrust his staff at Jack a second time. Still off-balance, Jack couldn't avoid the strike and was caught in the stomach. He doubled over with pain. Kazuki went for the final blow, hoping to knock Jack into the water. But Jack managed to raise his *bō* at the last second and block the strike. He then whipped his own staff round in an arc, aiming for Kazuki's head. Kazuki ducked and swept his *bō* low across Jack's boat. Jack was forced to jump and barely avoided getting cracked across the shins.

Landing unevenly on the rails, Jack felt the little rowing boat rock dangerously. Yamato's right oar dug deep into the water and was snatched from his grasp. The boat lurched to one side. Jack teetered on the edge of the rail, arms cartwheeling manically. Only years of seafaring allowed him to regain his balance.

To no avail. As their boat keeled over and water rushed in,

Jack jumped to the other side, trying to level the boat before it capsized. But it was too little, too late.

Kazuki and Hiroto coursed ahead, laughing to one another. 'Hope you can swim!' Hiroto shouted back as Jack and Yamato floundered in the chilly waters of the pond.

By the time they'd righted their boat, clambered in and completed their penalty circle, three other boats had passed them by, including Takuan and Akiko.

Yamato grabbed the oars and began to row furiously, while Jack crouched low on the stern urging him on. They passed two of the boats before reaching the opposite bank. Takuan and Akiko were setting off on the return leg. Kazuki and Hiroto, however, had swapped positions and were already heading back towards the jetty. Jack took over the oars from Yamato, checked to see his friend was balanced, then dug the blades in.

With each stroke, they gained on the two lead boats. Takuan appeared balanced, but Akiko was not as accomplished a rower as Jack. He soon overtook their boat. Then Jack focused on catching up with Kazuki. Keeping the strength in his pull even and ensuring the blades didn't catch the pond's surface, he brought the boat cutting smoothly through the water until they were head-to-head with Kazuki and Hiroto.

But Kazuki was determined not to let them pass. Their oars clashed and he threatened to ram Jack's boat. Hiroto tried to dislodge Yamato with his staff, but Yamato was too quick and skilful with the *bō*. He neatly deflected the strike, cracking his staff across Hiroto's knuckles and forcing him to drop his weapon. Then he jabbed Hiroto hard in the chest and the boy flew off the stern. Kazuki cursed and broke off from the race.

Jack and Yamato let out a shout of triumph.

They'd won!

All of a sudden their boat came to a juddering halt, Yamato landing in a heap on top of Jack. Too intent on beating their rivals, they'd crashed into an ornamental rock. They could only watch as Akiko rowed calmly by.

Takuan raised his staff in salute. 'Your exploits have inspired me to compose a *haiku* in your honour . . .

> '*Spring hare runs too fast*
> *to cross the finish line first –*
> *hear the tortoise laugh.*'

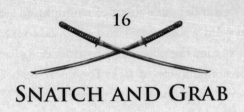

16

SNATCH AND GRAB

Jack, still wet from capsizing in the pond, trudged through Kyoto's side streets in the direction of the *Niten Ichi Ryū*. Yamato had stayed behind with Sensei Kano for his advanced *bōjutsu* practice, while the rest of the class, in high-spirits following the race, had taken a more direct route back to school.

But Jack was not alone. Yori had insisted on accompanying him.

'He's so full of himself!' muttered Jack, kicking at a loose pebble on the ground.

'Who?'

'Takuan.'

'Ah! The tiger returns,' said Yori, arching his eyebrow in a sage-like manner.

'What *are* you on about?'

'The tiger of jealousy, of course.'

'I'm not jealous,' declared Jack. 'Why on earth should I be jealous of him?'

'No reason. Good-looking, excellent at martial arts, impresses the sensei, a bit different, admired by Akiko . . .'

124

'OK, I might be a *little* bit envious,' admitted Jack.

Yori stopped walking. Jack turned round to see his friend shaking his head, a despairing look on his face.

'I was describing *you*.'

'Me?'

'Yes,' sighed Yori in exasperation. 'Jealousy is seeing the other person's blessings instead of your own. You *chose* to hear it as praise for Takuan. But I was pointing out why you've no reason to feel threatened by him.'

'I'm not . . . I'm just worried for Akiko's sake . . .' began Jack, but he trailed off under his friend's questioning gaze.

'Takuan is a nice person. He's just being friendly. He wants to be your friend too. Why don't you let him? Then he'll no longer be a threat; he'll be your ally.'

'You're right, as always,' said Jack, squeezing the water from the sleeves of his *kimono*. 'I don't know why I've been acting so irritably recently. Perhaps it's the pressure of the Two Heavens. It's *so* hard to learn. Even Masamoto-sama's admitted only a few students ever master the technique. What if I'm not one of them?'

'You will be,' assured Yori. 'You conquered the Circle of Three. Remember what the High Priest said. "If your spirit is strong, you can accomplish anything." It's just going to take time. Besides, a fruit that falls without shaking is too ripe for eating.'

'Have you swallowed Sensei Yamada's prayer book or something?' exclaimed Jack, laughing.

'It means good things only come through hard work.'

'But Kazuki and Akiko seem to be progressing so much faster than me.'

'There you go again, comparing yourself to others. Don't worry about what anyone else is doing. Concentrate on your own progress.'

Yori paused a moment, his fingers lightly tapping his chin as he contemplated what to say next.

'It's like today on the pond. You were so focused on beating Kazuki that you forgot the purpose of the race. It's the same with the Two Heavens. If you waste your energy thinking about others, you'll end up on the rocks again. Focus on rowing your own boat and you will reach the shore.'

Yori gave a sagely nod of the head, clearly satisfied with his advice, and set off down the road again. Jack stared after his little friend. Yori may not possess the build of a warrior, but he certainly had the brains of a priest. Jack was glad of his friendship. He lifted the sodden folds of his kimono and hurried after him.

As they passed by a building with an arched roof of green tiles and dragon finials, Jack recognized they were in the outer courtyard of the *Ryōanji*, the Temple of the Peaceful Dragon. He'd been here several times before.

The previous year Jack had spotted Akiko mysteriously leaving the *Niten Ichi Ryū* at night. Being both curious and concerned by her unusual behaviour, Jack had followed her and arrived at this very temple. He'd discovered she was visiting a strange monk who had knife-like hands more suited for fighting than praying. To begin with, Akiko had given no credible explanation for her nocturnal wanderings or why she kept them so secret. At one point, Jack had even thought she was training to be a ninja. But Akiko had eventually confided in him that the monk was simply offering her spiritual comfort for the loss of her baby brother, Kiyoshi, some years ago. Jack knew Akiko still called upon the monk as he'd seen her leave the school grounds at night on a number of occasions since their return to school.

'GRAB HIM!' shouted a gruff voice.

Two men jumped from a side alley and seized Jack by the arms, disarming him of his staff. A third man shoved a bag over his head. Before Jack knew what was happening, they had dragged him off his feet and were carrying him away. As Jack struggled wildly to escape, he could hear Yori shouting.

'Stop! Or I'll —'

'Or what, little one?' snorted the gruff voice. 'Bite our ankles?'

The two men holding Jack began to laugh.

'I'm warning you,' said Yori, his voice trembling. 'I train at the *Niten Ichi Ryū*.'

'Don't make me laugh. They don't teach pet samurai.'

Jack heard a scuffle. One of the men swore loudly. There was a snap of wood as a staff broke, followed by the dull sound of a fist striking flesh. Yori groaned and Jack heard a small body fall to the floor. Forgetting his fear and fuelled by anger, Jack redoubled his efforts. He managed to free a leg and lashed out. His foot connected with someone's face. There was a satisfying crunch as a nose broke. Jack kicked again and freed his other leg.

'Damn *gaijin*!' the man growled, spitting blood.

Jack tried to get away, but the other man still held his arms tight from behind. He flung back his head in an attempt to knock his captor's teeth out, but something hard struck the back of his neck first.

Lights exploded in front of his eyes. He felt sick. Then blacked out.

17
Punishment

A musty smell of rotting straw filled Jack's nostrils. His head pounded, his neck was stiff and a large bruise throbbed below his right ear. Licking his lips, a wave of nausea rose in his throat. He opened his eyes, only to discover it was dark. How long had he been out for?

Then he realized his captors hadn't removed the bag from his head. His kimono was still damp, though, so he couldn't have been unconscious for long. He tried to remove the bag, but his hands were tied. In fact, he couldn't move at all. He was lying on his side upon a hard wooden floor, his feet and hands bound tightly behind his back.

'I say we kill the *gaijin*,' said a man to Jack's right. 'Far less hassle than delivering him alive.'

'True . . .' said the man with the gruff voice, standing behind Jack. 'But he's worth more alive.'

Jack tried to clear his head. He had to think his way out of this predicament. Who were his captors? They had to be ninja. Dragon Eye must have sent them to kidnap him. This was good news. It must mean the *rutter* was still not deciphered.

But he'd planned to face Dragon Eye on equal terms, both swords in hand – not as a prisoner.

'The only good *gaijin* is a dead *gaijin*,' spat a third man to Jack's left.

The wooden floorboards creaked as someone stepped closer. A cold steel blade was pressed against his throat. Bound and helpless, Jack couldn't avoid his fate.

Snatching a last breath, he squeezed his eyes shut and prayed to God. In those final moments, his mind filled with all the memories of his life, his mother and father, of little Jess, the voyage around the world, his time in Japan, of the *Niten Ichi Ryū* and Masamoto, of Akiko and his friends. He realized he'd be leaving them all behind and desperately wanted to live.

'Stop!' shouted the gruff-voiced man.

The blade hesitated on Jack's skin.

'But *daimyo* Kamakura's ruling clearly stated that any *gaijin* found in his domain are to face punishment,' said the man with the knife.

'Yes. But we're not in his province – yet. Kyoto belongs to that soft-headed, Christian-loving *daimyo* Takatomi. Besides, this *gaijin* is no ordinary foreigner. He's pretending to be samurai! How perverse is that? If we deliver him alive to *daimyo* Kamakura in Edo, our reward would be tenfold. We wouldn't be masterless *ashigaru* any more. He'd make us samurai!'

The blade was withdrawn and Jack let out an unsteady sigh of relief. Though it was only a short reprieve, he'd live to see another day.

Jack reassessed his situation. His captors weren't ninja. They were foot soldiers looking to better themselves. They were seeking the reward Kazuki had talked about during the opening ceremony of the Hall of the Hawk. He also knew he was still in Kyoto, so there was a slim chance he'd be able to escape before they moved him to Edo.

'A good point,' agreed the man to Jack's right. 'We can't kill him. Not yet, anyway.'

'Fine, but the *daimyo*'s decree allows us to punish *gaijin* in other ways besides death.'

The man with the knife wrenched Jack to his knees. Jack groaned under the strain, his bonds tightening painfully round his wrists.

'He's coming to. That's good. He can hear his choices,' the man said with glee.

He whipped the bag off Jack's head. Jack squinted against the sudden brightness. Once his eyes grew accustomed to the light, he saw he was being held in a featureless room with a single high slit for a window. There was dirt and straw on the floor and the roof had a hole in it. The surrounding walls were made out of rough planks of wood and the only door he could see was the one straight in front of him.

The man with the knife crouched before him, grinning maliciously while turning the blade before Jack's eyes. He had a flat ugly face with pockmarked skin. Both eyes were ringed black and blue and his nose was flattened like a trampled mushroom, the nostrils caked with dry blood. Jack had obviously executed a perfect stamping kick in his attempt to escape, since both the man's front teeth were missing too.

Glad to see I improved your looks, thought Jack, allowing himself a little smile of satisfaction.

'You won't be smiling when I've finished with you, *gaijin*,' gloated Broken Nose. 'Maybe I can't kill you. But you have a choice of punishment – branding, nose-slitting, amputation of the feet or castration. What will it be?'

'You can't brand him,' said the man to Jack's right. He was heavy-set with a bald head and thick muscular arms.

'Why not?'

'We haven't got a hot iron or fire, stupid.'

'Then perhaps I should cut off his feet?' Broken Nose allowed the knife to wander down Jack's body.

'I wouldn't if I were you,' said Jack, trying not to tremble. 'I'm Masamoto-sama's adopted son.'

'So what? I've no idea who Masamoto is.'

'He's the greatest swordsman in Japan and he'll slice you into eight pieces if you harm me.'

'I've heard of him,' said the leader with the gruff voice, who still stood behind Jack unseen. 'He's that samurai who uses two swords, isn't he?'

Jack nodded furiously. Masamoto's reputation had saved him once before with some local drunks and he hoped to God it would again.

'I doubt his story's true. No respected samurai would dishonour their family name by adopting a *gaijin*. Slit his big nose,' he ordered the man with the knife. 'A nose for a nose. The *daimyo* would surely consider that just punishment.'

Broken Nose excitedly raised his *tantō*. Jack tried to turn his head away, but was grabbed by the hair from behind and forced to face the blade.

'Hold still, *gaijin*. This won't take long.'

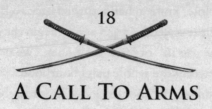

18

A CALL TO ARMS

There was a rap on the door. The knife hovered over the bridge of Jack's nose.

'Gag him,' said the leader, passing Broken Nose a dirty piece of cloth. 'And you, see who it is.'

The bald-headed foot soldier got to his feet and went to the door.

Jack retched as the filthy rag was stuffed into his mouth. Broken Nose drew closer, spittle plastering Jack's face as he spoke, 'Make a single sound and it'll be your *throat* I slit.'

Jack stared back, wide-eyed with panic. The unexpected visitor was his sole chance of escape, but bound and gagged as he was, he was helpless. He could only pray that the caller would look in and see him.

'It's just some blind beggar,' said the bald-headed soldier, parting the door a crack.

Jack's hope of rescue vanished.

'Tell him we're not a temple. We don't give out alms,' ordered their leader.

'Go away!' shouted the bald-headed soldier, closing the door in the beggar's face.

Broken Nose, knife in hand, turned back to Jack. His gap-toothed smile revealed his eagerness to begin the punishment.

'Leave the gag in,' ordered the leader. 'We don't want his screams attracting the whole neighbourhood.'

All of a sudden the door exploded inwards, the splintering wood knocking the bald-headed soldier off his feet. Jumping to his feet, Broken Nose was confronted by a tall bearded man.

Sensei Kano.

Jack would have cried out for joy if not for the gag.

Broken Nose ran at the *bō* master with his knife. Sensei Kano, hearing his attacker cross the wooden floor, whipped his staff hard and high into the man's face. It caught Broken Nose on the jaw and he dropped like a stone.

Meanwhile, the bald-headed soldier had scrambled to his feet and snatched up his *katana*. He charged at Sensei Kano, aiming to slice through his neck. The *bō* master sensed the attack and ducked beneath the blade. He brought the other end of his staff cracking down on to the man's skull. The soldier reeled under the blow and dropped his sword. Then Sensei Kano thrust the tip of his *bō* into the man's gut. The soldier fell to his knees, croaking for breath. A third strike knocked him flat on his back, where he lay unconscious.

Jack wondered where the leader was in all this. Hearing a clattering sound to his left, he spied a discarded *saya* out of the corner of his eye. Sensei Kano turned to face his adversary.

But the leader appeared to Jack's right instead, sneaking silently towards the blind samurai. This was the first time Jack had caught sight of the man. Red-eyed, with a moustache consisting of two tufts of thick black hair either side of his nose, he looked as mean as a devil – and was as devious as one. Sandals in one hand, he crept round the edge of the room so as not to make the boards creak. In the other hand, he held his *katana*, its blade chipped and battleworn. Throwing a sandal close to where his *saya* had fallen, he moved even closer to Sensei Kano.

Sensei Kano held his staff out in the direction of the noises, unaware of the approaching man behind.

Tossing his other sandal into the far corner as a final distraction, the soldier thrust his sword into Sensei Kano's back. But the *bō* master had already dropped to his knees and simultaneously driven his staff backwards into the groin of his attacker. The soldier, bent double with agony, didn't stand a chance as Sensei Kano swivelled round and struck him a mighty blow across the temple with his *bō*. The man collapsed in a pile.

So intent upon the fight, Jack had failed to notice that Broken Nose had come to. The man was crawling towards him. His mouth hung ghoulishly open, all blood, gums and shattered teeth.

'Die, *gaijin*!' he spat.

Jack tried to wriggle away, but Broken Nose was already on his knees lifting the blade to drive it into Jack's chest.

Suddenly a staff shot across the room like a spear, striking Broken Nose in the side of the head. His eyes rolled in their sockets and he fell face first to the wooden deck. Jack heard a crunch as several more teeth were knocked out of the man's mouth.

Yamato ran into the room.

'Are you all right?' he asked, removing Jack's gag.

'I am now,' coughed Jack. 'Thanks to Sensei Kano's *bō*.'

'That was my *bō*!'

'*You* threw it?' said Jack, impressed at his friend's skill.

'New trick I learnt today,' he replied, grinning with pride while he undid Jack's bonds.

'But one only to be used as a last resort, since you sacrifice your weapon,' reminded Sensei Kano, dragging the three unconscious soldiers into a pile. 'Yamato-kun, restrain these men with the rope. Masamoto-sama will decide their fate.'

'You were lucky to survive, Sensei,' said Jack, sitting up and rubbing at his wrists. 'I thought that last one had you fooled.'

'Luck had nothing to do with it,' said Sensei Kano. 'The man hadn't washed for a month. It was I who fooled him.'

'But how did you ever find me?'

'Yori ran back to the Eikan-do Temple and told us what had happened,' Yamato explained as he tied the three men's hands together. 'To begin with, it was a simple matter of following the water dripping from your kimono. But then the trail dried up. Fortunately, Sensei Kano could smell you nearby.'

'But I had a bath yesterday,' protested Jack.

'Foreigners have a different odour to Japanese,' explained Sensei Kano, wrinkling his nose and giving a great big belly laugh.

Sensei Kano escorted Jack, Yamato and the prisoners back to the *Niten Ichi Ryū*. As soon as they returned, Masamoto summoned Jack to the Hall of the Phoenix.

'Despite my efforts on behalf of *daimyo* Takatomi, *daimyo*

Kamakura's campaign against Christians and foreigners continues to gather support,' began Masamoto solemnly, sitting cross-legged upon his dais.

A maid brought in a pot of *sencha* and poured them each a cup before being dismissed. Masamoto now toyed with his, appearing too deep in thought to drink any.

'We had been aware that he was offering rewards to those delivering so-called justice upon Christians. *Daimyo* Takatomi, being a recent convert to Christianity, was not best pleased. I, however, was not concerned for your personal safety, Jack-kun. It was a local ruling. Kyoto and every other province were unaffected by it. But I'd not counted on *ronin*.'

'*Ronin*?' asked Jack.

'Masterless samurai,' explained Masamoto as he sipped his tea, only to find it had become too cold for his liking. 'Ever since the Battle of Nakasendo brought an end to civil conflict ten years ago, many soldiers have been out of service. *Ronin* seek a *daimyo* to serve, to fight for, to die for. The cause rarely matters, so long as they have food in their stomachs and a standard to bear.'

Masamoto put down his cup and studied Jack. He gave a weary sigh, clasping his hands beneath his chin as if deliberating on whether to disclose something troubling.

'There's been a call to arms,' he finally revealed. '*Daimyo* Kamakura is openly recruiting *ronin, ashigaru* and the support of any *daimyo* sympathetic to his mission. The man's made his intentions clear. It's a worrying development.'

'Are you suggesting I should leave?' asked Jack, both hopeful and anxious of his guardian's answer.

Returning home to England was his hope, his dream.

Alone, he had no chance of making the long journey south through Japan to the port of Nagasaki. But with Masamoto's help, he'd have his guardian's guidance and protection. Yet Jack was now in two minds about going. He wasn't ready. He hadn't mastered the Two Heavens and Dragon Eye was still a threat. Most importantly, he had yet to recover his father's *rutter*, though he was beginning to lose hope of ever finding it. Masamoto's sources had still not heard anything.

'NO!' shouted Masamoto vehemently. 'That man will not drive you away. You are my adopted son. You are family. You are samurai!'

Jack was taken aback by his guardian's passionate outburst. This was the other reason for his growing reluctance to leave. He now had family here in Japan. A father figure in Masamoto and a brother in Yamato. He'd also made good friends in Yori and Saburo. And there was Akiko, who'd become so much part of his life that he couldn't imagine being without her. Japan had got under his skin, found a place in his heart, and the idea of leaving was becoming harder with each day.

'Besides,' continued his guardian, 'I suspect there's much more to *daimyo* Kamakura's campaign than a simple hatred of foreigners.'

Jack was intrigued. Having met the man himself, he'd been struck by how cruel, power-hungry and sadistic the samurai was. Jack had once witnessed the beheading of an elderly tea merchant, merely because the old man hadn't heard the command to bow as *daimyo* Kamakura passed by. What worse could *daimyo* Kamakura be planning than the exile and murder of all foreigners?

'But I'll be making an announcement about that this evening. First, I must see to the punishment of the three *ashigaru* who kidnapped you.'

Masamoto got to his feet and picked up his swords.

'Are you going to kill them?' asked Jack, not certain he really wanted to know the answer.

'I've seriously considered it. But Sensei Yamada convinced me they'd be more useful as messengers. They'll ensure everyone they meet knows the province of Kyoto will not tolerate racial persecution.'

'So what will you do?'

'Let's just say they won't be able to count higher than eight – with either their fingers or toes!'

19

THE ANNOUNCEMENT

'WAR sits upon the horizon like a thundercloud,' proclaimed Masamoto.

The announcement sent a wave of stunned astonishment through the rows of young samurai kneeling before him in the *Chō-no-ma*, the dining hall named after its panelled walls of painted butterflies. For some, it was a shock; for others, it brought the promise of honour and glory. For Jack, who'd witnessed battles first-hand at sea against Portuguese warships, it meant days and nights of fear, pain and death.

Masamoto held up his hand for silence. He was wearing his ceremonial flame-red kimono, its five golden phoenix *kamon* glimmering in the lamplight like armour. His face was brooding and severe, his scarring a dark red.

'You'll all be aware of *daimyo* Kamakura's campaign to drive out Christians and foreigners from our land. He considers them a threat to our nation.'

Jack felt the eyes of his fellow students upon him. Most were sympathetic to his plight, but a number were openly hostile.

'*Daimyo* Takatomi, however, believes the way forward is a unified Japan that welcomes guests from other lands. He doesn't see religion as a barrier to a samurai's duty to their Emperor. Indeed, he is a convert to Christianity. He has, therefore, been seeking a peaceful solution to the situation, confident that his old comrades-in-arms will realize a campaign against foreigners would divide Japan, not strengthen it. For if *daimyo* begin to take sides, the whole of Japan could be dragged into another civil war.'

There was an anxious murmur among the students. Jack glanced over in Kazuki's direction. His rival was smirking at the announcement, no doubt pleased to hear war was a real possibility. So far Kazuki's Scorpion Gang had only been a focus for their bullying of him, but now it threatened to fulfil its true purpose – 'Death to all *gaijin*' – that the gang had pledged during their secret *irezumi* initiation ceremony. Jack shuddered at the thought.

'But do *not* be fooled by *daimyo* Kamakura's crusade,' warned Masamoto, slamming his fist upon the table. 'His call to arms suggests this isn't *just* about banishing a supposed enemy from our country. We now have good reason to suspect he's playing upon prejudice to raise an army, not only to expel our foreign friends, but to overthrow all of Japan and rule it for himself.'

There was a collective gasp of disbelief.

Masamoto had evidently informed his sensei of the news beforehand, for they showed no surprise. They sat impassively either side of Masamoto upon the wooden dais, studying their students with the steely determination of warriors ready to do battle.

'We should therefore be prepared for war, if needs must. That is when I will turn to you, my young samurai. I trust I can count on your loyal service.' He paused, gazing intently at the rows of trainee warriors. 'In the meantime, we'll intensify our battle training and await *daimyo* Takatomi's command.'

Unsheathing his *katana* from its *saya*, he held the gleaming blade aloft and cried, 'Learn today so that you may live tomorrow!'

The school thundered its response.

'MASAMOTO! MASAMOTO! MASAMOTO!'

The conversation during dinner was animated. Clusters of students discussed the prospect of war in excited whispers, while others silently picked at their food, coming to terms with the news.

Jack sat between Akiko and Yamato only three tables down from the dais where Masamoto and his sensei ate. With a few more years' training they would earn the right to sit at a table directly in front of the sensei. That was if they *had* a few more years to train. Or, for that matter, to live.

'Do you think we'll *all* have to go to war?' whispered Yori, who sat opposite Akiko and Kiku, anxiously biting on his lower lip.

'Probably,' said Yamato. 'It's what we were born to do.'

'But a lot of the students haven't come of age yet,' pointed out Kiku.

'I don't think the younger trainees will have to go,' said Akiko. 'But those at the top table certainly will.'

'What about us?' asked Saburo, the only one not to have

lost his appetite, tucking into the bowls of rice and steamed fish with gusto.

'Perhaps we get to choose,' said Yori hopefully.

'There's no choice in war,' Jack stated, his eyes fixed on a grain of rice that had got stuck to the end of his *hashi*. 'War chooses us.'

Reflecting on his own predicament, he crushed the rice grain between the tips of his *hashi*. He was caught between two conflicts and had chosen neither. Portugal had been at war with England for as long as he could remember, but the only Portuguese person he had ever met was Father Lucius. Yet he was still their sworn enemy. And now he found himself trapped in the centre of another power struggle, one in which his race and religion were being used as pawns in the fight for Japan's throne. Jack realized that as one of Masamoto's students, he too would be called upon to fight. Not only for his survival, but for Japan's future as well – one he had a vested interest in preserving.

'You *were* right, Jack,' said Kiku. '*Daimyo* Takatomi was talking about war when he'd described the Hall of the Hawk as a beacon of light in dark times. He must have already known of *daimyo* Kamakura's plans.'

'But what about the Emperor? Doesn't he rule Japan?' asked Jack, finding he had little stomach for dinner, and put down his *hashi*. 'I thought *daimyo* Kamakura, as a samurai lord, was supposed to fight *for* him, not against him.'

'He wouldn't be taking power from the Emperor,' explained Akiko. 'The Emperor is the symbolic head of our country. The real power resides with the Council of Regents.'

'So who are the Regents?'

'They're the five most powerful samurai lords in Japan. *Daimyo* Takatomi from Kyoto Province, *daimyo* Yukimura from Osaka Province, *daimyo* Kamakura from Edo Pro—'

'But if Kamakura's already in charge,' interrupted Jack, 'why would he want to start a war?'

'The Council is only governing Japan on behalf of the ruler-in-waiting, Hasegawa Satoshi.'

'What do you mean "in waiting"?'

'Satoshi isn't old enough to rule yet. His father, who became Japan's leader following the Battle of Nakasendo, died only a year after the war. Satoshi was six at the time. And our *daimyo* Takatomi, not wanting Japan to descend back into civil war, set up the Council of Regents. They were to act as Japan's government until Satoshi came of age. When he does next year, the Council will end and Satoshi will rule Japan alone.'

'So that's why *daimyo* Kamakura's building an army now,' said Yamato. 'He's intending to take over Japan before Satoshi does.'

'So, if it does come to war,' said Jack, lowering his voice and glancing over at Kazuki's table, 'would *everyone* here fight on *daimyo* Takatomi's side for Satoshi?'

'Of course!' said Akiko, astonished Jack would even ask such a question.

'Even Kazuki?'

'Yes. Everyone at this school has sworn their allegiance. We're all students of Masamoto-sama.'

'But don't you remember what I told you about his Scorpion Gang?'

Akiko sighed. 'And remember how you falsely accused Kazuki of cheating during the Circle of Three?'

Jack nodded reluctantly.

'Kazuki may not like you, but he's not always as black as you paint him. He is a *true* samurai. As a student of the *Niten Ichi Ryū*, his duty is to Masamoto-sama. He is honour-bound to follow him. Besides, his family fought alongside *daimyo* Takatomi's forces at Nakasendo.'

Jack still had his doubts. Locking eyes with Kazuki on the opposite table, he knew his rival wasn't to be trusted. Despite Akiko's reassurance of Kazuki's obedience to the code of *bush-ido*, Jack knew what he'd heard that night in the *Butokuden* when Kazuki, following in his father's footsteps, had sworn his allegiance to Kamakura's cause.

Dinner over, the young samurai left the *Chō-no-ma* and made their way to the Hall of Lions for bed. Summer was at an end, so there was a chill to the night air and few students dawdled long outside. Jack noticed some of them glancing in his direction. They seemed to be talking about him as they passed. Jack wondered whether they were blaming him for the growing troubles, being the only foreigner in the school.

'Jack!' called Takuan, strolling over. 'I think we should increase our number of horseriding lessons. If there's to be a war, you'll need to know how to ride well.'

'Thanks,' said Jack, forcing a smile.

Though he appreciated Takuan's help, he wasn't looking forward to more lessons. They'd started practising the trot and

Jack had great difficulty matching his horse's rhythm. By the end of a session, his bones were pounded so much he could barely walk.

'By the way,' asked Takuan casually, 'have you seen Akiko recently?'

'She's gone to ninja training,' replied Jack, only half-joking. Takuan was always asking after Akiko. It irritated him, though he tried not to show it.

'Really?' replied Takuan, his mouth falling open in astonishment.

'No,' said Jack, laughing. 'She sees her priest at this time.'

'So that's where she's always off to!' A puzzled expression then formed on Takuan's face. 'Don't you think it's a little odd? Why not the normal morning prayers?'

Jack shrugged. Though her timing did seem a bit strange, now he thought about it.

'Well, it's good to know Akiko's a devout Buddhist,' said Takuan cheerily, before turning towards the *Shishi-no-ma*. 'See you tomorrow at the usual time.'

Only a few pockets of students remained in the courtyard now. From bitter experience, Jack didn't want to end up alone out here. He'd seen enough trouble for one day.

As he was making his way to the *Shishi-no-ma*, Jack spotted a lone boy sitting on the steps of the *Butsuden*. Wandering over, he discovered that it was Yori.

'Are you all right?' asked Jack.

Yori nodded, but wouldn't meet his gaze.

'Are you sure?' Jack insisted. 'You hardly said anything during dinner.'

Yori merely shrugged and concentrated on folding a small piece of *origami* paper with his hands.

'Don't think much of your bodyguard,' shouted a voice from the other side of the courtyard.

Jack turned to see Kazuki heading towards the Hall of Lions with Nobu and Hiroto.

'I heard he scurried away like a mouse at the first sign of danger!' Nobu chortled, mimicking a panicked escape. 'Oh, help! It's a lowly *ashigaru*!'

'We should be thanking him for leaving the *gaijin* to die,' sneered Hiroto. 'It would have been a gruesome death!'

'Go away!' said Jack, seeing Yori hang his head in shame.

'That's what *you* should do,' said Kazuki, stopping beside the entrance to the Hall of Lions. 'If you stay here, you'll burn.'

'He'll be roasted alive along with the rest of them,' taunted Hiroto gleefully. 'Anyone fancy *gaijin* for dinner?'

The three of them disappeared inside the hall, laughing to themselves.

'Sorry, Jack,' mumbled Yori, in a voice so quiet Jack had to crouch down to hear his friend.

'Sorry for what?'

'I'm ashamed I failed you.'

Jack looked into Yori's face. He had tears in his eyes and was trembling.

'You didn't fail me. You got help.'

'But I couldn't save you,' he sniffed, wiping his nose with the sleeve of his kimono. 'I *did* try to fight, but the men just laughed at me. One of them snapped my staff and punched me in the face. I'm a pathetic joke of a warrior.'

'No, you're not,' insisted Jack. 'If it wasn't for your quick thinking, Sensei Kano would never have found me.'

'It doesn't matter what you say,' said Yori, making a final fold in the paper to form a small *origami* mouse. 'When we go to war, I won't stand a chance.'

He closed his fist round the little paper creature and threw the crushed remains to the ground.

20

KIAIJUTSU

'What is your true face, which you had before your father and mother were even born?' asked Sensei Yamada, twirling his wispy grey beard between his bony fingers.

Perched before the great bronze statue of the Buddha in the *Butsuden*, the old monk reposed upon his *zabuton* cushion like an amiable toad. He grinned impishly, enjoying the quizzical expressions upon his students' faces.

'*Mokuso*,' he instructed, lighting a stick of incense.

The scent of jasmine floated through the air as the class settled into their meditation for the day. Sitting in the lotus position, they calmed their breathing and let their minds contemplate Sensei Yamada's *koan*.

The Buddha Hall became silent with thought.

Jack shifted awkwardly upon his cushion, sore from all his horseriding lessons. He had never found his Zen master's riddles easy, but this had to be the most perplexing of them all. The sad thing was that Jack was already having trouble remembering what his parents' faces looked like. With each passing day he lost another detail, his memory of them washing away like sand with the incoming tide.

How on earth was he supposed to know his true face?

Jack let his mind drift to Jess. The last time he'd laid eyes upon his sister, she'd just turned five. Blessed with curls of mousey-blonde hair and sharing the same sea-blue eyes as Jack, she was a pretty girl, more summer buttercup than English rose. Jack wondered what his little sister looked like now. After four years away from home, she wouldn't be so little. And when he finally did make it back to England, after another two years at sea, would he even recognize her? Jess would be ten, going on eleven. A grown-up girl. He could only imagine how different she looked. Then again, he must appear utterly transformed himself. What a bizarre sight he would make back in London, an English boy dressed as a samurai warrior!

'*Mokuso yame!*' announced Sensei Yamada as the last piece of ash fell from the stick of incense. Laying his hands in his lap, he waited for an answer to his *koan*.

The students all sat there, mute.

'Does anyone wish to make a suggestion?' Sensei Yamada asked. 'Kiku-chan?'

Kiku shook her head.

'Emi-chan, perhaps?'

The *daimyo*'s daughter bowed apologetically.

'How about you, Takuan-kun? It's a good opportunity for you to make your first contribution to my lesson.'

Jack looked over his shoulder at Takuan, who was sitting between Emi and Akiko. All the girls in the class were watching him and listening expectantly. For once, Takuan didn't appear comfortable with all the attention.

After a long pause, he finally answered:

'An empty cup waits:
Filled to the brim with thought
now too full to drink.'

There was some respectful applause at Takuan's answer, though many were bemused that he'd replied to a *koan* with a *haiku*.

'That's a very imaginative way of saying you don't know,' Sensei Yamada chortled. 'But I was looking for an *actual* answer.'

The girls gave a disappointed sigh. Jack offered Takuan a sympathetic shrug. Since Yori's chat with him, Jack no longer felt threatened by Takuan. Even though it still bothered Jack every time Takuan asked after Akiko, the boy had really helped him with his horsemanship. In the past month, Jack had learnt to canter and soon, Takuan promised, he would be galloping. Not that this made the slightest impression on his *kyujutsu* teacher, who still insisted he train on the wooden dobbin, much to his continued frustration and embarrassment.

'Doesn't anyone have an answer?' Sensei Yamada asked, looking around hopefully.

Greeted with silence, the Zen master turned to Yori.

'Yori-kun, what do you think?'

'Does it *really* matter?' Yori replied grumpily.

Sensei Yamada's eyes almost disappeared into his head as his face crinkled in utter astonishment. The monk hadn't expected his most promising student to respond with such discourtesy. Nor had the rest of the class, who stared aghast at Yori's attitude.

'We're going to war! What's the point in answering a *koan*, or composing a *haiku*,' Yori continued, picking angrily at the sleeves of his kimono. 'Shouldn't we be learning to fight instead?'

Sensei Yamada took a long slow breath and steepled his fingers beneath his chin. The class waited on tenterhooks for his response.

'I appreciate your concerns, Yori-kun,' he said, fixing Yori with a steely glare, 'but I am surprised that *you* of all my students question the purpose of my classes.'

Yori swallowed guilty and looked as if he was about to burst into tears.

'Let me make clear the crucial importance of these lessons.' The Zen master's tone was measured but severe, delivered like a rap across the knuckles. 'The *Niten Ichi Ryū* does not train ignorant thugs. You are following the Way of the Warrior and this entails mastering *all* the Arts. You're not a mercenary. You're not a dim-witted *ashigaru*. You are samurai. Now act like one!'

Yori bowed his head in shame, his little rebellion over. Sensei Yamada turned his attention upon the rest of the class.

'That goes for all of you. A nation that draws too broad a difference between its scholars and its warriors will have its thinking done by cowards and its fighting done by fools!'

The Zen master stood up and strode over to a large bowl. Made of hammered bronze, the singing bowl was seated upon an ornamental cushion and red lacquer stand. When struck, the bowl rang like a heavenly gong, its resonance pure and rich. Jack had heard its harmonious tones during the *Ganjitsu* celebrations at New Year.

'Perhaps you need a more practical demonstration of the

esoteric spiritual arts?' said Sensei Yamada, sounding the bowl with a large wooden striker. It rang loud and clear, echoing endlessly throughout the Buddha Hall. 'Maybe it's time I taught you *kiaijutsu*.'

All of a sudden the students were abuzz. Jack looked around, wondering what was going on.

Saburo leaned over and excitedly whispered, 'It's the secret art of the *sohei*!'

The *sohei*, as Jack knew, were the legendary warrior monks of the Enryakuji Temple. It was rumoured that using *ki*, their spiritual energy, they could defeat their enemies without even drawing their swords. The *sohei* became the most powerful Buddhist sect in Japan, until forty years ago the samurai General Nobunaga gathered together a massive force and destroyed them. It had been thought that no warrior monks survived the attack. Jack, however, had discovered that Sensei Yamada himself had once been *sohei*. But only he, Akiko and Saburo had known this. Until now.

As the singing bowl's ring faded to nothing, so too did the students' chatter. Sensei Yamada seemed pleased to have their undivided attention.

'What purpose has a *kiai* in a fight?' he asked the class.

Several hands shot up, all eager to respond.

'It's a shout that scares your opponent,' said Kazuki.

'A battle cry to help focus and strengthen your attack,' suggested Yamato.

'The yell confuses your enemy,' blurted Saburo.

Sensei Yamada pointed to Akiko, who was waiting patiently to give her answer.

'It helps you to overcome your fear.'

153

Sensei Yamada nodded, waving the other students' hands down.

'Yes, it is all those. But what you're describing is purely a shout — a *kakegoe*. A *kiai* is something deeper. It is the projection of the fighting spirit into the voice.'

The class all looked bemused.

'How do you do it?' asked Saburo eagerly. Jack smiled to himself. Never before had he seen his friend so animated during one of Sensei Yamada's classes.

'In essence, you channel your inner energy, *ki*, through a battle cry, and strike at your enemy's own spiritual energy. When mastered, *kiaijutsu* can be a weapon as devastating as any *katana*.'

Though no one would dare question Sensei Yamada, there were many incredulous looks and a few snorts of disbelief.

'You don't believe me?' he said, a mischievous twinkle in his eye.

Walking to the other side of the hall, the old monk turned to face the singing bowl and took a deep breath as if preparing for meditation. Without warning, a shout exploded from him. It was so forceful and unexpected, several students screamed.

On the other side of the hall, the bowl rang out as if struck by a mallet.

The class was stunned into silence.

'The *sohei* developed secret mantras for the most dangerous *kiai*,' explained Sensei Yamada. 'I will teach you these words of power, but they should never be used except in battle. With a *kiai*, you directly attack your opponent's spirit and their will to fight. The shout literally shocks him into defeat.'

From personal experience, Jack knew Sensei Yamada was capable of unbelievable feats of martial arts. After all, it had been the Zen master who'd taught him the devastating butterfly kick. But to Jack's Western thinking, this was something else. A skill beyond belief.

'Sensei,' said Jack, raising his hand, 'a person is completely different from a bell. How can a *kiai* possibly defend against a sword attack?'

'Perhaps you need a little convincing?' said Sensei Yamada, smiling playfully. 'Attack me with your *bokken*.'

Jack hesitantly got to his feet and approached the Zen master. He now regretted expressing doubt at his teacher's powers. Looking into the monk's eyes, he could see the *sohei* spirit in him.

'But didn't you say a *kiai* should only be used in battle?'

'Yes, I did, but don't worry. I've done this many times before. I won't kill you.'

'Shame!' muttered Kazuki under his breath.

Jack ignored the comment, too nervous about what Sensei Yamada might do to him.

'The first *kiai* you'll be taught is "YAH!",' Sensei Yamada lectured as Jack withdrew his sword and prepared to attack. 'This power word represents the sound and force of an arrow being released. With this *kiai*, you penetrate the opponent's spirit just like an arrow.'

He beckoned Jack to begin. 'Do not hold back.'

Jack charged at Sensei Yamada.

'YAH!'

One moment Jack was striking with his *bokken*. The next he was flying backwards, all the power knocked out of his attack.

Jack landed on the temple floor, stunned. It was as if someone had punched him in the gut. His body felt tight and he found it hard to breathe. He flashed back to the time Dragon Eye had executed *Dim Mak* on him, blocking and destroying his *ki*. That Death Touch had almost killed him.

'The feeling of constriction will pass,' said Sensei Yamada, noting Jack's distress. 'I held back from using a full *kiai*.'

'That *was* impressive,' said Kazuki. 'Can you do it again?'

'No! The risk of internal injury is simply too great,' explained Sensei Yamada. 'A single demonstration is fine, but two attacks like that could kill.'

He helped Jack back to his feet.

'Now I want everyone to attempt this *kiai*.'

A mixture of excitement and concern consumed the class.

'Don't worry,' said Sensei Yamada, holding up his hand. 'In these lessons, you'll only practise on the singing bowl.'

Groans of disappointment emanated from Kazuki and his gang.

'Remember, this is a skill to be used in battle, against your enemy. Now line up, so each of you can have a go.'

The students formed an orderly queue. The first in line was Saburo. Sensei Yamada positioned him a single pace from the bowl.

'To perform this *kiai*, you must act like a bow and arrow. Inhale and draw your *ki* into the *hara*,' he explained, indicating the area just below Saburo's stomach. 'This action is like an archer drawing back the bow. Then exhale, tightening the stomach and letting out a "YAH!". This should have the feel of firing the arrow.'

Saburo screamed at the top of his lungs, his face turning bright red with the exertion. 'YAAAAAAAAH!'

The bowl remained stubbornly silent.

'Very good, Saburo-kun, full of intent,' praised Sensei Yamada, 'but you must ensure the sound isn't forced out of the throat. The *kiai* should come from the *hara* and that way it will contain your *ki*.'

Saburo nodded keenly and hurried to the back of the line for another attempt.

'As everyone's skill grows, you'll be able to make the bowl sing. With practice, you'll move further away from the target until you can defeat your enemy at any distance.'

The rest of the afternoon was filled with a cacophony of shouts, yells and battle cries. When it came to Jack's turn, he bellowed as loud as he could. But just as it had with everyone else's attempts, the singing bowl remained unmoved.

Next, Yori meekly stepped up to the mark.

Jack watched as his friend took a breath and . . . squeaked.

The whole class erupted with laughter at the pathetic sound he'd produced. Even Sensei Yamada couldn't help but smile.

Yori didn't know where to look. Curling up with shame, he seemed to shrink into himself. Like a startled mouse, he scurried out the doors of the Buddha Hall.

21

WEAPONS WALL

'Choose your weapon,' ordered Sensei Kyuzo, picking Jack from the line of students in the *Butokuden*.

The *taijutsu* master stood in the centre of the *dojo*, his tiny rock-hard fists planted firmly on his hips. Not much bigger than a child, he was dwarfed by the huge pillars of cypress wood that supported the *Butokuden*'s immense vaulted ceiling. Yet, as every student in the *Niten Ichi Ryū* knew, this teacher of unarmed combat was not to be underestimated. He was as mean and dangerous as a pit viper.

Sensei Kyuzo's beady black eyes followed Jack's progress across the *dojo* to the Weapons Wall. Jack gazed in awe at the collection of armaments. There were the familiar *bokken* and *katana* swords, plus a good selection of deadly *tantō* knives. Jack also spotted a couple of *nodaichi* – their *saya* extra long to accommodate the huge blades. He recalled Masamoto facing one during a beach duel and how his guardian had been forced to use an oar to overcome the *nodaichi*'s deadly reach.

To his left hung several bows and arrows, alongside numerous wooden staffs of varied lengths. On his right a neat rack of spears promised a multitude of gruesome deaths – some had simple spikes to skewer; others had sharpened edges to slice and hack; and a number had trident-shaped prongs to inflict the greatest possible damage on impact.

Spread throughout the display were more specialized weapons. Jack wasn't surprised to see a Japanese fan among the arsenal. He'd faced one of these innocent yet deadly weapons when a *kunoichi*, a female ninja, had tried to club him to death with one – the spine of a *tessen* being made of reinforced metal. But there were also *manriki-gusari* chains, several curved-bladed *naginata*, sickle-shaped *kama* and a large oak club encased in iron with vicious-looking studs.

'Move it! There'll be a war on before you've made your mind up,' grunted Sensei Kyuzo, the tuft of moustache beneath his nose twitching impatiently.

Jack decided to go for the club. If Sensei Kyuzo wanted a weapon then he'd get one.

But the club was so heavy Jack discovered he could hardly lift it. It went crashing to the floor, crushing his foot. The class burst into fits of giggles as Jack hopped around in agony.

'You need real muscles to wield a *kanabō*, *gaijin*!' snorted Sensei Kyuzo. 'Choose something suited to your limited capabilities.'

Irritated, Jack grabbed the nearest thing to him. A *tantō*.

As usual, Sensei Kyuzo had picked on him to be his *uke*, demonstration partner. Jack, therefore, knew he was about to suffer the customary abuse and humiliation of being thrown, kicked, pinned and punched across the *dojo* floor. But this was the first time they'd used weapons in a *taijutsu* class and Jack wasn't looking forward to the consequences.

'A predictable choice,' said Sensei Kyuzo, 'but a practical one for demonstrating how to disarm an opponent. Stab me in the stomach.'

Jack blinked in surprise.

'Do it!' commanded Sensei Kyuzo.

Jack thrust the blade at the sensei's gut. The *taijutsu* master slipped to the outside and slammed his fist on to the back of Jack's wrist while simultaneously striking Jack in the throat. The *tantō* dropped to the floor a moment before Jack did.

'The first principle of disarming is to get out of the way,' lectured Sensei Kyuzo as Jack lay gasping for breath. 'Even if the technique is executed poorly, you'll have avoided immediate danger.'

Jack slowly got to his feet, massaging his throat. As he was still conscious, it meant Sensei Kyuzo had pulled the strike. But the blow had *definitely* been harder than necessary.

He spotted Akiko with her head in her hands, dismayed at his treatment by their sensei.

'Choose another weapon,' ordered the sensei, without giving Jack time to recover.

Jack decided upon a *bokken*. By selecting the wooden weapon he was familiar and quick with, he might stand a chance of getting his own back. Jack turned to face his teacher.

'A sword-bearing samurai is harder to disarm,' explained the sensei, nodding at Jack to begin. 'Distance and timing are crucial.'

With lightning speed, Jack cut down at Sensei Kyuzo's head.

Only because the *taijutsu* master knew what to expect was he able to evade the sword so easily. Stepping to Jack's right-hand side, he blocked and grabbed Jack's elbow and wrist, executing a lock on him.

'The second principle is to inflict pain, thereby distracting and maybe even disabling your opponent,' Sensei Kyuzo explained as he added pressure to the lock and made Jack's face contort with agony. 'In this instance, you can follow through with the sword and cut your opponent in half.'

Forcing the *bokken* down and round, he freed the sword from Jack's grasp and drove the blade up between his legs. The class all winced as the *kissaki* of the *bokken* was then drawn from his groin up to his chest. Even though the contact was light, it still hurt and Jack was very glad he hadn't selected a steel *katana*.

'If you can gain control of your opponent's weapon, even better. This is the third principle,' lectured Sensei Kyuzo, ignoring Jack's suffering. 'Now, come at me with a spear.'

Infuriated, Jack picked the lethal trident-shaped spear and charged at his sensei. Calmly, the *taijutsu* master dodged the sharpened prongs and kicked Jack in the shins. Grabbing hold of the spear, he twisted it out of Jack's hands and slammed him in the jaw with it. Jack was floored a second time.

'Get up!' sneered Sensei Kyuzo, showing no sympathy. 'I'll give you one last chance to get me. Unless you're too feeble.'

Shaking his head clear, Jack staggered back to his feet. He could see Akiko now had her eyes covered with her hand, unable to watch any more. Yamato was silently willing him to give up while he had the chance.

Though Jack knew his sensei was baiting him, his blood was boiling and he couldn't resist a last attempt. Scanning the wall, he looked for a weapon that would keep his sadistic teacher at bay. He picked up a length of chain with a weight on the end. This had to be it.

Whirling the *manriki-gusari* above his head, he advanced on the *taijutsu* master. Jack was pleased to see Sensei Kyuzo immediately backing away.

'Such a weapon is very difficult to disarm,' said the sensei, retreating further. 'You cannot block it. You cannot grab it. You cannot easily avoid it.'

Jack grinned. For the first time, he *had* Sensei Kyuzo. He'd beaten him. And now he would strike . . .

'Your only option is *kuki-nage*,' shouted Sensei Kyuzo, whirling towards Jack. 'An air throw!'

Jack whipped the chain round as fast as he could. Sensei Kyuzo, arms outstretched, spun within its arc. His lead hand caught Jack in the head and, using the momentum of Jack's strike, he whipped him off his feet. The other hand took control of the chain and drove Jack towards the ground. Jack flew through the air and landed hard upon the *dojo* floor for a third time, his arm trapped in a painful lock.

'The air throw is based on the principle of the sphere: a sphere never loses its centre,' explained Sensei Kyuzo. He disarmed Jack of the *manriki-gusari* but kept the lock on, despite Jack's submissive taps. 'In this case, you cannot resist the force. You have to go with it, throwing your attacker in the air.'

Jack tapped louder, the pain in his arm growing unbearable. But Sensei Kyuzo continued to ignore his calls of submission.

'You've now seen the four disarming techniques that you'll be working with. These could save your life in a battle. Pair up. Choose a weapon. Then practise on one another.'

He finally released Jack, discarding him like an unwanted toy.

Rubbing his aching elbow joint, Jack joined Akiko and the others at the Weapons Wall.

'Why do you let him goad you like that?' said Akiko, glancing at Jack with concern as she weighed a spear in her hand.

'I never *volunteered* to be the *taijutsu* punchbag,' protested Jack. 'He always has it in for me. But at least I know whose side he'll be on, when there's a war.'

'Jack, don't say such a thing,' she scolded. 'You can't question his loyalty to Masamoto-sama. If Sensei Kyuzo heard you talking like that, he'd give you punishment for a month.'

Jack shrugged. 'He'll punish me anyway.'

'This *is* heavy,' grunted Saburo, trying to lift the *kanabō* for himself. 'It would certainly crush a skull or two!'

Yamato was swinging the chain in his hand. 'Jack, this was a good choice of weapon, but if you wanted distance, why didn't you use a bow and arrow against Sensei Kyuzo?'

'Good idea, he'd *never* be able to defend against that!' puffed Saburo, the iron club in his hands.

'Wouldn't I?' challenged the *taijutsu* master, who'd suddenly appeared behind Saburo.

'Well . . . surely, it would be impossible,' Saburo stammered, dropping the *kanabō* with a loud bang.

'It's merely a matter of reflexes.'

'But how could you *stop* an arrow?' exclaimed Saburo, taken aback by Sensei Kyuzo's blasé attitude.

'With your hands.'

Saburo snorted incredulously.

Sensei Kyuzo glared at him for his impudence, but then noticed that his students had all gathered round. They were looking expectantly at him, wanting to see this great feat.

He snatched a bow from the Weapons Wall. 'I need someone who can fire an arrow straight. Akiko-chan, I instruct you to shoot me in the heart.'

Sensei Kyuzo walked to the other end of the *Butokuden*, ignoring Akiko's protests.

'What are you waiting for?' he snapped. 'We're wasting valuable lesson time.'

Despite the samurai's impatience, Jack thought his sensei was relishing the opportunity to display his martial arts skills. The man was conscious of his diminutive size and loved proving he was stronger, quicker and more skilled than anyone else.

Akiko nocked an arrow and drew back on the bow. Her hands were shaking slightly as she took aim.

A tension hung in the air. No one moved. Everyone waited to see what Sensei Kyuzo would do.

Akiko released the bowstring and the arrow flew towards their teacher.

Sensei Kyuzo didn't move a muscle.

The arrow shot past his shoulder and struck a pillar behind.

'I told you to aim it at me!' he shouted angrily. 'There's no point in me trying to stop an arrow that isn't a threat.'

Akiko licked her lips nervously and strung a second arrow. This time, she aimed for the heart.

Jack knew she wouldn't miss. They were about to witness the death of their sensei.

The arrow flew through the air, straight and true.

At the very last second, Sensei Kyuzo caught the arrow with his right hand.

The students gasped in astonishment.

Sensei Kyuzo took a moment to enjoy the stunned expressions of all the young samurai, before striding triumphantly back up the *dojo* and handing Akiko the arrow.

'Any further questions?'

22

LOVE POETRY

'Have you heard the news?' said Saburo, hurrying across the courtyard the next day.

Jack, Yamato and the others were heading to the Hall of the Hawk for a *haiku* lesson. They stopped as Saburo gathered his breath.

'Last night someone set fire to the Catholic church next to the Imperial Palace!'

'The war's started then,' said Kiku, her face blanching slightly.

'No, it was a one-off attack. The sensei think a passing *ronin* did it on his way to Edo. I heard *daimyo* Takatomi's furious about it.'

'Was anyone hurt?' asked Jack tentatively.

Saburo gave a solemn nod of his head. 'A priest was trapped inside.'

They all fell silent. Jack felt *daimyo* Kamakura's noose tighten another notch. It seemed that every week they had word of another foreigner or priest who'd been persecuted, but this was the first religious attack to have occurred within Kyoto itself.

'What about the *ronin*?' asked Yamato.

'No one knows. But apparently the Tokaido Road north to Edo is crowded with samurai and *ashigaru*, responding to the call to arms.'

'Where are they all coming from?' said Kiku. 'Kamakura's army is going to be unstoppable.'

'Don't forget the four other Regents of the Council all have armies of their own,' said Akiko, trying to calm her friend. 'Together, they'll easily outnumber Kamakura's forces.'

Jack was about to ask another question when he spotted Yori emerging from the Buddha Hall. 'Where have you been?' he exclaimed.

They ran over to Yori who was now slumped on the steps of the *Butsuden*, a small brass bowl in his lap. He gazed up at them and offered an exhausted but untroubled smile.

Saburo plonked himself down beside Yori.

'You missed the most amazing *taijutsu* lesson yesterday. Sensei Kyuzo caught an arrow with one hand!' he said, snatching an imaginary one from the air.

Yori raised a weary eyebrow in acknowledgement of his friend's enthusiasm.

'Are you all right?' Akiko asked, kneeling down in front of him. 'We've been worried about you, ever since you ran out of Sensei Yamada's lesson.'

'I've been apologizing to Sensei,' Yori replied quietly.

'For over a day?' said Kiku, exchanging a worried glance with Akiko.

'Sensei Yamada had words with me. Quite a few, in fact. Then he made me polish the bronze Buddha to give me time to think about what he'd said.'

'But that statue's huge!' said Jack, inspecting Yori's tiny hands black with grime. 'That's unfair. You only left his lesson.'

'No, I was highly disrespectful,' reminded Yori. 'Sensei Yamada was right to punish me. Besides, I'm feeling better now he's explained things.'

'What did he say then?' asked Yamato.

'Sensei Yamada said that as samurai, we must devote ourselves with equal passion to both fighting *and* the creative arts. It is our duty to ensure we have a peace worth fighting for.'

Yori raised the little brass bowl and cushion out of his lap.

'He's also given me this singing bowl to practise on. *Kiai-jutsu* isn't about how loud the shout is; it's about how focused the *ki* is,' explained Yori, his eyes sparkling with determination. 'Sensei Yamada said that even the smallest breeze can make ripples on the largest ocean.'

Sensei Nakamura returned Jack's attempt at *haiku*. She gave him a single despondent shake of the head that sent a shudder down her mane of snow-white hair.

'You insist on putting your own opinion into the poem,' she said, her tone cold as the grave. '*Angry* sea. *Pretty* blossom. How many times have I told you not to use words that impose your personal response on the moment you're describing? The reader of your *haiku* might not have the same reaction as you.'

'*Hai*, Sensei,' replied Jack with a weary sigh. He still didn't understand. He thought poetry was all about love, emotion and passion. That's why that playwright William Shakespeare was so popular in England. 'Shall I compare thee to a summer's day? Thou art more beautiful . . .' or something like that. The Japanese, on the other hand, seemed so detached from their emotions that they weren't even allowed to express them in a poem.

Sensei Nakamura moved on to Yori. With a dour expression, she studied his page.

'A fair attempt. You show promise,' she began.

Yori smiled hopefully. Her praise, though, was short-lived.

'But you must avoid saying the same thing twice in your *haiku*. You begin here with *cold* dawn and then go on to observe the *chilly* breeze. Not good. You've wasted a word and haven't told the reader any more about your subject. Try again.'

Abashed, Yori took back the *haiku* and began to rewrite it.

Sensei Nakamura worked her way through the students, admonishing them for their various faults and very occasionally offering faint praise.

'Kazuki-kun, recite your *haiku* to the class. I would like to commend yours.'

Standing, paper in hand, Kazuki proudly read aloud:

> *'Take a pair of wings*
> *from a dragonfly, you would*
> *make a pepper pod.'*

There was a generous round of applause, but Sensei Nakamura cut it short with a stern look. 'I said I *would* like to commend it. But this isn't in the spirit of a *haiku*. The boy has killed the dragonfly. To compose a *haiku*, you must give life to it, you should say:

> *'Add a pair of wings*
> *to a pepper pod, you would*
> *make a dragonfly.'*

A collective hum of understanding filled the hall as Kazuki sat back down, his moment of glory quashed.

'I had hoped by autumn that this class's attempts at *haiku* would be of a higher standard,' she sighed. 'Nonetheless, most are now passable so I will risk organizing a *kukai* for the start of winter. That should give those falling behind in class enough time to improve.'

Sensei Nakamura was met with a roomful of puzzled looks. She tutted loudly, her eyes widening in exasperation at their ignorance.

'A *kukai* is a *haiku* contest. I will be inviting the renowned poet Saigyo-san to preside over the *kukai*, so ensure the poems you present are only those of the highest quality!'

She dismissed the class with a wave of her hand. After tidying away their ink blocks, paper and brushes, the students filed out of the hall.

'It's very exciting, isn't it?' enthused Yori as they were slipping on their sandals in the courtyard. 'I mean, to have the great Saigyo-san come here, to our school! He's my favourite poet.'

'I think I'll enter,' said Saburo, to everyone's surprise.

'You?' said Akiko, giving him an incredulous look. 'There won't be any prizes for poems about bodily functions.'

'I'll write one about love then!'

'What do *you* know about love?' laughed Akiko.

Saburo suddenly looked flustered. 'As much as anyone here.'

'Akiko!' called Takuan, beckoning her to join him.

'Though probably not as much as some people,' he muttered under his breath, and strode off in the direction of the *Chō-no-ma* for lunch.

Jack heard the comment and glanced over at Akiko and Takuan talking.

'Let's go, Jack,' said Yamato, chasing after Saburo. 'Otherwise there won't be any rice left after the Poet of Love's finished!'

While Jack found his sandals, he overheard Takuan say, 'I was thinking of entering this *haiku* into the competition and I'd value your opinion.'

'It's lovely,' said Akiko, bending closer to read the paper he held. 'The mountain image is so clear. I can just imagine myself there.'

'It's yours to keep,' Takuan offered.

Akiko flushed, bowing humbly. 'But this is your entry for the *kukai*.'

'I can write another,' he said, placing it into her hands. 'The greatest honour is that *you* appreciate it.'

'Thank you,' she said, bowing and accepting the *haiku*.

'Come on, Jack!' shouted Yamato impatiently from the other side of the courtyard.

Jack followed him into the *Chō-no-ma*, though his appetite had gone.

'Are you going to enter the *kukai*?' asked Jack, gazing out of Yori's tiny bedroom window at the stars glimmering in the night sky.

'Yah!' squeaked Yori.

'Do you think I should?'

'Yah!' squeaked Yori again.

'Are you even *listening* to me?'

'Yah!'

Yori stood in one corner of his room, shouting at the small singing bowl perched on a stand in the other. He was determined to make it ring. Since his chat with Sensei Yamada, he'd been convinced that *kiaijutsu* was his undiscovered talent and the martial art would save him in the forthcoming war. So far the bowl had remained silent.

Jack caught a movement outside in the courtyard. He spotted Akiko leaving the *Niten Ichi Ryū* by its back gate. No doubt visiting the monk at the Temple of the Peaceful Dragon.

'Sorry, Jack, what were you saying?' gasped Yori, trying to get his breath back.

'I said, are you going to enter the *kukai*?'

'Hopefully, if I can compose one worthy enough for Saigyo-san. He'll expect something special. What about you?'

'There's not much point, is there? I'm useless at *haiku*. Unlike Takuan.'

Yori gave Jack a sideways glance.

'I'm not jealous,' insisted Jack, turning away from Yori. 'It's just that I saw Takuan give a *haiku* to Akiko.'

'If you're so desperate for a poem, I'll write you one,' said Yori, suppressing a smile.

'You know that's not what I mean,' Jack replied tetchily. 'Doesn't it have some sort of significance in Japan? In England, that would be seen as *love* poetry.'

'Not with Takuan,' assured Yori. 'I saw him compose a *haiku* for Emi the other day. He's probably written one for each of the girls. They like such gallant gestures. That's one reason why he's so popular. If it's bothering you, why not write Akiko a *haiku* yourself?'

'You know that I'm no good at *haiku*. She'd just laugh.'

'No, she wouldn't. I'll help you,' said Yori kindly, pulling some paper from a pile.

Jack reluctantly took the paper. 'But this isn't a love poem, right?'

He felt his cheeks flush and hoped Yori wouldn't notice.

'No, of course not,' said Yori, his face the picture of innocence. 'It's just practice for the *kukai*.'

Despite denying being jealous, Jack realized his feelings for Akiko amounted to more than just friendship. If he was honest with himself, *she* was the reason he was having second thoughts about leaving Japan.

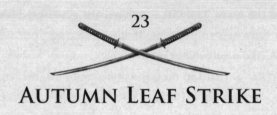

23

AUTUMN LEAF STRIKE

'*Hajime*,' commanded Masamoto, beginning the Two Heavens *kata* between Jack and Taro.

The two of them cautiously approached one another from opposite sides of the Phoenix Hall *dojo*, until the tips of their *katana* touched, their *wakizashi* held in a low guard.

Suddenly Taro exploded forward. Without lifting his sword, he drove his blade along the length of Jack's *katana*, pushing it aside and striking at Jack's heart. Taro displayed perfect control over the attack, and Jack felt only the lightest pressure of the *kissaki* hitting his chest.

'Excellent, Taro-kun. A faultless Flint-and-Spark strike,' commended Masamoto. 'Your turn, Jack-kun.'

Maintaining contact with Taro's sword, Jack now thrust the tip of his *katana* at his opponent's heart. But the end of Taro's blade jabbed into Jack's stomach before he could reach his target. He hadn't deflected Taro's sword wide enough.

'If that had been a steel blade, Taro's *katana* would've cut straight through you,' said Masamoto, a grim expression on his scarred face. 'Jack-kun, you *must* execute this strike with great certainty. Put more strength into your feet, body and hands, and strike quickly with all three at once.'

'*Hai*, Masamoto-sama,' replied Jack, glumly kneeling back in line with the rest of the students. He'd been the only one in the class not to manage the Flint-and-Spark attack.

'We'll move on to the Autumn Leaf strike,' Masamoto announced. 'An appropriate Two Heavens technique for the season, I think. The heart of this attack is to strike down upon your opponent's lead sword, disarming him and picking it up yourself. Watch carefully.'

Masamoto and Sensei Hosokawa withdrew their swords. As Sensei Hosokawa moved to attack, Masamoto surged forward, hitting Sensei Hosokawa's *katana* twice in quick succession with his *kissaki*. The sword clattered to the floor.

'This technique will only work if you don't let up for a second during the attack,' he explained, ushering the class to take up fighting positions in the *dojo*.

'Practise until you've mastered it.'

Glad to escape the training pressure of Masamoto's *dojo*, Jack stood alone on the veranda of the Southern Zen Garden. He gazed thoughtfully at a long rectangle of white sand raked to look like miniature waves. This formed the central feature of a garden decorated with large granite standing stones and meticulously pruned shrubs. In the far corner, like a frail old man, grew an ancient pine tree, its branches so twisted and bent by the elements that its trunk had to be propped up by a wooden crutch.

Jack took a deep breath, hoping the tranquil setting would lift his spirits.

By the end of a morning's training, he'd still been struggling with the Autumn Leaf strike. Why couldn't he do it? He was skilful enough with a single sword. But when he held two, he lost his control and accuracy. It frustrated him that after three months of Two Heavens training, he seemed to be getting worse rather than better.

Jack was certain the simplicity of the forms was hiding a deeper secret within. One Masamoto had yet to reveal. Or one he'd entirely missed. Whatever, he wouldn't give up. With the possibility of war and Dragon Eye still out there, the Two Heavens was the key to his survival.

Taro emerged from the Hall of the Phoenix and, spotting Jack on the veranda, joined him in the Southern Zen Garden.

'Don't be disheartened by your lack of progress,' said Taro. 'The Two Heavens is known to be the hardest sword style in Japan. Learning it is like climbing a mountain with your feet tied together and your hands bound.'

'But you can do it,' said Jack. 'What's the secret?'

'I once asked Masamoto-sama that,' said Taro, laughing. 'He said, "The secret is there *is* no secret."'

'I don't understand. There has to be.'

'Exactly what I said. He just replied, "The teacher is the needle, the student the thread. As a student, you should practise without end." I suppose *that's* the secret. Continuous hard training.'

He gestured to the Zen garden with a sweep of his hand.

'The Two Heavens is like this garden. I've no idea how the gardener created this. It looks beautiful, perfect and, at the same time, so simple. But I'm certain a great deal of time, thought and skill were put in to achieve this.'

'So how long did it take you to master the technique?' asked Jack.

Taro chuckled at the idea. 'I'm barely a beginner. The Two Heavens takes a lifetime to master.'

Jack's face dropped. 'But I don't have a lifetime. There's a war coming.'

Taro nodded gravely. Studying Jack out of the corner of his eye, he said, 'I can see you're determined like me. If you want more practice, I'd be willing to train with you outside class.'

'When?' said Jack, bowing his appreciation.

'You *are* keen. This evening?'

Jack nodded eagerly.

'See you after dinner,' said Taro, bowing and heading off in the direction of the *Shishi-no-ma*.

Jack remained behind in the garden. With Taro as a training partner, he was already feeling much more optimistic. He could learn from the boy's mistakes and improve at a faster rate. Hearing a *shoji* slide open, he turned round. Sachiko, Mizuki and Akiko were now leaving the Hall of the Phoenix.

'Akiko!' called Jack, running over to her.

She bowed as he approached. 'That was a hard lesson, wasn't it? The Autumn Leaf strike is almost impossible.'

'Yes,' agreed Jack. 'But Taro's offered to give me extra Two Heavens practice this evening. Would you like to join us?'

'Thank you, Jack,' replied Akiko. 'That's very kind of you, but Takuan's offered to help me with my *haiku* for the competition. Maybe another time.'

'I understand,' he replied, trying to hide his disappointment.

'Great. I'll see you later at lunch,' she said, smiling breezily. 'I'd better go, Sachiko and Mizuki are waiting for me.'

Returning to the garden, Jack sat down on the veranda, his head in his hands. He could hear Yori's voice in his head, telling him that Takuan helped lots of people, including Jack himself. So there was no reason for him to be upset. Why, then, did he feel as if he'd suddenly sunk to the bottom of the ocean?

'You look sad, *gaijin*,' said Kazuki, leaning nonchalantly against one of the veranda pillars. 'Jealous Akiko's got a prior engagement?'

'No!' replied Jack. 'Takuan's just helping her with her *haiku*.'

Kazuki grinned, realizing he'd got under Jack's skin. 'I can understand what Akiko sees in Takuan. He's handsome, intelligent, not really a fighter but a fine horseman nonetheless. And, of course, he's *Japanese*. Are you certain it's just his *haiku* she's interested in?'

'What do you mean by that?' Jack scrambled to his feet, his hand on his sword.

'Willing to defend her honour. How noble!' Kazuki snorted. 'If you're so up for a fight, how about a little extra Two Heavens practice?'

Kazuki withdrew both his *katana* and *wakizashi* from their black-and-gold *saya*. These were the *daishō* Kazuki's father had given him for successfully entering the Circle of Three. Their blades gleamed devilishly in the light.

Jack was wearing his steel *daishō* too, a privilege allowed all Two Heavens trainees. In class, though, these swords were only used for solo *kata* practice. Sparring was always done with wooden swords for safety. Jack wasn't confident enough with both blades yet to rise to Kazuki's challenge.

'Or maybe you lack the guts?' baited Kazuki, seeing Jack hesitate. 'You see, that's the difference between you and Yamato. He has honour and courage. He isn't afraid to take a risk. That's what makes him samurai and you *not*!'

Jack's hand tightened round the hilt of his sword, but he refused to respond.

'Your sort are spineless. I don't blame Akiko for wanting to be with a *real* samurai.'

In spite of himself, Jack was goaded by Kazuki's taunts.

'Take that back!' he exclaimed, unsheathing his swords.

'But it's the truth. It's obvious she prefers Takuan to you.'

Jack could hold back no longer. He attacked, aiming for Kazuki's head.

Kazuki was ready for him. He blocked Jack's sword with his *wakizashi* and at the same time drove forward with the tip of his *katana*. It was the most basic of the Two Heavens techniques – a simple 'parry and strike' – but it worked.

Jack barely avoided the blade and would have been choking on the *katana*, if Kazuki hadn't aimed a fraction too wide. He retreated before Kazuki retaliated.

'Is *that* the best you can do?' spat Kazuki.

Riled, his emotions getting the better of him, Jack went on the offensive again. Their *katana* clashed in mid-air. Before Jack could react, Kazuki drove forward, striking with his blade twice upon the back of Jack's weapon. The *katana* was knocked from Jack's grip and clattered to the wooden decking. Kazuki held the tip of his sword to Jack's neck.

'Would you believe it?' gloated Kazuki. 'The Autumn Leaf strike works!'

Jack still had his *wakizashi*, but there was nothing he could do to save himself. A single thrust from Kazuki would end his life. His rival was about to claim his so-called prize for defeating Yamato.

Kazuki forced Jack back off the veranda and up against a standing stone.

'I'll *always* defeat you with the Two Heavens,' said Kazuki, savouring the panic in Jack's eyes.

'You wouldn't dare!' breathed Jack.

'Again, that's the difference between a true samurai and a *gaijin* like you. I most certainly would,' said Kazuki, pressing until a pinprick of blood appeared on Jack's skin.

Jack grimaced, feeling the razor-sharp steel pierce his flesh. He pulled back, but had nowhere to go. Kazuki grinned vindictively, a cruel intent in his eyes.

'But I'll spare you, this once,' he said, retracting the blade.

Jack breathed an unsteady sigh of relief, then tensed in shock as Kazuki's steel *katana* flashed before his eyes. It skimmed past his nose, the blade slicing him across his left cheek.

'*That*, though, will serve as a reminder of what awaits you!'

Kazuki left Jack in the garden, blood trickling down his face and dripping red spots on to the pure white sand.

24

THE SPY

'Your cut's bleeding again,' said Takuan as he and Jack led their horses back to the school stables the following evening. 'It must have opened up during that last gallop.'

Jack's hand went to his cheek where a raw red line now marked his skin.

'You'll have a good scar when that's healed,' observed Takuan. 'Though you still haven't told me how you got it.'

'Two Heavens training,' Jack replied, not wishing to elaborate further.

'I'm glad I'm not in that class!'

'What do you mean?'

'Akiko injured herself during one of those lessons too.'

Jack stared blankly at Takuan.

'Haven't you noticed the bandage round her arm?'

Jack shook his head. As far as he was aware, nobody had been hurt during Two Heavens practice. Though *he* hadn't revealed the whole truth about his own injury, why would Akiko lie about hers? And *how* had she got it in the first place?

'I have to go,' said Takuan, passing Jack the reins to his

horse. 'You don't mind stabling them both, do you? I'm due to help Akiko with her *haiku*.'

'No, of course not,' replied Jack, forcing a smile.

'Thanks. We'll work on improving your seat position next time.'

Bowing, Takuan headed back to school.

Dusk had fallen by the time Jack had unsaddled the horses and tethered them in their stalls. He'd have to hurry. Taro would be waiting for him in the *Butokuden* to start their extra Two Heavens practice. Jack much preferred that to horse-riding. Their first session together had proved very helpful and, by the end, Jack had nearly mastered the Flint-and-Spark strike. Taro was a natural teacher, so they'd arranged to meet every evening to build on this initial success. At breakfast that morning he'd enthused about Taro to Akiko in the hope she'd join them, but to no avail. She was already busy. Now he knew why – Takuan.

As Jack put some extra hay into the horses' troughs, he heard the back door of the stable block open.

'So what have you found out?' breathed a girl's husky voice.

'My father's told me *daimyo* Kamakura now has some fifty thousand troops at his command.'

Jack instantly recognized the voice as Kazuki's.

'Fifty thousand!' squealed the girl excitedly.

Creeping into an adjacent empty stall, Jack peeked through a gap in the wood. Kazuki was sitting close to Moriko, her pale face ghost-like in the darkness. The floor had recently been swept and like all Japanese stables was spotlessly clean.

'So our lord's ready to attack,' she said in eager anticipation.

'We can finish off the *gaijin*! Exterminate him like a rat!'

'Not yet.'

Moriko's face dropped.

'Don't worry. His time will come. I left him with a scar so he wouldn't forget his fate.' Kazuki smirked as he ran finger across his own left cheek.

Moriko's eyes lit up with sadistic glee. 'He must now look even uglier!'

Jack felt his cut throb as the two of them laughed at his expense. *Moriko has some nerve to call me ugly*, he thought. *She has black teeth!*

'But when will *daimyo* Kamakura strike? When can the Scorpion Gang begin its work?'

'Patience, my Moriko,' said Kazuki, resting a hand on her knee. 'Our lord is waiting for more samurai to come to his side. My father told me *daimyo* Satake of Dewa Province has recently joined his ranks. But *daimyo* Kamakura needs *all* the northern lords to pledge their allegiance to him.'

'Why? He already has enough samurai to drive out every *gaijin* in our country.'

'But *not* enough to take over the country.'

'So the rumours are true?' she breathed.

Kazuki nodded.

'How do you know this?'

'My father's one of *daimyo* Kamakura's most trusted samurai.' Leaning closer to Moriko, he lowered his voice conspiratorially. 'I've been asked to carry out a special mission. By order of Kamakura himself.'

Moriko gasped. 'What do you have to do?'

'The clever hawk hides its claws,' he replied.

'I don't understand,' she said, her face screwing up in puzzlement.

'It means a great warrior doesn't reveal his true strength until the time calls for it. But *daimyo* Kamakura will reward me for my service when I do.'

'What with?'

'My own castle!'

Moriko could barely contain her excitement.

'You'd be made a *daimyo*!' she fawned.

Jack had heard enough. Whatever Akiko had said about the Oda family fighting alongside *daimyo* Takatomi, that was no longer true. He *had* to tell Masamoto.

Slipping unnoticed out of the stables, he ran back to school.

As he hurried across the courtyard, Jack spotted his guardian entering the *Butsuden* with Sensei Yamada. Taking the steps two at a time, he found them standing before the large bronze Buddha, deep in conversion. Barging through the doors, he dashed over to them.

'I overheard Kazuki . . . talking in the stables . . .' blurted Jack, in between snatches for breath. 'His father's on *daimyo* Kamakura's side —'

'We know,' interrupted Masamoto, holding up his hand.

Jack was stunned into silence.

The two samurai looked at each other gravely for a moment, before Sensei Yamada said, 'I don't think we have any choice but to tell him.'

Masmaoto turned to Jack. 'We're about to trust you with a highly sensitive secret. Do you understand?'

Jack bowed to show he appreciated the gravity of his guardian's words.

'Oda-san's actually on our side. He's keeping us informed of *daimyo* Kamakura's plans,' Masamoto explained.

'Kazuki's father's a spy?'

Masamoto nodded. 'In order that Kamakura wouldn't suspect a thing, Oda-san's entire family had to pledge their allegiance, including Kazuki-kun. Even they don't know.'

Jack realized Kazuki was totally convinced by the set-up. Dangerously so.

'Don't worry about Kazuki-kun,' said Masamoto, seeing the concern on Jack's face. 'Oda-san will tell his son the truth when the time comes. But, until then, you mustn't say a word of this to *anyone*. If *daimyo* Kamakura ever found out, Oda-san and his family would be put to death instantly.'

'I promise I won't,' replied Jack, understanding the seriousness of the situation. 'But if you know *daimyo* Kamakura intends to take power, why aren't the Council stopping him now?'

'It isn't as simple as that,' said Masamoto. 'Even though we know this coming conflict isn't just a question of faith, publicly *daimyo* Kamakura insists he's only interested in expelling Christians and foreigners. As a key member of the Council, he claims to be acting in Satoshi's best interests. He's defending Japan against the supposed threat of *gaijin* and fighting in the Emperor's name.'

'But he's killing innocent people. Isn't that justification enough?' implored Jack.

Masamoto sadly shook his head.

'Unfortunately not,' he sighed. '*Daimyo* Kamakura is as cunning as a chess player. Until he directs his forces against a Japanese *daimyo*, no one can act against him. Otherwise the

Council become the aggressors. If we start the conflict, then *we* are the enemy of the Emperor.'

'So war is inevitable,' said Jack.

'Not necessarily. It depends upon *daimyo* Kamakura getting the support he needs. Though his army is large, it's still no threat to the Council's combined forces.'

Despite Masamoto's assurance, Jack remained unconvinced.

One thing was certain, the impending war wouldn't aid Jack's search for the *rutter*. And the logbook definitely wouldn't be a priority for Masamoto, whose enquiries had still come to nothing. But there was little he could do about that. He would have to hope the logbook remained undeciphered. In the meantime, his priority was to learn the Two Heavens. He had to be prepared for the future – however uncertain it was.

25

LAST SAMURAI STANDING

Jack sat upon his wooden horse among the decaying brown leaves.

Autumn was over and the trees lining the *Yabusame* course of the Kamigamo shrine were almost bare. The threat of war, once so sharp and terrifying, had now dulled and hung on the horizon like a distant storm. Though news continued to trickle in of foreign persecution and *ronin* drifting northwards, *daimyo* Kamakura had yet to attack a Japanese lord and the conflict itself had failed to materialize. Many students considered the danger had passed. Jack realized such complacency was hazardous with a man as devious as Kamakura. But even he was beginning to hope the *daimyo*'s crusade had lost its momentum and that the samurai lord hadn't got the support he needed.

'In-yo, In-yo,' said Jack half-heartedly, as he went through the motions of drawing an arrow, nocking it on his bow and shooting the wooden target.

He could do this now with his eyes closed. He knew the exact height of the mark. He could hit the target from any distance and any angle. He knew precisely how long it would take him to nock an arrow, fire and prepare for his next shot.

And he knew the *jindou* arrows with their blunt wooden ball heads had a tendency to drop slightly during flight. But he still had no idea whether he could do this on a galloping horse.

Jack watched enviously as the rest of the class thundered down the *Yabusame* track on their steeds. Emi went by, taking out the first two marks but missing the final one. Despite the months of training, no one – apart from Takuan – had struck all three targets in a single run. Occasionally, a student took a tumble in the dirt, but Sensei Yosa didn't relegate them to training permanently on a wooden horse – as she had with Jack.

'Takuan tells me your horsemanship has improved greatly in the last month,' said Sensei Yosa, startling Jack as she approached him from behind.

'Really?' he replied, snatching at this glimmer of hope. Though he was surprised to hear this, considering Takuan spent more time watching Akiko's prowess on the course than observing his riding skills.

'He says you're ready to learn how to ride without using the reins,' she told him, patting the head of Jack's dobbin affectionately. 'If you make good progress, we'll have you on a real horse for *Yabusame* by springtime. Now come over to the track, I have an announcement to make.'

Jack sighed at the thought of staying on his wooden horse for another three months. Dismounting, he kicked it in its unresponsive rear before trudging after Sensei Yosa.

'How's your mighty steed?' said Saburo as Jack knelt down between him and Yamato. 'Still eating sawdust?'

'Very funny, Saburo.'

'So when are you going to join us on a real horse?' asked Yamato.

'Not until spring!'

'But that's ages away!' he exclaimed.

Jack nodded despondently. At least someone took his situation seriously.

'You'll have been on that dobbin so long, you'll be getting splinters!' said Yamato, his face cracking into a grin.

Seeing the funny side, Jack joined in the laughter. Sensei Yosa raised her hand for silence and the three of them stifled their giggles.

'I'm very pleased with everyone's progress. In the light of this, I've proposed a *Kyosha* against two of the local samurai schools, the *Yagyu Ryū* and *Yoshioko Ryū*. This competition shoot will take place as the first blossom forms on the *sakura* trees. In the meantime, I'll be assessing everyone's abilities and will select three riders to compete for the honour of the *Niten Ichi Ryū*.'

There was excited chatter among the students as they left the Kamigamo shrine and returned to school.

'I wonder who'll be chosen?' asked Kiku.

'Takuan will be,' said Akiko. 'He's the best archer and rider.'

'That's kind of you to say, but there are many other fine riders in the school,' replied Takuan, smiling warmly at her. 'You would be my choice.'

Saburo rolled his eyes at Jack, who tried to ignore the exchange but couldn't help noticing Akiko's face flush in response to Takuan's compliment. Jack realized Kazuki had been right. Akiko clearly had feelings for Takuan.

'I also reckon you've got a chance, Jack, with all that target practice you've had,' added Takuan over his shoulder.

'Well, unless there's a category for wooden horses, it won't be me,' replied Jack, doing his best to hide his hurt. 'Sensei Yosa said I have to wait until spring to do *Yabusame* on a real horse.'

'You're lucky,' said Takuan. 'I know one student at my old school who was made to train on a wooden horse for three years before he was allowed to ride a real one!'

Jack could well believe it. Judging by his experience of Sensei Kyuzo, there were clearly some very cruel sensei in Japan.

'Don't worry, Jack,' said Yori, trotting alongside him. 'When you do get on a real horse, your *Yabusame* technique will be so superior, you're sure to be selected for the team.'

'I wouldn't get too excited about the *Kyosha*,' interrupted Kazuki from behind.

'What do you mean?' asked Yori.

'There'll be a war on by then.'

Yori looked shocked. 'But . . . but it's almost winter and nothing's happened. Surely the threat's passed.'

Kazuki shook his head. 'It takes time to gather an army. My father says this is just the calm before the storm.'

'But why would Sensei Yosa be planning an inter-school contest for the spring, or Sensei Nakamura a *kukai*, if there's still going to be a war?' said Yori, a note of desperation entering his voice.

'Competitions keep morale high and our minds off the coming conflict.'

Kazuki gave Jack a hard stare.

'Nice scar,' he said, before striding on ahead.

★　★　★

The knife flashed towards Jack's stomach. He neatly slipped to Kazuki's outside guard, struck the back of his wrist and disarmed him. But before Jack could enjoy the victory, a *bokken* sliced towards his head.

Jack evaded the blade's arc, closing in on his second attacker, Goro, and grabbing hold of his arm. Applying a crippling lock, he disarmed the sword and drew the blade up between his legs.

Alerted by a shout from behind, Jack turned to see a spear ready to impale him through the chest. Barely avoiding the sharpened steel tip, he kicked his third attacker, Nobu, in the shins and took hold of the spear's shaft. A quick twist and the end was driven into his face.

Jack turned to face his final adversary. But before he had the slightest hope of executing an air throw, Hiroto released the *manriki-gusari* and the chain wrapped itself round his body. A moment later, Jack was yanked off his feet.

'And you were doing *so* well until then,' commented Sensei Kyuzo sarcastically. 'Fail!'

Jack shrugged off the chain, stood and bowed to his four attackers. Though no bones were broken, he could already feel a painful bruise forming where the weighted end had thumped into his back. Being the final combatant in the weapon-disarming exercise, he returned the *manriki-gusari* to the Weapons Wall and rejoined the rest of the students kneeling in a line. They'd had an entire morning of *taijutsu* trials, assessing their fitness, fighting technique, grappling skills, breaking ability and disarming methods, all in preparation for the possibility of war.

'Some of you have proved exceptional in your *taijutsu*

training,' said Sensei Kyuzo, glancing in the direction of Kazuki. 'A few are disappointing, to say the least.'

Jack felt Sensei Kyuzo's beady eyes upon him.

'However, I consider you're all ready for the final test of your hand-to-hand fighting skills – Last Samurai Standing.'

Sensei Kyuzo's stern face broke into a fiendish grin.

'All stand.'

There was an uneasy murmur among the class as they got to their feet. Sensei Kyuzo was smiling. This could not be good.

26

ZANSHIN

It was utter chaos.

The *dojo* turned into a battle zone as fights broke out all over the *Butokuden*. Students began to pummel their nearest neighbour. Everyone was now a potential enemy.

Sensei Kyuzo had set a simple but brutal challenge. A fight between every samurai in the *dojo*. Defeat was judged as being knocked or thrown to the ground. The only rule: no weapons.

Jack ducked as a hook punch came out of nowhere. Retaliating with an elbow strike to the stomach, he winded his attacker. Then, reaching up, he grabbed the other's arm and executed a *seoi nage*. The shoulder throw brought his opponent crashing to the ground.

She cried out as all the breath was knocked from her.

'Sorry,' said Jack, realizing he'd just floored Cho, one of Emi's best friends. Then again, she *had* just tried to knock his head off.

Jack spotted Akiko on the other side of the *dojo*, effortlessly dispatching all challengers. She whirled through the air, executing a spinning back kick that sent Renzo, one of the toughest young samurai in their class, flying into a pillar. Suddenly Jack sensed someone behind him. He spun round to be confronted by Yori. He looked terrified.

'Don't worry,' said Jack, dropping his guard. 'I won't fight you.'

'*Please* throw me,' pleaded Yori, glancing fearfully in the direction of Kazuki and his gang. 'At least I know you won't hurt me.'

The four of them were cutting a swathe through their opponents and they weren't holding back. Using his bulk to his advantage, Nobu would grab a student, then Kazuki and Hiroto beat him to the floor while Goro covered their backs.

Jack understood. He picked Yori up round the waist, performing an *o-goshi*, and gently hip-threw his little friend to the ground.

'Thank you,' whispered Yori, pretending to be winded so that Sensei Kyuzo wouldn't suspect he'd evaded the test.

Jack winked at his friend and prepared for his next challenger. Beside him, Yamato was locked in combat with Emi's other best friend, Kai. As soon as she saw Jack, Kai disengaged from Yamato and attacked him instead.

She came in with a blistering combination of kicks. A front kick followed by a roundhouse, then a back kick, finished off with a brutal side-kick to the ribs. Jack rapidly retreated under the onslaught. But, as Kai went for a spinning hook kick to his head, Jack dropped low to the floor. Mirroring her turn, he executed a spinning ankle sweep and Kai went crashing to the ground.

'Kai really had it in for you!' said Yamato, his mouth open

in astonishment at her vicious attack. 'What did you do to upset her?'

'I don't know,' gasped Jack, 'but we have to stick together. Otherwise, Kazuki's gang will win.'

On the other side of the *dojo* Kazuki, Hiroto and Goro were battling their way towards Akiko. They had just taken out Saburo and Kiku. Bypassing the other students, Jack and Yamato ran over to even up the fight. As they approached, Jack spotted Nobu targeting Takuan. Nobu had noticed the new boy was out of his depth and was about to seize him from behind. Jack owed it to Takuan to save him, in return for all his horseriding lessons.

'Watch out!' he shouted, charging past Takuan and front-kicking Nobu in the gut.

Nobu staggered away, though he remained on his feet.

'Thanks,' said Takuan, both of them now unsure whether they should fight one another or not.

But they didn't have time to ponder the issue. Jack, having been distracted with his rescue of Takuan, was immediately attacked from the rear.

The punch to the kidneys almost dropped Jack there and then, but somehow he managed to keep his feet. Stumbling round, he threw up his guard, but a lightning kick blasted through his defences and caught him full in the face. Knocked senseless, Jack fell on his backside. Whoever had attacked him hadn't held back.

'That's for using me to get inside my father's castle!' exclaimed Emi.

'I . . . I said I was sorry,' stammered Jack.

He sat there stunned, the shame of his past attempt to

protect the *rutter* once again coming back to haunt him. No wonder Cho and Kai had been so keen to fight him. The *daimyo*'s daughter held a serious grudge, though. The incident had been over a year ago.

'And I thought you liked me,' she said in a harsh whisper.

Emi then noticed Takuan and threw him a coy smile. Takuan was so captivated by her that he was totally unaware of Hiroto until it was too late. The boy kicked Takuan across the stomach, doubling him over. A forearm strike to the back of the neck dropped him into Jack's lap.

Emi was outraged.

'Leave Takuan alone!' she shouted, palm-heel striking Hiroto in the chest.

Shocked by the suddenness of the assault, Hiroto was completely unprepared for *tomoe nage*, the sacrificial stomach throw. Emi grabbed him by the lapels of his *gi* and rolled backwards. Jack and Takuan could only gawp as Emi tossed Hiroto high into the air and sent him crashing on to the *dojo* floor.

Jack winced in sympathy for Hiroto. Emi's foot hadn't planted itself in Hiroto's stomach. It had been much, much lower. Hiroto rolled around on the floor, his hands between his legs, whimpering in his high-pitched voice.

Jack realized he'd been lucky to get away with a kick to the face.

Emi flipped to her feet and shot Takuan another demure smile. A moment later, she was bowled over by Nobu who charged into her.

Jack, now defeated, looked around the hall to see who remained standing. Akiko had just leg-swept Goro, finishing him off with a hammerfist strike to the stomach.

Meanwhile, Nobu was seeking his next victim. The only other samurai still standing were Yamato and Kazuki, who were battling it out in the centre of the *dojo*.

Yamato was putting up a strong defence, but over the course of two years Kazuki had received so much additional *taijutsu* training from Sensei Kyuzo that there was no one in the class to rival him. Jack could only watch as Kazuki systematically demolished his friend's guard. A crippling roundhouse to the thigh dropped Yamato to one knee. Kazuki followed up with a crushing elbow strike to the head. Only a last-second block prevented Yamato getting a broken jaw, but the force of the blow sent him reeling across the *dojo* and on to the floor.

Nobu, sweating heavily from his exertions, was now circling Akiko. He kept a wary distance, occasionally feigning an attack so as to keep her attention on him, while Kazuki advanced on her blind side.

Jack, along with the rest of the class, held their breath as they waited for the outcome of this match. He knew Nobu was not the best fighter, his immense size having saved him from getting thrown so far. He'd also toughened up in recent months and so was able to absorb any blows that once would have floored him.

Despite the rigors of the battle and the threat Nobu posed, Akiko looked calm and collected. The real danger for her was Kazuki.

However much Jack disliked Kazuki for his bullying, he couldn't deny the boy was a skilled and clever fighter. His innate talent at the Two Heavens was as impressive as it was annoying for Jack. His abilities at archery and horseriding were strong. He was good at the *bō*, lethal in unarmed combat and had proved his worth by conquering the Circle of Three. Kazuki was developing into a supreme samurai warrior.

Kazuki gave a subtle nod of the head to Nobu and as one they attacked Akiko. Kazuki going for the head, Nobu for the stomach.

Unfazed, Akiko stood her ground. Suddenly she exploded upwards, jumping clear of Kazuki's front kick and Nobu's roundhouse punch. Rising above them, she simultaneously kicked out with both feet and planted them into Kazuki's and Nobu's gawping faces. Taken by complete surprise at such an advanced and agile technique, the two of them staggered backwards then collapsed on the floor.

Akiko landed lightly in a fighting guard and surveyed the scene. She stood alone in a *dojo* littered with fallen and groaning bodies. The ones who'd been watching the final fight greeted her victory with stunned silence.

'Who taught Akiko *that* move?' whispered Takuan to Jack, an incredulous look on his face.

'No idea,' replied Jack, shrugging. *But no one in this school, that's for sure*, he thought.

Sensei Kyuzo strode over to her. As he approached, she bowed her respect. Without stopping, Sensei Kyuzo brought his arm up hard across her chest and, twisting, threw her over his hip. She landed in a dazed pile beside Jack. Everyone stared in shock at the *taijutsu* master, bewildered by his unwarranted attack.

'This exercise was not simply to test your *taijutsu* skills,' justified Sensei Kyuzo, his expression once again severe and pitiless. 'It was to see how you reacted under pressure of battle. It also tested *zanshin* – your awareness of your surroundings and enemy. If you are to have any hope of surviving a war, you must apply *zanshin* at all times.'

'But Akiko had won!' exclaimed Jack, incensed by his teacher's vindictiveness. 'She was –'

'No,' snapped Sensei Kyuzo, cutting Jack off with a withering look. 'She wasn't the Last Samurai Standing. I am.'

27

KUKAI

Snow blanketed the *Niten Ichi Ryū*'s courtyard, its crisp white surface peppered with footprints that crossed from the *Shishi-no-ma* to the *Chō-no-ma* and on to the Hall of the Hawk. The tiered roofs of the buildings were caked in snow and the eaves hung heavy with glistening icicles. Even the ancient pine tree in the Southern Zen Garden struggled to hold its shape, the branches drooping like a cascade of frozen miniature waterfalls.

Inside the *Taka-no-ma*, the students shivered despite their thick winter kimonos, their breath misting in the chill air. Sensei Nakamura sat with her guest, the renowned poet Saigyo, upon the polished wooden dais furthest from the door. Saigyo was a small, unassuming man with sleepy eyes and large rounded ears. He wore a plain bowl-shaped hat and by his side was a weatherworn bamboo walking stick. Taking time to admire the mural of the swooping hawk on the ceiling, he warmed his hands in front of a clay *hibachi*. The students gazed enviously at the small charcoal brazier that Sensei Nakamura had reserved for their honoured guest.

> *'Glowing coals*
> *melt away the icicles —*
> *Ah! I have hands.'*

A serene smile spread across the poet's face at his composition, and so light and feathery was his voice the *haiku* seemed to float on the air.

Sensei Nakamura initiated a polite round of applause, which quickly spread throughout the hall. The clapping was enthusiastic, mostly because it provided an opportunity for the students to warm their own numb hands.

'We shall commence the *kukai*,' said Sensei Nakamura with solemn ceremony. 'Those who consider they have a *haiku* of merit may step forward. Each of you in turn will present your poem to our esteemed guest. Saigyo-san will deliver his verdict and announce the winner once all the *haiku* have been heard.'

Several students rose to their feet and began to form an orderly line down one side of the hall.

'Are you coming up, Jack?' asked Saburo, wielding a crumpled piece of paper in his hand.

'You must be joking,' replied Jack. 'You know what Sensei Nakamura thinks of my efforts.'

Saburo laughed. 'Well, wish me luck. I think you'll like mine!'

As Saburo eagerly joined the queue, Yori crept past.

'Good luck!' whispered Jack.

'Thanks,' replied Yori in nervous excitement and joined the queue.

'Let the first poet deliver their *haiku*,' announced Saigyo, rubbing his thighs in eager anticipation. 'May it be a drop of dew in an autumn pond.'

Sensei Nakamura beckoned Akiko forward. Bowing low in respect, she took her *haiku* out of the pocket sleeve of her kimono. Jack thought Akiko looked even more anxious than when she'd shot the arrow at Sensei Kyuzo.

'Winter was my inspiration,' she began.

> *'The purple iris*
> *beneath the white blanket sleeps —*
> *there sprouts hope!'*

Having read her *haiku*, Akiko bowed again and awaited the poet's verdict. Saigyo took a deep breath and gazed out of the window at the falling snowflakes. Akiko glanced in Jack's direction, her brow furrowing in concern at the poet's lack of response. Jack smiled back, trying to comfort her, then realized she was looking past him to the end of the *haiku* line where Takuan was nodding his head earnestly. Akiko seemed reassured. Jack felt a pang of envy at the exchange.

'Like spring, your *haiku* is fresh, clear and promises much,' spoke Saigyo eventually, much to Akiko's relief. 'Yet will it be the best blossom of the day? We shall see.'

He gave Akiko a polite clap, then beckoned the next contestant over. Akiko sat back down as Emi took her place before the poet. Saigyo listened attentively before giving an equally profound response to her poem. Two more *haiku* were heard. Then it was Saburo's turn.

'This one is about love,' he declared.

> '"She may have only one eye
> but it's a pretty one,"
> says the go-between.'

A burst of laughter broke from the class. Jack grinned at his friend's humorous verse, while Akiko rolled her eyes in despair. The amusement was silenced by a stern look from Sensei Nakamura.

'*That* was not an appropriate entry,' she fumed, wiping the smile from Saburo's face.

'Sensei,' interrupted Saigyo gently, 'the verse may have been somewhat coarse, but our young poet here is certainly novel. His entry amused me. Like a plant needs sun as much as rain, so a poet needs laughter as much as tears.'

Sensei Nakamura inclined her head in acknowledgement of his judgement. Saburo returned to his place beside Jack.

'You'll be writing that one out *two* thousand times, at least!' hissed Akiko over her shoulder.

Saburo grinned as if he didn't care.

Jack gave his friend a wink. 'I thought it was great.'

The following entries proved to be less inspiring and, at one point, Jack thought the old poet had gone to sleep. Then Yori shuffled up. He nervously flattened the piece of paper in his hands and, in a voice so soft even Saigyo had to lean forward to hear it, he said:

> '*Squatting by the tree
> an old frog observes the faces
> hidden in the clouds.*'

The poet's face lit up like the dawn, his sleepy eyes bursting awake. 'Why, that's a *haiku* worth waiting for! My favourite topic is frogs!'

Yori bowed and guiltily whispered, 'I've always admired your *haiku* about the frog jumping into the old pond. I wished to write one like it.'

'And so you have,' said Saigyo, beaming at him. 'You have spirit, little poet. And so does your *haiku*.'

Yori, looking relieved, sat back down next to Jack.

'Well done,' said Jack, patting him on the back. 'You've won.'

Emi leant forward and hissed, 'Takuan has yet to read his *haiku*!'

Takuan bowed to Saigyo and in a clear, confident voice recited:

> *'Temple bell*
> *a cloud of cherry blossom*
> *Heaven? Hanami?'*

Emi applauded loudly and the rest of the class soon joined in.

Saigyo nodded appreciatively, a deeply satisfied smile on his face. 'Your style is pure like white jade. Without ornament, without carving, you get straight to the heart of the moment. This is *haiku* at its finest.'

Takuan bowed his gratitude at the poet's praise and returned to his place next to Emi. Sensei Nakamura's characteristically sombre expression softened for a moment as she glowed with pride at her son's achievement.

A growing sense of excitement filled the room while Saigyo

conferred with Sensei Nakamura. A few moments later, Sensei Nakamura turned to the class.

'Saigyo-san has deemed the winner to be . . .'

28

THE GRACIOUS LOSER

'. . . impossible to decide,' Sensei Nakamura announced.

'Like peas in a pod, we have two poets of equal worth,' explained Saigyo.

The hall was instantly abuzz with excited chatter as to who could be the most likely *haiku* candidates. Jack hoped Yori was one of them. It was just the sort of confidence boost his friend needed.

Once the news of a draw had sunk in, Saigyo continued 'I propose a *maekuzuke* between the two best entrants.'

The class sat rigid, no longer from cold but with anticipation.

Sensei Nakamura stepped forward to explain the rules.

'Our honoured guest will provide a short two-line verse to which the participants must add a *haiku* of their own, and so form a complete *tanka* poem. The joining verse will be judged on its originality and relevance to the given phrase. The participants must compose their contribution on the spot.'

The difficulty of the challenge triggered an astonished gasp from the students.

'Yori-kun and Takuan-kun, step forward.'

Yori froze, looking startled as a rabbit caught out in the open.

Jack whispered, 'Don't worry. You're a natural with words.'

Takuan jumped up and strode to the front. The class waited patiently while Yori, finding his feet, reluctantly joined him.

Saigyo greeted Yori with a reassuring smile.

'Your opening phrase is a simple dilemma:

> *"I want to kill him,*
> *I don't want to kill him . . ."*

Surprise registered on Yori's face at the verse's brutal bluntness, but Jack could see Takuan was already composing his response.

'My friend who's fond of frogs,' announced Saigyo, 'you will go first.'

Yori glanced around in panic at all the expectant faces. Jack thought he was about to bolt from the Hall of the Hawk, the pressure too much for him. But all of a sudden Yori's face lit up as he found inspiration. He spoke his *haiku* so fast, his tongue almost tripped over his words:

> *'Given a choice:*
> *revenge can be sweet*
> *but mercy greater.'*

Yori breathed a sigh of relief at having managed a response.

Saigyo pursed his lips considering the *haiku*, then turned to Takuan. 'What is your joining verse for the *maekuzuke*?'

Takuan replied without hesitation:

> *'Catching the thief*
> *and seeing his face,*
> *it was my brother!'*

Giving a noncommittal nod of the head, Saigyo gazed into the glowing coals of the *hibachi* as he mulled over the two verses.

'Such a decision as this is like choosing between two types of *saké*. Though possessed of different flavours, they are both refreshing and potent,' he explained, rubbing his chin. 'Yori-kun, yours resounded with the spirit of *bushido*, but it lacked a poetic twist. Takuan-kun, your response was as unexpected and memorable as a red rose in winter. I, therefore, declare you the winner!'

There was an excited squeal of delight from the girls, followed by enthusiastic clapping from everyone. Takuan went up to receive a scroll from Saigyo within which the poet had personally penned a *haiku* for him as a prize.

The competition over, Sensei Nakamura called an end to the class and ushered Saigyo towards the Hall of the Phoenix for a private audience with Masamoto-sama. Outside, the students all crowded round Takuan to congratulate him on his inspired response and well-deserved victory. Emi and Akiko were at his shoulder reading the prize *haiku*.

Jack spotted Yori wandering off on his own and crunched through the snow after him.

'Are you all right?' Jack asked tenderly, hoping his friend wasn't too upset.

Yori turned round, a contented grin on his face.

'Of course I am. I came second. How amazing is that?'

'But . . . but you lost. Aren't you disappointed that Takuan beat you?'

'Why should I be? I never expected to win, let alone reach the final two. I just wanted to meet the great poet Saigyo. And he *liked* my frog *haiku*!'

'I still don't understand how you can't be even a little upset that you lost,' continued Jack, later that evening in Yori's bedroom at the *Shishi-no-ma*. 'If that was me, I'd be really disappointed.'

'But I'm not you,' replied Yori, setting up the little singing bowl for his nightly *kiaijutsu* practice. 'If I was comparing my achievements with Takuan, then I would be a loser. But I was comparing them with my own ambition to be the best poet I can be. Therefore, I *am* a winner.'

Jack couldn't argue with his friend's wisdom, so he sat down in a corner of the room and picked through the various scraps of paper that bore the efforts of his own poetry. Having heard the other *haiku* during the competition, Jack felt none of his were in any way good enough to present to Akiko.

'They're terrible,' he moaned. 'Takuan's are so much better. Perhaps I should just get him to write one for me.'

'Stop comparing yourself to Takuan,' admonished Yori as he began his *kiai* breathing exercises. 'Akiko will appreciate your *haiku* more, simply because of the effort you've put in.'

'Do you think so?'

Yori nodded and shouted at the singing bowl. The squeak that came out left the bowl unmoved. He grimaced in frustration and tried again.

Settling down, Jack redoubled his efforts to write a decent *haiku*. Once again, Yori's insight had helped him to see things clearly. He would write a poem that meant something for him – and would mean something to Akiko. She had given him a black pearl. He saw this *haiku* as his personal gift to her.

'Have you heard the announcement?' said Saburo, bursting into the room.

Jack and Yori shook their heads.

'Akiko, Emi and Takuan have been selected as the riders to represent our school at the forthcoming *Yabusame* competition.'

'Great,' mumbled Jack to himself, putting down his writing brush. 'Takuan will be spending even *more* time with Akiko.'

'I don't know what you're complaining about,' retorted Saburo, suddenly defensive. 'You spend most of your time training with my brother!'

'What do you mean by that?'

'You should hear yourself at breakfast. Taro this. Taro that. I'm sick to death of hearing about how great he is!'

'Sorry,' said Jack, shocked by his friend's sudden outburst. 'I didn't know you were . . . jealous.'

Saburo gave a tired shake of the head. 'My apologies, Jack. It's what I have to put up with from my parents. *Taro's done this and he's achieved that. When are you going to do something worthy of a samurai, Saburo?* I'm tired of having to measure up to my brother all the time.'

'You shouldn't worry about that. You need to stop comparing yourself to your brother and have your own ambitions,' said Jack. He spotted Yori silently laughing at hearing his own advice being repeated. 'Taro may be skilful with two swords but, if I'm honest, he can be a bit dull. It's all he ever goes on about. He's not funny like you.'

'Thanks' said Saburo, the smile returning to his face as he picked up a discarded *haiku*. 'What's this? I thought you hated writing *haiku*.'

'Give it back!' said Jack, panicking that Saburo might read the poem and guess it was for Akiko.

He snatched the paper from Saburo's hands, pushing his friend out of the way so he could gather up the rest of the *haiku*. Saburo stumbled backwards, accidently stamping on Yori's foot in the process. Yori let out a sharp cry.

The singing bowl pinged.

Jack and Saburo stared in amazement at Yori and then at the bowl.

'I did it,' whispered Yori in awe of himself. 'I really did it.'

'It's certainly a hive of warrior activity in here,' commented Kazuki, poking his head through the doorway. 'Are we in the girls' corridor? Squabbles, poetry and a *kiai* only a moth would be scared of. We'd better watch out, boys, they'll be asking us to join their flower-arranging class next!'

Hiroto, Goro and Nobu burst into laughter before carrying on down the corridor to their rooms. Insulted, Jack and Saburo ran to the door. But unable to think of a suitable comeback to Kazuki's abuse, they could only glare after them.

Yori remained where he was, transfixed by the bowl still humming away.

29

THE FRIAR

Akiko's defence crumpled under Masamoto's onslaught.

Having already lost her *wakizashi* to an Autumn Leaf strike, she valiantly tried to sustain her attack. But Masamoto's skill was unassailable. He drove forward, knocking Akiko's *katana* from her grasp and bringing his sword down upon her head. In a fit of apparent insanity, Akiko slammed her hands together either side of the sword.

There was a gasp of utter astonishment from the Two Heavens students standing down one side of the Hall of the Phoenix.

Akiko had caught Masamoto's blade with her bare hands!

'Not the recommended defence for a samurai,' said Masamoto, strangely unfazed by Akiko's miraculous skill. 'You could easily lose your fingers.'

Akiko let go, suddenly self-conscious of her feat. She picked up her swords and rejoined Jack in line. Jack couldn't believe what he'd just witnessed. Blocking a sword like that was a technique far beyond their samurai training. But before he could question Akiko, Masamoto summoned him on to the floor. Immediately the training duel began.

Jack struggled to defend himself against Masamoto's double sword attack. Blocking the cut to his head with his *wakizashi*, Jack thrust his *katana* in a counterstrike at his guardian's throat. But Masamoto effortlessly sidestepped the threat, bringing his own *katana* slicing across Jack's chest.

Their swords clashed.

Without thinking, Jack struck down hard upon Masamoto's blade with his *kissaki*. Twice.

The sword clattered to the *dojo* floor.

All the students now stared in wide-eyed amazement at Jack, apart from Taro who bore a proud grin.

It took a moment for Jack to realize what he'd done.

He'd disarmed the legendary swordmaster, Masamoto Takeshi.

He'd accomplished a perfect Autumn Leaf strike.

'I did it!' breathed Jack. 'I've mastered the Two Heavens.'

But the duel wasn't over. Masamoto still had his *wakizashi*.

Before Jack could exploit his advantage, Masamoto had changed grip on the short training sword and threw it at Jack. The hilt struck him hard in the chest. Staggering backwards, his heel caught on the edge of the dais and he crashed to the floor.

'You're dead,' stated Masamoto, ending the duel.

Breathless and exasperated, Jack tried to protest, 'But *that* . . . wasn't sword fighting . . . You threw it at me.'

'Mountain to Sea,' replied Masamoto, offering Jack no sympathy. 'In order to break through your double guard and win, I had to change tactics. I had to attack in a manner that wouldn't be expected. In other words, move from the Mountain to the Sea. Learn from this, young samurai.'

Jack got to his feet and returned Masamoto's *wakizashi* to him.

'It's satisfying to see you've grasped the Autumn Leaf strike at last, but do *not* confuse individual sword techniques with the Two Heavens style as a whole,' reprimanded Masamoto, his scarred face stern and unsmiling.

Jack bowed his head in acknowledgement. Carried away by his brief success, it had been foolish to think that he'd suddenly mastered the technique.

'The true Way of this style is not solely about handling two swords,' Masamoto explained, now addressing the whole class. 'The essence of the Two Heavens is the spirit of winning – to obtain victory by any means and with any weapon. Understand this and you'll be well on the way to mastering the Two Heavens.'

With the snow now gone, the early spring sunshine had encouraged people on to Kyoto's streets. Jack and Yamato, late as they were for their *Yabusame* class, had to push their way through the crowds. In the marketplace, Jack noticed a tense, edgy atmosphere as harassed shoppers bought provisions. After no word for months, rumours were now spreading that Kamamura's army was on the march and many people were stocking up in case of war.

'So how's the Two Heavens training going?' asked Yamato.

Jack was taken by surprise at the unexpected question. His friend usually avoided talking about it. Despite Yamato's prowess in other classes, it reminded him of his failure to live up to his father's expectations.

'Good and bad,' replied Jack. 'I've just discovered the Two

Heavens is as much to do with battle strategy, as it is with skill —'

Suddenly a hand shot out from a side alley and grabbed Jack by the arm. His immediate thought was of *ronin* seizing him for punishment again and he shouted to Yamato for help. At the same time, he instinctively twisted his hand round and put the attacker into a crippling lock. The man fell to his knees, crying out for mercy. In a flash Yamato was by Jack's side, sword drawn.

'Don't kill me!' pleaded the man as he grovelled on the ground. 'I mean you no harm.'

'What do you want then?' demanded Yamato.

Dirty and dishevelled, the man wore a tattered cowl and cloak, his face was haggard, and his eyes sunken and bloodshot. But the most remarkable thing about him was that he wasn't Japanese.

'I . . . I'm Friar Juan de Madrid,' he stuttered, his Spanish accent thickly tainting his Japanese. 'I'm a Franciscan monk from the Church of St Francis in Edo. I saw this boy and thought he could help me.'

'What could I do?' asked Jack, wondering how the friar had got into such an appalling state.

'You're European. I thought you may be attached to a Spanish or Portuguese vessel.'

'No. I was shipwrecked here. I'm English.'

'English!' exclaimed the friar, stunned. Jack nodded. 'No matter. In these dreadful times, we must be allies, not enemies. As I said, I've come from Edo in the north where I've been for many years, had a faithful congregation, but now that's all gone . . . gone . . .'

Tears welled up in his eyes.

'Come to the *Niten Ichi Ryū*,' suggested Jack, kneeling down to try and comfort the friar. 'You'll be safe there.'

'No. No one's safe,' the friar shot back. '*Daimyo* Kamakura's army has destroyed all Christian churches and burnt down our houses, even as we slept in them! Those friars and Jesuit priests that didn't die by the fire were slaughtered by the sword . . .'

The friar was convulsed in sobs as he relived the horror of the massacre.

'But why weren't you killed?' demanded Yamato, his sword still at the ready.

'I don't know. Somehow I managed to escape. But I've lost everything, save the clothes on my back. I'm trying to get to Nagasaki. I have to leave this godforsaken land.' Clasping Jack's arms, the friar exclaimed, '*Daimyo* Kamakura and his army are headed this way as we speak! We have no time to lose. You should come too! He will kill *you* for sure.'

Looking around in a wild panic, he tried to stand, but his legs gave way under him.

'You need to rest,' said Jack, putting his arm round the friar. 'Let us take you to Sensei Yamada, our Zen master. He'll look after you.'

It was early the following morning that Sensei Yamada and Jack bid farewell to Friar Juan de Madrid.

'You're welcome to stay longer,' said Sensei Yamada.

'No, you've been too kind already,' said the friar, bowing humbly. 'Thank you for the food and fresh robe, but it's too dangerous to linger.'

Looking at Jack, he implored, 'Are you *certain* you won't come with me?'

'Jack-kun will be safe here with us,' assured Sensei Yamada.

With that, the friar set off down the road. Jack watched him shamble away, keeping to the shadows. With confirmation that *daimyo* Kamakura's war had begun in earnest, Jack realized he'd have to give up all hope of retrieving his father's *rutter*. Fighting a single ninja, even one as ruthless as Dragon Eye, was entirely different from battling a whole army. His greatest concern now was his own life. With each passing day, the threat drew ever closer.

The friar disappeared round the corner without looking back.

'Perhaps I should have joined him,' reflected Jack.

Sensei Yamada slowly shook his head.

'You're safer in the lion's den than in a field of snakes,' replied the Zen master. 'The road to Nagasaki is hard and dangerous. I doubt the friar will even make it to Kōbe, and that's barely three days' journey from here. In these uncertain times, there will be few who will take him in and many who will want to take his head. Masamoto-sama, though, can protect you, Jack-kun. The *Niten Ichi Ryū* is the safest place you can possibly be.'

30

KYOSHA

The *taiko* drum boomed to the thunder of horses' hooves pummelling the air as the competing archers galloped past. The students jostled for position along the roped-off length of the *Yabusame* course, cheering and applauding their teams. Jack, seeing Akiko, Emi and Takuan fly by, gave a great shout of encouragement.

Spring had finally arrived and with it the exquisite *sakura* blossom that heralded the inter-school archery contest. But in the month that had passed since the friar's unexpected appearance, many more stories of persecution and massacre, of branding and public burnings, had reached Kyoto. So far, the cleansing and Kamakura's army had remained within the boundaries of Edo Province. But there was a growing tension among Kyoto's citizens as more and more of his forces gathered on the border. Even though *daimyo* Kamakura had yet to directly attack a Japanese lord and his army was still seven days' march from the city, this didn't allay people's fears. The lord of Edo could strike at any moment.

Seated high upon the ceremonial wooden tower, Masamoto and Yoshioka, the heads of the *Niten Ichi Ryū* and the *Yoshioka*

Ryū, oversaw the proceedings. From their privileged position, they could view the entire course. A third *zabuton* cushion, set aside for the head of the *Yagyu Ryū*, *daimyo* Kamakura, remained ominously vacant.

'Would you like some chicken?' asked Saburo, offering Jack a bite of his *yakitori*.

Jack refused. They'd just had lunch.

'Don't you ever stop eating?' Taro demanded, giving his brother a despairing shake of the head. 'What will our father say, when you can't fit into your armour?'

Saburo glared at Taro. 'As if he'd notice with you flashing your two swords about —'

'Will you both please stop arguing?' interrupted Kiku. 'Emi's riding first for our school.'

Looking to the head of the course, the *daimyo*'s daughter was already mounted upon her steed. She was anxiously adjusting her quiver and arrows as she awaited the signal to start. The crowd quietened in anticipation.

Lots had been drawn to determine the order of the three riders from each school. They were competing for two prizes, one to be awarded for the best archer and another for the school with the highest number of targets struck and broken.

An official waved a large paper fan with a single red sun emblazoned on it and Emi was off, her horse galloping at a breakneck speed down the track. She let go of the reins and reached for her *jindou*. Nocking the wooden-tipped arrow, Emi cried out '*In-Yo!*' and took aim at the first target.

But her horse veered slightly on the approach and she had to grab for the reins. There was a groan of disappointment as she shot by the mark. Jack had to admire Emi's skilled horsemanship, though. She recovered quickly and readied herself for the second target. Letting fly her arrow, she struck it dead centre and a cheer erupted from the *Niten Ichi Ryū*.

Now into the flow, Emi smoothly strung a *jindou* for the final target. But her horse was galloping at such a pace that she was soon alongside the mark. Quickly aiming and firing, her arrow caught the edge of the wooden board, breaking off the bottom corner.

The crowd applauded her run. Sensei Yosa took Emi's horse by the reins and congratulated her. Two strikes was a fine achievement. Masamoto-sama seemed pleased too, bowing his head respectfully in Emi's direction.

Next up was a boy from the *Yoshioka Ryū*. He appeared more confident than Emi. The signal fan went up and at once he spurred on his horse. Flying down the course, he took out the first target with practised ease.

But his over confidence got the better of him. Standing high in the saddle, he lost his balance before the second mark. His horse stumbled slightly and the boy went tumbling to the ground, bouncing a couple of times through the dirt before rolling to a stop.

There was a moment of uncomfortable silence as the crowd waited to see if he had survived the heavy fall. Then, with the aid of a couple of officials, the boy got to his feet and limped to the sidelines. The students all gave him a sympathetic round of applause, but Yoshioka-san in the tower looked thoroughly displeased with his archer's performance. He flicked his paper fan closed so violently that the spine broke. Jack noticed Masamoto leant over to offer words of condolence, but the samurai ignored him.

'Did you know that Masamoto-sama and Yoshioka-san once duelled?' Taro whispered furtively into Jack's ear.

'No,' said Jack.

Saburo nudged Jack with his elbow and rolled his eyes at the prospect of hearing yet another of his brother's sword stories. He went back to munching on his *yakitori*, while a boy from the *Yagyu Ryū* took up position at the head of the course.

'When Masamoto-sama first arrived in Kyoto, he was an unknown swordsman,' explained Taro. 'In order to make his name, he decided to challenge the most renowned school in Kyoto, the *Yoshioka Ryū*.'

There was a cheer as the *Yagyu Ryū* archer took out the first target.

'To everyone's surprise, Masamoto-sama defeated the head of the school, Yoshioka-san, with only a *bokken*!' said Taro, shaking his head in amazement at such an accomplishment.

A groan filled the air, the boy having missed the next target.

'This was so humiliating for the school that Yoshioka-san's younger brother now challenged Masamoto-sama to a duel. Once again, Masamoto-sama won, this time gravely injuring his opponent.'

Applause broke forth as the *Yagyu* boy completed his run. He'd struck two out of the three targets.

'Incensed at their failure, Yoshioka-san ordered his son to regain the family honour,' continued Taro, no longer paying attention to the *Yabusame* competition. 'Despite being only a young lad, the son agreed and issued a final challenge at the Kodaiji Temple. But he was devious. He laid a trap for

Masamoto-sama. Dressed in full battle armour, he arrived with a party of well-armed retainers determined to kill him.'

Jack listened as the next competitor from the *Yoshioka Ryū* lined up her horse.

'Masamoto-sama, however, was cunning. Having turned up late to the first two duels, he arrived early this time. Discovering it was an ambush, he concealed himself. Just as they were setting the trap, Masamoto-sama cut a swathe through the retainers and broke the lad's shoulder with his first attack. Yoshioka-san's son hasn't been able to wield a sword since.'

The girl from the *Yoshioka Ryū* sped down the course and improved the fortune of their team by taking out two targets and clipping the third, though it didn't break. Yoshioka applauded loudly, shooting Masamoto a haughty look down his nose.

'Despite the intervening years, Yoshioka-san has never got over the shame and still refuses to speak with Masamoto-sama.'

'Will you please be quiet?' said Kiku in exasperation. 'It's Akiko's turn.'

Akiko patted the neck of her white stallion, calming it before the run. Jack crossed his fingers for her. He knew Akiko had been training hard for this moment.

The signal fan went up.

Akiko spurred on her horse.

Jack found himself holding his breath as she nocked, aimed and shot her first *jindou*. It struck the very centre of the target, exploding it into pieces. The *Niten Ichi Ryū* cheered her on.

Approaching the second mark, Akiko gripped the stallion with her thighs to steady herself for the shot. The *jindou* flew straight and true, cracking the target in two. Again, there was rapturous applause and Jack punched the air with delight.

All eyes were on Akiko for the final mark.

But by the time she'd raised her bow, her horse had overshot the last target. A disappointed groan rose from the crowd, but Akiko hadn't given up. Turning round in her saddle, Akiko fired backwards, demolishing the last target.

The *Niten Ichi Ryū* went wild.

Unable to contain himself, Jack ran down to congratulate her. By the time he got there, she'd dismounted and was making her way back up the course.

'You were amazing,' said Jack. 'That final shot was unbelievable.'

'Thank you,' replied Akiko, smiling bashfully. 'But I can't take all the credit. Takuan taught me that technique.'

Jack could have guessed Takuan would be involved somehow.

'Well, we'd best go and wish him luck then,' suggested Jack as gallantly as he could. 'He has a lot to live up to after your performance.'

As they passed the start, the second *Yagyu Ryū* student set off. Only polite applause greeted the boy when he reached the end of the course. He'd failed to hit a single target.

'We're going to win!' said Jack. 'The *Yagyu Ryū* have only broken two targets; the *Yoshioka Ryū* have three; we've got five already.'

'There's still a rider from each school to go,' reminded Akiko, nodding in the direction of a tiny girl from *Yoshioka Ryū* mounting her horse.

'I'd be amazed if she can even reach the target, let alone hit it!' said Jack. 'Besides, you're bound to get the prize for best archer.'

The girl, though smaller than the saddle she sat upon, had a fierce look of determination about her. The signal fan went up and she urged her horse into a gallop. Careering down the track, she could hardly stand up in her stirrups. But, incredibly, she managed to nock an arrow and shatter the first target. The second was demolished soon after.

Akiko gave Jack a knowing look.

The girl went for the final mark, but she lost grip of her arrow and it fell to the ground.

'Told you,' said Jack, a look of triumph on his face. 'You're going to win.'

'You've forgotten Takuan, and also the final *Yagyu Ryū* rider. *She* might be good enough to win best archer,' said Akiko, with uncharacteristic malice.

Making final adjustments to her saddle was Moriko. The girl had viciously beaten Akiko during the *Taryu-Jiai* contest two years ago, a fact Akiko had not forgotten. She was talking earnestly with Kazuki, who stood close by. Taken off-guard by Akiko and Jack's sudden appearance, the two of them seemed furtive and embarrassed by the interruption.

'Good luck,' mumbled Kazuki, bowing.

'You too,' she replied, flashing a blackened smile at him.

Kazuki pushed past Jack, ignoring him. Jack wondered if he'd been passing on more news from his father, unaware the samurai was really on Masamoto's side.

Moriko mounted her black steed and headed towards the start.

'Nice pony trick,' hissed Moriko, giving Akiko a withering look as she passed by. 'Shame it won't count.'

'What do you mean?' said Akiko, rising to the bait.

'You'd ridden past the end of the course,' gloated Moriko. She trotted off, leaving Akiko stunned and unable to protest.

'Ignore her,' said Jack, seeing the concern in Akiko's eyes. 'The official's flag went up. It must have counted. Anyway, who cares if she gets all three targets, we still have Takuan. He won't fail us, will he?'

FALLEN RIDER

Moriko's horse pounded down the track, snorting under the exertion. But she rode with calm confidence, her eyes locked on the first target. Standing up in her saddle, she maintained perfect balance. With no sense of urgency, Moriko nocked an arrow, drew back on the bow, fired and destroyed the first mark with brutal proficiency.

The next target was also obliterated.

Approaching her final mark, Moriko waited until she was almost alongside before releasing her *jindou*. The wooden-tipped arrow struck dead centre and annihilated the target, splinters of wood flying in all directions. A huge cheer erupted from the students of the *Yagyu Ryū*.

Akiko shook her head in dismay. '*That* was impressive,' she admitted.

'But shooting backwards surely proves you're the more skil-ful archer,' said Jack.

She smiled kindly at Jack's belief in her. 'Let's wish Takuan good luck. He'll need it after that display.'

They followed the path round to where the horses were tethered.

'What's wrong?' said Akiko, rushing over to Takuan, who lay on the ground, groaning and clutching his side.

'I was saddling my horse . . .' he gasped, wincing with each breath, 'when I stepped back and knocked into another horse. It kicked me in the ribs. I think they're broken.'

'Will the last rider for the *Niten Ichi Ryū* please come forward?' announced an official.

'Do you think you can still ride?' asked Jack.

Takuan tried to sit up, but the effort was too much. He shook his head feebly. 'It hurts like hell. I can hardly breathe.'

'Final call for the *Niten* archer!' shouted the official.

'But the schools are tied on points,' said Jack. 'You only need to hit one target for us to win.'

'You do it,' Takuan wheezed.

'But I've not trained on a real horse!' protested Jack.

'You let go of the reins last week,' said Takuan, giving Jack a pained smile.

'And I fell off!'

'Jack, don't worry about it,' said Akiko, kneeling down beside Takuan. 'It's just a competition. It's more important we look after Takuan.'

Jack realized an opportunity to impress Akiko was about to slip through his fingers. Kazuki was right. Akiko wanted a real samurai, one who wasn't scared to take a risk.

'No, I'll do it,' he said, untying Takuan's horse.

He led it to the start line, not daring to look back in case Akiko saw the fear on his face.

Jack gazed down the length of the *Yabusame* course and swallowed nervously. It appeared to stretch on forever, the targets impossibly small. He shifted in his saddle, trying to get a better grip with his thighs. Takuan's stallion was so much bigger than his wooden dobbin. Not only that, it had legs! There was simply no way he could do this.

The faces of hundreds of young samurai stared expectantly in his direction. Jack spotted Saburo gawping back at him in shock, a half-eaten stick of *yakitori* hanging from his open mouth. Sensei Yosa came up on the pretext of checking the bridle on Jack's horse.

'Where's Takuan?' she hissed, her eyes fiercely glaring up at him.

'A horse kicked him,' Jack whispered.

The official raised his red sun fan, signalling Jack to start.

Sensei Yosa took a deep breath and sighed. 'Well, it's too late now. Just don't break your neck!'

Giving Sensei Yosa an uneasy smile, Jack urged his horse on. The stallion quickly built up speed and was soon galloping down the track. Jack gripped the reins and his bow so tightly his knuckles went white.

All too soon, the first target loomed into view. Willing himself to let go, Jack reached behind for one of Takuan's arrows. Jolted around by the movement of the horse, he struggled to nock the *jindou*. At the last second, he fumbled it into place and took a desperate potshot at the target.

Jack was so wide of the mark, he almost hit one of the officials. He caught the sound of laughter as he hurtled past. He realized he would have to stand up in his stirrups to have any hope of keeping steady long enough to strike a target.

His horse powered on. Jack snatched another *jindou* from his quiver as the second target rushed towards him. Throwing caution to the wind, he released the reins and stood. He managed to match the rhythm of his horse and took aim. But an unexpected jolt threw him off balance and Jack went tumbling forward. In desperation, he lunged for the horse's neck.

There was more laughter from the ranks of young samurai as the *gaijin* flew past, hanging on for dear life. For Jack, it felt like he was back on-board the *Alexandria,* wrestling to stay upright on the yardarm in some fearsome storm.

That was it! Jack realized. He just needed to find his sea legs again.

Imagining the horse was the yardarm and forgetting his fear, Jack stood up in his stirrups. He allowed his body to bend and bounce, absorbing the movements of the galloping stallion as if they were waves.

With one more target left, Jack only had moments to prepare. All the training on the back of the dobbin, however, now paid off. Remembering what Sensei Yosa had taught him a year before – '*When the archer does not think about the target, then they may unfold the Way of the Bow*' – he no longer focused on the final target. He simply let his body go through the motions of nocking, drawing and shooting the arrow. On the wooden horse, he knew he could hit the mark every time, even with his eyes closed. Jack had to trust his instincts.

He let the arrow fly.

His horse thundered on, galloping past the end of the course as Jack reached in vain for the reins hanging below its neck. His first indication that he'd actually struck the *Yabusame* target came when he heard a distant cheer. But by then Jack was deep into the woods.

★　　★　　★

'You were hilarious,' said Saburo, later that evening at the school celebrations in the *Chō-no-ma*. 'You almost killed an official, strangled your horse, then rode off into the next province!'

'But he *still* broke the target,' reminded Takuan, who sat opposite Jack, his ribs bandaged tightly, surrounded by several concerned girls.

'It was a team effort,' said Jack, toasting Takuan with a cup of *sencha* that Akiko had just poured him. 'I couldn't have done it without you.'

'Modest to the last,' said Yamato. 'He usually takes *all* the glory!'

Yamato gave Jack a friendly nudge in the ribs to let him know he was teasing.

'How are you feeling, Takuan?' asked Emi.

'Much better,' he replied, bowing his head to her as she joined them at their table. 'Sensei Yamada says it's probably only a cracked rib. The bruising is already fading thanks to the herbal ointment you gave me.'

Emi smiled coyly. 'It's just something my nurse had to hand.'

Saburo looked pointedly at Jack, then whispered in his ear, 'How does he do it? Even the *daimyo*'s daughter is running round after him!'

Suppressing a grin, Jack took another sip of his green tea.

'*Kohai!*' called Masamoto from the far end of the Hall of Butterflies.

The students ceased their chattering and turned to the head table.

'Once again, young samurai, you have made me proud.

Triumphing against the *Yagyu Ryū* and *Yoshioka Ryū* proves we are the greatest samurai school in Kyoto!'

The students gave an almighty cheer.

'We are doubly fortunate to also have the best *Yabusame* archer in Kyoto,' he added, inclining his head in Akiko's direction.

Akiko bowed humbly and Jack beamed at her with pride. The *Yabusame* officials had awarded her the prize in light of her exceptional rear-facing shot. It had been the first time any student had successfully executed such a technique in an inter-school *Kyosha*. Moriko had fumed at the decision and later Jack had spotted the girl snapping her arrows in a fit of temper while Kazuki tried to console her.

'As tradition dictates,' said Masamoto, lifting his cup of *sencha* in a toast, 'winning the *Kyosha* brings good fortune on the *Niten Ichi Ryū* for the rest of the year. May it last. *Kampai!*'

'*Kampai!*' replied the students, returning the toast.

All of a sudden, the doors to the *Chō-no-ma* flew open. A girl ran in, screaming, 'The Hall of the Hawk is on fire!'

32

FIRE OF THE HAWK

The magnificent *Taka-no-ma* was lit up like a bonfire against the night sky. The students formed a line from the school well to the blazing hall, frantically passing buckets to one another. At the front, Jack was dousing the flames on the veranda. The heat was so intense that the hairs on the backs of his arms were all singed and he had to shield his eyes from the fire. Smoke swirled around him and Jack began to choke.

'Jack-kun, come away!' ordered Sensei Yosa.

Jack stumbled off the veranda, coughing and spluttering. He crouched down in the middle of the courtyard, drawing deep breaths of clean air as the other students continued to battle the flames.

Through eyes stinging with smoke, Jack noticed a movement near the school gates. A huge shadow, distorted by the flickering glow of the fire, slipped along the outer wall. It shrank to nothing as a figure furtively approached the entrance and pulled back the bolts. Jack rubbed his eyes. Squinting, he saw more shadows enter through the open gateway.

Ninja! thought Jack. Dragon Eye had finally come.

But then Jack spotted the samurai swords, glinting in the firelight. How stupid to think it was Dragon Eye. The ninja would be more covert with his mission. This could only be *daimyo* Kamakura's army. But how could he have got his forces here so quickly? They were supposedly still encamped on Edo's borders, several days' march away. Whatever, Jack knew the fire was a diversion and the *Niten Ichi Ryū* was under attack.

'*ENEMY!*' screamed Jack at the top of his hoarse lungs.

But the fire of the Hawk roared so loud, few heard him.

Jack ran back to Sensei Yosa, pulling on her arm and pointing to the invading force. Her keen eyes spotted the danger immediately.

'Get your weapons!' she ordered, before hurrying to inform Masamoto and the other sensei. Since they'd all been attending the formal celebrations, none of the students were carrying swords.

Jack grabbed Saburo and Yori.

'We're under attack! Tell everyone to arm themselves.'

Jack sprinted off towards the *Shishi-no-ma* to retrieve his *daishō*. Arriving at the entrance, he discovered the doors were jammed and he couldn't get in. He kicked hard, but the thick wooden panels wouldn't budge. What was going on? These doors were never barred.

With dread horror, Jack realized the enemy had planned the attack in advance. Ensuring the *Niten Ichi Ryū* were unable to defend themselves, it was to be a massacre.

Searching for another way in, Jack found an unshuttered window, but it was too high and too small for him to clamber through. Scanning the courtyard, he spotted Yori trying to warn the other students of the attack. Many were still battling the fire, unaware of the danger.

'Yori!' screamed Jack, beckoning him over.

The little boy sprinted across, his face black with smoke and his eyes wide with fear.

Jack hurriedly explained the situation. 'I'll lift you up. You climb through and open the door from the other side.'

Yori nodded obediently and Jack hoisted him up until he was standing on Jack's shoulders. Stretching for the sill, Yori wriggled himself through the opening and disappeared inside.

Jack ran back to the entrance and waited for what seemed an age. Masamoto and his sensei were now engaged in heavy combat with the intruders, trying to break through the lines so the rest of the school could reach the Weapons Wall in the *Butokuden*. Many students, however, had been forced into hand-to-hand combat, relying solely on their *taijutsu* training to survive.

The door scraped open and Yori's face appeared. Jack burst in, pushing past him to retrieve his swords. But glancing down the girls' corridor, he caught sight of a figure enter a room at the far end. A flame flickered in the darkness.

'Yori,' Jack whispered. 'Get Yamato, then collect as many weapons as you can!'

Yori, terrified by the sudden turn of events, could only nod.

'Go!' urged Jack and pushed his friend out of the door.

Jack ran silently down the girls' corridor. As he approached the last room, he slowed and peered round the door. Inside, a shadowy figure was bent over an oil lamp, about to set fire to the paper walls. Jack had discovered the culprit. Preparing to attack, he crept closer but the intruder spun round.

'You're too late, *gaijin*!' snarled Kazuki. 'The Scorpions have struck.'

Jack was stopped in his tracks and stared open-mouthed at his rival.

'Kazuki? What . . . ? Why burn down your *own* school?' Jack exclaimed.

'As *daimyo* Takatomi said, the Hall of the Hawk should be a beacon of light in dark times,' Kazuki mocked, imitating their lord. 'And it's now *daimyo* Kamakura's time!'

'But your father's on *our* side!' said Jack urgently.

Kazuki laughed. 'That's what Takatomi is meant to believe, but my father's always served *daimyo* Kamakura.'

Jack felt his temper rising at the betrayal. 'What about your loyalty to Masamoto-sama?'

'He lost my respect the day he adopted you,' spat Kazuki, standing to face him. 'But he's still the best swordsman in Japan, so my father ordered me to stay to learn the secret of the Two Heavens.'

Grinning, Kazuki raised the oil lamp. 'Now I know it. School's over!'

'NO!' screamed Jack, lunging to stop him.

He collided with Kazuki, but the lamp was already sailing towards the wall. It smashed open, spilling burning oil across the room. Jack drove his shoulder into Kazuki's chest. They both crashed to the floor.

Jack, having the advantage, landed a solid hook punch across Kazuki's jaw. Spitting blood, Kazuki retaliated with a series of devastating body blows. Jack grimaced, trying to absorb the punches so he could stay on top. But Kazuki's skill at grappling meant Jack was soon dislodged.

They both scrambled to their feet amid the burning room. Smoke clogged their vision and Jack didn't see the roundhouse kick until it was too late. It caught him in the ribs, sending him staggering sideways. A moment later, Kazuki front-kicked him in the chest. Jack flew against the burning paper wall and crashed through to the next room.

Jumping after him, Kazuki aimed to land a stomping kick to the head. At the last second, Jack rolled out of the way. Turning back, he drove his body into Kazuki. Grabbing hold of his rival's leg, he twisted it and swept him to the floor. Jack was up first, kicking Kazuki in the back as he tried to stand. It was only then that he noticed the sleeve of his kimono had caught fire.

Panicking, Jack slapped at the flames to extinguish them. But the momentary distraction allowed Kazuki to recover. Flipping to his feet, he backfisted Jack in the nose. Then, grabbing Jack's smouldering arm, he executed a *seoi nage*, throwing him through the next wall.

Jack lay there dazed, staring up in a blur at the burning ceiling. The Hall of Lions cracked and creaked under the strain of the spreading fire. Kazuki stepped through the flames, his fists clenched, his eyes blazing with hatred. He looked down at Jack.

'I've waited a long time to finish you,' he said, kicking Jack several times in quick succession.

Jack doubled up, trying to protect himself, but a kick to the head took all the fight out of him. Crippled with pain, he could only watch helplessly as the room became consumed in flames.

Smiling cruelly, Kazuki gave the door frame an almighty

kick. It splintered and snapped. The room began to collapse around Jack. A beam dropped from the ceiling and landed across his back, flattening him. Crying out, he tried to rise but the beam was too heavy.

'Burn, *gaijin*, burn,' said Kazuki, leaving Jack to his fate.

33

MORIKO

Jack lay there, pinned beneath the beam.

The flames grew more intense and the whole building groaned, threatening to collapse around him.

He felt a wave of utter despair at the realization he'd never get to say goodbye to Akiko, or any of his friends. He'd never see his little sister again. Never set foot on English soil. After all the struggles he'd been through, all the lessons he'd learnt and all the challenges he'd overcome, he was to die alone. Burnt alive.

He cursed Kazuki, his Scorpion Gang and everything he stood for. Jack had been right all along about that boy. Intense anger now replaced his despair. Kazuki would not beat him like this. Jack strained with all his might against the beam.

But it refused to budge. He tried again.

'Jack!' shouted a familiar voice as he felt the weight of the beam lift.

He crawled forward, his back scraping against the wood.

'Hurry!' urged Yamato. 'I can't hold it any longer.'

Yamato dropped the beam just as Jack snatched his legs out

from underneath. Getting to his feet, Jack stumbled with Yamato into the corridor now thick with smoke.

'Where's Kazuki gone?' Jack gasped.

'He pushed past me saying he hadn't seen you!'

'Kazuki's a traitor!' replied Jack as they burst out of the *Shishi-no-ma* and into the courtyard.

Outside, the school grounds were a war zone. Blades flashed in the firelight. Battle cries of samurai and the screams of the wounded filled the air. A small group of *Niten Ichi Ryū* students were fighting in a tight circle beside Sensei Hosokawa and Sensei Yosa, fending off the intruders – the whole scene hellishly distorted by the blood-red glow of the buildings.

Yamato was staring at Jack in shock. '*Kazuki?* A traitor?'

Jack nodded. 'Yes, and his Scorpion Gang.'

Looking around, Jack noticed many of the intruders were actually young samurai like themselves. He recognized two of them by their immense size – Raiden and Taro, Kazuki's hulking cousins from Hokkaido. Jack now realized the truth. The *Niten Ichi Ryū* wasn't being attacked by *daimyo* Kamakura and his army but by the students and sensei of the *Yagyu Ryū*. That was how Kamakura had managed to launch a surprise attack without giving Masamoto any warning of their advance. The enemy had been residing in Kyoto all along.

Akiko, Saburo and Kiku came running over.

'Where's Yori?' Jack demanded.

'We haven't seen him,' replied Akiko.

A dread realization fell upon Jack. 'He was getting our weapons.'

Jack turned to run back inside the Hall of Lions.

'NO!' shouted Yamato, grabbing hold of him. 'It's too dangerous.'

As if in confirmation, the roof over the girls' section of the *Shishi-no-ma* collapsed, sending a huge cloud of sparks into the night like a swarm of fireflies.

'Yori!' cried Jack, struggling to break free from Yamato.

They all looked on in desperation as another section of the roof gave way. Jack went limp in Yamato's arms, as he realized his friend had no hope of surviving the blaze.

Then a moment later, Yori came stumbling out, smoke and ash billowing around him. On his back he carried a large bundle of weapons, wrapped in Jack's ceremonial kimono. Panting, his eyes red with smoke, Yori dumped the pile at their feet.

'I grabbed everything I could,' he gasped.

Jack hugged his friend with relief. Yori, unaccustomed to such displays of affection, tensed his body in surprise.

'Great work, Yori!' said Yamato, snatching up his staff.

Akiko picked up her bow and quiver. Jack spotted his own two swords among the weapons, the golden phoenix *kamon* glinting in the darkness.

'Look out!' Saburo shouted, pushing Jack violently to one side.

An arrow aimed at Jack's heart whistled past. It struck Saburo instead and he slumped to the ground, the steel tip piercing his left shoulder.

Kiku was immediately by his side. 'He's dying!,' she cried.

'No, he's only bleeding,' said Yamato, ripping a strip from the spare kimono and applying pressure to the wound.

'What's *she* doing here?' exclaimed Akiko.

Jack looked over to see Moriko, the *Yagyu Ryū* girl, standing beside the flaming Hall of the Hawk with her bow in hand. With no sense of urgency, as if still competing in a *Yabusame* competition, Moriko reached for another arrow.

Akiko hurried to string her own bow, but stopped to stare in horror at her arrows. 'These are *jindou*!'

'That was *my* archery prize,' screeched Moriko above the noise of battle. She took aim at Akiko and fired.

Dropping to one knee, Akiko drew back on her bow and released the blunt *jindou*. Moriko's arrow skimmed past Akiko's ear, catching a lock of her hair as it shot by. The *jindou*, however, didn't miss. It struck Moriko squarely in the chest. She stumbled backwards under the blow.

Akiko withdrew another *jindou*. Moriko, winded but unhurt, went to nock another steel-tipped arrow. Jack watched, powerless, as the two of them raced to shoot first. Akiko was ready a second before Moriko. She let loose her *jindou*. It flew straight and true, striking Moriko directly in the forehead. Stunned, Moriko reeled towards the blazing Hall of the Hawk before collapsing, unconscious.

'No, it was my prize,' said Akiko, allowing herself a smile of satisfaction at her shot.

Before any one else attacked them, Jack grabbed his swords from the weapon pile, then passed Yori, Kiku and Akiko the three remaining *katana*.

'It's time we rejoined the fight.'

In the far corner of the courtyard, Takuan and Emi were surrounded by enemy samurai. Takuan, weakened by his injury, could hardly lift the sword he'd found. Akiko immediately let loose a *jindou*, knocking his attacker to the ground.

Yamato, staff twirling, hurried to their aid. Akiko was right behind him, stringing her bow as she ran. Jack was about to follow when he noticed Moriko getting to her feet. She swayed unsteadily as she nocked an arrow.

Jack ran to stop her, but he knew he'd never make it in time.

'Die!' shrieked Moriko, targeting Akiko in the back.

34

HANGING

The Hall of the Hawk finally surrendered to the flames. The roof fell in and the wooden superstructure disintegrated with a resounding *crack*.

Moriko had little chance.

The building suddenly collapsed sideways, consuming her in an avalanche of fire, blazing wood and scalding ash. Jack saw her pale face stricken with fear as her hair burst into flame, her blackened mouth opening in an unheard scream. Then she disappeared beneath the smoking ruins, her bow and arrow still in her hands.

Beyond the remains, Kazuki stared in anguish at where Moriko had fallen. Through the haze of smoke and fire, Kazuki locked eyes with Jack. His face consumed with hate, Kazuki stormed off in the direction of the *Butokuden*.

Jack would not let him get away this time. Leaving Yori and Kiku tending to Saburo, he skirted the remains of the hall, evading several ongoing fights as he made for the *Butokuden*'s back entrance.

Peering in, he found the *dojo* eerily deserted. The light from the fires chased shadows round the pillared hall and the noise of battle echoed in the high-vaulted ceiling like the spirits of warriors past.

Kazuki was in the ceremonial alcove. He was splashing lamp oil over the walls, clearly intent on burning the whole school to the ground.

Drawing both his swords, Jack crept inside. Carefully stepping over a couple of weapons discarded by students in their haste to arm themselves from the Weapons Wall, he crossed the *dojo* floor and approached Kazuki from behind.

Now was his chance to make Kazuki pay for all the bullying and harassment he'd suffered these past three years. In just a few more steps, he could run his rival through with his sword.

But his hand was stayed by the memory of Masamoto's words of welcome that first day at the *Niten Ichi Ryū*.

The Way of the Warrior means living by the samurai code of honour – bushido – at all times. I demand courage and rectitude in all your endeavours.

Jack realized the right thing to do here was *not* to kill Kazuki out of any sense of personal revenge. That was wrong. Jack had to bring this traitor to justice. Masamoto would want to deal with him personally.

'Surrender, Kazuki,' said Jack, placing the tip of his *katana* to Kazuki's back.

Kazuki slowly turned round and raised his hands above his head.

Jack hadn't expected Kazuki to give in without a fight.

A devious grin spread across his rival's face.

Out of nowhere, a chain flicked through the air and wrapped itself round Jack's neck. He was yanked backwards off his feet, both swords flying out of his hands. Hidden behind a pillar, Hiroto held the other end of the *manriki-gusari*. He began to drag Jack across the *dojo* floor.

'Come on, good little *gaijin* dog!' he squealed.

Choking on the chain, Jack tried to force his fingers between it and his throat. He managed to get some slack and rolled on to his knees. But Hiroto wrenched the chain again, throwing him face first to the floor.

Dragging him in the direction of a low beam, Jack realized Hiroto intended to hang him. Struggling harder, Jack clutched desperately at the polished wooden blocks of the *dojo* floor, but it was futile.

Then his hand came across a discarded *tantō* knife. He snatched it up. At least he would die fighting.

Moments later, he heard the clunk of the *manriki-gusari* being flung over the beam. All of a sudden, his head was yanked upwards. Jack gagged and had to stand on his toes to relieve the pressure. Hiroto, bracing himself against a pillar, hauled Jack off his feet.

Jack could no longer touch the floor. He hung there, his legs kicking spasmodically as Hiroto laughed at his torment. The boy's grinning face faded in and out of focus, Jack on the verge of blacking out. In a last-ditch effort, he threw the knife at Hiroto. The *tantō* struck Hiroto in the stomach.

Screaming, Hiroto let go of the *manriki-gusari*. The chain came loose and Jack hit the ground at the same time as Hiroto. Jack heaved air into his oxygen-starved lungs. Hiroto didn't stop screaming, horror-struck at the blood gushing forth from his wound.

Jack crawled away, knowing he had to reach his swords

before Kazuki saw what had happened and attacked him. He could hear the lumbering thud of footsteps getting closer. Only at the last second did Jack catch a glimpse of the iron-studded club. It came hurtling towards his head. He rolled to one side and the *dojo* floor exploded, splinters flying everywhere.

Standing over him, Nobu raised the *kanabō* again.

'I'm going to squash you, *gaijin*!' he growled.

Jack scrambled away as the club came crashing down a fraction behind him. He desperately needed a weapon, but the only thing close to hand was a discarded *tessen*. Picking up the iron fan, Jack stood to face his attacker.

Nobu looked at Jack's tiny weapon and then at his own massive club.

'What are you going to do? Fan me to death?' he said, giving a great belly laugh.

As he lifted the club for another strike, Jack flicked the fan shut and drove its reinforced spine into Nobu's gut. Winded, Nobu dropped the *kanabō*. It crashed to the ground. With lightning speed, Jack struck a second time, catching Nobu across the temple. The boy flopped to the floor, groaning and unable to stand.

Jack stepped away, breathing hard. His throat throbbed, his head pounded and his body ached from all the bruises.

But the fight was far from over.

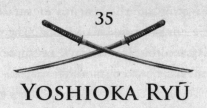

35

YOSHIOKA RYŪ

Only *zanshin* saved Jack's life.

Sensing an attack from behind, Jack ducked. The *katana* blade whistled through the air, barely missing his head. Kazuki swore in frustration and followed up with his *wakizashi*. With no time to evade the short sword, Jack turned on the spot, blocking the thrust to his stomach with the iron spine of the *tessen*. He deflected the strike, but lost his grip on the fan and it went clattering to the floor.

Kazuki came at Jack again. Jack dived out of the way, rolling across the *dojo*. Without a weapon, he had little hope of defending himself against two swords. He could see his own *katana* and *wakizashi* lying tantalizingly on the far side of Kazuki, but every time he tried to run for them his rival blocked the way.

Jack feigned a desperate rush for his swords. Kazuki jumped in his path. At the last second Jack switched directions, sprinting for the Weapons Wall instead. He seized the only remaining *katana*. Jack didn't even have time to unsheath the sword before Kazuki's blade cut at his neck.

Jack blocked the strike, the *saya* of his *katana* shattering on impact. Shaking off the remains of the scabbard, he hurriedly retreated and raised his weapon. The sword didn't compare to Masamoto's. It was heavy, unbalanced, its blade chipped and the handle worn smooth from constant training practice.

Kazuki noticed the uncertainty in Jack's stance and attacked. A whirlwind of blades sliced through the air. Jack tried to defend himself, but his second-rate weapon put him at a disadvantage. He deflected a thrust to the stomach and countered with a strike to the neck, but Kazuki easily evaded the blade. Stepping off to one side, he smashed his sword on top of Jack's, snapping off the tip of the battleworn blade. Jack stared at his broken weapon in shock.

Kazuki drove forward, shoulder-barging Jack into a nearby pillar. Jack crumpled against it as Kazuki's *katana* came round in a great arc to cut him in half. In desperation, Jack swung his own sword across and the two weapons clashed and locked. Jack tried to disengage, but as he pulled away Kazuki executed a perfect Autumn Leaf strike, disarming Jack of his *katana*.

'Defeated yet again!' gloated Kazuki, placing the sword's *kissaki* to Jack's neck. 'On your knees, *gaijin*!'

With no alternative, Jack did as he was told. It appeared that Kazuki was going to force him to commit *seppuku*. The thought terrified him. How could anyone slit open their *own* stomach?

Kazuki looked over at Hiroto, still screaming in the corner.

'Will you be quiet! You're not dying. It's only blood.' Kazuki shook his head in irritation. 'Nobu, over here.'

Nobu sat up, rubbing his head. When he saw Jack on his knees, defeated with Kazuki's blade to his throat, his face lit up with glee.

Kazuki studied Jack a moment, seeming to be in two minds whether to kill him or not.

'You're not samurai. *Gaijin* don't deserve to die *honourably* by the sword,' he sneered, drawing the blade away and flicking the *kissaki* across Jack's right cheek. Jack grimaced as a thin line of blood oozed to the surface. 'That should even up your scars, for a start.'

Nobu lumbered over, the *kanabō* on his shoulder, and awaited Kazuki's command.

Sheathing his swords, Kazuki grabbed Jack by the throat.

'You killed Moriko!' he said, a tremor seizing his voice. 'You *will* suffer for it.'

'I didn't –' protested Jack, but Kazuki cut him off.

'Nobu, break his legs. We don't want him getting away this time. I want the *gaijin* to burn, just as she did.'

Nobu obediently raised the *kanabō* to shatter Jack's ankles.

'Stop!' said a timid voice from the doorway.

Yori ran in, his sword drawn.

'If you hurt Jack, I'll kill Kazuki,' he threatened, pointing his sword at Kazuki's heart. Despite the courage of his words, Yori's sword arm trembled.

'Nobu, do what he says,' said Kazuki, bowing his head in defeat.

Nobu, his podgy face wrinkling in bemusement, was about to lower his club when Kazuki struck. With lightning speed, he withdrew his *katana* and knocked Yori's sword to the ground.

'Yet again, your little bodyguard fails you, *gaijin*,' sneered Kazuki, poking Yori in the chest with his finger. 'Go on, Yori, run away like you always do.'

Yori stood there, his lip trembling. He sobbed in great gulps of air and looked like he was about to cry.

Kazuki walked away, laughing coldly. 'Nobu, after you snap the *gaijin*'s legs, crush the mouse.'

Grinning, Nobu raised the *kanabō* above his head.

All of a sudden, an ear-splitting *kiai* filled the *Butokuden*.

'*YAH!*'

Nobu staggered backwards, a confused expression on his face. All his strength evaporated and he dropped the *kanabō* on his head. Lurching like a Daruma Doll, he crumpled to the floor again, this time unconscious.

Kazuki spun round, his eyes wide with shock. Drawing his swords, he charged at his enemy.

'*YAH!*'

Kazuki stopped in his tracks. He tried to lift his *katana* again.

'*YAH!*'

Kazuki dropped to his knees, his face ashen, groaning as if a spear had been thrust through his body.

'No more! You'll kill him,' shouted Jack.

Yori, his lungs full for another attack, slowly released his breath. Jack got to his feet and retrieved his swords.

'Are you all right?' he asked, seeing Yori shuddering.

Yori blinked, as if awoken from a trance, and nodded weakly. In a tiny voice he replied, 'I couldn't fail you again.'

'And you didn't,' said Jack, putting his arm round Yori. 'I guess Sensei Yamada was right, even the smallest breeze can make ripples on the largest ocean.'

Jack indicated the immense Nobu out cold on the floor and they both laughed from a combination of exhaustion and relief. But they stopped when they noticed Kazuki had managed to stagger to the doorway.

Leaving Hiroto still groaning in the corner and Nobu unconscious, Yori and Jack hurried after Kazuki. By the time they reached the door, the traitor had disappeared among the chaos of battle.

A huge cry sounded as a fresh wave of young samurai poured in through the *Niten Ichi Ryū* gates.

At the head of the column was Yoshioka.

Masamoto rallied his students together in front of the Southern Zen Garden, each group led by a sensei. Jack and Yori ran over and joined the ranks to face their new enemy from the *Yoshioka Ryū*. Tired, battleworn and vastly outnumbered, Jack realized there was little hope for them now.

'We'll fight to the last samurai standing!' shouted Sensei Kyuzo, raising his *katana*.

The *Niten Ichi Ryū* bellowed in response, firing up their courage for the final assault.

The *Yagyu Ryū,* confident of victory, roared back. But the students of the *Yoshioka Ryū* didn't join in the battle cry. Instead, they unsheathed their swords and attacked the students and sensei of the *Yagyu Ryū*.

Suddenly the invaders were on the defensive and being driven back. The tide of battle had turned.

Their advantage lost, the *Yagyu Ryū* beat a hasty retreat.

The *Niten Ichi Ryū* cheered their unexpected allies and joined in routing the enemy. Soon the courtyard was cleared and the gates closed against further attacks.

Jack and the others lowered their swords with relief, glad to have survived the raid.

But the cost of victory had been high. Sensei and young samurai of both schools lay bleeding and dying in the court-yard, while all around the *Niten Ichi Ryū* continued to burn.

36

AFTERMATH

The dawn sun bled through the smoke-laden sky, staining the clouds a watery red. A solemn silence hung over the *Niten Ichi Ryū* as the survivors tended to the wounded and salvaged what they could from the burnt-out buildings.

Jack kicked aside the smouldering ruins that had been the *Shishi-no-ma*. His room had been completely destroyed, his *bokken*, *bonsai* and clothes ravaged by the fire. For once he was glad Dragon Eye had the *rutter*. It would have been burnt to a cinder otherwise. But now he possessed nothing save the kimono on his back and Masamoto's *daishō*.

Crouching down, he spotted a charred scrap of paper buried in the ash. Pulling it free from the blackened *inro* case, he held the remains of a child's drawing. His sister's scribble of their family. The picture had been obliterated. Jack let the scrap fall back into the dying embers.

He could no longer hold out hope of returning home to Jess. Not when a war threatened to consume Japan. It wasn't just the fact that battles would bar his way. The *Niten Ichi Ryū* had been attacked and, having vowed to follow the Way of the Warrior, it was his duty to defend his school's honour. Bound by the code of *bushido*, his loyalty to Masamoto and his friends had to take priority over his long-held dream of going home.

The *inro* that had contained the picture was all but destroyed. Tossing the case aside, he heard a rattle as it landed. Picking it up again, he found Akiko's pearl inside. Miraculously, it had survived the fire. Allowing himself a weary smile, he slipped the precious gift inside the folds of his *obi*. It would serve as a reminder of everything that was good about Japan and why he must fight to protect it.

He was about to return to his friends, when he noticed a glint of steel. Brushing aside the ash, he uncovered the *tantō* he'd taken from the ninja in the bamboo forest. The lacquered *saya* had cracked under the heat, but the knife itself was undamaged. In fact, the fire seemed only to have further tempered the steel, for Jack's little finger was dripping blood. He must have cut it while clearing away the embers. Very carefully, Jack tucked the demon blade into his belt.

'Jack!' called Yori, scurrying over.

Rising slowly to his feet, Jack greeted his friend. He felt sore all over, his muscles bruised and battered and his neck aching from his near-hanging experience. But he was one of the fortunate ones. At least he could walk.

Yori, his face streaked black with smoke and dried tears, handed him a small round bundle wrapped in a piece of cloth.

'This is yours,' he said proudly.

Opening it, Jack found himself staring at his Daruma Doll.

'It was lying on top of the kimono I used to collect the weapons,' Yori explained. 'I know the wish it contains means a lot to you, so I rescued it along with your swords.'

'Thank you,' replied Jack, patting his friend on the shoulder. 'But I don't think this Daruma Doll works. It's been nearly three years since I made that wish.'

'Daruma wishes *do* come true. You can't give up hope, Jack.'

Yori's pleading eyes looked up at him. Jack realized his friend was barely holding himself together. The sudden attack and the brutality of the fighting had left him shocked and on the verge of falling apart. Yori was looking to Jack for reassurance.

'We survived, didn't we?' replied Jack, smiling. 'And it was your loyalty that saved me. My mother used to say, "Where there are friends, there's hope." You're a true friend, Yori.'

Touched by his words, Yori bowed his head. 'It's my honour.'

Crossing the courtyard, they passed a group of *Yagyu* students guarded by samurai from the *Yoshioka Ryū*. Patched up but looking thoroughly defeated, Nobu and Hiroto were among the prisoners, their heads hung in shame. Jack noticed Kazuki was not with them, the traitor having escaped amid the confusion of battle. News of his defection had spread rapidly among the students. Masamoto had been furious to discover the truth of Kazuki's father's treachery. Vowing to punish Oda-san, he'd sent a patrol in search of his son. But so far Kazuki had evaded capture.

Beside the main gate, the bodies of the fallen had been gathered for cremation at various temples. Akiko stood nearby.

'You go on, I'll join you shortly,' said Jack to Yori.

His friend nodded in understanding and headed inside the *Chō-no-ma*.

As Jack approached Akiko, she looked up, her eyes red from crying.

'I may not have liked her, but she didn't deserve to die like this.'

Akiko gazed down at the lifeless Moriko.

'It was all my fault,' she sniffed, her voice cracking slightly.

'No, it wasn't,' Jack insisted, trying not to look at the charred corpse. 'You didn't know the building was about to collapse. Besides, if you hadn't knocked her out with your *jindou*, she would have killed us both.'

'But is this what war *really* means?' asked Akiko, waving a despairing hand at the pile of dead bodies. 'None of our training prepared us for *this*.'

Jack understood what she meant. They'd been so focused on the training, they'd never really thought about the consequences – of actually taking a person's life. But the onset of war had forced them into using their skills. From this day forth, they would have to face up to their responsibilities as samurai.

'You told me once that being a samurai means "to serve",' said Jack. 'That our duty is to our Emperor, our *daimyo* and our family. I didn't understand at the time, but I now know what duty means. As samurai, we may have to kill, or be killed, if we want to protect those we serve and love.'

'You're right, Jack,' sighed Akiko. 'It doesn't make it any easier, though.'

'No, but it's a peace worth fighting for.'

And with those words, Jack realized he'd willingly lay down his life for Japan and those he loved.

★   ★   ★

Inside the *Chō-no-ma*, injured young samurai lay upon the cleared tables, Sensei Yamada and Sensei Kano administering to their wounds. The other teachers were in conference with Masamoto and Yoshioka in the Hall of the Phoenix.

'Wait till our parents hear about this!' exclaimed Taro as Jack and Akiko approached their friends.

Taro stood over his brother. Saburo was laid out on a table, his shoulder bound in bandages, a patch of blood oozing through.

'Leave him alone, Taro,' said Jack, rushing to Saburo's defence. 'He's been through enough as it is.'

'Jack, you misunderstand me. He'll be a hero in their eyes. Saburo sacrificed himself for another samurai.'

Saburo grinned proudly, 'And I'll have a real battle scar!'

'You need to rest,' insisted Kiku, helping him sip some water and wiping his brow.

'Has anyone found out what's going on yet?' said Yori.

Yamato nodded. 'A student from the *Yoshioka Ryū* told me there have been surprise attacks all over the city. *Daimyo* Kamakura has begun his rebellion.'

'But why did the *Yoshioka Ryū* help us?' asked Jack.

'Yoshioka-san is a loyal subject of *daimyo* Takatomi,' explained Taro with an air of authority. 'His duty to his lord outweighs any personal grievance against Masamoto-sama. He was most likely commanded to come to our aid. Besides, by rescuing us, Yoshioka-san has regained the status he lost in his duels with Masamoto-sama.'

The *shoji* by the head table flew open and Masamoto strode in, flanked by his sensei. All the students stopped what they were doing and knelt down. Masamoto took his place in the centre of the dais, put his swords to one side and fixed his students with a stern gaze. The scarring down his face throbbed an angry red and there was a vicious cut above his right eye. Sensei Hosokawa was beside him, a tourniquet wrapped round his left bicep. A tense silence fell over the hall.

'WAR has been declared,' stated Masamoto.

Still in shock from the battle, the students could only stare back in numb horror. Yori glanced nervously at Jack. His worst fear had come true.

'No longer is *daimyo* Kamakura targeting just foreigners and Christians. He is attacking any *daimyo* and their samurai who will not submit to his rule, whether they are sympathetic to foreigners or not. We believe *daimyo* Kamakura has organized coordinated strikes across Japan. The city of Nagoya has fallen, the Tokaido Road to its north is in his control and his army is marching south as we speak.

'We've received word that samurai loyal to the Council and Hasegawa Satoshi, our ruler-in-waiting, are combining forces at Osaka Castle. From there, they intend to face down and destroy this enemy of the Emperor. By the order of *daimyo* Takatomi, we leave for Osaka today.'

It was midday by the time all the preparations were complete. Horses were saddled, supplies were gathered and samurai armed. Not all the *Niten Ichi Ryū* students were going. The younger trainees were being sent back to their families, while the wounded would remain at the school until fit to fight. Those destined for battle now stood in formation in the courtyard, awaiting the command to leave.

'*Gambette*,' said Saburo, wishing them luck. Despite Kiku's protests, he'd insisted on coming to say goodbye to his friends. He bowed stiffly.

Kiku, who'd volunteered to stay behind to look after the wounded, wiped a tear from her eye and bowed too. Akiko, Yamato and Yori returned the bow. Saburo glanced over at Jack, then pulled him into an awkward hug. Wincing from the pain in his shoulder, Saburo blurted, 'Keep your head down. Don't do anything stupid. Watch out for ninja. Make sure you eat all your rations –'

'I'll miss you too, Saburo,' said Jack sincerely. Then, with a grin, 'I'll have no one to take an arrow for me now!'

Saburo laughed. Then he pulled away, the smile on his face fading into sorrow. 'Take great care, my friend.'

'OSAKA AND VICTORY!' shouted Sensei Hosokawa, signalling for the column of young samurai to begin marching out of the school gates.

Shouldering his pack, Jack wondered if he'd ever return to the *Niten Ichi Ryū* again. He gazed around at the mighty *Butokuden* where he'd defeated the sword and been pummelled every day as Sensei Kyuzo's *uke* in *taijutsu*; at the beautiful *Chō-no-ma* where he'd been introduced to the dubious pleasure of grilled eel's liver and celebrated New Year; at the Southern Zen Garden, his favourite place to relax and be alone with his thoughts, and where he'd first learnt the archery skills of *kyujutsu* from Sensei Yosa; at the *Butsuden* in which Sensei Yamada had set his impossible *koans* and once shown him the legendary butterfly kick; and finally at the burnt shell of the *Shishi-no-ma* that had been his home for the past three years.

He recalled how overawed he'd been the first day of his

arrival at the school. How terrifying and invincible the students had appeared. He remembered lying on his *futon* in his tiny bedroom, alone in an alien land, the prey of a one-eyed ninja, and feeling like a lamb going to the slaughter.

Heading off to war now, he didn't feel much different. Except this time, he knew how to fight. He may have arrived as a lost English boy, but he was leaving the *Niten Ichi Ryū* as a trained samurai warrior.

37
OSAKA CASTLE

After three days' hard march the students arrived in Osaka, the political and economic centre of Japan. Jack hadn't known what to expect from this great city. But, like Kyoto, it was a long way from the realities of English urban life with its putrid stench of dunghills and tanneries, its potholed roads and its gangs of footpads and wild youths.

Osaka was teeming with people who politely bowed as they passed. The shops and houses were all staggeringly clean. The roads were wide, swept and free of rubbish. Even the air was fresh.

But nothing could prepare Jack for Osaka Castle.

Dominating the skyline was a fortress of unimaginable size. The Tower of London looked pitiful in comparison, and Jack thought several Hampton Courts could fit within its walls. Soaring up from the centre of the castle was a *donjon* – the main keep – eight stories high, with the walls painted a stark heron white and curved roofs overlapping at each level, their green tiles decorated with gleaming golden gables.

As they passed through the outskirts of the city, the column of young samurai joined other troops heading towards the castle, until there was a steady stream flowing up the main thoroughfare. They approached a gigantic stone gateway set into a towering wall of interlocking battlements and bastions. The portcullis was raised and the huge iron-plated door opened to welcome their arrival.

Jack's ears were assaulted by the tramping of hundreds of marching feet as they crossed the long wooden drawbridge that spanned a wide moat. Glancing to his right, Jack noticed the outer defensive rampart stretched for at least a mile before it turned north. Its sheer walls sloped directly into the waters of the moat and appeared unscalable. Each block of stone in its construction was taller and wider than he was and had to weigh as much as ten cannon combined. Along the top, like the backbone of a dragon, ran a series of turrets that faced the wide, open plain of Tenno-ji to the south. As they passed through another gateway, equally formidable, Jack was astonished to discover the walls were several metres thick.

At the next gate, the road bore right and they headed down a wide avenue lined with heavily fortified houses. Their route then doubled on itself through another portcullis and over a second large moat.

Taro indicated for Jack to look up. Staring down at them from the battlements and parapets above were hundreds of soldiers. There were more on foot, guarding the gates, patrolling the thoroughfares and training in open courtyards, or tending to horses in the stables. There were samurai everywhere, by the thousand.

'Whoever controls Osaka Castle, controls the heart of this country,' whispered Taro.

Jack could well believe it and his heart lifted. The castle

appeared impregnable and the army invincible. Maybe there *was* hope after all.

Jack soon lost his bearings in the labyrinth of stone steps and roads, and was glad when they finally halted in a large treelined courtyard with a building reminiscent of the *Butokuden*. Masamoto ordered his students to line up and there they waited while he disappeared with Sensei Hosokawa in the direction of the *donjon*.

The keep was nearer now, but still appeared to be some ten minutes' march away. Jack reckoned they'd entered the inner defences of the castle, but the area was still large enough to contain a small town. Off to one side was a carefully tended garden with little bridges and a tiny stream that ran into a pond. Blossoming *sakura* trees offered shade and across from where the students stood was a small well. Aside from the availability of water, Jack had noticed along their route a plum grove and numerous storehouses being stocked with rice, salt, soya beans and dried fish. It was clear those in the castle would not only be safe, but self-sufficient against any siege.

Sensei Hosokawa returned, calling them sharply to attention. He was swiftly followed by an entourage of fully armed samurai warriors. In its midst was *daimyo* Takatomi, accompanied by Masamoto, several retainers and a young boy.

'Kneel!' commanded Sensei Hosokawa and all the young samurai dropped to one knee and bowed their heads.

Daimyo Takatomi stepped forward to speak.

'It is with great honour that I present to you his lordship Hasegawa Satoshi, Japan's rightful heir and ruler-in-waiting.'

The boy, surrounded by the retainers, nodded his head in

acknowledgement. Jack risked a glance up. Satoshi appeared not much older than himself. Maybe sixteen. He had a thin unblemished face with the early signs of a moustache faint upon his upper lip. His hair had been pulled into a topknot and he wore the full regalia of a commanding *daimyo*. What surprised Jack the most was the small silver Christian cross that hung from the boy's neck.

'Your young samurai are most welcome in my castle, Masamoto-sama,' piped Satoshi. 'With each passing day, more loyal troops arrive. Our army will soon number over a hundred thousand. With such a force, we will crush *daimyo* Kamakura and his illegitimate campaign.'

Moving with the gracious airs of one brought up in nobility, Satoshi inspected the lines of young samurai. He stopped before Jack.

'And who is this?' he asked, taken by surprise at the unexpected mop of blond among the rows of black-haired Japanese.

Jack bowed. 'Jack Fletcher, at your service.'

Satoshi laughed heartily. 'This will certainly put the fear of God into our enemy. A foreign samurai!'

His retainers joined in the laughter. Except one. Close behind the boy stood a man of European descent, tall and slim, with dark-olive skin and slicked-back hair. Jack hadn't noticed him before because he wore the same formal attire as the rest of the retainers. The man's eyes flared a moment on seeing Jack, then appeared to regain their composure. A tight smile formed on his thin lips. He whispered something in Satoshi's ear as the entourage moved on.

Jack wished he could have overheard what the man said. The foreigner clearly had some influence over Satoshi to be part of his private entourage. And Jack should have been comforted by the presence of another European face, but he couldn't shake the uneasy feeling in the pit of his stomach.

Having completed his inspection, Satoshi nodded his approval to Masamoto and departed, his retainers and samurai guard following swiftly behind. *Daimyo* Takatomi and Masamoto headed towards the garden, deep in discussion, leaving Sensei Hosokawa in charge.

'These are to be our barracks,' announced Sensei Hosokawa, indicating the building behind them. 'Deposit your kit, then follow me to the armoury.'

There were no beds inside, just a large empty hall separated at one end by a *shoji* screen. Jack followed Yamato and Yori, while Akiko headed to the other side of the screen with the rest of the girls. Finding a space in the far corner, Jack put down his pack. It contained little beside the Daruma Doll, the ninja's *tantō* and a spare blanket and kimono he'd managed to acquire from the school stores. His two swords were now permanently on his hip.

The students were slow to take their places, morale low since the attack on the *Niten Ichi Ryū*. The damage Kazuki had inflicted upon the school was proving to be greater than the burning of a few buildings. His defection had struck at the very heart of the *Niten Ichi Ryū*. The school was splitting into cliques, the students no longer trusting one another, and a great sense of shame hung round everyone's necks, the dishonour of a samurai-turned-traitor tainting them all.

'Mind if I join you?' asked Takuan, who looked exhausted after the long march.

'Of course not,' said Jack, making a space for him. Any

sense of rivalry over Akiko now seemed irrelevant at a time of war. 'How are you feeling?'

'Awful,' he replied, grimacing as he dropped his kit. 'My pack rubbed against my ribs all the way –'

'Hurry up!' shouted Sensei Kyuzo from the doorway.

Outside they were taken to a large storeroom and supplied with armour. A gruff soldier handed Jack a skirted breastplate consisting of overlapping layers of lacquered leather scales, two large rectangular shoulder pads, a metal helmet with three curved plates that shielded the neck, a pair of heavy gauntlets to protect his hands and, lastly, an ugly metal mask. It covered half of Jack's face and had a large pointed nose and thick black moustache.

'What's this for?' asked Jack.

'It's a *menpō*,' growled the soldier irritably. 'It protects your throat and scares the enemy. Not that you need one with a face like yours!'

He belly-laughed at his own joke. 'Next!'

Jack joined the others in the courtyard who were trying on their new equipment for size. Studying the array of armour, Jack had no idea where to start.

'Do you need some help?' asked Akiko, who was already fully clad in a magnificent turquoise-blue set.

'How did you put it on so quickly?'

'I often helped my father with his; even on the day he left for the Battle of Nakasendo. That was the last time I ever saw him.'

A sadness passed across Akiko's face. Jack knew she still felt the death of her father keenly despite the intervening years. He supposed the loss at such an early age had been one of the reasons Akiko was so intent on becoming a warrior herself. With no older brother in the family, it was her responsibility to take his place and maintain the family honour. Jack could understand her sense of loss. There wasn't a day that went by when he didn't think of his own father. But he had a different reason for becoming a samurai – the threat of Dragon Eye.

Akiko passed the breastplate over Jack's head and was about to tie it in place, when giggles burst forth from the other side of the courtyard. They turned round to see Yori swamped by his armour. His arms were not much longer than the shoulder pads and his breastplate almost touched his knees. But the feature that was generating the most amusement was his helmet. When Yori had put it on, his whole head had disappeared inside and he was now staggering around blind. Yamato rushed to his rescue.

Once fully kitted, Yori having exchanged his helmet for a smaller, but equally ill-fitting one, they stored their armour with their other belongings and headed over to the communal kitchens for food. The long march from Kyoto to Osaka had left Jack starving and he was looking forward to a proper meal. But the only provisions were several balls of cold rice and a watery fish soup.

The students gathered in disgruntled groups to eat their dinner. Yori sat down next to Jack in the courtyard, appearing thoroughly depressed. He picked at his rice, but didn't eat any.

'I know it's not up to the standard of the *Chō-no-ma*, but at least here we have great views of the castle,' said Jack, trying to encourage a smile from his friend.

'We're really going to war, aren't we?' Yori whispered, staring into his soup.

'Don't worry, Yori,' Akiko soothed. 'We won't be on the frontline.'

'Then why give us armour?'

'We're the reserve. That's why we've been stationed in the inner bailey. It's the safest place before the keep itself.'

'But what if the enemy gets in?'

'That won't happen. You saw the defences. No army can cross two moats and scale these fortified walls. Osaka Castle will never fall.'

As they were talking, four castle guards approached Jack. The lead guard addressed him.

'Jack Fletcher, you are to accompany us to the keep.'

38

FATHER BOBADILLO

Jack was frogmarched along a narrow road, the walls closing in on either side of him as they approached a huge iron-clad timber gateway, guarded by foot soldiers with spears. The doors swung open and they entered an inner courtyard bordered by plum and *sakura* trees. The keep was much closer now and Jack had to incline his head to see the uppermost floor.

Passing a tea garden with an oval pond, then a central well house, they crossed to the main entrance of the keep. As they approached the large fortified doorway set into its immense stone base, samurai guards challenged them, their hands ready on their swords. The Council were clearly taking no chances with Satoshi's safety. Jack also noticed a patrol circling the *donjon*. The lead guard gave the password and the gate was opened.

Once inside, the guards kicked off their sandals and Jack did likewise. The wooden interior was dark and it took a few moments for Jack's eyes to adjust. Off to one side, Jack spotted a storeroom stacked with gunpowder, muskets, arquebuses and spears. Expecting to find stone steps leading up to the main floor, Jack was amazed to discover there were three levels within the base of the keep alone. Ascending several wooden staircases, they passed more guards and countless rooms, but only when they reached the fourth floor were there any windows.

The sun was now low on the horizon and Jack could see for miles across the Tenno-ji Plain. Below were the three main encircling walls of the castle and beyond that the city, stretched out like a patchwork quilt to the harbour and the sea. It was so tantalizingly close. Perhaps, thought Jack, when this was all over, he could find a Japanese ship in the harbour bound for Nagasaki and from there make his way home.

His escort abruptly halted before a large wooden door on the fifth floor. There were no guards here and Jack had no idea what to expect. The samurai hadn't spoken a word to him since the barracks, so Jack didn't know whether he'd been arrested or was about to meet the ruler-in-waiting. The uneasy sensation in his stomach returned as the door was pulled back.

'Come into my study,' said a voice, thick and oily as tar.

Before him stood the European man from Satoshi's retinue, his hair slick and shiny in the lamplight. No longer dressed in a Japanese kimono, he wore the distinctive buttonless cassock and cape of a Portuguese Jesuit priest. Jack tried to suppress the surge of fear he felt at discovering a sworn enemy of England held a position of power in the castle.

Jack entered the priest's study and was momentarily disorientated. It was as if he'd stepped to the other side of the world. The room was fashioned in an entirely European manner. The walls and ceiling were wood-panelled. A heavy oak table with intricately carved legs dominated the room. Upon its surface were two silver candleholders and a pewter jug containing water. Behind was a large wooden chair, in which the priest now seated himself, its headrest decorated in the floral swirling pattern so popular among the courts of Europe. In one corner was a dark mahogany casket secured with a large lockplate. Above it on the wall was an oil painting, a portrait of St Ignatius, the founder of the Jesuits; and in a recess were a number of thick leatherbound books. The furnishings were so wholly un-Japanese that Jack experienced an overwhelming pang of homesickness.

'Sit down,' instructed the priest as the door was closed.

Jack instinctively knelt down on the floor.

'In the chair,' the priest said, waving in exasperation at the wooden high-backed seat behind Jack. 'You've clearly forgotten who you are. Not that I blame you. One can only live among the Japanese for so long before going completely mad. That's why I insisted on having my own piece of Portugal here. This room is my sanctuary from all their suffocating rituals, formality and etiquette.'

Jack sat down, still dumbfounded by the appearance of the room.

'Do you understand me?' enquired the priest, slowly enunciating the words as if Jack was an idiot. 'Or would you prefer me to speak . . . English?'

Jack snapped to attention, immediately wary of the man. Despite his apparent friendliness, there was something snake-like and conniving about his manner. He'd not told the priest where he was from, so clearly the Jesuit was well aware of how he'd come to be in Japan. Though Jack desperately wanted to speak English after all these years, he needed to make clear he wasn't to be taken for a fool.

'Japanese is fine. Or Portuguese, if *you* prefer,' replied Jack, thankful his mother, a teacher, had taught him some of the language.

The priest smiled thinly. 'It is pleasing to discover you're educated. For a moment I was worried you were a lowly ship's boy. But we shall speak in English. I'm sure you've missed your mother tongue.

'My name is Father Diego Bobadillo, a brother of the Society of Jesus, the protectorate of the Catholic Church and the head of the missionaries here in Japan. I am also a key adviser to his lordship Hasegawa Satoshi.'

Jack realized this was the very man Father Lucius, the Jesuit priest in Toba, had asked him to deliver the Japanese–Portuguese dictionary to.

'I was meant to find you,' interrupted Jack. 'I knew Father Lucius.'

The priest raised an eyebrow, but otherwise seemed unsurprised at the news. Father Lucius had evidently informed his superior of their meetings.

'His dying wish was for me to give you his dictionary. I'm sorry to say it was stolen.'

'That is a great shame, but don't trouble yourself over it,' replied the priest, dismissing the issue with a wave of his hand.

Jack was both relieved and astonished by the priest's indifference. 'But it was Father Lucius's life's work. It took him over ten years. He said it was the only one in existence –'

'What's gone is gone.'

'But Dragon Eye, the ninja, stole it.'

'I can't say I've heard of the man,' replied the priest, his brow furrowing. 'Besides, what would a ninja want with a dictionary?'

'He wasn't after the dictionary, he was after . . .'

Jack stopped. This priest was cunning. He had a way of leading him on. By talking in English, he'd got Jack to drop his guard. If Jack wasn't careful, he would reveal too much.

'Go on,' encouraged Father Bobadillo.

Jack suddenly seized on the idea that this influential Jesuit might be able to instigate an official search for Dragon Eye and this could lead him to the *rutter*.

'He was after . . . me,' repeated Jack, correcting his answer. 'But Father Lucius insisted the dictionary was crucial for the Brotherhood to spread your faith in Japan. Surely you want to get it back from the ninja?'

'If you haven't noticed, we're faced with the possibility of war,' said Father Bobadillo, his voice thick with sarcasm. 'A dictionary is the least of my concerns. *You*, however, are a concern.'

'What do you mean?'

'I'm right to believe that Father Lucius was unsuccessful in persuading you to follow the true path, am I not?'

Jack answered ardently, 'I'm already following the true path.'

Father Bobadillo sighed. 'We're not here to discuss semantics, or lost causes. I have made his lordship aware of the traitorous tendencies of the English.'

He held up his hand, warning Jack not to interrupt.

'I want to make it very clear that your presence in this castle is only tolerated because of your adoption by Masamoto-sama.

When his lordship's forces win this war, the Society of Jesus will be made the state religion and heretics like yourself will not be welcome on these shores. Ever.'

Jack wondered how the priest could be so certain of the Jesuits' rise to power, then remembered the silver cross around Satoshi's neck. The priest must have ingratiated himself into Satoshi's inner circle and become his spiritual adviser.

'I will not lie to you, Jack Fletcher. You're clearly resourceful to have survived this long on your own in Japan.'

Resting his elbows on the table and steepling his fingers, Father Bobadillo continued. 'As an Englishman and Protestant, you're an enemy of my country and the Brotherhood. But given your age and willingness to fight for his lordship, I wish to make a proposition. If you do not cause me any trouble, then once this war is over I'll personally guarantee your safe passage back to England. That's what you *really* want, isn't it?'

Jack was taken aback. He was being promised the one thing he'd desired above all else these past three years. But he was being offered his dream by a Portuguese Jesuit priest, his country's arch-enemy. 'How can I trust you?'

'I swear upon the Word of God. I have ships at my disposal and will seal a letter with my insignia to ensure your safe return.'

Jack found himself nodding numbly to the proposal.

'Good. It's decided. You will not speak about this conversation to anyone and if you should meet his lordship, or one of his retainers, you will not discuss the conflicting religion or politics of our countries. Understood. You may now leave.'

In a daze, Jack got up from his chair, bowed and turned to

depart. As he did so, his eyes passed over the bookshelf and there was a flicker of recognition.

He looked again. Among the leatherbound tomes, there was a Bible, a collection of sermons and, nestled between them, Father Lucius's dictionary.

39

THE ENEMY

'I'm certain it was the same dictionary,' said Jack as he sat with Akiko and Yamato in the star-studded darkness of the barracks' garden.

The three of them had slipped out of the hall and found a secluded spot to talk. The moonless night was silent save for the trickling of the stream beneath them. In the distance glowed the lanterns of the keep and the silhouettes of soldiers patrolling the battlements.

'You only caught a glimpse of it,' said Akiko. 'How can you be so sure?'

'I'd recognize that binding anywhere. It's exactly like my father's *rutter*.'

'But couldn't this just be another dictionary, compiled by one of his priests?'

'No, Father Lucius said his book was unique.'

'Perhaps Dragon Eye, having stolen the wrong book, got rid of the dictionary and Father Bobadillo acquired it by fortune,' she suggested.

'Then why didn't he say he had it?' Jack countered. 'Father Bobadillo wasn't concerned about the dictionary's theft because he's already got it! Which means he might have my *rutter* too.'

'That's absurd!' exclaimed Yamato. 'Are you seriously suggesting a key retainer of Hasegawa Satoshi *and* his spiritual adviser is responsible for hiring Dragon Eye to steal your father's *rutter* and murder you?'

'Yes,' stated Jack emphatically.

'But he's a priest. Aren't stealing and killing against his religious vows? I know Jesuits are your country's enemy, but he's on *our* side. You even said he's promised to help get you home. He seems to be a compassionate man, not a thief or a murderer.'

Jack sighed with exasperation. It was all so clear to him. 'Remember when Father Lucius was on his deathbed, he'd asked my forgiveness, saying that it had been his duty to tell someone but he hadn't realized they'd kill for it? He *must* have been talking about the *rutter* and his superior, Father Bobadillo.'

Akiko gazed thoughtfully at the sky, the starlight sparkling in her eyes. 'You cannot accuse his lordship's adviser of theft or hiring an assassin without proof. We need evidence. First, we must confirm that the book you saw *was* Father Lucius's dictionary –'

'What are you suggesting?' interrupted Yamato, worried where the conversation was leading. 'That we simply march up to a heavily guarded keep, walk into the priest's room and take a look.'

Akiko smiled. 'That's *exactly* what we're going to do.'

It was a full week before the three of them had an opportunity to attempt the break-in. An afternoon given over to untutored weapons practice. Until that moment the sensei of the *Niten Ichi Ryū* had been drilling the young samurai hard, teaching them battle formations and getting them used to combat in full armour. The regime was relentless, the sensei knowing their students' lives depended upon the quality of their training.

With each day that passed, more and more troops loyal to Satoshi arrived. They brought news of skirmishes breaking out across the country and of a huge force advancing upon Osaka. Jack was astounded at the number of foreigners and Japanese converts now gathered inside the walls of the castle. *Daimyo* Takatomi's crusade had evidently driven all the missionaries to seek refuge with Satoshi. The presence of so many European faces should have been comforting to Jack, but none appeared to be English or Dutch. Bar the occasional trader or merchant, everyone was either a Spanish friar or a Portuguese Jesuit.

'This is suicidal,' whispered Yamato as they approached the first set of gates. 'My father will disown me for this.'

He and Akiko, dressed in full armour and with *menpō* covering their faces, escorted Jack up the narrow road towards the inner courtyard.

'Just march like you've got every reason to enter and don't stop,' hissed Akiko.

One of the foot soldiers, spear in hand, stepped into their path.

Before he could even challenge them, Akiko ordered, 'Open the gates!'

The man hesitated, taken aback at hearing a girl's voice from behind the mask.

'Now! This boy's a guest of Father Bobadillo.'

Her tone was so authoritative that the bewildered man hurried to the door. The guards all bowed as the three of them passed through.

'I told you it wouldn't be a problem,' said Akiko smugly. '*Ashigaru* follow orders. They don't question them.'

They crossed the courtyard to the main entrance of the keep. Two samurai guards blocked their way. Jack realized this would be an entirely different matter. They weren't lower-status *ashigaru*.

'Password,' demanded the one on the right.

Yamato gave them the answer Jack had heard his guard utter the previous week.

'That's an old password,' stated the samurai.

Yamato stood there, speechless, unsure what to do next. The other guard reached for his sword. Jack began to sweat. While their attempt to enter the keep was unlikely to result in a fight, they would have some serious explaining to do.

'How annoying!' complained Akiko, pulling off her mask. 'Saburo-san has given us the wrong password. I bet he's done this on purpose to embarrass us.'

The guards looked at her, taken by surprise to discover a young girl behind the *menpō*. Jack and Yamato exchanged worried glances, as bemused as the guards by Akiko's outburst.

'We're going to be the laughing stock of the school!' she said, directing her irritation at Yamato. 'Our first assignment as samurai warriors for *daimyo* Takatomi and we can't even escort a boy to Father Bobadillo!'

One of the guards smirked at her anguish. Akiko turned to

him, her eyes pleading. 'Please let us pass. The boy's been summoned to the keep before. You can't forget a face like *his*, can you?'

Grimacing and wrinkling up her nose, she pointed to Jack's much bigger one and the guards fell about laughing. Jack wasn't so impressed. He wondered if she really did think that.

Lowering her eyelashes, Akiko gave the man an innocent look. 'It'll be so shameful to return without accomplishing such a simple order.'

The guard's resolve weakened under her gaze. He looked again at Jack and grunted in recognition.

'Fifth floor, but no further. Beyond that are his lordship's personal guard and they're not so understanding.'

'Thank you,' she said, bowing and replacing the *menpō*.

The three of them entered the keep. Slipping off their sandals, they ascended the stairs, Yamato taking the lead.

'I hope I didn't offend you,' whispered Akiko in Jack's ear.

'No, of course not,' replied Jack quickly, feeling his face flush.

'Which way now?' asked Yamato as they reached the fifth floor.

'Um . . . left,' said Jack, a little flustered in case his friend noticed his reddened face.

They walked down the main corridor towards Father Bobadillo's study. A couple of guards passed by. For a moment Jack thought they'd been caught, but the two guards ignored them and descended the stairs. There were no other samurai around.

'What if he's in his room?' asked Yamato.

'Only one way to find out,' said Akiko, indicating for them to wait in a side corridor.

She knocked on the door. There was no answer.

Akiko beckoned the two of them to rejoin her.

'We'll stand guard here,' she said to Jack. 'We'll warn you if anyone comes.'

Jack nodded his agreement and slipped into Father Bobadillo's study. The weird sensation of crossing the world struck him again. In a single step, he'd gone from East to West.

A few shafts of afternoon sun seeped through a shuttered window, giving the impression this darkened room was full of secrets. Crossing over to the recess, he looked for the dictionary. It was easy to spot. The binding was exactly as he remembered, worn from his constant use and slightly damaged on the lower edge where he'd once dropped it. Opening up the book's pages, his suspicions were confirmed. Father Lucius's name was clearly written in black ink on the first plate.

Jack had all the proof he needed. Father Bobadillo was the devil behind Dragon Eye. How else could he have got the dictionary? Why deny all knowledge of it? A cold realization fell over Jack. If this Jesuit priest had the dictionary, then he must have the *rutter* too. A surge of anger coursed through Jack. If Father Bobadillo was responsibile for hiring Dragon Eye, then he was as guilty of his father's murder as the assassin himself.

Jack's right hand clasped the ninja *tantō* tucked into his *obi*. He gripped the handle of the demon blade so tightly that his knuckles went white. Thoughts of revenge pulsed like fire through his veins.

'What are you two doing here?' said a voice outside the room.

Jack went cold. They'd been discovered. He shoved the dictionary back on the shelf.

'Guard duty, officer,' responded Yamato, sounding nervous.

'You're on the wrong floor. I requested a change of guards for Father Bobadillo's guest on the fourth floor.'

'But —' said Akiko.

'No arguing. Follow me!'

'*Hai!*' responded Akiko and Yamato, and Jack heard them all march away.

Jack let go of the knife. He had to think clearly. Revenge was not an option. Father Bobadillo was too powerfully connected and there was still the chance Jack could be wrong in his assumption. Besides, his priority was to find the *rutter*. Jack realized it could even be in this very room. He hunted through the other books, but with no success. He looked on the table. Then he spotted the locked casket in the corner.

Jack knelt before the immense chest and unsheathed the *tantō*. Carefully inserting its tip into the lock, he jiggled the blade round. When his little sister had lost the key to their own chest at home, his father had shown him how to pick such a lock. But this one was stronger and wouldn't budge. His knife slipped. As he tried again, Jack got the unnerving sensation he was being watched. Looking round, he saw a man's dark eyes stare accusingly down at him, but it was only the portrait of St Ignatius.

All of a sudden, the lock gave and Jack pulled it free from the plate. Lifting the heavy top, he looked inside. There were papers, silver coins, some jewellery, a thick velvet robe and three books. Jack snatched them up, but none were the *rutter*. He hunted the depths of the casket. Where would Father Bobadillo keep it? Had he given the logbook to someone to decipher? Perhaps Dragon Eye hadn't even delivered it to him? Having discovered its true worth, the ninja may have kept the *rutter* for his own purposes. Through the rush of thoughts, Jack became aware of footsteps coming down the corridor. They stopped directly outside the door to the study.

'Please thank *daimyo* Yukimura for his time today,' said an oily voice.

It was Father Bobadillo.

Jack was trapped. Hurriedly replacing the contents of the casket and slipping the lock back on, he looked round in a wild panic. There was nowhere to hide.

Then Jack spotted a slither of light running down the opposite wall. He ran over to discover a *shoji* disguised as a wooden panel. He slid it open, barely making it through before Father Bobadillo opened the main door. As the priest stepped inside, Jack shut the *shoji* behind him.

Jack discovered he'd entered a prayer room. Furnished in a Japanese style, the floor was richly carpeted with *tatami* mats and the walls were constructed of *washi* paper. Thankfully, the room was empty save for a simple altar and wooden crucifix, beside which was a discreet door. To his right was a *shoji* leading to the main corridor.

Jack heard Father Bobadillo opening the shutters to his room. Holding his breath, Jack put an eye to the crack in the door. Father Bobadillo was not alone.

'I believe that went rather well, don't you?' said a small, rotund man of Portuguese origin. Balding, with deep-brown eyes and a prominent nose, he wore the cassock of a Jesuit priest.

Father Bobadillo nodded. 'The threat of war often makes men more pious. Before this is over, I expect to have *all* the ruling lords converted.'

'His Holiness will reward you in Heaven for such faithful service.'

'I hope a little sooner than that,' replied Father Bobadillo, a wry smile upon his lips. 'I would, after all, be bringing the whole of Japan under his authority.'

He sat down in his high-backed chair, offering the other seat to the priest.

'But we still have one small thorn in our side that must be dealt with.'

'I thought you'd already spoken with the boy.'

'Father Rodriguez, every day that English heretic is in this castle he's a threat to our holy mission. We must dispose of him.'

'You mean *murder* him?' replied Father Rodriguez, his eyes widening in alarm. 'Have mercy!'

'Of course not, I'd rot in Hell,' relented Father Bobadillo. 'But his death would be convenient.'

'What harm can a mere boy do to us?'

'The greatest harm. We've always presented the Church as united in faith and doctrine. We cannot have his lordship discovering there's dissent among Christians. Imagine if the boy revealed to Satoshi the truth of the matter. He may question his faith in us and Christ. The boy could undermine *everything* we've worked towards in Japan.'

'So what do you propose?' asked Father Rodriguez, shifting uncomfortably in his seat. 'Surely Masamoto-sama would question the boy's disappearance?'

'We need a reason to discredit Jack Fletcher,' replied Father Bobadillo, looking thoughtfully out of the window. 'Something that will guarantee his banishment. Then again, a war might solve the problem for us. After all, it's a dangerous time to be a samurai . . .'

The priest trailed off to stare quizzically at the recess. Jack followed his gaze and cursed himself silently at his stupidity. He'd returned the dictionary to the wrong place on the shelf. The Jesuit's eyes flickered round the room. Getting out of his chair, he strode over to the casket and bent to examine the lock. In the cold light of day, even Jack could see the deep score mark where his *tantō* had slipped.

'What's wrong?' asked Father Rodriguez.

Without replying, Father Bobadillo stood up slowly and approached the portrait. He studied it, appearing to be deep in thought. All of sudden he made for the door behind which Jack crouched.

Jack turned to run. But he knew he'd never make it to the *shoji* in time.

'Your Eminence!' cried someone, urgently hammering on Father Bobadillo's study door.

'Yes! What is it?' demanded the priest, so close Jack thought he was in the room with him.

'The enemy are here! *Daimyo* Kamakura's army has been sighted. His lordship requests your immediate presence on the battlements.'

Father Bobadillo seemed to hesitate on the other side of the *shoji*.

'We shouldn't keep his lordship waiting,' reminded Father Rodriguez.

Then Jack heard the study door open, slam shut and several sets of footsteps receding down the corridor. Jack remained where he was, his heart pounding within his chest.

Not only was the enemy outside the castle walls, he was also within.

40

SIEGE

Cannonshot rained down on the walls of Osaka Castle. The bombardment had been unceasing for three days. The noise of exploding gunpowder rolled like thunder over the castle compounds and the acrid stench of burning filled the air. A haze of smoke now hung over the plains of Tenno-ji like morning mist, obscuring much of *daimyo* Kamakura's vast encampment. The size of a small city, its regimented rows of tents, pavilions and canvassed barracks stretched for miles into the distance. Masamoto had estimated some two hundred thousand troops were mustered outside the walls of the castle.

Jack stood on the inner battlements with the other young samurai. He was stunned at the sheer firepower of the enemy. Where had Kamakura got his cannon from? Osaka Castle possessed no such heavy weaponry and Satoshi's forces gave no return fire. Jack realized if this had been a ship, they'd have been sunk a thousand times over by now. But as shot after shot pounded the fortifications, the robust stonework proved invulnerable to the barrage.

In lulls between the cannon battery, *daimyo* Kamakura's troops mounted attacks on the castle gates. But they were repelled each time. Mangonels upon the ramparts hurled huge rocks and fireballs into the midst of the advancing force. Volleys of arrows fell like hailstones, killing and wounding row upon row of *ashigaru*. Any battalion that did make it through was then faced with the challenge of crossing the moat. Most were killed as they attempted to row across on rafts or tried to fill it in to create a crossing. The few samurai who did reach the walls had little hope of scaling the steep incline of their bases. They were picked off with arrows and arquebus shot, scalded with boiling oil, or battered by rocks dropped from murder holes.

Osaka Castle was proving impregnable.

It became obvious that *daimyo* Kamakura's only option was to lay siege.

'How long can we hold out for?' asked Yori, his voice trembling as he peeked fearfully over the edge of the rampart.

'Months, maybe even a year,' replied Taro, dressed in full battle armour like the rest of the students.

'But won't we run out of food before then?' asked Jack. Despite the numerous storehouses, he was certain one hundred thousand troops would consume their supplies very quickly.

'I wouldn't worry. The *tatami* in the castle are made out of vegetable roots. We can eat those if the situation gets desperate.'

Taro grinned at Jack, but the serious look in his eyes made Jack realize he wasn't joking.

'Hopefully, it won't come to that,' said Takuan, who stood stiffly beside Emi and Akiko, his injured ribs still giving him trouble. '*Daimyo* Kamakura will soon realize the futility of this battle and give up.'

'But his army outnumbers us two to one!' squeaked Yori, ducking down as cannonshot exploded on a nearby tower.

'He'd have to draw our forces out into open combat to have any chance,' replied Taro, unperturbed by the volley. 'With the fortifications standing, there's no reason for us to meet him on the plain.'

'I'd heard *daimyo* Kamakura was already getting desperate,' said Emi. 'My father told me he'd sent a messenger this morning to bribe *daimyo* Yukimura with the offer of Shinano Province! It was bluntly refused, of course.'

'But isn't Shinano governed by Kazuki's father?' enquired Takuan.

'Yes,' laughed Emi. 'That's why we know he's getting desperate.'

'Well, a province will be the least that traitorous family lose if I ever meet Kazuki again,' seethed Yamato, his eyes narrowing.

Jack wondered what had happened to Kazuki. Even though Masamoto had sent out a search party for him, the traitor had never been recaptured. His defection was no longer openly discussed among the students. Nonetheless, it remained in everyone's minds like an infected splinter under the skin.

'Stand down!' commanded Sensei Hosokawa, appearing on the battlements. 'You're all summoned to the barracks.'

The young samurai took up position in the courtyard, each unit headed by a sensei.

Masamoto stood before them, his face grave.

'I've called you together to discuss a matter of great concern.'

Jack exchanged worried looks with Akiko and Yamato. Was this about the break-in? During the commotion created by the arrival of *daimyo* Kamakura's army, the three of them had managed to return to the barracks unnoticed. But Father Bobadillo remained a problem. He knew someone had been in his room and Jack was certain the priest would suspect him. It was just the excuse Father Bobadillo needed to discredit him. Had Father Bobadillo spoken with Masamoto?

'With war on our doorstep, we must face the prospect that we'll be going into combat.'

At Jack's side, Yori began to tremble like a leaf.

'We must be a united force,' he declared, striding along the lines of young samurai, his hand upon the *saya* of his sword.

'Be committed without a shred of doubt. Be able to trust one another – with our lives.'

Masamoto stopped in front of Jack's line. Taking a deep breath, the samurai seemed to struggle with his emotions for a moment. Jack began to perspire. He realized he was in serious trouble.

'The traitorous actions of one of our students has undermined the morale of the *Niten Ichi Ryū*.'

Jack breathed a silent sigh of relief. The summons could only be about Kazuki's defection.

'This is a dangerous state of affairs for warriors about to engage in war. Sensei Yamada, please inspire our young samurai with your wisdom.'

Leaning upon his walking stick, Sensei Yamada shuffled forward and addressed them.

'Every tree has one bad apple, but that doesn't mean the tree itself is rotten.' He twirled the tip of his long grey beard between his fingers as he spoke, his gentle words somehow carrying above the noise and thunder of the raging battle. 'Testing times such as these feed the very roots of our strength as a school.'

'Your quiver, please?' said Sensei Yamada, approaching Akiko.

Bemused, Akiko unslung her arrow case. Sensei Yamada removed one of the arrows and passed it to Yamato.

'Break it in half.'

Yamato blinked in surprise at the order, but Sensei Yamada nodded his assurance. Everyone watched as Yamato took the wooden shaft in his hands and, without much effort, snapped the arrow in two.

Sensei Yamada now took three arrows from the quiver and put them into his hands.

'Break all three at once.'

Holding the shafts before him, Yamato glanced apologetically at Akiko as he prepared to ruin more of her precious hawk-feather arrows. He started to force his hands together. But the wooden shafts refused to yield – even when he put his knee against them. However hard he strained, the arrows wouldn't break. Sensei Yamada indicated for Yamato to stop trying.

'A samurai alone is like a single arrow. Deadly but capable of being broken,' he explained, returning the quiver to Akiko.

He now held the three arrows aloft.

'Only by binding together as a single force will we remain strong and unconquerable. Remember this, young samurai of the *Niten Ichi Ryū*. By the seven virtues of *bushido*, you're forever bound to one another.'

'*HAI*, SENSEI!' roared the students, the fervour of loyalty exploding from them. 'LONG LIVE THE *NITEN ICHI RYŪ*!'

As their cry echoed off the walls of the castle courtyard, the cannon bombardment suddenly stopped.

41

MOON-VIEWING PARTY

'*Kachi guri?*' enquired Yori, his face beaming in the pale white light of the full moon.

He held out a small plate of brown nuts to Jack, who was leaning thoughtfully over a wooden bridge in the tea garden of the keep, observing the golden carp swim peacefully beneath.

'They're dried chestnuts,' explained Yori, popping one into his mouth. '*Kachi* also means victory. That's why his lordship's provided them for the party. We've won, Jack! We've won without having to fight!'

Jack smiled warmly at his friend's enthusiastic relief and tried one of the chestnuts. It tasted sweet, like victory.

A week had passed since the hostilities had ceased. *Daimyo* Kamakura had sent a peace agreement confessing his folly at attempting to capture Osaka Castle. Unexpectedly repentant, he promised that all those loyal to Satoshi would be safe from attack, his lordship's reign be unchallenged and that his campaign against the 'foreign invaders' would end. He'd even sealed the document with a *kappan*, a blood-stamp from his own finger, which rendered the agreement sacred and binding.

Everyone within the castle was stunned by this turn of

events. In particular Masamoto, who couldn't quite believe their enemy had surrendered so easily. The conflict had barely begun. Cautious as ever, Masamoto insisted the *Niten Ichi Ryū* continue their battle training.

Yet *daimyo* Kamakura seemed true to his word. The next day his colossal army struck camp and began to retreat in the direction of Edo Province. There was great rejoicing among Satoshi's forces. They'd won the war without having to engage in direct combat.

As a token of his appreciation for his troops' support, Satoshi ordered *saké* and extra rations to be given out. For the *daimyo* and samurai generals who'd rallied to his cause, he'd decided to hold a celebratory moon-viewing party in his tea garden. The invite had been extended to the students of the *Niten Ichi Ryū* with whom he felt a certain affinity, being of similar age.

Satoshi welcomed each *daimyo* in an open-sided tea house set on an island at the heart of the garden. The guests wandered round the meandering paths and bridges, chatting amiably and appreciating the clear night sky, the stars bright as diamonds.

Father Bobadillo was there too, making the most of the opportunity and circulating among the key members of the Council. Occasionally he would glance in Jack's direction, his eyes narrowing. Jack tried to ignore the priest and kept his distance.

Across from Jack and Yori, on the far side of the oval pond, Takuan sat surrounded by a group of young samurai. Akiko and Emi were either side of him, admiring the reflection of the moon upon the still surface of the water. Inspired by its ethereal beauty, Takuan was composing impromptu *haiku* to keep everyone entertained.

'Did you know that a rabbit lives in the moon?' said Yori, gazing up at the night sky. 'If you look closely at its surface, you can see him making rice dumplings.'

The sound of appreciative applause floated across the pond. Jack heard Akiko laughing lightly and found himself gazing at her, not the moon.

'Look, there he is!' said Yori, pointing gleefully at the nebulous outline of a rabbit.

'I'll now compose a poem in honour of each of you,' Takuan announced, his voice carrying clearly through the night. 'Akiko, you'll be my muse.'

There was more delighted clapping and Akiko gave Takuan a bashful bow of her head.

Yori tugged on Jack's sleeve. 'Can you see it, Jack? The rabbit's got a wooden hammer.'

'You're suffering moon madness,' said Jack, irritably pulling his arm away. 'Everyone knows it's a man in the moon, not a rabbit!'

Startled by Jack's curt reaction, Yori took a step back, his eyes showing hurt. Jack immediately felt ashamed. Bowing to Yori, he muttered an apology and strode off towards the well house to be on his own.

Sitting upon the lip of the well, he stared glumly through the open door at all the guests enjoying the party. Why had he snapped at Yori like that? Jack realized he could no longer deny that Takuan's ever-growing closeness to Akiko upset him. The more time she spent with Takuan, the more Jack realized how important Akiko was to his life. He didn't want to lose her as his best and most trusted friend.

Nor did it help his mood having Father Bobadillo around.

He felt threatened by the man's presence. Having confirmed his suspicions about the dictionary, Jack was convinced the priest was in league with Dragon Eye and responsible for his father's death.

With the war now over, Father Bobadillo would insist upon arranging his passage back to England, arguing that it was in Jack's best interests. But Jack could never trust such a man. The priest surely intended to double-cross him – perhaps lock him in a Portuguese prison; or put him on a ship only to have him thrown overboard; or maybe even send Dragon Eye to torture or kill him.

Although Jack despised his old rival Kazuki for his prejudice and bullying, he could appreciate the boy had been right about certain foreigners' corrupt intentions to usurp the rule of Japan. Even now, Jack could see Father Bobadillo working his charm upon various *daimyo*, bowing and scraping, delivering honeyed words of praise and wheedling his way into their trust. A zealous Jesuit and a cunning diplomat, Father Bobadillo was a dangerous man.

But such political matters were beyond Jack's influence. As a mere boy, any warnings would go unheeded. The greatest harm he could inflict upon Father Bobadillo's cause was to get his father's *rutter* back. If only for his father's sake, Jack couldn't let someone as evil as Father Bobadillo possess such knowledge of the seas and, therefore, such power.

But where could the *rutter* be? The hurried search of the priest's study had come up with nothing, except the dictionary. He was certain Father Bobadillo knew where the logbook was. But the Jesuit was definitely keeping an eye on him and Jack couldn't risk going back a second time.

Yori poked his head round the door. 'Can I come in?' he asked timidly.

Jack nodded and Yori perched beside him. Staring at the floor, Jack searched for the right words to apologize properly to his friend.

'This well house is called the Gold Water Well,' said Yori, attempting to fill the awkward silence. Looking into the well, he continued, 'It's fed by a tunnel from the inner moat, but to improve the taste Satoshi's father sank bars of gold into the well's depths.'

Jack looked down. A slither of moonlight danced upon the clear water below.

'I can't see any gold,' replied Jack, relieved Yori had broken the tension by speaking first. 'But I did see your rabbit in the moon. Sorry for being so rude to you.'

'Don't worry,' said Yori, smiling. 'I know it was the tiger talking and not you.'

'What do you mean?' replied Jack, uncertain what he was referring to.

'I saw the way you looked when Takuan made Akiko his muse.'

'It's nothing to do with that,' mumbled Jack, glancing over at Takuan and his group of followers. They were strolling round the garden, Emi now at his elbow.

Yori smiled knowingly. 'You really should show Akiko your *haiku*. I'm sure she'd like it.'

'My *haiku*?' said Jack, his brow creasing in puzzlement. 'But it was destroyed in the fire.'

'No, it wasn't,' replied Yori, pulling a crumpled piece of paper from the sleeve of his kimono. 'I spotted it when rescuing your Daruma Doll and slipped the paper into my *obi*.'

'What were you thinking?' exclaimed Jack, staring at Yori aghast. 'The school was being attacked, the *Shishi-no-ma* ablaze, and you were saving my poetry!'

'Don't you remember what Sensei Yamada said? *It is our duty to ensure we have a peace worth fighting for.* Your *haiku* is exactly what Sensei Yamada meant by a peace worth fighting for. It is, therefore, *your* duty to present this poem to Akiko.'

Jack sat there, dumbstruck by Yori's suggestion.

Yori sighed with exasperation. Jumping down from the well, he pulled Jack towards the garden.

'Go on,' he urged, seeing Akiko wander away from the group and enter the *sakura* trees bordering the tea garden.

Jack felt Yori shove him in the small of the back and he stumbled in Akiko's direction. He walked in a daze over the bridge, his *haiku* in hand, and followed her into the trees. Glancing back, he saw Yori smiling and nodding his head in encouragement.

Akiko had found a quiet bench in the lee of the castle wall. There was no one around and it was quite dark here, but the stars and moon were brighter and looked even more beautiful because of this. Her face was turned towards the sky in peaceful contemplation. Jack remained at a distance, hidden in the shadows, trying to pluck up the courage to approach.

'I simply don't trust Kamakura,' said a voice in the darkness.

Startled, Jack slipped behind the trunk of a tree as three *daimyo* walked by. He recognized the voice as Emi's father, *daimyo* Takatomi.

'He's laid a trap and we've fallen for it.'

'I agree,' said another gravely. 'My scouts have informed me that his army is encamped but a day's journey from here. There's no doubt he intends to return.'

'But *daimyo* Kamakura's bound to the terms of the peace agreement by his own blood,' noted the third *daimyo*.

'Yes,' replied *daimyo* Takatomi, 'but you're also aware he left a battalion of troops behind, demolishing the castle's outer wall and filling in the moat. In light of the treaty, their captain said, there was no longer any need for the defences to stand!'

'But they were eventually stopped, weren't they? Repairs are already under way.'

'And that's when the trap was sprung,' said Emi's father with a weary sigh. 'By ordering the walls to be rebuilt, his lordship played right into *daimyo* Kamakura's hands . . .'

Jack strained to hear their conversation as the three *daimyo* rounded the corner.

'. . . our enemy will proclaim that we've broken the spirit of an inviolable agreement . . . He'll declare war again, but with Osaka Castle now dangerously weakened . . .'

Jack couldn't believe what he'd just heard. If Emi's father was right, then this false peace was merely the calm before the storm.

'Spying, are we?' hissed a voice in Jack's ear.

Dropping his *haiku* in shock, Jack spun round to be confronted by the malignant face of Father Bobadillo.

'N-no,' stuttered Jack, trying to get away.

'It looked like it to me,' said the priest, grabbing Jack by the scruff of his kimono. 'Skulking behind a tree. Listening in on private conversations. Do you make a habit of poking your nose into places you shouldn't?'

Father Bobadillo glared into Jack's eyes, hunting for a glimmer of guilt. Jack shook his head.

'You do know spying is punishable by *death*?' uttered Father Bobadillo, emphasizing the last word with relish. A thin smile formed on his thin lips. 'I'm afraid I'll have to report this.'

Jack realized he had little chance against the priest. Father Bobadillo would do everything in his power to discredit him, using the excuse of spying to have him killed or, at the very least, banished. It would be his word against a retainer of the ruler-in-waiting.

'Jack!' called a voice merrily.

The smile dropped from Father Bobadillo's face at the interruption. Over the priest's shoulder, Jack glimpsed Takuan striding through the trees towards them. He'd left his friends upon a bridge watching the carp in the pond.

'There you are!' he exclaimed. 'We finished playing *kakurenbo* ages ago. Thank you, Father, for finding him. Jack always wins hide-and-seek!'

Father Bobadillo eyed Takuan suspiciously, then glared at Jack.

'My pleasure,' he muttered, letting go of Jack's kimono collar.

The priest marched off in the direction of the tea house.

'Thanks,' said Jack, breathing a sigh of relief.

'What did that man want? I saw him follow you into the trees. It looked like you were in trouble.'

'It's nothing,' replied Jack, not wishing to involve Takuan. 'We just have a conflict of religion.'

Takuan nodded his understanding. 'Well, come and join the party. You've been missing all the fun.'

Jack glanced over to where Akiko still sat in darkness. He'd have to give her the poem another time.

'What's this?' asked Takuan, bending down to pick up the piece of paper at Jack's feet. 'A *haiku*!'

Jack snatched at the paper.

But Takuan was too quick. He danced out of reach and read the poem out loud:

> '*In my own garden*
> *English rose, sakura flower*
> *growing together.*'

'Is this yours?' asked Takuan.

'Give it back,' Jack pleaded, embarrassed.

'But this is wonderful! I didn't realize you were such a poet.'

'I'm not . . . it's nothing like your *haiku*.'

'No, this is better. You must have been very inspired —'

Takuan stopped in mid-sentence. He'd spotted Akiko on the bench. Looking at Akiko, then at the *haiku* and finally at Jack, an enlightened smile formed on his handsome face.

'Rose? *Sakura?* This is you and Akiko, isn't it?'

'No . . .' protested Jack feebly. He felt horribly awkward and exposed. Takuan was surely going to taunt him about it and tell everyone. This was worse than being caught by Father Bobadillo.

'I must apologize to you, Jack,' said Takuan, handing him back the *haiku* with a low bow. 'I've been insensitive. I had no idea you felt that strongly for Akiko. If I had, I wouldn't have expressed interest in her. I've acted dishonourably. You must hate me.'

'Not at all, you misunderstand . . .' insisted Jack, realizing now that Takuan was not only an honourable person, but a samurai of great integrity. 'It's not like you think. We're just friends.'

'*Just* friends,' said Takuan, arching his eyebrows. 'All she ever does is talk about you.'

'Really?' Despite himself, Jack felt his heart lift.

'I think I should leave you to deliver your *haik-k-k—*'

Takuan appeared to be choking. He collapsed into Jack's arms.

Piercing his neck was a small poison dart.

42

NIGHT ATTACK

'Akiko!' cried Jack, struggling to drag Takuan behind a tree for cover.

His eyes hunted the darkness for ninja, but if there were any, their black *shinobi shozoku* concealed them.

A moment later, Akiko was by his side.

'What happened?' she gasped as she helped Jack lower Takuan to the ground.

'Blow dart,' replied Jack, pulling the poisoned tip from Takuan's neck.

Akiko glanced around. 'Up there!'

A shadow flitted like a ghost on top of the castle wall.

Hearing a twig snap upon the path, Jack and Akiko spun round.

'Takuan, we're all waiting for you . . . TAKUAN!' Emi screamed, seeing him slumped in Jack's arms.

She rushed to his side. 'Are you all right?'

Takuan tried to focus on her face. His breathing was shallow and his lips had turned blue. He attempted to speak, but his voice was barely a croak. Emi leant in closer and Takuan graced her cheek with a kiss.

Then his eyes closed and his head lolled sideways.

Emi took hold of his hand. 'Stay with me . . .' she sobbed.

But Takuan had stopped breathing.

'Akiko, you must warn the others,' said Jack, gently resting Takuan's head upon the ground. In the distance, the sound of musket fire could be heard and Jack realized *daimyo* Takatomi's suspicions were right. '*Daimyo* Kamakura has returned with ninja!'

She nodded and ran back through the trees.

Jack heard Masamoto shout, 'We're under attack! Samurai of the *Niten Ichi Ryū*, guard the inner gate!'

This was followed by further shouts of 'Protect his lordship! All *daimyo* to the keep!'

Feet pounded across the wooden bridges and samurai were called to arms. Jack heard *daimyo* Takatomi's voice above the clamour. 'Emi-chan? Where are you?'

'There's nothing we can do for Takuan now,' said Jack, pulling the weeping Emi away from his lifeless form. 'You must go to your father.'

Jack urged her towards the garden, then ran in the opposite direction.

'Where are you going?' she called.

'To find Takuan's killer!' Jack replied, heading for the stone staircase that led up to the inner castle walls.

Jack took the stairs two at a time. As he emerged on to the walkway of the ramparts, he drew his *katana*.

The wall was eerily deserted. Where had all the guards gone?

Suddenly there was a thunderous explosion to the east of the castle, followed by a second volley as if a hundred guns had been fired all at once. All over the castle compounds, lights were doused.

Hurrying to the parapet, Jack stumbled over something in the darkness. A dead samurai lay slumped on the floor, his throat slit open. At least he now knew where all the guards had gone.

From his position on top of the inner bailey wall, Jack could see endless lines of flaming torches advancing upon the great outer gate.

Daimyo Kamakura's army had returned in full force.

The attack had begun.

Thousands of Satoshi's troops converged on the main gate to man the battlements and defend the barricades. But they didn't realize the enemy was already within the castle compounds.

A three-pronged grappling hook sailed through the air and the *kaginawa* caught upon the edge of the parapet where Jack stood. Jack cut down with his *katana*, severing the climbing rope. The grappling hook clattered to the stone floor as the rope slithered away into darkness.

Looking over the edge, Jack could barely make out a thing. Then he realized this was exactly what the enemy wanted. The gunfire had been a diversion, not only to draw the defenders to the east gate but to force them to extinguish all the lanterns in the castle so the keep didn't become a target for repeated cannonfire. Any black-cloaked ninja was now virtually invisible in the darkness.

Jack stared into the void and couldn't believe what he saw. Moonlight, reflecting off the waters of the inner moat, revealed shapes walking *across* the surface. Below him, shadows were scaling the walls like spiders.

Suddenly two eyes appeared out of the darkness. A flash of steel whistled through the air. Jack threw himself backwards, the *shuriken* barely missing his throat. A ninja scrambled over the parapet.

Without hesitating, Jack retaliated with his *katana*, cutting across the assassin's legs. But the ninja jumped high into the air and somersaulted over his head. He landed behind Jack to kick him in the kidneys. Jack crumpled against the parapet as pain seared up his side. He heard a swooshing noise and instinctively rolled to one side. A heavy lead weight cracked into the stonework where his head had just been, sending shards of rock flying into the air.

Jack scrambled away, his sword out to defend himself. The ninja held a sickle and chain and was spinning the weighted end above his head. Releasing his grip, the chain whipped out at Jack. With nowhere to go on the narrow walkway, Jack cut down with his sword blocking the chain. It wrapped itself round Jack's blade and the ninja yanked the *katana* from Jack's grasp.

The ninja hissed at Jack. Leaving the sword where it had fallen, he advanced on him, the chain once again spinning above his head. In his other hand, the assassin held the curved blade of the sickle, primed to kill Jack once he'd ensnared him with the chain.

Jack backed away. He still had his *wakizashi* and the ninja *tantō*, but he'd be dead by the time he drew them. The ninja wound up to strike. Jack timed his move perfectly, stepping inside the arc of the chain and executing *kuki-nage*.

The ninja was taken completely by surprise, the air throw whipping him off his feet. Just as Sensei Kyuzo had done to

Jack on countless occasions, Jack now spun round using the attack's momentum to fling his assailant into the air. The ninja flew over the side of the parapet and disappeared into the blackness, his screams ending in a faint splash as he hit the waters of the moat.

Retrieving his *katana*, Jack didn't have time to appreciate his perfect *kuki-nage*. During the fight, several more *kaginawa* had appeared on the wall. Jack began to cut the ropes, but three ninja further along the battlement had already clambered over. They went unchallenged, the guards all dead from the advance raiding party. Using the cover of darkness, the ninja crept towards the keep.

Jack realized Satoshi and the Council must be the target. With every defender focused on *daimyo* Kamakura's forces outside the walls, the ninja would be silently assassinating the heads of state within. For all Jack knew, some of the assassins were already hidden inside the keep awaiting the Council's retreat.

He had to warn Masamoto.

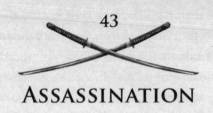

43

ASSASSINATION

Jack bounded down the stairs. He ran through the now deserted tea garden to the inner gate of the bailey, where he found Yamato and the rest of the *Niten Ichi Ryū* students on guard.

'Where's your father? Where's Masamoto?' demanded Jack, breathless.

'He's escorting *daimyo* Takatomi to the keep.'

'We have to stop him!' said Jack, pulling Yamato from his post.

'But our orders are to man the gate,' he protested.

'Ninja are in the bailey and may have broken through to the keep,' explained Jack hurriedly. 'Our duty is to protect your father and *daimyo* Takatomi. Are you *ashigaru* or samurai? Now come on!'

Grabbing his staff, Yamato sprinted after Jack.

Yamato glanced around the moonlit courtyard as they ran. 'I can't see any ninja. How did they evade the wall guards?'

'The guards are all dead.'

As they approached the *donjon* entrance, samurai armed with spears and swords rushed to confront them.

'Who goes there?' challenged the lead guard.

'Samurai of the *Niten Ichi Ryū*,' replied Yamato. 'We must speak with Masamoto-sama.'

'No one's to enter.'

'But this is Masamoto-sama's son,' insisted Jack.

'Our orders are to let *no one* through.' The guard's hand went to his sword.

'But ninja may already be inside!'

'Impossible. The enemy hasn't even breached the outer walls.'

'What's going on?' demanded a voice. It was Sensei Hosokawa.

'Sensei!' cried Jack, waving frantically to their swordmaster.

'Let them pass,' he ordered and the guards reluctantly backed off.

Jack and Yamato ran through the gates and up the steps to Sensei Hosokawa.

'You have to warn Masamoto-sama. There are –'

Masamoto descended the second-floor staircase at that very moment.

'What are you two doing here?' he demanded. 'Why are you not at your post?'

'The attack outside's a diversion,' blurted Jack. '*Daimyo* Kamakura has hired ninja to assassinate the Council.'

'Trust Kamakura to resort to such tactics,' he growled. 'Sensei Hosokawa, inform all the patrols and have a sentry posted at each window. Double the guard round the Council on the sixth floor and –'

'It's too late for that,' said Jack. 'I think they're already inside.'

'Are you certain?' asked Masamoto, his eyes narrowing.

Jack nodded furiously. 'I saw several ninja and all the guards on the battlement had been killed before the alarm was raised.'

Masamoto didn't wait to hear any more. 'Come on!'

He turned and thundered up the stairs. Jack and Yamato hurried after him, while Sensei Hosokawa barked orders to the guards. They raced along the corridor, up another staircase, past patrols of samurai and up to the sixth floor. By the time the two of them caught up with Masamoto, he was already speaking with the head guard.

'No, Masamoto-sama, all's quiet,' replied the samurai. 'The *daimyo* and his lordship are safely in their rooms. I've stationed guards outside each door.'

'Organize an immediate search. Begin with his lordship Satoshi's floor.'

The guard bowed and ran off.

'We'll start on this level,' Masamoto said, addressing Jack and Yamato. '*Daimyo* Takatomi is our priority.'

They headed down the corridor and bore right. The hallway was dark and shadowy. With all the torches doused, the only light came from the soft glow of candles seeping through the inner paper walls and the pale moonlight that filtered through the slatted windows of the keep. Danger appeared to lurk in every darkened corner. Masamoto led the way.

'Stay alert,' he whispered. '*Daimyo* Takatomi's room is down the next corridor.'

As they hurried along the hallway, an alarm bell rang in Jack's head. *Didn't the samurai say he'd put guards on every door?*

All of sudden Jack slipped on the polished wooden floor

and landed with a thump. Masamoto spun round, his two swords at the ready.

'I told you to stay alert!' hissed Masamoto, glaring at him.

Not bothering to wait, he ran on, Yamato close on his father's heels. As Jack scrambled to his feet, his hand touched something sticky and wet. His palm came away slick with blood. He followed the trail, shiny in the moonlight, to a small wooden door. As he undid the latch, out fell the body of a guard, his throat slit open exactly like the sentries on the wall.

'Back here!' shouted Jack, trying to stifle his shock.

Masamoto and Yamato turned on the spot and saw the corpse hanging out of the storage room. They ran back down the corridor as Jack slid open the unguarded *shoji* to an inner room. A man lay sprawled across the *tatami*-matted floor, a large pool of blood staining the fine rush straw a deep red.

'*Daimyo* Yukimura!' exclaimed Masamoto, pushing past Jack.

The *shoji* to the adjoining room was ajar. Masamoto flung it aside, only to discover a second member of the Council spreadeagled across the *tatami*, a garrotte wrapped round his throat.

Hearing a cry for help, the three of them ran back into the hallway and sprinted for *daimyo* Takatomi's corridor. The two guards that had been posted outside his door lay dead. Masamoto burst in.

Three ninja surrounded *daimyo* Takatomi who lay wounded on the floor, blood pouring from a cut to his sword arm. Emi was by his side, a *tantō* in her hand poised to defend her father to her last breath.

Masamoto charged, cutting down the first ninja with his

katana before the assassins had time to react. The second ninja made a lunge for *daimyo* Takatomi with his sword, but Masamoto slammed his *wakizashi* on top, deflecting the thrust away from his lord. The ninja retaliated, now attacking Masamoto and driving him through a wall into the next room.

Seizing the opportunity, the third ninja rushed at *daimyo* Takatomi with a *tantō*. Jack was too far away to stop him. But Yamato used the reach of his staff. As the assassin thrust his knife at their *daimyo*, he swiftly brought his *bō* down on to the ninja's wrist. There was a crack of bone and the *tantō* was knocked from his grasp, barely a blade's breadth from *daimyo* Takatomi's startled face.

The ninja's reactions, though, were lightning fast. He kicked Yamato in the chest, sending him flying backwards. Reaching for the *ninjatō* strapped to his back, the ninja now rushed to impale Yamato on his blade.

Jack leapt to his friend's defence. At the same moment, Emi buried her knife into the assassin's leg. The ninja screamed in pain. Outnumbered and injured, he fled through the door.

'After him!' ordered Masamoto as he drove his *katana* through his opponent.

Jack pursued the assassin into the corridor. The ninja turned the corner. But when Jack reached the outer hallway, the ninja had disappeared.

'Where did he go?' said Yamato, running up behind Jack.

Jack searched the shadows, wary of any recesses where the ninja might be hiding. Yamato then spotted a smear of blood on the window sill. One of the wooden slats to the window was missing. Jack pulled himself up and through the gap. More splashes of blood stained the roof tiles.

'Do you know how high we are?' exclaimed Yamato, going pale at the thought of having to follow him.

Jack knew his friend was petrified of heights. 'Stay here, in case any other ninja try to escape this way.'

Finding his footing on a ledge, Jack stepped out on to the curved roof. The ground was a long way down, an inky-black sea in the darkness. Although he wasn't afraid of heights, he knew a single mistake could result in a fatal fall.

Further along, the ninja was shuffling towards the crest where the roofs of the sixth and fifth floors met. Keeping his centre of gravity low, Jack crept after him. As the ninja reached the ridge, he spotted Jack following him. This time the assassin chose to fight rather than flee and grabbed a blowpipe from his waistbelt.

Jack realized he had seconds before the ninja would fire. With no other choice, he ran across the tiles and threw himself at the assassin. They collided, forcing the ninja to drop his blowpipe. But the two of them now began to slide down the roof towards the eaves, picking up speed as they got closer and closer. Jack snatched out for anything he could. At the last moment, his fingers found purchase on one of the decorative golden finials and he clung on for all his life.

But the ninja kept going, his broken wrist preventing him getting a grip on anything. He tumbled down the slope and disappeared. There was silence, then a distant thud as a body hit the ground.

Pulling himself back up to the ridge, Jack breathed a sigh of relief. He secretly hoped that had been the ninja who'd killed Takuan.

Suddenly there were shouts from above.

'Assassin!'

'Save his lordship!'

Then a loud bang and smoke billowed from the uppermost windows.

A moment later, a black hooded figure emerged on to the roof and ran with cat-like ease along the tiles. Jumping to a lower floor, he zigzagged his way down the roofs of the *donjon*.

Getting to his feet, Jack drew his *katana* and waited. For once, he had the element of surprise. The ninja certainly wouldn't be expecting to meet a samurai on the roof.

44

NEVER HESITATE

The assassin rounded the corner of the building. Through the slit in his black hood, a single green eye flared with fury and amazement.

'A samurai who thinks he's a ninja!' hissed Dragon Eye, emitting a callous laugh.

Jack's sword arm wavered. He hadn't expected to meet his arch-enemy.

The ninja took a step towards him.

'Stay where you are!' ordered Jack, steadying his *katana*.

'You've caught me off-guard,' admitted Dragon Eye, still approaching. 'My surprise at your appearance is matched only by my amazement at your continued survival. I trust your friend didn't take too long to die.'

'*You* killed Takuan!'

'I've killed countless samurai,' shot back Dragon Eye. 'But I don't stop to ask their names first.'

Jack felt his anger boil over at the ninja's coldness. 'But why murder him? What did he mean to you?'

'Nothing. *You* were the target, but your friend got in the way. You're the reason he died.'

Jack wrestled with his conscience. Was it his fault again that he'd put his friends' lives in mortal danger? Surely not. This raid had nothing to do with him. The ninja's mission was to assassinate the Council and Satoshi.

'Don't you work for Father Bobadillo? Why attack the side that pays you?'

'I work for no one,' Dragon Eye spat. 'But I *kill* for anyone who pays.'

A glimpse of steel flashed from the ninja's hip. On instinct alone, Jack cut down with his sword. It met a *shuriken* head on. The lethal star was deflected off into the night. Dragon Eye ran at him, but Jack brought his blade up, stopping the ninja in his tracks. Jack held the *kissaki* to his throat.

'Yet again you impress me, *gaijin*,' said Dragon Eye, seemingly unconcerned at his predicament. 'A long sword wouldn't be my choice of weapon on a roof, but you handle it well. Your talents as a samurai are wasted. I could teach you so much more if you were ninja.'

'Just tell me where the *rutter* is.'

'I don't have it. But you know who does. Ask him yourself.'

'So Father Bobadillo *did* hire you?'

Dragon Eye nodded imperceptibly. 'Not only to steal the *rutter*, but to kill *you* too.'

Jack felt his blood run cold at having his suspicions confirmed.

'Some priest he is,' laughed Dragon Eye. 'The question is, do you have what it takes to kill *me*?'

Staring into the eye of the assassin, Jack saw no fear, no guilt, no remorse in the man's soul. This was the very ninja responsible for murdering his father, garrotting him before

Jack's own eyes. For killing the innocent maid Chiro and assassinating Yamato's brother, Tenno. Dragon Eye had destroyed not only his life, but those of his friends too. All the pain, suffering and loss he'd experienced since being in Japan welled up inside him, threatening to explode in a burst of murderous fury.

This was the moment he'd been training for.

'*Yes*, I do,' breathed Jack, pressing the tip of his blade against the ninja's neck.

'I don't believe you,' goaded Dragon Eye. 'If you had, you would have done it by now. I told you once before, *never hesitate!*'

Out of nowhere, a ninja materialized from behind and grabbed Jack. He was yanked backwards off his feet and thrown down the other side of the ridge. Losing his grip on the *katana*, the sword clattered down the slope and disappeared over the side.

Jack dug his heels into the tiles, somehow managing to halt his fall. A moment later, the ninja pounced alongside him, landing on the narrow ledge between the wall and roof. Jack scrambled to his feet and threw up his guard. But, stood on the slope, he was at a dangerous disadvantage.

Dragon Eye appeared on the ridge above him. Silhouetted against the full moon, he looked more terrifying than ever. A black ghost in the night.

'Your time has come, *gaijin*,' he hissed, the blade of a *tantō* glinting in his hand. 'You've nowhere to run.'

Jack peered over the eaves. It was a long, long way down.

'Up there!' came a faint shout.

A volley of arrows hurtled towards them. Jack dived for

cover, the steel-tipped arrows clattering against the walls and tiles of the keep. When he looked up again, Dragon Eye had vanished.

The other ninja was fleeing along the ledge.

Jack pursued the assassin as more arrows were mistakenly fired at him. The ninja leapt down to the next level, gliding through the air like a bat. Only as Jack reached the eaves did he realize just how far it was between the roofs. But it was too late to change his mind.

Jumping down, he landed heavily. The tiles broke on impact and Jack lost his footing. He tumbled down the slope, past the ninja, towards the edge.

The ninja dived for him, catching hold of his arm as he went over.

Jack now hung from the eaves, swinging high above the ground. Below him, he caught a glimpse of Dragon Eye leaping from the *donjon*'s lower level to the roof of a nearby building. The distance seemed impossible, but the assassin landed with stealth and disappeared into the night. Jack wouldn't be so fortunate if he fell from his height.

His heart hammering in his chest, he looked up to see a gloved hand holding his wrist tightly. As he swung in the darkness, two eyes gazed down at him through the slit of the ninja's hood. There was a moment of recognition.

Then the ninja let go.

45

DOUBLE LIFE

Jack plummeted through the air, screaming in terror as the wind whipped past him. A second later he crashed, not into the ground, but on to a lower roof of the keep.

He lay there a moment, too shocked to move.

As he recovered from the fall, he noticed a gleam of steel beside him. His *katana* was caught in the gap between two rows of tiles. Cautiously, he shuffled to the edge and grabbed hold of the handle. With his sword back in hand, he felt his strength return.

Jack got to his feet and sheathed his *katana*. He now had to climb all the way back up to the sixth floor via the precipitous maze of interconnecting roofs. He carefully made his way along the ledge to the corner of the keep. Peering round, he spotted the ninja coming towards him. Unseen, Jack crouched low, hiding in the shadow of the eaves above. He withdrew his *tantō* and waited to ambush the assassin. As the ninja turned the corner, Jack jumped out. He forced him against the wall, holding his knife to the ninja's throat. The demon blade shone white in the pale moonlight, hungry for blood.

'No!' cried a girl's voice.

Stunned, Jack stared into the ninja's eyes, black as ebony.

'*Akiko?*' he breathed, almost too scared to utter her name.

The ninja nodded once. Pulling off the hood, Akiko's long dark hair fell round her shoulders.

'I . . . I can explain,' she stuttered, glancing fearfully at the knife still held to her throat.

'You're a *traitor* . . . like Kazuki!' said Jack, his hand starting to tremble in shock.

'No, No! I'm on our side.'

'Then why dress like a ninja? Why save Dragon Eye?'

'No, I saved *you* back there,' Akiko insisted. 'Dragon Eye had the *tantō* up his sleeve. He was about to kill you.'

'But I had my sword to his throat. And you attacked me! Why should I believe you? You dropped me off the roof!'

Akiko shook her head vigorously. 'If I'd wanted you dead, I'd have simply let you fall. Instead I swung you to safety,' she explained, her eyes pleading with Jack to believe her. 'Remember the ambush in the bamboo forest? I was the third ninja who saved you.'

Jack felt his heart being torn in two. He dearly wanted to believe her, but his eyes couldn't deny the truth.

Akiko was a ninja. The enemy.

'Why not just warn me that Dragon Eye had a knife?'

Akiko looked away, unable to meet his gaze. 'I couldn't let you kill him.'

Jack's mind reeled. Not only was she a ninja, she was protecting Dragon Eye, his father's murderer. Jack felt a throb of rage and the demon blade in his hand seemed to beg him to draw its razor-sharp edge across her throat.

'Please take that devil knife away,' she whispered, terrified by the look in his eyes. 'I'll explain everything.'

Jack suddenly became aware of what he was doing. This was Akiko. His best friend. He had to trust her. As if a spell had been broken, he felt his anger ebb away.

'You can't kill Dokugan Ryu,' she said as Jack slowly lowered the blade and put it away. 'He's the only person who knows where my brother is.'

'But Jiro's in Toba,' challenged Jack.

'I'm talking about my baby brother, Kiyoshi.'

'You told me he was dead.'

'I said he was no longer with us,' corrected Akiko.

'But you pray for him at the Temple of the Peaceful Dragon.'

'Yes, I pray for his safe return. Dragon Eye kidnapped him the same night he killed Tenno.'

There were shouts from below and they both crouched further into the shadows to avoid being spotted by the archers.

'My family was visiting Masamoto-sama in Kyoto at the time. I was woken by a noise in the garden and opened the *shoji* to see a black ghost standing over Tenno. He had a *tantō* in his hand. I was only a little girl at the time. I couldn't save him. I just watched as the ninja thrust the blade through his heart.'

Her eyes filled with tears at the memory and she clenched her fists in frustration. Jack knew what she was going through, having felt that exact same sense of helplessness. It pained him every day to think how he'd stood there, frozen with fear, as Dragon Eye throttled his father with a wire garrotte. He too had been powerless to prevent the murder.

'Dragon Eye looked at me, blood dripping from his knife. I remember how it left a trail of red spots like rose petals on the white stone path. I ran. I know I shouldn't have left Kiyoshi all alone, but I was scared. By the time I'd woken Masamoto-sama, Dragon Eye was gone. So too was my brother.'

'I'm so sorry,' said Jack, reaching for her hand to comfort her. 'But why become a ninja?'

'That was Masamoto's idea.'

Jack stared in shock at Akiko. 'He *knows* about this?'

Akiko nodded. 'He's the one who introduced me to the monk at the Temple of the Peaceful Dragon. The monk's a member of the Koga clan and is a ninja grandmaster. Well, he used to be until he became a priest. In return for a donation to the temple, he was willing to teach me the secret arts of the ninja.'

'I always suspected that monk!' exclaimed Jack, remembering the man's hands that looked like knives. 'And it certainly explains all your hidden talents! But I can't believe you lied to me all this time. You could've trusted me, you know.'

'I trust you more than anyone in this world, Jack,' said Akiko, her hand taking his in earnest. 'And I never lied to you. It's just a different version of the same truth. I *did* receive spiritual comfort from the monk, but I also got training in *ninjutsu*. It was vital to my safety that no one knew I was leading a double life.'

'But why did Masamoto-sama even want you to learn the Way of the Ninja?'

'After we prevented *daimyo* Takatomi's assassination by Dragon Eye two years ago, Masamoto-sama realized the tide of peace was turning. He believed that in order to know your enemy you must become your enemy.

'I jumped at the chance. I felt certain Dragon Eye hadn't killed Kiyoshi. And I became convinced when the monk told me of a rumour about a boy of samurai status entering a ninja clan in the Iga mountains. I thought if I could infiltrate the ninja, I might find my brother.'

'But how would you even recognize him after all this time?'

'I'd never forget Kiyoshi. Even if they shaved off all his hair and called him by another name, I'd always know him. Besides, he has a birthmark like a petal of *sakura* blossom on his lower back.'

She smiled at the thought.

'So does Masamoto-sama expect you to be an assassin?' asked Jack tentatively.

Akiko shook her head. 'My only task is to gather information from the enemy.'

An arrow clattered above their heads.

'I think it's time to go,' she said, slipping her hood back on.

With that, she ran off the edge of the roof and disappeared into the night.

46

THE BLESSING

The following morning, dressed in battle armour, Jack stood beside Yamato and Yori in the square of the Hokoku shrine. A light rain fell from the weeping clouds and mixed with the tears of the young samurai gathered before the funeral pyre of Takuan.

Masamoto-sama and the sensei of the *Niten Ichi Ryū* formed a semi-circle round the body, now wrapped in a stark-white kimono. Sensei Yamada wafted incense and chanted a *sutra* as the feeble light of dawn entered the courtyard. In the distance, the rumble of cannonfire rolled on.

Once Sensei Yamada had completed the burial rituals, Masamoto addressed the school.

'The Way of the Warrior is found in death. Takuan was the first to fall. He won't be the last. But he will always be remembered.'

Jack could hear Emi sobbing. He too had a lump in his throat as he thought of Takuan, his generosity of spirit, his kind-heartedness and, of course, his *haiku*.

Sensei Nakamura stepped forward, her stricken face as pale as her ice-white hair. She gazed at her son one last time, then, with a trembling hand, put a burning taper to the pyre. The wood caught and the flames grew until they consumed Takuan's body, smoke and ash rising in a cloud towards the heavens.

The students all bowed their heads in his honour and the rain stopped, as if the sky had cried all it could. The sensei then led them in a slow march back up to the barracks, where they formed into their units and awaited Masamoto's address.

'Takuan did *not* die in vain,' announced Masamoto. 'His death warned us of the ninja attack and saved his lordship Satoshi from assassination. It is such sacrifice and loyalty that may be asked of *all* of you this day.'

Jack already knew Satoshi had survived. After Akiko had left him, he'd managed to climb back up the roofs to Yamato, where his friend had greeted him with relief and revealed that Dragon Eye had failed in his mission. The explosion on the upper floor had only been a smoke bomb, allowing the ninja to escape. And although two members of the Council had been killed, *daimyo* Takatomi had survived, his wound not fatal.

'My sources reveal that the enemy intend to mount another assault on the keep tonight,' said Masamoto, glancing in the direction of Akiko, who stood near the back after joining the ranks last. There were dark shadows under her eyes and Jack wondered if she'd had any sleep at all.

'We now know the ninja entered the castle during the day by impersonating the samurai of *daimyo* Yukimura, and hid in a storehouse until nightfall. They surprised us once and escaped, but they won't again. The orders of the Council are to meet the enemy on the plains. We are to take the battle to them. Students of the *Niten Ichi Ryū*, we march – FOR GLORY!'

As one, the school roared back, 'FOR GLORY!'

Sensei Hosokawa called the students to attention. Each unit then strode out of the courtyard, headed by their sensei.

'This is a dangerous move,' muttered Taro as he donned his helmet and *menpō*.

'What do you mean?' said Jack.

'The castle walls must have been breached for the Council to risk open combat like this. I truly hope they know what they're doing.'

The cannonfire got louder as they crossed the inner moat. Winding their way through the outer defences of the castle, Jack noticed the walls and battlements were bedecked with hundreds of flags and banners. Alongside the multitude of family crests belonging to the samurai fighting in Satoshi's name, the standards bore images of the Holy Cross, Jesus Christ and even of St James, the patron saint of Spain. The walls were awash with Christian symbols, colourful and defiant against the grey stone of Osaka's ramparts. Jack could just imagine how incensed *daimyo* Kamakura would be at seeing such a blatant show of Christianity.

As they neared the main gate, the devastation of the battle made itself apparent. At first, it was the odd wall damaged by cannonshot, then a few battleworn samurai with blood splattered on their armour. As the students joined the vast column of troops heading towards the plain, they passed growing numbers of wounded. Men with sword cuts to their faces, others with arrows protruding from their torsos, and some dying slowly, limbs missing or guts spilling out. Moving among them with solemn grace, a number of Franciscan friars and Jesuit priests performed the last rites on those near death.

The young samurai now marched along a road parallel to the outer wall. Above them on the ramparts, archers sent volley after volley of arrows into the sky, while soldiers loaded mangonels and launched rocks and fire pots into the thick of the battle. Jack realized it wouldn't be long before they too entered the conflict.

All of a sudden, the Tenno-ji Plain appeared through a hole blown in the fortifications and Jack caught a glimpse of the fighting. A haze of smoke. A flash of cannonfire. A moving forest of steel swords and fluttering flags. Screaming samurai by the thousand. A corpse floating in the moat. Then the hellish vision disappeared.

Approaching the main gate, Masamoto called a halt. A Shinto priest greeted them and offered prayers to the war god Hachiman, asking for his divine help in securing victory and protecting the young samurai.

Along with the Shinto priest, several Jesuits and friars stood either side of the entrance, blessing the soldiers with Christian prayers as they passed across the final bridge and on to the plain. Jack was surprised to see Father Bobadillo at the gate. Spotting Masamoto, the priest immediately hurried over and spoke with him.

Jack wondered what the treacherous snake was up to now. Though he'd told Akiko and Yamato about the priest's dealings with Dragon Eye, there hadn't been an opportunity to warn his guardian. The problem was he still had no real proof. The fact that Dragon Eye, a master of deception, had told him would be laughed out of court by Father Bobadillo. Besides, Jack's main concern was to find the *rutter*.

'By the will of his lordship Hasegawa Satoshi,' announced Masamoto, 'Father Bobadillo is to personally bless the students of the *Niten Ichi Ryū* before you go into battle. It's a great honour for the school to have our lord's own priest perform such a rite. Please kneel.'

The rows of young samurai bent down on one knee and lowered their heads. Father Bobadillo stepped forward and raised the wooden cross that hung round his neck.

'Lord, grant that these souls are blessed and protected with your love. May you deliver them from harm this day and carry them safely in your arms. Amen.'

He then walked the rows, annointing the heads of each. As he passed Jack, he surreptiously skipped over him, leaving him unblessed. Jack cursed the man. Even in the final moments of war, he could not extend the love of God to a sworn enemy of his country.

The blessing complete, Masamoto mounted his horse, as did Sensei Yosa, carrying her powerful bow in her hand. The other sensei remained on foot. Sensei Nakamura wielded a vicious-looking *naginata*, Sensei Kano his long white staff, Sensei Hosokawa his two swords, but Sensei Yamada and Sensei Kyuzo were unarmed, Sensei Kyuzo trusting in his hand-to-hand *taijutsu* skills and Sensei Yamada, resting upon his walking stick, serenely relying on himself.

'Young samurai!' bellowed Masamoto, 'Are you ready to face the enemy?'

Once again, the students roared their commitment. Apart from Yori, who began to quiver within his oversized armour.

'Stay close to me,' whispered Jack, 'and you'll be fine, I promise.'

328

He really didn't believe his own words, though they seemed to comfort Yori, who attempted a brave smile through his *menpō*.

'The school maxim is *Learn today so that you may live tomorrow*,' Masamoto proclaimed.

He raised his *katana* aloft, its steel blade glinting in the morning light.

'Tomorrow is upon us. Long live the *Niten Ichi Ryū*!'

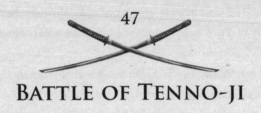

47

BATTLE OF TENNO-JI

No amount of training could have prepared the young samurai for the chaos of war. Thousands upon thousands of samurai swamped the plain, the two sides clashing like monstrous waves in a seething ocean. Each and every samurai bore upon his back a colourful *sashimono*. The small rectangular banners, painted with their *daimyo*'s *mon*, rippled with the aftershock of each attack.

The sounds of battle assaulted the students' ears. Explosions of cannon, the crack of arquebus fire, the clash of swords and the screams and shouts of samurai filled the air. The onslaught of two hundred thousand enemy troops determined to fight to the death chilled the young samurai to their bones.

Their unit stood at the rear overlooking the plain. They were part of the reserve force, awaiting the command to join the fight. To their left on a distant rise, Satoshi's top general issued orders directing the movement of all their troops. The instructions were conveyed to the other generals through a combination of *nobori* signal flags, ear-splitting blasts from conch horns and *taiko* drums, and runners bearing the distinctive golden *sashimono* of a messenger.

As yet, the reserves had not been called for.

The waiting was the hardest part. The adrenalin that had kicked in upon exiting the castle had faded, leaving only the dull throb of constant fear. Every student was agitated, caught between a determination to fight and an urge to flee.

'Are we winning?' asked Yori, trying to snatch a look between Jack and Taro.

'The battle's barely begun,' replied Taro.

'But how are we doing? I can't see anything in this stupid helmet.'

'Take it off,' Akiko suggested, helping him untie the cord round his chin. 'It's going to do you more harm than good.'

Yori stared in fear at the grey sky. 'What if an arrow hits me?'

'We're standing behind Sensei Kyuzo. He'll catch it for you!' jested Yamato.

A ripple of nervous laughter broke from the ranks of young samurai.

'Stay focused,' growled Sensei Kyuzo, pacing the lines.

Taro scanned the plain, giving them a running commentary of the battle as it progressed.

'It's too early to tell who has the advantage. But a division of our troops are attacking the centre of the enemy's frontline. See the ones with the black-and-white-striped *sashimono* — they're trying to smash their way through to *daimyo* Kamakura's personal guard.'

'Why on earth attempt that?' said Yamato. 'That's where his army is most concentrated.'

'I think it's a distraction. To draw their forces inwards. Look! Over to the left, there's huge movement of our troops.

I think Satoshi's planning to strike Kamakura's ranks from the rear.'

'So . . . the enemy are losing?' asked Yori hopefully.

'No, they're putting up heavy resistance. Kamakura's cannon and arquebus fire are slaughtering our right flank.'

Jack could see wave upon wave of their *ashigaru* charging at the enemy, but each advance was decimated by a hail of gunshot. *Daimyo* Kamakura had trained his troops to shoot in coordinated ranks, ensuring at least one row was firing while another reloaded. Behind the gunners, an immense division of samurai was poised to launch a counter-attack.

'They could break through at any moment,' said Taro.

The optimistic smile on Yori's face dropped.

The light rain of dawn returned and began to fall in earnest as the morning progressed. By noon, it had turned into a torrential downpour. The sounds of battle became lost in the deluge and the fire from cannon and arquebus petered out. The plain was churned into a quagmire of mud and blood, slowing the advance of both forces. Samurai not only had to fight the enemy, but also the ground as it sucked at their feet and dragged them off-balance. Meanwhile, the reserve troops, soaked to the skin and shivering with cold, slowly lost their resolve to fight.

'Have we won yet?' asked Yori, tugging on the sleeve of Taro's armour.

'No,' replied Taro irritably. 'Stop pestering me.'

'Then why have the enemy stopped firing?'

'He's right,' said Yamato, their view across the plain obscured by rain and smoke. 'Have they surrendered?'

'It doesn't look like it,' Taro said, pointing to a contingent of *daimyo* Kamakura's army fighting tooth and nail with Satoshi's samurai. 'Though they are no longer shooting at our right flank.'

Jack grinned. The reason was apparent to him from his experience of loading the cannon on-board the *Alexandria*. 'Gunpowder doesn't ignite when wet!'

'Of course! It should give us the advantage,' said Taro, slamming a fist to his breastplate in satisfaction. 'Look! Our troops are already starting to break through their frontline.'

Jack watched as a battalion of crack troops engaged with *daimyo* Kamakura's personal army. A diamond formation of black-and-white *sashimono* was cutting deep into a sea of Kamakura's blue-and-yellow flags. Soon they would be within striking distance of *daimyo* Kamakura's own bodyguards.

'We might just win!' uttered Taro in disbelief.

48

THE RED DEVILS

Out of the east came a terrifying sight.

As if the horizon itself was bleeding, an army of red marched on to the battlefield. Not only were their *sashimono* a brilliant scarlet, but their helmets, body armour and even their mounted troops' harnesses were the colour of blood. Fearing his imminent loss, *daimyo* Kamakura had summoned his reserve army, his secret weapon.

'The Red Devils of the Ii,' breathed Taro, his face going deathly pale.

Jack turned to him for an explanation, though their hellish appearance had already sent an involuntary shudder of fear through him.

'They're the most ruthless, brutal and bloodthirsty samurai in all of Japan. Without mercy, they'll kill us to the last samurai standing.'

The Red Devils entered the fray, launching a blistering counter-attack and laying waste all those before them. Like a floodgate opening, the black-and-white banners of Satoshi's forces were washed aside by a surge of red.

The tide of battle had turned and, as if the war god Hachiman were now on the Red Devils' side, the rain ceased and the blasts from cannon and arquebuses commenced once more.

'Samurai of the *Niten Ichi Ryū*!' cried Masamoto, riding along their frontline. 'Prepare for battle!'

The students exchanged nervous glances and unsheathed their swords. Jack grasped the handle of his *katana*, the *menuki* grip digging deep into his palm. He was hesitant to withdraw the blade, terrified he'd suddenly forgotten all his training. A hand clamped on his shoulder and Jack turned to see Yamato, his staff planted firmly in the ground beside them.

'Five years ago I lost a brother,' said Yamato, staring gravely at Jack. 'I don't want to lose another.'

The significance of his statement touched Jack to his heart. He drew Yamato into a tight embrace.

'I never had a brother until I came to Japan,' he replied, letting Yamato go. 'And I'll willingly lay down my life to save yours.'

'I hope it won't come to *that*,' said Akiko.

She stood beside them, her bow at the ready. In her other hand, she held three arrows. Without prompting, Yamato and Jack grasped the shafts either side of her outstretched hand.

'Only by binding together will we remain strong,' she said, recalling Sensei Yamada's words.

For a moment Jack believed they were invincible, the bond between them unbreakable. Yamato let go. But Jack didn't want to. He realized this might be the last time they'd be together. He held Akiko's gaze, the connection between them seeming stronger than ever, the shared secret of her ninja identity somehow bringing them even closer.

'Forever bound to one another,' she whispered, smiling at him.

'Forever bound to one another,' repeated Jack, meaning every word.

Feeling a tug on his armour, he looked down to see Yori, his eyes red and welling with tears.

'Jack, I'm scared,' he blurted. 'I know I'm samurai, but we're too young to die.'

Trying to comfort his friend, Jack could only think of repeating his mother's phrase again. 'Remember, where there are friends, there's hope.'

His words sounded weak and insipid in the midst of battle. But if the truth be told, he was just as terrified. The Red Devils were drawing ever nearer, leaving a bloodbath in their wake. Yori began to tremble uncontrollably. Panic seizing him, he dropped his sword and looked ready to flee.

'Yori-kun!' said Sensei Yamada, shuffling over to them. 'Have you figured out my *koan* yet?'

Yori blinked in bafflement at his sensei, completely taken off-guard by the unexpected question.

'What is your true face, which you had before your father and mother were even born?'

'I'm sorry, I don't know,' replied Yori, shaking his head.

'But you are wearing it *now*,' replied Sensei Yamada, smiling kindly at his protégé. 'When confronted with death, a samurai's true face is revealed. And I see in you strength, courage and loyalty. With those *bushido* qualities, you *will* survive the forthcoming fight. Just like you survived the attack on our school. I hear you mastered *kiaijutsu*.'

Yori nodded.

'Then you'll understand what I meant, that even the smallest breeze can make ripples on the largest ocean.'

Sensei Yamada wandered away, seeking out other students to counsel in the final moments.

Yori picked up his sword, a newfound strength within him.

49

SACRIFICE

'Hold the line!' ordered Sensei Hosokawa, as the Red Devils thundered towards them.

The *Niten Ichi Ryū* were positioned at the top of a rise and their sensei was determined they shouldn't lose the advantage by entering the battle too soon. Closer and closer came the murderous red samurai, cutting a swathe through the ranks of *ashigaru*.

Jack began to hyperventilate, his breathing sounding loud and panicky inside the helmet and *menpō*. His heart thudded against his breastplate. Despite all his training, all the duels he'd won, all the challenges he'd faced, he'd never been so scared in all his life.

He wished his father were still with him. Even in the most treacherous of storms, he'd been reassured by his presence. His father's sense of strength and unwavering confidence had always given him hope where there appeared to be none. Here he was, facing an army of bloodthirsty warriors, about to sacrifice his life for a Japanese lord. What hope did he have?

There was a flicker of movement in the sky and he spotted an arrow flying at him. Fear having nailed his feet to the ground, he could only watch as the steel tip hurtled directly towards his head.

At the last second, a hand snatched the arrow from the air.

Sensei Kyuzo glared at Jack with contempt. 'I haven't trained you to die before the fight even starts, *gaijin*!' he sneered. 'You're a pathetic excuse of a samurai!'

Jack felt a wave of anger rise in him at his teacher's abuse. It broke his paralysis. He confronted his sensei, *katana* in hand.

'*That's* the fighting spirit I'm looking for,' snapped Sensei Kyuzo, seeing the indignation in Jack's eyes.

Jack suddenly realized Sensei Kyuzo had goaded him on purpose. To impel him into action.

'LONG LIVE THE *NITEN ICHI RYŪ*!' bellowed Masamoto, brandishing his sword and spurring his horse into the thick of the enemy.

Roaring a battle cry, the students and sensei charged down the slope at the advancing Red Devils. The two sides met head on, swords and spears clashing. Jack found himself surrounded by warring samurai, mounted and on foot. An *ashigaru* fell at his feet, blood spewing from his mouth as the sharpened points of a trident pierced his chest.

Behind the soldier stood a Red Devil. Ripping the spear out of the dying man, the samurai advanced upon Jack. He thrust the trident at his belly. Jack's *taijutsu* training kicked in and he swiftly evaded the weapon. But the Red Devil snatched back his spear too quickly for Jack to grab hold. The samurai lunged at him again. Jack jumped to the other side, swinging his *katana* round to chop the Devil's head off. The samurai ducked and drove his shoulder into Jack, knocking him backwards. Jack stumbled over the dying *ashigaru* and fell to the floor.

The Red Devil rushed to stand over him, the blood of his previous victims dripping from his armour. His helmet had two great golden horns and he wore a terrifying *menpō* with fierce saw-like teeth cut into it. Only the samurai's eyes showed, glinting with bloodlust as he raised his trident to skewer Jack into the ground.

A wooden staff rocketed out of nowhere, deflecting the spear's lethal points into the muddy earth. Yamato, jumping over Jack, kicked the thwarted samurai hard in the chest. The Red Devil staggered backwards and lost his grip on the trident. Unsheathing a *katana*, he now charged at Yamato but was stopped in his tracks by an arrow. Akiko's shot penetrated the samurai's breastplate.

But a single arrow would never be enough to fell such a warrior. Grunting in pain, the Red Devil snapped off the shaft and recommenced his attack. As Yamato battled with the samurai, Akiko hurriedly restrung her bow. Jack jumped to his feet and rejoined the fight.

An experienced warrior, the Red Devil drove them both back. His blows were so violent that Jack's arms shook with each strike. Akiko let loose another arrow, but the samurai was ready this time, cutting it in half in mid-air. Yamato, stunned at the feat, was knocked to the ground by a surprise front kick. Jack cut at the warrior's head with his *katana*, but his strike was blocked and he was driven away. The Red Devil, retrieving his trident, raised it aloft to kill the fallen Yamato.

All of a sudden, the glistening tip of a sword thrust out of the samurai's chest. The Red Devil staggered, coughing up blood, and collapsed to the ground, dead.

'Best avoid those with the golden horns,' Sensei Hosokawa advised. 'They're the elite warriors.'

He then returned to fight beside Masamoto, who'd dismounted and was decimating any Red Devil who came near with his Two Heavens technique. Sensei Yosa, though, was still on horseback, riding through the battle and picking off the enemy with her deadly arrows. To Jack's right, Sensei Kyuzo was taking on two Red Devils at once. In an impressive display of *taijutsu*, he disarmed them both before impaling them on one another's spears. A flurry of snow-white hair revealed where Sensei Nakamura was fighting, tears of grief running down her face as she exacted revenge upon the enemy, her *naginata* swooping through the air like a steel bird of prey. Nearby, the immense form of Sensei Kano could be seen twirling his *bō*, the enemy dropping like flies around him. The only centre of calm in the midst of this chaos was Sensei Yamada, who stood in the middle of a circle of fallen bodies. Jack watched as a Red Devil charged at the Zen master then suddenly dropped to his knees. A second *kiai* from Sensei Yamada finished the warrior off.

Jack spotted Yori wandering unscathed through the fighting, as if in a daze. His sword was raised but no one was engaging with him. He was simply too small to be considered a threat. A Red Devil bumped into Yori, saw the tiny warrior, then laughed. A moment later, the smile had been wiped off the man's face as Sensei Yosa planted an arrow through his throat.

Breaking through the masses, a number of Red Devils on horseback bore down on the *Niten Ichi Ryū* students. Yori was directly in their path and about to be trampled underfoot. Jack screamed a warning, but he couldn't be heard above the noise of battle. He sprinted at his friend, shoulder-barging him out from under the horses' hooves.

Jack dragged Yori to his feet. 'I told you, stick with us.'

Yori nodded meekly. 'But no one wants to fight me.'

'And you're complaining!' exclaimed Jack.

'No, of course not,' said Yori, giving a nervous laugh. His eyes suddenly widened in fear. 'Behind you!'

Jack turned to see a Red Devil charging at them. Having dropped his *katana* in the mud saving Yori, Jack went to draw his *wakizashi* but knew it was too late. The samurai was already bringing his sword round to decapitate him.

'*YAH!*'

The Red Devil's eyes rolled into the back of his head and he collapsed face first in the mud.

Yori, breathing hard from the exertion of his *kiai*, grinned at Jack.

'No wonder no one wants to fight you, Yori. You're lethal!' said Jack, picking up his *katana* before another samurai could attack them.

'I think I only knocked him out,' Yori replied, tapping the body with his foot. The Red Devil moaned feebly.

'Jack!' cried Akiko, frantically beckoning them to join her and Yamato.

The two of them ran over, only to discover Emi lying on the ground, an arrow protruding from her thigh. She was pale, blood soaking through her leggings and *hakama*.

'We must protect Emi, at all costs,' said Akiko, raising her bow.

They immediately formed a defensive circle round the *daimyo*'s daughter, driving back the advancing Red Devils. But there were simply too many. *Daimyo* Kamakura's forces were now smashing their way through every rank and file of Satoshi's army.

The battle had become a massacre.

Encircled by Red Devils, Sensei Nakamura wielded her *naginata* with brutal abandon, her snow-white hair whirling amid a sea of red. Suddenly she disappeared, swallowed up by the enemy.

A soldier bearing a golden *sashimono* ran towards them.

'RETREAT TO THE CASTLE!' screamed the messenger.

A moment later, he was slain by a Red Devil from behind, his blood splattering the golden banner.

'Fall back!' commanded Masamoto, cutting his way through the mass of enemy troops with Sensei Hosokawa, Yosa and Kyuzo.

'Leave me,' Emi groaned, unable to stand. 'Save yourselves.'

'No,' said Jack. 'We're *all* bound to one another, remember?'

Sheathing his swords, he lifted her to her feet. Emi almost passed out with the pain.

'Time to go!' said Akiko urgently, firing off several arrows.

The five of them retreated in the direction of the castle with thousands of other fleeing troops, fighting a rearguard action. But their progress was hampered, not just by the wounded Emi but by the churned-up terrain. The Red Devils were rapidly closing in, threatening to cut off their escape route to the main gate.

'We're not going to make it,' said Yamato, as a squad of Red Devils broke free and charged at them. Taking Emi's other arm, he helped Jack carry her, hoping that together they could outrun the enemy.

Taro, who'd already reached the bridge, spotted them struggling towards safety. He ran back, both swords raised high.

'Keeping going,' he said. 'I'll hold them off as long as possible.'

He stood his ground as the squad of Red Devils bore down on him. His *katana* and *wakizashi* became a blur, the Two Heavens technique annihilating any samurai who ventured near. But reinforcements were not far behind and Taro was in danger of being overwhelmed before the five of them could reach the bridge.

'Taro needs help,' said Yori, running off.

'No!' screamed Jack, but it was too late.

Yori took up position beside Taro, yelling *kiai* after *kiai* at the advancing force. The two of them slowed the enemy's progress enough for Jack, Emi, Yamato and Akiko to cross the bridge.

'Yori! Taro, come on!' shouted Jack.

They turned and ran.

Exhausted and out of breath from the fight, Yori's little legs wouldn't carry him fast enough.

The enemy were closing in on him.

He slipped and fell.

Taro stopped and, turning back, withdrew his swords.

'What's does he think he's doing?' exclaimed Yamato.

'He's sacrificing himself for Yori,' said Akiko, a tear running down her cheek.

Taro made his final stand upon a small rise.

Red Devil after Red Devil fell, as he held back the tide of enemy samurai. Then an immense Red Devil with twisted gold horns drove a spear into him. Taro staggered under the blow, but kept fighting. He managed to take out a few more of the enemy, before the gold-horned samurai cut him down with the massive blade of a *nodaichi* sword. Taro crumpled to his knees. Showing no mercy, the samurai chopped Taro's head from his shoulders. The Red Devils swarmed over him and advanced on the castle.

Jack could only stare at where Saburo's brother had fallen, shocked by the sudden and brutal loss.

But Yori was still on the plain, running for all he was worth.

'COME ON!' screamed Jack.

The thought of his loyal and courageous friend suffering such a gruesome death was too much to bear.

Suddenly the massive doors of the outer wall began to close.

'Wait!' he begged the guards. 'Yori's still out there.'

'I'm under orders,' growled the gatekeeper.

Yori was flagging, his strength sapped by all his *kiai* attacks.

The gates were drawing ever closer.

Jack willed his friend on.

Through the narrowing gap, he saw Yori stumble on to the bridge.

But behind, an avalanche of red samurai threatened to engulf him.

The doors slammed shut with a thunderous clang.

'Noooo!' cried Jack, hammering his fists against the barred gates.

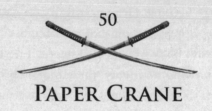

50

PAPER CRANE

Barging the guards out of the way, Jack dashed up the stairs of the gate tower to the ramparts. He discovered hundreds of soldiers firing arquebuses, launching arrows, and hurling rocks at the enemy. On the plain, stranded knots of Satoshi's samurai fought bravely on, while *daimyo* Kamakura's forces continued their advance, bringing up their siege machines and cannon.

Below him, a seething mass of Red Devils launched an assault on the castle gate. The drawbridge had been raised, but they'd begun to fill in the moat with the bodies of the slain, piling them higher and higher.

Jack looked desperately around, but Yori was nowhere to be seen, his friend's body lost among the corpses.

'We have to go,' said Akiko, resting her hand upon his shoulder. 'Masamoto-sama's ordered us to regroup at the barracks.'

'Why close the gates?' raged Jack, slamming his fist upon the parapet.

'The enemy was about to overrun us.'

'But he was *on* the bridge!'

Jack shook with fury, then broke down in tears, weeping, 'I'd promised to look after him.'

'And you did,' said Akiko, drawing Jack away from the rampart. 'But it was Yori's decision to help Taro. His sacrifice saved us.'

When they reached the barracks, Jack was shocked to see that barely half the students had made it back. Many were injured, while others sat around with a dazed, faraway look in their eyes. Their losses had been heavy. Not only had Sensei Nakamura fallen in battle, but Sensei Yamada and Sensei Kano were missing too. Jack wandered over to where Emi lay, her leg now bandaged. Cho was by her side.

'Where's Kai?' he asked, though he feared the answer.

Cho gave a sad shake of her head and wiped a tear away.

'Jack,' said Emi, trying to sit up to greet him. 'Thank you for saving my life.'

'It's the least I could do after endangering it last year,' he replied.

Emi smiled warmly at him. 'I forgive you for that.'

'And so do I,' said a voice from behind.

Jack turned round to see *daimyo* Takatomi, his arm in a sling, accompanied by two of his bodyguards.

'Jack-kun, I must thank you and your friends for bringing my daughter back to safety. I'm sorry to hear of the loss of Taro and Yori,' he said, bowing his head in respect. 'Once this little battle's over, please join us again for *cha-no-yu* at my castle. We will toast their bravery and remember them.'

'It would be an honour,' said Jack, bowing low as the *daimyo* departed with Emi, borne away by his bodyguards.

Though he had to suppress a weary smile; only *daimyo* Takatomi would think about holding a tea ceremony in the middle of a war.

'Samurai of the *Niten Ichi Ryū*,' said Masamoto, looking battleworn yet defiant. 'We may have suffered great losses. But the enemy has *not* broken the spirit of the *Niten Ichi Ryū*.'

The scars on his face flared with the emotion of his statement.

'The virtues of *bushido* you displayed on the field of battle are to be commended. Your courage in the face of danger, and the loyalty shown by those who died to save their comrades will forever be remembered. Such heroism is the cornerstone of our school and why we will *never* be defeated. Remember Sensei Yamada's words, only by binding together will we remain strong.'

Jack, Akiko and Yamato looked at one another. Though Yori was on all their minds, they realized their continued survival relied upon their trinity remaining intact.

'As I speak, the Council are planning our counter-offensive. In the meantime, ensure you get some rest. You'll need your strength for the forthcoming assault. Long live the *Niten Ichi Ryū*!'

The students shouted their response. But with so many of them missing, the battle cry sounded hollow as it echoed off the castle walls. Masamoto and the remaining sensei strode out of the courtyard in the direction of the keep. Jack followed Yamato and Akiko into the barracks.

Settling down in the far corner, he tried to get some sleep. But the distant rumble of cannonfire was a constant reminder that the battle was not yet over. And the empty bed between him and Yamato was the cruel, painful proof that Yori was no longer with them.

Jack tried to occupy his mind with memories of home, but he always came back to Yori. Just as he was drifting to sleep, he noticed a small white paper crane peeking from Yori's pack. Reaching over, he pulled it out. Holding the little bird in his palm, he recalled Yori giving him one when he'd fought Sasaki Bishamon, an arrogant samurai on a warrior pilgrimage. That *origami* model had been Yori's thousandth crane. As legend dictated, it contained a wish and Yori had wished for Jack's protection during the duel. Hoping this crane would bring him the same good fortune, Jack put the little bird inside his own shoulder bag next to the Daruma Doll that Yori had rescued from the fire.

Jack would never forget his loyal friend.

51

THE KEEP

A huge explosion woke Jack.

Yamato was gone. So too was Akiko.

He ran outside to see all the students dashing to the top of the inner ramparts. Climbing the stairs two at a time, he found Akiko and Yamato on the battlements. The sun was low on the horizon, the sky a bloody red. In the fading light, Jack could see the Tenno-ji Plain was crawling with *daimyo* Kamakura's troops, their cannon and siege machines continuing to bombard the defences.

'Kamakura's forces have crossed the moat,' Yamato explained. 'They're setting off barrels of gunpowder to destroy the outer wall.'

Another almighty explosion rocked the castle fortifications. Smoke and dust rose from a collapsing outer battlement and the Red Devils could be seen surging through the gap.

'So it's over?' said Jack.

'Not yet. They still have to fight their way through the castle complex,' replied Akiko. 'Remember, no one has *ever* taken Osaka Castle.'

The students watched as Kamakura's army fought a war of

attrition. Fierce sword battles broke out between thousands of samurai in and around the battlements as the two sides fought for ground. The Red Devils were intent on reaching the inner bailey, but their progress was slowed by the winding narrow roads of the castle's outer fortifications. Every gate and outpost was hard won and their losses quickly mounted up.

By the time the sun was dipping behind the horizon, *daimyo* Kamakura's advance had come to a standstill.

'Look! The castle's on fire!' said Cho, pointing to the west side of the inner fortifications.

'But the Red Devils haven't even breached that section,' said Yamato in astonishment. 'We must have a traitor.'

'It's more likely to be ninja,' corrected Akiko, giving Jack a knowing look.

Flames rose from the area of the castle kitchens, an ominous orange glow against the darkened sky. Fanned by the wind, the fire spread rapidly, causing confusion and panic among Satoshi's troops. *Daimyo* Kamakura's forces took immediate advantage of the chaos, breaking through the defensive lines and forcing their way into the inner bailey.

Suddenly the parapet to Jack's right exploded in a hailstorm of rock and cannonshot. The students all threw themselves to the ground as another cannonball demolished a large section of the rampart. Jack dragged Akiko and Yamato to their feet and they stumbled down the damaged staircase. Screams and shouts of panic erupted from the young samurai. Masamoto and his sensei ran into the courtyard, rallying the students.

'To the keep!' he bellowed.

Grabbing their weapons and packs from the barracks, the young samurai followed. They ran through the inner bailey towards their final stronghold. Jack glanced behind. The Red Devils were already battling their way through the rearguard. As the students raced up the cobbled road, Jack knew the safety promised by the keep was only a few more turns away. But the enemy were closing in. Fast.

'Hurry!' urged Jack, seeing Cho fall behind.

The Red Devil with the twisted gold horns hacked his way past the remaining guards, his *nodaichi*'s immense blade slicing straight through three of them in a single sweep.

The road narrowed as the students neared the keep's inner courtyard. Masamoto was at the gateway, ensuring they all made it to safety.

Jack risked another glance over his shoulder. The gold-horned Red Devil was now hefting a long spear, launching it at the retreating young samurai.

'Look out!' screamed Jack to Cho.

The spear spiralled towards her.

At the last moment, Yamato pushed Cho out of the way.

Its cruel barb struck him instead and he fell to the ground.

The Red Devil roared with satisfaction and, wielding his *nodaichi*, bore down on the wounded Yamato.

Jack turned and ran back to his fallen friend.

Yamato was crawling desperately towards him, the spear still protruding from his side.

Drawing both his swords, Jack charged at the enemy.

The Red Devil was ready for him. As Jack cut down with

his *katana*, the samurai sliced upwards at the same time. Jack barely avoided the lethal length of the blade, managing to deflect it with his *wakizashi* at the last second. But he lost his grip on the *katana* when the Red Devil's forearm smashed across his wrist. The samurai swiftly followed up with his armoured fist, punching Jack in the face. If it hadn't been for his *menpō*, Jack would have been killed. The facemask cracked and his helmet was knocked from his head as he flew into the wall.

Stunned, Jack expected to feel the hard steel of the *nodaichi* cut through his throat at any second. But the Red Devil had halted his attack to stare at Jack.

'A *gaijin* samurai!' he exclaimed, shocked at seeing Jack's blond hair and bright blue eyes.

An arrow shot through the air striking the Red Devil in the gap between his helmet and *menpō*. He staggered backwards, blood pouring from his eye socket.

'Never hesitate,' said Jack, snatching up his *katana*.

But the samurai didn't die.

Screaming in agonized rage, he charged at Jack. Another arrow penetrated his chest as Akiko was joined by Sensei Yosa at the gate. Yet still he attacked. Jack dodged the Red Devil's wild strike, and a moment later Masamoto was by his side.

'Go!' ordered Masamoto, attacking the seemingly indestructible samurai with vengeful fury.

Jack ran over to Yamato. Removing the spear, he helped him to his feet and they staggered towards the gate. Behind them, hundreds more Red Devils stormed up the road. Akiko and Sensei Yosa launched arrow after arrow, trying to stall the enemy's advance.

Masamoto, disarming the Red Devil with a lightning fast Autumn Leaf strike, thrust his *wakizashi* into the samurai's gut. The Red Devil groaned and fell to his knees.

'That's for my son!' declared Masamoto.

He then brought his *katana* slicing across, decapitating the gold-horned Red Devil. The man's head fell from his shoulders and bounced down the road.

'And that's for Taro!'

As soon as Masamoto was inside the inner courtyard, the guards slammed the gates shut against the Red Devil horde. The enemy hammered against the other side, but the re-inforced doors held. For the time being at least.

Jack laid Yamato on the ground. Akiko knelt beside him, her face etched with worry.

'I'm fine,' wheezed Yamato. 'It's not deep.'

Akiko gently rolled him to one side to inspect the wound.

'How is he?' asked Masamoto, standing over them.

'He's bleeding badly, but his armour's taken the brunt of the blow.'

'Can you stand?' asked Masamoto of his son.

Yamato nodded.

'Good,' said Masamoto. 'Take him to the keep and get him bandaged up.'

Even now, Masamoto's austerity prevented him showing the love and approval Yamato desperately needed. Jack realized his guardian probably thought it a sign of weakness to display any emotion in front of his students. But Jack saw how Yamato's head dropped when there was no recognition of his valour in saving Cho.

Taking Yamato by the arm, Jack and Akiko helped him across the courtyard.

'Thanks . . . for saving . . . me,' said Yamato between spasms of pain. 'I owe you both my life.'

'It's Akiko we should be thanking,' replied Jack. 'If it wasn't for her archery skills, we'd both be dead by now.'

'It was a terrible shot,' said Akiko.

'What do you mean?' exclaimed Jack. 'You got him straight through his left eye!'

'I was aiming for his right.'

The three of them burst into laughter.

'Stop it,' groaned Yamato. 'It hurts to laugh.'

Inside the keep, *ashigaru* rushed past, ferrying arquebuses and gunpowder to the troops on the inner walls. The three of them headed up the stairs to the second floor. *Daimyo* Takatomi was there, giving orders to the surviving generals. He broke away from the group as soon as he saw that Masamoto's son was wounded.

'Take Yamato-kun to my quarters immediately. He can use my personal physician.'

As they climbed the stairs to the sixth floor, the sound of cannonfire appeared to be getting closer. Through a window on the fourth floor, Jack glimpsed the battle outside. *Daimyo* Kamakura's troops were closing in on all sides, sending flaming arrows over the walls. Satoshi's forces, however, were still keeping them at bay with a constant barrage of musket fire and arrows.

Passing the fifth floor, Yamato stopped.

'Are you all right?' asked Jack.

Nodding, Yamato whispered, 'Look! Father Bobadillo's door is open.'

Down the corridor, the wood-panelled walls of the priest's study were visible, an oil lamp flickering in one corner.

'This could be your only chance,' said Yamato, looking meaningfully at Jack.

'But what about you?'

'I'll be fine with Akiko's help,' he said, taking his arm off Jack's shoulder. 'Just find your father's *rutter*.'

52

DIVINE JUSTICE

Jack crept towards Father Bobadillo's study. Despite the raging battle outside, the corridor was eerily deserted. Most of the guards were engaged in fighting on the battlements. Standing to one side of the door frame, Jack peeked in and immediately drew his head back.

Father Bobadillo was in the room.

But he had his back to the door.

Jack risked another look. The priest was frantically emptying the most precious contents of his casket into a bag. Moving to the recess, he pulled the books off the shelf and slid open a hidden compartment in the wall.

Jack almost gasped aloud. This *had* to be where he kept the *rutter*.

But Father Bobadillo only palmed more jewels and silver coins into his bag. Shouldering his booty, the priest hurried towards the prayer room.

Jack was about to follow, when Father Bobadillo suddenly stopped as if he'd forgotten something. Turning, he considered the oil painting of St Ignatius.

Surely he isn't thinking of taking that, thought Jack.

But the priest returned and lifted it off the wall. Putting the portrait to one side, he pressed one of the wooden panels and there was a soft click.

Behind the painting lay another secret compartment.

Father Bobadillo reached inside and pulled out the *rutter*, still wrapped in its protective oilskin.

Jack, stunned to actually see it again, couldn't contain his anger at the priest.

'So it *was* you!' said Jack, stepping into the room and drawing his sword. 'You stole the *rutter*! You murdered my father!'

Father Bobadillo spun round, the momentary shock on his face quickly replaced by a sneer.

'I stole nothing,' he replied, ignoring the threat the sword posed. 'I only took back what was rightfully ours.'

The priest calmly settled into his high-backed chair and eyed Jack.

'This *rutter* is the property of Portugal,' he said, placing the logbook on the table. 'Before your father acquired it by ill means, it belonged to a Portuguese pilot. Your father was not only a Protestant heretic, he was a *thief*.'

'You lie!' shouted Jack, his outstretched blade quivering with fury at the accusation.

'Have you never questioned how your father, an Englishman, came by such vast knowledge of the oceans?' said the priest, laying his hands in his lap.

Jack faltered, unable to answer the priest's question.

'Let me enlighten you. Your father was a pirate. He plundered the seas and stole our *rutter*. I didn't kill your father. He condemned himself. I was merely administering justice on behalf of my country. Having dared sail to the Japans, I

358

thought it fitting his executioner should be a ninja.'

Jack didn't know what to think. Father Bobadillo must be lying, but the priest had sown a seed of doubt in his mind. His father had never spoken of how he'd come by the *rutter*. He'd just said the logbook was obtained at great cost to life and limb. Jack had assumed he was referring to the dangers of exploration, not piracy. Anyway, he couldn't remember a time when his father *hadn't* possessed the *rutter*. It had to be his father's.

At the same time, he knew the logbook contained more information than one man could obtain during a lifetime at sea. It even detailed the Pacific Ocean where his father had never sailed before. The more Jack thought about it, the more questions were raised.

'So what are you going to do, young samurai? Cut me in half?' said Father Bobadillo, enjoying the play of emotions and doubt on Jack's face.

As Jack lowered his sword, the priest smiled cruelly.

'Or perhaps I should try you for treason. Charge – attempted murder. Verdict – guilty. Sentence – death.'

Father Bobadillo rose from his seat, a wheel-lock pistol in his hand.

He aimed the gun at Jack's heart.

'Even a samurai can't avoid a bullet.'

53

SHADOW WARRIOR

Jack tensed but the shot never came.

Father Bobadillo was staring past him, an eyebrow raised in surprise.

'I was just about to do *your* job,' he said disdainfully, lowering the gun. 'But now you're here, you can finish what I paid you to do.'

Dragon Eye slipped from the shadows.

Jack felt an icy slither of fear run down his spine. He was trapped between his two worst enemies. Knowing the pain Dragon Eye could inflict upon him, he now wished Father Bobadillo *had* shot him.

'So the *rutter* has been decoded. Entirely?' enquired the ninja.

'Of course! I wouldn't have ordered you to kill the boy otherwise.'

Father Bobadillo rolled his eyes in exasperation.

'Good,' replied Dragon Eye.

Ignoring Jack, the ninja approached Father Bobadillo.

'Then I'll take the *rutter*,' he stated, holding out his hand.

'What?' exclaimed Father Bobadillo, his manner now indignant. 'Are you out of your mind?'

The ninja gave a single shake of his head. '*Daimyo* Kamakura has need of it.'

'But you stole it for *me*,' snarled Father Bobadillo.

'Now I'm stealing it back,' replied Dragon Eye.

Jack glared at the priest. The man must have been lying about his father. The *real* thief was Father Bobadillo.

'You can't. It's mine. I paid you for it,' he protested. Then, pointing an accusative finger at Dokugan Ryu, he growled, 'I also paid you to kill the boy.'

Jack could see Father Bobadillo was trying to regain control of the situation by diverting the ninja's attention from the *rutter* back to him.

'His time will come,' replied Dragon Eye, giving Jack a cursory glance. 'But not before yours.'

The ninja took a step towards the priest. Jack couldn't believe it. The assassin had turned on his paymaster.

'Stop,' exclaimed Father Bobadillo, his eyes widening in terror. 'I'll give you whatever you want. Money, jewels, guns . . .'

The priest threw his shoulder bag on the table, its contents scattering across the surface. Glittering gemstones and silver coins cascaded to the floor.

Dragon Eye shook his head in disgust, unmoved by the priest's pleas.

'*Daimyo* Kamakura is offering *far* more than you, a pitiful excuse for a priest, could ever give me.'

'Whatever it is, I'll double it, treble it,' said Father Bobadillo in desperation.

'Highly unlikely, considering you're on the losing side,' sneered Dragon Eye. 'He's promising me Yamagata Castle and a return to power.'

Jack's mind flashed back to the old woman's story in the temple.

'So you *are* Hattori Tatsuo?' he breathed.

Dragon Eye's head snapped round, his single green eye boring into Jack.

'You *really* should be a ninja!' he hissed. 'I need a spy like you.'

'But . . . but Masamoto-sama chopped your head off!' stuttered Jack, staring at Dokugan Ryu in disbelief.

'Yes, he did,' laughed Dragon Eye cruelly. 'At least, he thought he did. That murdering samurai actually killed my shadow.'

'Your shadow?' said Jack, utterly bemused.

'A *kagemusha*. A Shadow Warrior,' explained Dragon Eye, humouring him. 'I came across a man who looked identical to me. Apart from having two eyes, of course. But I soon remedied that. He was more than willing to become my shadow in return for sparing the lives of his family. So you see, your almighty Masamoto actually killed an innocent man.'

Jack was astounded at the ninja's cunning and cold-blooded nature.

'Clever, but ultimately futile,' sneered Father Bobadillo, now aiming the gun at Dragon Eye.

As he fired, the ninja instinctively leapt aside.

The bullet cracked into the wooden panel behind.

Dragon Eye charged at Father Bobadillo, striking him with the tips of his fingers in rapid succession. The priest's face froze into an expression of total panic, his eyes rolling in their sockets. He was completely paralysed.

'Samurai might not be able to avoid bullets, but ninja can,' whispered Dragon Eye into his victim's ear.

Father Bobadillo was now juddering slightly, a wet choking sound issuing from his lips. His breath rattled in his chest and his skin burst out in red patches.

'You no doubt recognize these symptoms, *gaijin*.'

Dim Mak. Jack wouldn't wish the Death Touch on anyone, even his worst enemy. In a previous encounter with Dragon Eye, Jack had personally experienced its crushing agony. The burning sensation that grew like a forest fire in the veins. The feeling of the heart trying to punch its way through flesh and bone. The tight constricting suffocation as the lungs began to fail. The pressure building and building until eventually the victim's heart burst within his chest.

'Unlike you, I doubt he'll survive,' said Dragon Eye, lifting up Father Bobadillo's lolling head by the hair.

The priest's eyes were now bulbous and streaked dark red.

Jack heard a distant pop like a stone being thrown into a pond. A moment later, blood spewed out of the Jesuit's mouth.

Father Bobadillo crumpled to the floor like a rag doll.

Sickened by his enemy's gruesome death, Jack forced himself to act, before he became the ninja's next victim. Snatching the *rutter* from the table, he sprinted out of the study into the prayer room.

To his right was the closed *shoji*, while to his left the door beside the altar was open.

With Dragon Eye hot on his heels, he fled through the open door.

Entering a deserted corridor, Jack realized he'd discovered Father Bobadillo's private access to his lordship Satoshi. The floor was laid with fine *tatami* mats and the walls richly decorated. This section was also isolated from the rest of the keep, with only a flight of stairs leading upwards.

Dashing up the staircase, Jack could hear the soft pad of the ninja's footsteps closing in on him.

54

REVENGE

Cannonshot shrieked through the air and fireballs whizzed by, almost scorching Jack's skin as he stood upon the balcony overlooking all of Osaka. On any other day the view from the top tower would have been magnificent, reaching far beyond the city, over the Tenno-ji Plain to the sparkling ocean itself.

But on this night, all Jack could see was devastation and destruction. Fires raged throughout the castle compounds. Bodies littered the burning ramparts. The enemy swarmed over broken battlements, firing cannon and arquebuses at the stronghold of the keep. Below, the Red Devils had smashed their way through the last gateway into the inner courtyard. They were now engaged in brutal hand-to-hand combat, as Satoshi's troops made their final stand.

By contrast, the private meeting chamber on the *donjon*'s eighth floor was a haven of peace. The room, lit by elegant free-standing oil lamps, was exquisitely decorated in gold leaf and framed by dark wooden beams. A mural of samurai lords adorned the walls, showing them hunting, meditating and enjoying tea beneath leafy green trees, all scenes recalling a more harmonious episode in Japanese life.

When Jack had reached Satoshi's personal chamber on the seventh floor, he'd discovered the ruler-in-waiting and all his retainers dead. There had been no sign of a struggle, but the *tatami* was soaked through with their blood and beside each of them lay a *wakizashi*. Realizing his forces faced defeat, Satoshi had taken the only honourable course of action available to a vanquished samurai lord. He'd committed *seppuku*. Bound by duty, his retainers had followed him into death, ritually disembowelling themselves with their own swords.

'Your time has come,' said Dragon Eye, appearing in the chamber behind Jack. 'Hand over the *rutter*.'

'No!' said Jack, defiantly slipping the logbook into his pack.

'I don't intend to disappoint *daimyo* Kamakura. Give it to me now!'

'If you *really* are Tatsuo,' challenged Jack, 'why are you helping *daimyo* Kamakura? He betrayed you at Nakasendo.'

'It's a decision he regrets,' replied Dragon Eye gravely. 'But he's made amends by waging war for me.'

'For *you*?' exclaimed Jack in astonishment.

Dragon Eye gave a self-satisfied nod.

'But this war's about expelling Christians and foreigners from Japan.'

'For *daimyo* Kamakura it is,' replied Dragon Eye. 'For me, it is about revenge.'

'Against whom?'

'Masamoto,' said the ninja, spitting the name with venom.

'You must be mad!' said Jack, stunned by the revelation. 'You've dragged Japan into civil war for a *personal* vendetta?'

'THAT SAMURAI KILLED MY SON!' shouted Dragon

Eye, his icy calm demeanour breaking for the first time.

'And you murdered *his* son, Tenno!' shot back Jack.

'An eye for an eye,' replied the ninja, regaining his composure. 'But that's not nearly enough. His lord, his family, his beloved school, his entire samurai way of life must be destroyed. I won't kill *him*, though. Masamoto must suffer the torment I've had to endure all these years. He'll spend the rest of his life grieving for all that he's lost. And I will *finally* have my revenge.'

Jack realized Sensei Yamada had been right that time in the Zen garden two years ago when he'd told him that revenge was self-defeating. It had eaten away at the ninja until there was nothing left – but hate.

'Now give me the *rutter*,' demanded Dragon Eye.

'Never!' said Jack, reaching for his swords.

He'd decided to take a stand. There would be no more running. No more hiding. It was indeed his time. Jack was ready to face his nemesis, once and for all.

'I've no quarrel with you, *gaijin*,' said the ninja, all of a sudden changing tack. 'In fact, I've come to admire you. So I'll give you one last chance. Hand over the *rutter* and I'll let you live.'

In spite of the proposal, Dragon Eye still unsheathed a fearsome *ninjatō* from the *saya* upon his back.

Kuro Kumo.

Black Cloud. The last and greatest sword to be forged by Kunitome. The steel shimmered in the reflected light of the castle's fires, the *hamon* on its blade swirling like a thunderstorm of clouds.

'My final offer,' he growled. 'Join me. I'll teach you the Way of the Ninja.'

'I'd never become a ninja!' retorted Jack, almost laughing out loud at the idea. 'Masamoto's no murderer. *You* are. *You* killed my father. *You* will always be my enemy.'

'So be it,' said Dragon Eye.

With lightning speed, Black Cloud cut through the air.

Drawing both his swords, Jack rushed to stop Dragon Eye slicing him from head to toe. He cross-blocked the *ninjatō* between the blades of his *wakizashi* and *katana*. In the flickering light, the name etched into the steel of his swords glinted in direct challenge to Black Cloud.

Shizu.

Dragon Eye snarled his frustration and kicked Jack in the chest. Jack went flying backwards, crashing against the rail of the balcony. Below him, the war raged on as Dragon Eye advanced on him, wheeling the *ninjato⁻* in a lethal arc towards his neck.

Jack blocked the attack with his *katana*, letting the force of the blow whip his own blade round in a counterstrike at Dragon Eye's head. The assassin ducked, dropping into a spinning leg sweep. He caught Jack's ankle and sent him crashing to the floor. Dragon Eye jumped into the air. Jack rolled out of the way as the ninja drove the shaft of his sword down at Jack's chest. Black Cloud pierced the decking as if the wood were no thicker than paper.

Flipping to his feet, Jack went on the attack. He cut across with his *wakizashi*, at the same time slicing down with his *katana*. Dragon Eye backflipped out of danger. But he was forced to retreat under Jack's unrelenting onslaught. Feverishly blocking the blur of blades, he was driven across the chamber. Jack almost had him backed into a corner when the ninja kicked over a lamp, sending flaming oil across the floor. The *tatami* caught alight in an instant and flames began to lick the walls, blistering the painted mural.

'Masamoto has taught you well,' sneered Dragon Eye, circling away from Jack and the spreading fire. 'But the Two Heavens will only prolong your inevitable death.'

The ninja thrust forward, almost impaling Jack through the heart. Jack deflected the strike at the last moment and countered with his *wakizashi*, catching Dragon Eye across the chest and slicing through the ninja's clothing. A line of blood appeared. Though the cut wasn't deep, Dragon Eye glanced down in surprise that he'd been wounded at all.

Jack, taking advantage of the ninja's lapse in concentration, sliced upwards with his *katana*. Dragon Eye's reactions were razor sharp, and he leant away from the lethal blade, bending like a reed in the wind.

But he wasn't quite fast enough.

The *kissaki* of Jack's sword cut through the hood of the ninja's *shinobi shozoku*.

Until that moment Dragon Eye had always been a faceless one-eyed nightmare to Jack. Now the assassin stood before him, exposed.

Hattori Tatsuo might have been a handsome man, for he possessed a strong jawline and well-defined cheekbones, worthy of admiration at any lordly court in Japan. His face, though, was a terrible sight to behold. Ravaged by the smallpox of his youth, the skin was horrifically scarred with lesions as if the flesh had rotted away. And, where his poxed eye had once been, was now a ragged black hole.

Dragon Eye glared at Jack with his remaining green eye.

'To look upon my face is to look upon death itself,' he snarled. 'Die, young samurai!'

Attacking Jack with insane ferocity, he slashed with Black Cloud, seeking to decapitate him. Jack brought his *katana* across to block the strike.

Their two swords clashed.

Black Cloud shattered the Shizu blade in two.

As Jack stared in shock at the useless stub of sword he now wielded, Dragon Eye kicked him in the chest.

Landing upon a blazing *tatami*, Jack screamed as his hand entered the flames, forcing him to drop his *wakizashi*. He rolled away from the fire, but was stopped by the edge of a blade.

'Kunitome swore on his life that this was the best sword he'd ever made,' said Dragon Eye, inspecting Black Cloud with grim satisfaction. 'He was right. Now kneel, *gaijin*.'

Faced with the *kissaki* of the *ninjatō*, Jack got to his knees.

He'd failed. Despite all his Two Heavens training, Dragon Eye had proved too powerful an adversary.

Dragon Eye raised Black Cloud aloft, pausing a moment to allow a malicious grin to spread across his ruined face.

'I'm going to take immense pleasure in beheading you.'

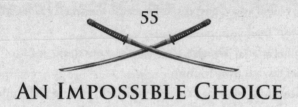

55

AN IMPOSSIBLE CHOICE

Recalling Masamoto's Two Heavens training – *obtain victory by any means and with any weapon* – Jack silently slipped the ninja *tantō* from the back of his *obi*.

'You once told me,' said Jack, as Dragon Eye relished his coming moment of triumph, '*Never hesitate.*'

Jack sliced the demon blade across the ninja's leg.

Crying out in shock and pain, Dragon Eye staggered back.

Jack jumped to his feet, knife in hand. But Dragon Eye recovered faster than he'd expected. Black Cloud flashed like a bolt of lightning towards his neck.

All of a sudden the wall to their right exploded as a cannon-ball ripped through the chamber. The hunting scene was obliterated and flaming chunks of wall flew through the air, knocking Jack and Dragon Eye off their feet.

Jack landed on the devastated balcony, pieces of gold leaf falling around him like snow. Completely disorientated, his head ringing, Jack stared down at the ground eight floors below. He could see Red Devils swarming like ants across the courtyard and Jack felt a sickening wave of vertigo pulling him over the edge.

He rolled away, gasping for breath, the deadly *tantō* still in his grasp.

To his left lay Dragon Eye, barely conscious.

He crawled over to him.

'Now *your* time has come,' said Jack, raising the knife to deliver the killing blow.

He would avenge his father's death.

End the nightmares.

Kill the ninja.

The Devil blade seemed to pulse in Jack's hand like a heartbeat.

The name etched into the steel glinted red in the fires, calling to him.

Kunitome. *Kill. Kill. Kill!*

Far in the recesses of his mind, Jack heard the warning of the tea-house owner.

Such a weapon hungers for blood, impels their owner to commit murder.

Jack felt its power.

The bloodlust was almost overwhelming.

Jack held the *tantō* high above his head.

But his hand was stayed by the memory of Sensei Yamada on the night Jack had chosen to follow the Way of the Warrior. His Zen master had explained the essence of *bushido* and what it meant to be samurai.

The Way of the Warrior is not to destroy and kill, but to foster life. To protect it.

Jack realized that, however much pain and suffering Dragon Eye had caused, he could not be ruled by vengeance.

He wasn't a murderer like this ninja.

Indeed, sparing the ninja's life might save another's. Akiko's brother, Kiyoshi.

'NO!' screamed a voice as he brought down the knife.

Throwing the Devil blade over the balcony and into the night, Jack turned to see Akiko at the top of the stairs.

'I thought you were going to kill him,' she said, picking her way through the burning ruins of the chamber.

Leaving the comatose Dragon Eye where he lay, Jack rushed to meet Akiko, happier than ever to see her. 'I almost did,' he replied, glad to be rid of the *tantō*'s murderous influence. 'But he's worth more to you alive than dead.'

'Are you hurt?' she said, her eyes widening at the appalling state he was in.

Jack examined himself. Black with ash, his armour charred, a split lip where the Red Devil had punched him, his left hand burnt and his hair a tangle of dust and debris, he must have looked half-dead.

'It's nothing serious,' he replied, as she inspected his hand.

'When we found Father Bobadillo dead in his study, I was worried for you – WATCH OUT!'

Akiko shoved Jack to the floor.

Suddenly she was yanked off her feet and disappeared over the balcony.

Jack heard her screaming as she fell.

'My patience is at its end, *gaijin*,' hissed Dragon Eye. 'Give me the *rutter* or I let her go.'

Dragon Eye was holding on to a *kaginawa*. The hooked climbing rope, having wrapped itself round Akiko's body, was now snapped taut under her weight.

Jack's eyes flicked to the ninja's sword lying in the rubble between them.

'Don't even *think* about it,' said Dragon Eye, letting the

rope slip a little through his fingers. 'She'll be dead before you take your first step.'

Jack had no choice. He opened his bag and reached for the logbook.

'I'd hurry if I were you,' said Dragon Eye, a sadistic smile curling the corner of his twisted mouth. 'I'm losing my grip.'

Handing him the *rutter*, Jack demanded, 'Now give me the rope.'

'Certainly,' said Dragon Eye, letting go.

'NO!' screamed Jack, diving for the *kaginawa* as it rapidly uncoiled, the rope fast disappearing over the edge.

His hands caught hold, but the line continued to run through his fingers. The rope cut deep into his palms. But he'd suffered worse on the rigging of the *Alexandria* and clamped down harder, biting his lip against the pain.

Drawing on all his reserves of strength, he slowed the *kaginawa* to a stop. He heard Akiko cry out. At least he knew she was still alive.

Bracing himself against a balcony post, Jack began to haul her back to safety. Hand over hand he pulled up the rope, but his arms began to tremble with the effort and he felt the rope once again slipping through his fingers.

'Your efforts are heroic, but ultimately wasted,' said Dragon Eye, standing over Jack, the *rutter* in one hand, Black Cloud in the other.

'You've got the *rutter*!' gasped Jack, struggling to keep hold. 'What *more* do you want?'

'Revenge,' he replied, raising the sword. 'Now, shall I kill you? Or shall I cut the rope first and watch you suffer?'

There was a thud as a wooden staff struck the back of the

ninja's head. Reeling from the blow, Dragon Eye dropped the logbook and crashed into the balcony rail before toppling over it head first, Black Cloud disappearing with him into the night.

A bandaged Yamato hobbled up to Jack. 'I think Sensei Kano would consider *that* a last resort situation!' he grinned, retrieving his *bō*.

He glanced round at the devastation. 'Where's Akiko?'

Jack nodded towards the edge, too shattered to speak, as he started pulling her up again.

Yamato looked nervously over the balcony. 'I can see her! She's almost at the –'

A gloved hand shot from the darkness below, grabbing Yamato by the throat. Yamato desperately held on to the rail as Dragon Eye tried to pull him over. Jack lashed out with a stomping kick to the ninja's chest. But he sacrificed a length of rope in the process and strained hard not to lose Akiko completely. The kick failed to dislodge Dragon Eye, but it was enough to force him to let go of Yamato.

Moving away from the balcony, Yamato grabbed his *bō* with both hands and prepared to fight back. Dragon Eye flipped over the rail to land beside him. Targeting Yamato's wounded side, Dragon Eye roundhouse-kicked him in the midriff. But Yamato whipped his *bō* across, blocking the attack. Unde-terred, the ninja retaliated with a spinning-hook kick to the head. Once again, Yamato drove his staff at Dragon Eye's leg and stopped it.

He then lashed out with the end of his *bō*, aiming for the ninja's head. But Dragon Eye ducked beneath it, flipping away as Yamato followed through with a rising strike.

Jack could only watch as Yamato fought bravely on, his

staff twirling through the air in a series of devastating attacks. But Dragon Eye constantly ducked and dived, waiting for Yamato to tire and make a fatal mistake.

Yamato drove the tip of his *bō* at Dragon Eye's chest. The ninja, evading it, grabbed the end and at the same time side-kicked Yamato in the ribs. Yamato crumpled under the blow, blood soaking through his bandages as his wound reopened.

But Yamato would not surrender.

He rolled the staff over, trapping Dragon Eye's wrist in a lock. Bellowing a war cry, he drove the ninja backwards on to the balcony. Dragon Eye crashed against the now weakened rail and it gave way.

Yamato began to pummel Dragon Eye with his staff, striking him both in the head and sides. The ninja tried to block the barrage of blows, but they rained down on him from every direction.

'*You killed my brother!*' yelled Yamato, his fury and pain fuelling his attack.

As Dragon Eye was driven off the balcony, he made a final lunge for Yamato, catching hold of the boy's ankle. Yamato was dragged over the edge with him. There was a sharp crack as the *bō* caught between the two broken rail posts. A split appeared in the shaft, fracturing like ice along the grain.

'JACK!' cried Yamato, desperately clinging on.

But Jack was faced with an impossible choice.

He could rescue Akiko. Or save Yamato.

But he couldn't do both.

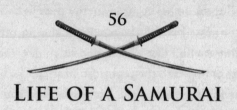

56

LIFE OF A SAMURAI

'Pull yourself up, Yamato!' urged Jack, frantically hauling in Akiko's rope.

'I can't,' he gasped, the staff splintering. 'Dragon Eye's climbing my leg!'

'Hold on, I'm coming,' said Jack, realizing if the ninja reached the balcony, no one would survive.

'No, save Akiko!' insisted Yamato, as a gloved hand clasped on to his *obi*.

'But you'll die –'

Yamato, his pale face suddenly resolute, nodded.

'But I'll die with honour.'

The staff cracked loudly on the verge of snapping.

'Tell my father I know what it means to be a Masamoto. It means sacrifice. For your lord, family and friends.'

Dragon Eye's malevolent green eye rose up behind Yamato's shoulder.

'You've been a loyal friend, Jack. *Sayonara*, my brother.'

With that Yamato let go, taking Dragon Eye with him into the darkness.

★　★　★

Jack pulled the sobbing Akiko into his arms.

She'd witnessed it all. Dragon Eye hanging off Yamato's leg, crawling up him like a black widow spider, then the two of them tumbling into the night.

'He died for *us*,' she croaked, her skin bruised and raw where the *kaginawa* had bitten in.

Jack could only hold her, his grief too great to speak, sorrow silencing his joy at her survival.

Masamoto had said the Way of the Warrior is found in death.

Jack now understood. Yamato was the very essence of *bushido*. His unwavering loyalty had saved both their lives. His decision to let go had taken great courage. And by fighting to the bitter end against the ninja who'd killed his brother, Yamato had died with honour.

He'd lived the life of a true samurai.

Among the ruins of the chamber, Jack spotted the torn hood of Dragon Eye's *shinobi shizoku* fluttering in the breeze.

He was surprised to feel nothing at the ninja's fate. No pleasure. No satisfaction. Not even a sense of relief. Just a numbness and the ever-aching emptiness in his heart at the loss of his father. Not even Dragon Eye's death could bring back his father. The wound in his heart hadn't been healed.

Jack realized it probably never would be.

Akiko, wiping her tears away, looked sadly up at Jack.

Jack knew she must be grieving, not only for Yamato, but for her brother too, her hope of discovering his whereabouts gone with Dragon Eye.

'Forever bound to one another,' she whispered, taking Jack's hand.

He was about to respond, when the keep was rocked by another cannonball blast to its walls. The chamber began to collapse around them burying his *wakizashi* and threatening to do the same to them.

'We have to go,' said Jack, pulling Akiko to her feet and putting the *rutter* back in his bag.

Jack may have found the logbook, but he'd lost almost everything else.

Masamoto's swords. His loyal friend, Yori. A samurai brother.

But he had *no* intention of losing Akiko.

His only thoughts were of escape.

57

SENSEI KYUZO

Jack and Akiko dashed down the stairs, past the corpses of Satoshi and his retainers. He snatched up two of the attendants' used *wakizashi* and gave one to Akiko, who'd lost her bow in the fall over the balcony.

On the sixth floor, they discovered *daimyo* Kamakura's ninja had breached the *donjon* itself. Four samurai lay dead at the foot of the stairs and further down the corridor ninja were slipping in and out of the shadows, silently assassinating the personal guard of the Council.

'*Daimyo* Takatomi!' said Akiko in alarm. 'He went to his room to check on Emi.'

She rushed off down a side corridor, Jack hot on her heels. Approaching the *shoji*, their worst fears were confirmed. His bodyguards were already dead, their throats slit.

Peeking through the open *shoji*, Jack glimpsed *daimyo* Takatomi preparing tea. It was a bizarre sight among such carnage. Beside him sat Emi, her bandaged leg outstretched, a cup in her hand. Surrounding them were four ninja. But they hadn't attacked. In fact, they appeared to be holding the two of them captive. It seemed *daimyo* Kamakura had alternative plans for his old friend.

Jack caught Emi's eye. But she seemed untroubled by their predicament. In fact, she gently shook her head when Jack made signs to rescue them. Smiling and raising her teacup, as if to her father, she mouthed '*Sayonara*, Jack.'

A samurai guard burst into their corridor pursued by two ninja. Hurrying the opposite way, Jack led Akiko back up to the sixth floor and down Father Bobadillo's private staircase.

They emerged from his study into chaos.

The Red Devils had broken through the last gate of the keep and Satoshi's forces were now fighting tooth and claw in a last-ditch attempt to hold the enemy back. A mean-looking Red Devil spotted Jack and Akiko and ran at them. Blood was splattered across his armour and, though smaller than most, he appeared as ferocious as a tiger.

They were about to flee, when the Red Devil ripped off his *menpō*.

It was Sensei Kyuzo.

Akiko breathed a sigh of relief and lowered her sword. But as their teacher got nearer, his expression hardened and he drew a *tantō* from his *obi*. Seeing the murderous intent in the man's eyes, Jack pulled Akiko away. Sensei Kyuzo was a traitor like Kazuki. He was on *daimyo* Kamakura's side and clearly determined to kill them.

'Jack-kun!' bellowed Sensei Kyuzo, throwing the blade at him.

Trapped between ninja, Red Devils and a crazed sensei, Jack had nowhere to run.

The knife shot past Jack's shoulder – making a fleshy thud

as it struck a ninja creeping up behind him. The assassin collapsed to the floor.

'Kamakura's ninja are everywhere,' scowled Sensei Kyuzo, pulling the *tantō* out and wiping its blade on the dead assassin. 'Now, where's Yamato-kun?'

Jack was too shocked to reply. He was also ashamed to have thought Sensei Kyuzo had betrayed them.

'He died,' said Akiko, her voice hoarse with emotion.

Sensei Kyuzo gave them a hard look before replacing his *menpō*. 'Masamoto-sama's waiting.'

He grabbed their swords and threw them away. Their *taijutsu* master didn't wait to explain. Seizing them both by the arms, he manhandled them down the corridor to a flight of stairs. Four Red Devils came charging up towards them. Jack and Akiko looked at one another in alarm.

'Keep going!' hissed Sensei Kyuzo, roughly pushing them on.

The enemy ignored the three of them as they thundered by.

Not stopping for anyone, Sensei Kyuzo escorted Jack and Akiko all the way to the ground floor entrance of the keep. They were almost through the gate, when a gold-horned Red Devil stepped into their path.

'Traitors for execution,' barked Sensei Kyuzo, by way of an explanation.

'It would be *my* pleasure,' said the Red Devil, reaching for his sword.

'No!' Sensei Kyuzo replied firmly.

The Red Devil glared at him. 'Are you challenging my authority?'

'These are for *daimyo* Kamakura,' explained Sensei Kyuzo, bowing his head respectfully. 'Our lord has requested any students of the *Niten Ichi Ryū*. He wishes to punish them personally. In particular, this *gaijin*.'

Sensei Kyuzo cruelly shook Jack by the arm.

The Red Devil backed down, glowering with disappointment.

'Very well,' he grumbled, waving them on.

Sensei Kyuzo didn't look back as he led them out of the gate.

Pockets of fighting were still going on throughout the courtyard. But he walked them straight across, taking a sharp right through the trees, past a dead samurai whose armour was missing.

'Masamoto-sama's holding off the enemy near the tea garden,' he whispered, taking off his helmet and *menpō*. 'By *daimyo* Takatomi's command, we're to get all surviving young samurai out of the castle –'

All of a sudden, he unsheathed his *tantō* and threw it into a tree. A second later, a ninja fell from the branches and crashed to the ground, dead.

'We don't have much time,' said Sensei Kyuzo, his eyes scanning the canopy. 'There's a hidden passage. Sensei Kano will guide you through –'

'Sensei Kano's alive!' exclaimed Jack.

'Yes,' snapped Sensei Kyuzo impatiently. 'The passage is how he got back in. We'll find you some weapons on the way.'

He stopped as six ninja dropped from the trees.

'Go!' ordered Sensei Kyuzo, pushing them in the direction of the garden.

'But it's suicide,' said Jack, realizing their sensei intended to fight the assassins single-handedly.

'Don't think I'm fighting for you, *gaijin*,' spat Sensei Kyuzo. 'My duty is to Masamoto-sama. Now I order you to go!'

Jack was astounded by his sensei's sacrifice. Bound by the code of *bushido*, Sensei Kyuzo didn't question his duty to protect the young samurai with his life, despite his personal hatred of Jack.

Risking a final glance back, Jack saw his *taijutsu* master encircled by the ninja, his fists raised, calmly beckoning them on.

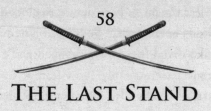

58

THE LAST STAND

Breaking from the treeline, Jack and Akiko ran through the tea garden and headed for the island. Masamoto and Sensei Hosokawa were protecting the bridge on the far side, their *katana* and *wakizashi* flashing like shooting stars in the night as they cut down any Red Devils who dared approach.

On the island, Sensei Yosa was launching arrow after arrow at enemy archers on the ramparts, while the surviving *Niten Ichi Ryū* students hurried across the bridge to the tea house. Inside, Sensei Kano was urging them through a concealed trapdoor into a secret passageway below.

Almost all the young samurai were safely through, as Jack and Akiko now crossed the bridge. Cho, the last of the students, was heading for the trapdoor, when a ninja on the battlements threw a fist-sized black ball into the tea house. It landed heavily and rolled to a stop next to Cho. The fuse on the round iron explosive crackled and burnt bright red in the darkness.

'Bomb!' she screamed, her eyes widening in panic.

Sensei Kano grabbed Cho and dragged her into the passage, slamming the trapdoor shut behind them.

A second later the incendiary device exploded and the tea house was blown apart. Sensei Yosa was blasted off her feet. Jack and Akiko dived for cover, as wood and rocks rained down on them.

Masamoto dashed over, his eyes fiery and alert. 'Are you hurt?'

'I don't think so,' said Jack, getting to his feet with Akiko.

'Where's Yamato-kun?' Masamoto demanded.

Unsure how to deliver the dreadful news, Jack bowed his head unable to look his guardian in the eye.

'No!' said Masamoto, his voice tight as a fist. He shook his head as if to deny the fact. 'Tell me it isn't true.'

'Yamato saved our lives,' explained Jack. 'He died with honour. Taking Dragon Eye with him.'

Masamoto's scars reddened with his distress and his swords trembled in his hands.

'Yamato asked me to tell you that he knew what it meant to be a Masamoto. Sacrifice.'

'NO, he doesn't!' snapped Masamoto. 'It should be *me* sacrificing myself for *his* life – and for yours – just as your father did.'

Tears welled in the samurai's eyes. 'My son . . . my Yamato . . . my brave boy. I'm so . . . proud of you.'

Masamoto took a deep breath and gave a great shuddering sigh.

'His sacrifice must *not* be in vain.'

Masamoto glanced at the devastated tea house, timbers and rock blocking any hope of escape. Sensei Yosa was back on her feet, but a shard of the iron had pierced her leg. As she hobbled over, Sensei Hosokawa came thundering across the opposite bridge, the Red Devils regrouping in preparation for another attack.

'Akiko,' said Masamoto, turning to her with urgency. 'Is there another way out?'

She shook her head.

'Think! You *must* have overheard something.'

'The ninja once mentioned a tunnel to a well,' she said, furrowing her brow as she tried to recall the details. 'But they decided against it.'

'The Gold Water Well,' blurted Jack, remembering Yori's story. 'Its tunnel leads to the inner moat.'

'That's it,' said Masamoto. 'To the well house!'

The three of them dashed across the bridge to the rear of the tea house, Sensei Yosa and Sensei Hosokawa following close behind as the Red Devils launched their attack. Arrows shot past as Jack, Akiko and Masamoto fled through the garden. There was a scream and Jack looked back to see Sensei Yosa falling to the ground, an arrow in her side, the Red Devils closing upon her fast.

'Keep going,' ordered Masamoto.

'But what about Sensei Yosa?' cried Akiko, making to turn back.

Masamoto grabbed Akiko. 'Sensei Hosokawa will look after her. He knows what he has to do.'

Sensei Hosokawa locked eyes with Masamoto and gave a respectful bow of the head.

Masamoto returned it with equal formality.

Jack realized more was said in that brief exchange than could ever be expressed in a lifetime of talking.

This was his swordmaster's final farewell.

Sensei Hosokawa ran back to save their wounded *kyujutsu* teacher. Roaring a battle cry, he drew his swords and cut a swathe though the Red Devils about to surround Sensei Yosa. His blades whirled though the air as he defeated each warrior in succession.

An arrow flew from the battlements, striking the swordmaster in the shoulder, but he kept his feet despite the agonizing blow. Another two Red Devils fell under his blade, before a second arrow knocked him to the ground.

But Sensei Hosokawa got back to his feet and drove his sword through the next samurai. More arrows flew at him, but he refused to go down.

Sensei Hosokawa defended Sensei Yosa to his last breath and held off the Red Devils long enough for Jack, Akiko and Masamoto to reach the well house.

'In another life, my friend, we will finish our duel,' said Masamoto under his breath. With that, he urged Jack and Akiko inside, intent on saving his last two young samurai.

'Are you certain?' said Masamoto, peering into the inky blackness of the well's depths.

'No,' replied Akiko. 'But there's only one way to find out.'

She climbed over the lip of the well and began to descend with the help of the bucket rope.

The shouts of the enemy could be heard getting closer.

'You're next, Jack-kun,' insisted Masamoto.

Jack clambered over and cautiously lowered himself until he found his first toeholds on the slippery rock wall.

'This way!' shouted a gruff voice in the darkness.

Masamoto drew his swords and strode to the entrance.

'You're not coming?' said Jack in disbelief.

'No, Jack-kun. This is where I make my last stand.'

'But we're going to escape!'

'Yes, *you* are,' replied Masamoto. 'But I must remain.'

'Why?' Jack protested, his emotions suddenly overwhelming him at the prospect of losing another father. His guardian had given him so much and asked for so little in return. How could he ever express the love and gratitude he owed this man? 'It's *me* that should stay! I should be sacrificing my life for yours.'

'Don't worry about me. I've lived my life. I don't fear death. But you *must* live to fight another day, young samurai.'

'But –'

'Jack-kun, I've taught you all you need to live this life,' he said, smiling with paternal pride. 'That's more than any teacher, or father, could hope for. You've come of age, my son.'

Masamoto bowed his head to Jack, then disappeared into the night.

'There he is!' came a shout from the garden.

The courtyard outside pounded with the sound of charging feet.

'Long live the *Niten Ichi Ryū*!'

Unable to let go of the well's lip, Jack had to know his guardian's fate.

He heard a clash of swords and a body crumple to the ground.

But the fighting didn't stop.

The steel of *katana* and *wakizashi* sang above the screams of dying samurai. Masamoto refused to yield.

'STOP!' shouted a brusque voice. 'Your men will all die before he's even shed his first drop of blood.'

Jack recognized the voice. It belonged to *daimyo* Kamakura.

'Leave Masamoto-sama to *me*!' he commanded. 'Complete your search. Kill all Christian traitors!'

59

THE WELL

Jack clambered down the well as fast as he could. But the walls were slick and hard to grip. Below him, Akiko had almost reached the bottom.

Hearing the shouts of the Red Devils echoing above, he hastened his pace. In the ever-deepening gloom, he misjudged a foothold and, despite his years on-board a ship, his fingers failed him on the slimy rock. Jack fell down the well, knocking Akiko off as he tumbled past.

They splashed into the water together and Jack found himself sinking to the bottom. He tried desperately to swim up, but his armour was weighing him down. Struggling against it, he kicked himself towards the surface. But it was no use. It was as if an anchor had been tied to his waist.

Then he felt Akiko's hands upon his armour, deftly undoing the ties. In moments he was free of the heavy breastplate. Shrugging off the rest, he burst to the surface and drew in a large gulp of air.

As he got his breath back, Jack looked around the solid walls of the well. 'Where's the tunnel?' he asked in a panic.

'Under the water,' Akiko replied, shedding her last bits of

armour. 'I almost swam down it looking for you. This must be why the ninja never used this route.'

'So how are we going to get out *now*?'

'We swim.'

'You're out of your mind!' exclaimed Jack, staring aghast at Akiko. 'We'll never make it.'

'It can't be *that* far,' she replied seriously. 'The well house is near the bailey wall. I've swum much further when I dived with the *ama*.'

'I'm no pearl diver, Akiko,' he reminded her, starting to shiver in the chill of the water. 'Drowning's a sailor's worst nightmare.'

'What other choice do we have?'

Jack didn't have an answer. Then he realized something was missing.

'The *rutter*!' he exclaimed. 'My pack! It came off with the armour.'

'Don't worry, I'll get it. It should be a lot easier to find than a pearl.'

Taking a deep breath, Akiko dived beneath the surface.

Jack was left alone in the darkness, only the sound of the water lapping against the walls and the echoing shouts of the samurai above to keep him company. It seemed an age before Akiko popped up again, the bag and *rutter* in her grasp.

'Got it!' she said, grinning. 'But surely it's ruined by the water?'

'No, the oilskin wrapping will protect it,' replied Jack, taking the bag from her.

Suddenly a large rock splashed down between them.

'There they are!'

Another stone bounced off the walls, nearly hitting Jack in the head.

Jack didn't need any further incentive. 'The tunnel it is,' he said, bracing himself for the long swim.

'Take lots of deep breaths and try to stay calm,' instructed Akiko.

More rocks crashed into the water as they dived beneath the surface, Akiko leading the way. The tunnel was pitch black and Jack couldn't see a thing as he felt his way along. It was a truly terrifying experience. He had no idea which way was up. And no indication of how far they still had to swim.

Jack kicked as hard as he could, struggling to keep up with Akiko. He lost contact with her and panic seized him. The fear of drowning wrapped its cold, clammy fingers round his throat. His heart beat harder in his ears and the pressure built up and up in his lungs. He already had a desperate urge to breathe out and suck down the icy water.

A light-headed calm began to wash over him. Realizing he wasn't going to reach the end of the tunnel, he stopped swimming. He let his breath bubble out. A heavy sleepiness seeped into his bones and he lost all care. Strangely, he almost welcomed the idea of drowning. At least he'd die with the *rutter*. He'd be able to return it to his father. He'd see his mother again.

Jack was peacefully resigned to his fate.

All of a sudden, he felt two warm lips press themselves against his. Air was forcibly blown into his mouth and his lungs welcomed the oxygen like a heady elixir. Jack felt his stupor lift and realized he'd been on the verge of blacking out, the reason why he'd so willingly given in to death. But he *wanted* to live.

The lips drew away and a hand clasped his wrist, pulling him along the tunnel.

Moments later, Jack and Akiko burst to the surface of the moat.

Jack gulped down air in heaving gasps.

'I thought I'd lost you,' said Akiko in a distraught whisper.

'You'll have to try . . . harder . . . than that,' replied Jack, hacking up water.

'Shh!' warned Akiko. 'The enemy are all around.'

Looking to the opposite bank, Jack saw hundreds of troops running through the darkness and became aware of countless dead bodies floating beside him and Akiko. They bobbed in the water like rotting logs. Stifling a cry as a headless corpse bumped into him, Jack followed Akiko who was swimming silently to the other side of the moat.

Slipping out of the water, they bolted for the cover of a nearby building. When the way was clear, they headed in the direction of the outer wall. Keeping to the shadows, they weaved their way carefully through the many courtyards and pathways of the outer bailey. Their going was painfully slow as they tried to avoid the enemy.

Suddenly a patrol of Red Devils came marching up the road towards them. Akiko pulled Jack into a nearby stable, startling its occupant. She gently stroked its mane, calming the horse as the samurai passed by.

'That was close,' Jack sighed with relief.

'It's getting too dangerous,' whispered Akiko. 'They're all on the lookout.'

She peered into the darkness of the street.

'I have an idea,' she said, slipping out of the stable and leaving Jack on his own.

Akiko returned, dragging the body of an enemy *ashigaru* killed during the attack on the castle.

'*Bakemono-jutsu*,' she said, in response to the shocked look on Jack's face. 'It's a ninja ghost technique.'

60

MOUNTAIN TO SEA

The quiet of dawn was more a deathy silence than a peaceful awakening. Osaka Castle had settled into an uneasy sleep during the night as the last few pockets of resistance were crushed and the fires brought under control. By the time the first rays of the morning sun broke through the smoke-laden sky, Kamakura's troops had fallen into a weary stupor. With the enemy now vanquished, many had dropped their guard and were dozing amid the ruined battlements while awaiting further orders. At the outer gateway, though, there was still a heavy presence of Red Devils.

'We'll never get past them,' hissed Jack, leading Akiko on the horse down the main road.

'It worked for Sensei Kyuzo,' Akiko whispered in reply. 'Just *don't* stop.'

Jack adjusted his helmet and *menpō*. 'It's too small. It keeps slipping off,' he complained.

He was dressed in the blue-and-yellow crested armour of the dead *ashigaru*. He also had the man's swords. Akiko had managed to find a bow and a quiver of arrows along with the armour of a high-ranking samurai loyal to *daimyo* Kamakura.

Her helmet, adorned with a half-moon emblem to show her status, fitted perfectly. But the foot soldier Akiko had found him evidently possessed a tiny head.

Despite his concerns their disguise wouldn't work, the dozing samurai barely raised their heads as they passed. Since there were other Kamakura troops entering and exiting the castle, the two of them didn't appear out of place. Besides, who would suspect such a bold and blatant escape as to walk straight out of the main gateway?

As they got closer, one of the Red Devils observed their approach. Akiko bowed her head in acknowledgement, low enough to show respect but curt enough to indicate her superior authority. The Red Devil dropped his eyes and humbly bowed back. He turned his gaze upon Jack instead. Jack bowed too, lower. The Red Devil returned the bow, his eyes narrowing slightly as he did.

Beyond the samurai, Jack could glimpse the Tenno-ji Plain. Freedom was but a gate, a portcullis and a drawbridge away. He was almost counting the steps they needed to make it across.

The Red Devil stared harder at Jack as they passed him.

'Blue eyes?' muttered the samurai to himself, as if he didn't quite believe what he'd seen.

Increasing his pace, Jack felt his helmet slip. A lock of blond hair became exposed. The Red Devil's eyes widened in disbelief. He seized Jack's helmet, pulling it off along with the *menpō*.

'*GAIJIN!*' he shouted, stunned at his discovery.

Without hesitation, Jack front-kicked the Red Devil in the chest.

Akiko helped Jack on to the back of her horse and spurred their steed on.

'Stop!' cried the Red Devil, recovering from the blow.

Samurai groggily got to their feet, bewildered by the sudden appearance of a blond samurai, but Jack and Akiko were already passing through the gateway.

'After them!' ordered the irate Red Devil.

Akiko glanced round at Jack. 'Take the reins!'

Grabbing her bow, she nocked an arrow, then turned and took aim at the roped locking mechanism of the portcullis. Calling upon all her *Yabusame* skill, she released the arrow.

It sliced into the rope. Under such tension, the line snapped and the portcullis came crashing down.

The pursuing samurai were stopped in their tracks and could only watch through the grille as their quarry galloped over the drawbridge to freedom.

Jack and Akiko rode out on to the plain, determined to get as much distance between themselves and the enemy. But they were halted by the horrifying sight before them.

As far as the eye could see lay thousands upon thousands of fallen samurai. Tenno-ji was literally carpeted with corpses. Behind them, the moat was so heaped with dead bodies that it could be crossed without getting wet. Crows picked at their remains and the moans of the few unfortunate souls who had yet to die filled the air.

Jack thought of poor little Yori, his body resting somewhere in this graveyard of Hell. How could so many lives be wasted for the will of one man, *daimyo* Kamakura?

'We should head east to my mother's in Toba,' Akiko

suggested, taking off her helmet and strapping her bow to the saddle pack. 'Kyoto won't be safe for us.'

Jack nodded, choking back the grief that threatened to overwhelm him. At least he and Akiko had escaped the carnage. There was some small joy in that thought. The future wasn't entirely bleak.

Akiko pulled on the reins, then jolted in her saddle before collapsing to the ground, an arrow in her side.

'AKIKO!' cried Jack, jumping down beside her.

The arrow had gone through her armour and blood was pouring from the wound. Jack ripped a flag from a dead samurai's *sashimono* and desperately tried to stem the bleeding. Akiko cried out as he applied the pressure.

NO! This can't be happening, he thought. *Not now. Not when we'd escaped.*

'That arrow was meant for *you*, *gaijin*!'

A chill ran through Jack's veins at hearing the samurai's voice.

Jack turned to see Kazuki striding towards them through the maze of dead samurai.

His old rival wore the armour of a Red Devil.

'*Kyujutsu* was never my strongest skill, but it's poetic justice for killing Moriko,' he said, discarding the bow in his hand. 'Now you will suffer, just as I promised you would.'

'It was *your* fire that killed Moriko!' shot back Jack.

'No. *You* are responsible,' said Kazuki. 'Japan was a pure land before your kind arrived uninvited. Now *gaijin* have rightly been banished.' He grinned sadistically. 'Or else they face punishment.'

399

Kazuki drew both his swords, a fresh smear of blood clearly visible upon the blade of the *katana*.

'As a loyal subject of *daimyo* Kamakura and the founder of the Scorpion Gang, it is my duty – and my pleasure – to sentence you to a dishonourable death, *gaijin*.'

Jack, leaving Akiko to hold her dressing, rose to unsheathe his swords as Kazuki bore down on him.

He'd barely got out his *wakizashi*, when Kazuki's *katana* cut across his chest. Jack deflected the blade and brought his own long sword round on Kazuki. But his rival blocked it with his *wakizashi* and drove Jack backwards. He kicked Jack in the gut, sending him tumbling over a dead body.

Scrambling to his feet, Jack hurriedly raised his guard as Kazuki charged again. Their swords clashed and Kazuki drove his *katana* along Jack's blade, pushing it aside and striking for his heart.

A perfect Flint-and-Spark strike.

A samurai not trained in the Two Heavens would have met his end. But Jack recognized the attack as it was happening and slipped to one side. Kazuki's *kissaki* glanced off his breast-plate.

Cursing Jack's skill, Kazuki retaliated with a blistering double sword strike. Jack countered with equal force using both his swords. Their opposing blades locked against one another.

For a moment they glared into each other's eyes, the battle now being fought in their minds. Jack saw the pitiless fury that was driving his rival. It reminded him of Dragon Eye's hateful vengeance. Kazuki would never quit until Jack was dead.

Then Kazuki surged forward, hitting Jack's *katana* and *wakizashi* simultaneously. Twice upon the back of the blades. Jack was disarmed of both swords in the blink of an eye.

A *double* Autumn Leaf strike.

Jack was left astounded by Kazuki's masterful sword skill.

'I said I'd always defeat you with the Two Heavens,' gloated Kazuki.

He kicked the defenceless Jack to the ground. Then, sheathing his *wakizashi*, he prepared to finish off Jack where he lay.

'You don't deserve a samurai's death,' said Kazuki. 'But you don't deserve to keep your head either.'

Jack glanced desperately in Akiko's direction. She was struggling to her feet.

'Wait! Answer me this one question,' demanded Jack, playing for time. 'Why do you hate me so much?'

'You're *gaijin*,' he spat. 'That's *more* than enough.'

'What wrong did I ever do to you?'

'My mother *died* because of a *gaijin* like you!' he replied, his sword trembling with rage in his hands.

'But what's that got to do with me?' asked Jack.

Kazuki snarled at Jack. 'Out of the goodness of her heart, she took in one of your foreign priests. All he gave her in return was his illness. Your kind are a pestilence in Japan. A disease that *must* be wiped out.'

'I'm sorry,' pleaded Jack. 'I've lost my mother to an illness too. I understand how you feel. Angry. Betrayed. Hurting.'

'That doesn't change a thing,' said Kazuki, his face a mask of hate. 'Now kneel!'

In her weakened state, Akiko had only just reached up to

the horse and was still struggling to string an arrow. As Jack got to his knees, his hand came across the broken pole of a *sashimono* flag. Grabbing its shaft, he swung it, moments before Kazuki cut down with his sword. Jack struck his rival hard across the jaw, knocking him to the ground.

Jumping to his feet, Jack kicked Kazuki's sword away. Raising the standard above his head, he aimed its pointed steel tip at the dazed Kazuki's chest.

'Mountain to sea,' said Jack, recalling the essence of the Two Heavens — *to obtain victory by any means and with any weapon*.

Kazuki's eyes widened in alarm as Jack drove the *sashimono* down into him. There was an almighty scream as the shaft went through his armour and buried itself deep into the earth below.

His scream faded into sobbing shock.

'I've seen enough death to last a lifetime,' said Jack, leaving Kazuki pinned to the ground by his armour.

Jack hurried over to Akiko. As he approached, she shakily raised her bow and released her arrow, before collapsing to the ground with the effort.

He heard an anguished cry behind. Kazuki, still pinned, dropped the *wakizashi* he'd been about to throw at Jack. He now stared in horror at the arrow that had gone straight through his sword hand.

Akiko was still breathing, but looked pale and weak.

'We have to go,' said Jack, spotting a troop of Red Devils leaving the castle.

Lifting Akiko up on to the horse, he gave a prayer of thanks to Takuan. He needed to ride fast. **Faster than he'd ever done** before.

As Jack galloped away with **the wounded Akiko between** his arms, he heard Kazuki **screaming.**

'I *will* have my revenge, *gaijin*!'

61

SHOGUN

Jack sat beneath the *sakura* tree, gazing at the ever changing colours of the sky as the sun set red over Toba. In the background he could hear the soothing trickle of the tiny waterfall feeding the stream that wound itself through the garden and into the lily pond. He was surrounded by glorious flowers and shrubs, all lovingly tended and pruned to perfection. The setting was so beautiful, so peaceful, that it was impossible to believe Japan was anywhere but Heaven.

For Jack, the garden was the healing his heart needed. He had to believe that there was still good in this world, still hope in his life. As Yori would say, a peace worth fighting for.

Above his head, buried in the trunk of the tree, was the arrow that had missed Dragon Eye three years before.

It's to remind us never to lower our guard.

Jack took hold of the shaft and pulled the arrow out.

The shadow that had hunted him was gone.

The assassin that had haunted Masamoto and his family would never return.

Jack snapped the arrow in half.

Such a haven as this was no place for a weapon of war.

An old man with a wispy grey beard tottered over the little bridge towards Jack, his walking stick tapping upon the wooden boards with each step.

'How is she?' asked Jack.

'Akiko's recovering well,' replied Sensei Yamada as his gaze fell upon the broken arrow in Jack's hands. 'It'll take more than a single arrow to defeat that young samurai.'

His Zen master looked older and more worn by life than Jack had ever remembered. The fighting had taken its toll on him and the horrors of battle seemed etched into every wrinkle on his face. Sensei Yamada groaned in pain as he eased himself on to the stone bench beside the stream.

'Are you all right?' Jack asked.

'The only thing that will kill me is time,' he replied wryly, rubbing his knees with a bony hand. 'The question is, are *you* all right?'

'I've survived,' said Jack, without enthusiasm. 'I know I should be thankful. So many of us didn't make it. But I feel . . . empty inside. Guilty too. Guilty that Yamato, my friends and our sensei died for my sake. And for what? *Daimyo* Kamakura won. What hope is there for a *gaijin* samurai in Japan now?'

'When it is dark enough, you can see the stars,' said Sensei Yamada, looking up into the sky.

Jack shook his head in bewilderment. Here he was admitting his pain, guilt and worry, while Sensei Yamada was stargazing.

'There's always hope, even in the worst of times,' said his Zen master, by way of explanation. 'Yes, we have lost some dear friends. But we must remember that many survived too, *because* of their sacrifice. Sensei Kano led our young samurai to safety. Sensei Yosa was spared by the enemy, out of respect to Sensei Hosokawa's loyalty and courage in defending her. I've had no word of Sensei Kyuzo's fate, but he's a wily old goat. I wouldn't be surprised if he's still alive.'

'But what about Masamoto-sama?' asked Jack, hoping against hope.

Sensei Yamado smiled. 'I have good news.'

His smile waned. 'And some bad.'

Jack held his breath.

'*Daimyo* Kamakura didn't kill Masamoto-sama. But neither did he allow him to commit *seppuku* and die with honour.'

'So where is he?'

'To subdue such a legendary swordsman was a matter of great pride for *daimyo* Kamakura. Masamoto-sama has been banished to a Buddhist temple at the peak of Mount Iawo. He's to remain there for the rest of his life.'

'Can't we rescue him?'

Sensei Yamada shook his head. 'I understand he has gone there of his own choosing. He was offered a post serving *daimyo* Kamakura himself, but he refused to take it in deference to those who died. Masamoto-sama would never serve such a tyrannical master.'

Jack was relieved and at the same time saddened by the news. His guardian was alive, but it seemed a shameful end for such a great and noble warrior.

'He'll be fine, Jack-kun,' said Sensei Yamada, seeing the disappointment in Jack's eyes. 'Masamoto-sama had often said he intended to live out his final years in contemplation. It's always been his intention to write down the techniques of the

Two Heavens for future generations of swordsmen. This may be just the opportunity he was looking for.'

Jack laughed. It was so like his Zen master to see the silver lining behind every cloud.

'Did you ever find out what happened to *daimyo* Takatomi and Emi?' he asked.

Sensei Yamado nodded. 'Emi-chan's safe. *Daimyo* Takatomi is a man of great wisdom. Ruthless as *daimyo* Kamakura is, he recognizes the need for such an astute lord as Takatomi in his new vision for Japan.'

'You mean *daimyo* Takatomi's serving him? He's betrayed us!' exclaimed Jack.

'Our lord is no traitor,' said Sensei Yamada sternly. 'We have lost the war. But *daimyo* Takatomi realizes he could do more good for Japan serving in the new government than he could as an exiled lord, or a dead one.'

'But surely Japan's heading for disaster? Shouldn't he be organizing a rebellion?'

Sensei Yamada thumped the ground with the tip of his staff. 'After the rain, the earth hardens.'

Jack stared blankly at his Zen master, wishing he wouldn't always speak in riddles.

'Japan is now stronger than it was before the war. Though many would prefer someone else, *daimyo* Kamakura is the one finally to unify our country. Nobunaga piled the rice, Hasegawa kneaded the dough, but *daimyo* Kamakura gets to eat the cake!'

Sensei Yamada initially laughed at his clever analogy. Then his expression became grave again.

'He has declared himself Shogun.'

'Shogun?'

'The supreme ruler of Japan. *Daimyo* Kamakura has seized *all* power, claiming a Minamoto bloodline. The Emperor becomes but a figurehead for our nation. Japan is now entirely in *daimyo* Kamakura's hands. Which brings us to your predicament, Jack-kun. Have you had any thoughts as to your future?'

'A few,' admitted Jack, 'but none of them offer me much hope.'

Sensei Yamada tutted and wagged his finger at Jack. 'I believe you were the one to tell Yori, "Where there are friends, there's hope." Very wise words.'

He glanced towards the house as a *shoji* slid open.

'Speaking of wise words, here comes a little wellspring of them.'

Yori bounded over the bridge, a tiny plant in his hand.

Jack was amazed at how resilient his friend had proven to be. The day after he and Akiko had fled the Tenno-ji Plain, they had come across Sensei Yamada and Yori retreating down the same road. It had been just in time too. With Akiko slipping in and out of consciousness, Jack was at a loss what to do. Sensei Yamada soon had the arrowhead out and treated Akiko's wound with herbs.

It was during their journey to Toba that Yori told Jack how he'd escaped. Almost trampled underfoot by the Red Devils, he'd thrown himself off the bridge and into the moat. He'd then had to hide beneath the bleeding and maimed corpses of fallen samurai to evade capture. At dusk he'd made his way all alone across the Tenno-ji Plain until Sensei Yamada found him.

Yori was so delighted to discover his friends alive that his faith in Buddha now burnt brighter than ever. Yet in spite of his outward appearance of joy, Jack knew Yori suffered terrible nightmares of his escape. He heard him crying out in anguish every night.

Yori, a brave smile on his face, approached Jack and presented him with the sapling.

'Uekiya says we can plant this *sakura* tree in honour of Yamato,' he announced. 'Akiko says you should choose the spot – as his brother.'

Choking back the tears, Jack took the little tree from him.

That evening, as the sun dropped below the horizon, Sensei Yamada, Yori, Akiko and Jack solemnly planted the *sakura* sapling.

As he tenderly filled in the hole, Jack said a prayer.

'With this tree, we plant not only a memory of our friend, but a hope for our future.'

62

THE WAY OF THE WARRIOR

Jack double-checked his pack.

The *rutter* was safely stashed at the bottom, protected within its oilskin. Next to it was his Daruma Doll, its single eye staring out at him in the flickering light of the oil lamp. Also in the bag were a gourd of water, two straw containers of cooked rice, a spare kimono and a string of coins. All these had generously been given to him by Akiko's mother, Hiroko, in addition to the blue kimono he now wore. Neither of the kimono had markings or *kamon*. Hiroko had chosen them specifically so that no one could identify him as a member of any family who may have fought against *daimyo* Kamakura.

The packing complete, Jack smiled to himself as he slipped Yori's good-luck gift of a paper *origami* crane into the wooden *inro* case secured to his *obi*. The little bird rested on top of Akiko's black pearl, guarding it as if the precious gem were an egg.

He was about to shoulder his bag when he remembered Sensei Yamada's offering. Picking up the *omamori*, he tied the Buddhist amulet to the strap of his pack. Contained within its tiny red silk bag was a small rectangular piece of wood upon which Sensei Yamada had inscribed a prayer. His Zen master had told him the *omamori* would grant him protection. He'd warned Jack never to open it, otherwise the amulet would lose its power. But by hanging the *omamori* on his bag, Sensei Yamada prayed the amulet would convince locals Jack was a Buddhist, and that as a result they would be more willing to help him on his journey.

Sliding open the *shoji* to his room, Jack stepped out into the garden.

It was dark, the sun still below the horizon. The air had that fresh cool taste as if the world had yet to breathe. Jack slipped on his sandals and walked across the wooden bridge in the direction of a small gate set in the garden wall. As he put his hand upon the latch, Jack was reminded of the very first time he'd run away from Hiroko's house. He'd got himself into serious trouble – though he had learnt a very useful Japanese word as a result. *Abunai*. Danger. Jack knew that by stepping through the gate this time he was guaranteed to encounter *abunai*.

'You're leaving without saying goodbye?' said a softly spoken voice.

Akiko stood behind him, her hands clasped in front of her *obi*, her hair neatly combed and in a single plait down her back. She gazed at Jack with sorrowful, almost accusative eyes.

It hurt him for her to look at him that way.

But he'd said his farewells to everyone the night before at dinner. Akiko had been strangely quiet, though Jack had put that down to her slow recovery. Hiroko had offered to let him stay in her house indefinitely. Sensei Yamada had suggested Jack join Yori and him when they departed for the Tendai Temple in Iga Ueno. But he'd made up his mind.

'It's time I went home,' said Jack, his heart breaking at having to say goodbye to Akiko.

'But your home can be *here*,' she said, a tremor entering her voice.

'I can't stay. If I do, I'll only endanger you and your mother further. Rumours are spreading fast that you're sheltering a *gaijin*. It won't be long before *daimyo* Kamakura sends a patrol looking for me.'

'But I can protect you –'

'No, let me protect *you*,' insisted Jack. 'It's time I took responsibility for my actions. My determination to safeguard the *rutter* at all costs put you, Yamato, Emi, Masamoto and *daimyo* Takatomi in great danger. I will *not* do such a thing again. Masamoto-sama said I've come of age. I must face these challenges on my own.'

Akiko looked deep into his eyes and saw the path he'd chosen to take. She bowed in acceptance of his decision. When her head rose again, the tearful expression on her face had been replaced by one of strength and determined independence, a look Jack knew so well.

'You cannot embark on a warrior pilgrimage without swords,' she said, glancing at his unarmed hip. 'Wait!'

As Akiko walked back to the house, Jack felt a wave of guilt at losing Masamoto's *daishō*. It had also been foolish of him not to retrieve the samurai swords after his fight with Kazuki. But Akiko had been his priority.

A *shoji* opened and Akiko returned, bearing a *katana* and *wakizashi*.

'Jack, you're samurai. You must carry a *daishō*,' she said, bowing and holding out the swords.

Jack was stunned by her gesture. In her hands, she held two magnificent swords with dark-red woven handles. They were sheathed within gleaming black *sayas* inlaid with mother of pearl.

'I can't take these,' protested Jack. 'They belonged to your father.'

'He'd want you to have them. I want you to have them. Our family would be honoured if these swords served you on your journey.'

She bowed lower, pushing the *sayas* into his hands.

Reluctantly, Jack accepted the *daishō*. He slipped the swords into his *obi*. Unable to resist, he then withdrew the *katana*. The sun, now peeking above the horizon, caught the steel of the blade. A single name glinted in the morning light.

Shizu.

The swords had a good soul.

Resheathing the *katana*, Jack realized he would be forever indebted to Akiko. He wanted to give something in return, however small the gesture. Jack reached into his pack and removed the Daruma Doll.

'This is all I have to offer you,' he said, handing Akiko the little round doll.

'But it contains your wish,' she protested.

'That's why I want you to look after it for me,' he replied, closing her hands round the doll. 'You're the only one I'd trust with my wish.'

Akiko stared back into his eyes, aware as much as Jack of their hands touching.

'It would be an honour,' she whispered. 'But how will I know if it's come true or not?'

'When I am home, you can fill in the other eye.'

Akiko nodded, understanding that she didn't need to ask how she would know when. She just would.

Both of them remained standing close to one another, hands wrapped round the little doll. Neither seemed to want to pull away. There was so much more that needed to be said. But Jack knew that words would never be enough. How could they express all the experiences they had shared? All the challenges they'd overcome together? All that they meant to each other.

Memories flashed through his mind.

A mysterious girl upon a headland in a blood-red kimono. Japanese lessons in the shade of a *sakura* tree. Stargazing in the Southern Zen Garden. Sharing the first sunrise of the year on Mount Hiei. Witnessing her conquer the waterfall in the Circle of Three. The gift of the black pearl. Her winning performance in *Yabusame*. Discovering she was a ninja. The moment beneath the water when she pressed her lips against his and breathed life into his lungs.

But the sea beckoned. Home and his sister were waiting for him.

If he did what his heart really desired, he knew he'd never leave.

'I have to go,' said Jack, pulling away. 'I must get a head start.'

'Yes,' Akiko replied, breathless and slightly flustered. 'You are right to travel by foot. A horse will draw too much attention. Don't trust *anyone* and keep off the main roads.'

Jack nodded, undid the gate latch and went through on to the dirt road that swept round the bowl of the valley, weaving though countless paddy fields before disappearing over the rise in the direction of Nagasaki.

Before he could change his mind, Jack turned to head down the road.

Then stopped.

'Yori would never forgive me if I didn't give you this,' he said, reaching for a slip of paper in the fold of his *obi*.

'What is it?' asked Akiko.

'A *haiku*.'

'You wrote one for *me*!' she said in astonishment.

'It's about sharing a moment . . . forever,' replied Jack.

Before Akiko could open the paper, he turned and walked away.

He'd reached the bend in the road before he heard her call his name.

Akiko stood, her back to the rising sun. She appeared to wipe a tear away, or perhaps she was waving goodbye. But her words floated to him clear and pure on the breeze.

'*Forever bound to one another.*'

She bowed to him.

Jack returned her bow.

When he looked up again, she was gone.

For several long moments, Jack gazed at the rising sun. He questioned if he'd made the right decision. But he knew in his heart of hearts that it was his only option. He couldn't stay. In Japan, the Shogun wanted him dead. In England, his little sister needed him.

Turning to face the long road ahead, Jack took his first step, alone, upon the Way of the Warrior . . . and home.

NOTES ON THE SOURCES

The following quotes are referenced within *Young Samurai: The Way of the Dragon* (with the page numbers in square brackets below) and their sources are acknowledged here:

1. [Page 86] 'He who works with his hands is a mere labourer. He who works with hands and head is a craftsman. But he who works with his hands, head and heart is an artist' by Louis Nizer (lawyer and author, 1902–94).
2. [Page 152] 'A nation that draws too broad a difference between its scholars and its warriors will have its thinking done by cowards, and its fighting done by fools' by Thucydides (Greek historian, 471 BC–400 BC).
3. [Page 405] 'When it is dark enough, you can see the stars' by Charles Austin Beard (American historian, 1874–1948).

The following *haiku* are referenced within *Young Samurai: The Way of the Dragon*. The page number are in square brackets below and the sources of the *haiku* are acknowledged here:

> Flying of cranes
> as high as the clouds —
> first sunrise.

[page 82] Source: *haiku* by Chiyo-ni, 1703–75

> Look! A butterfly
> has settled on the shoulder
> of the great Buddha.

[page 83] Source: *haiku* by Bashō, 1643–94

> Letting out a fart —
> it doesn't make you laugh
> when you live alone.

[page 87] Source: anon., seventeenth century

> Evening temple bell
> stopped in the sky
> by cherry blossoms.

[page 88] Source: *haiku* by Chiyo-ni, 1703–75

> Take a pair of wings
> from a dragonfly, you would
> make a pepper pod.

[page 169] Source: *haiku* by Kikaku, 1661–1707

> Add a pair of wings
> to a pepper pod, you would
> make a dragonfly.

[page 170] Source: *haiku* by Bashō, 1643–94

> *"She may have only one eye*
> *but it's a pretty one,"*
> *says the go-between.*

[page 203] Source: anon., *senryu*, seventeenth century

> *Temple bell*
> *a cloud of cherry blossom*
> *Heaven? Hanami?*

[page 204] Source: *haiku* after Bashō, 1643–94

> *I want to kill him,*
> *I don't want to kill him . . .*
> *Catching the thief*
> *and seeing his face,*
> *it was my brother!*

[page 207–8] Source: after *maekuzuke*, seventeenth century

Haiku Notes

The principles of *haiku* have been described in this book from the point of view of writing this style of poetry in English, so may not necessarily be accurate for true *haiku* written in *kanji* script.

Haiku is actually a late nineteenth-century term introduced by Masaoka Shiki (1867–1902) for the stand-alone *hokku* (the opening stanza of a *renga* or *renku* poem), but the term is generally applied retrospectively to all hokku, irrespective of when they were written. For purposes of clarity and to aid understanding for today's modern reader, the term *haiku* has been used throughout this book.

For further information on writing *haiku*, please refer to *The Haiku Handbook* by William J. Higginson (New York: Kodansha, 1989).

JAPANESE GLOSSARY

Bushido

Bushido, meaning the 'Way of the Warrior', is a Japanese code of conduct similar to the concept of chivalry. Samurai warriors were meant to adhere to the seven moral principles in their martial arts training and in their day-to-day lives.

Virtue 1: *Gi* – Rectitude
Gi is the ability to make the right decision with moral confidence and to be fair and equal towards all people no matter what colour, race, gender or age.

Virtue 2: *Yu* – Courage
Yu is the ability to handle any situation with valour and confidence.

仁

Virtue 3: *Jin* – Benevolence

Jin is a combination of compassion and generosity. This virtue works together with *Gi* and discourages samurai from using their skills arrogantly or for domination.

礼

Virtue 4: *Rei* – Respect

Rei is a matter of courtesy and proper behaviour towards others. This virtue means to have respect for all.

真

Virtue 5: *Makoto* – Honesty

Makota is about being honest to oneself as much as to others. It means acting in ways that are morally right and always doing things to the best of your ability.

名誉

Virtue 6: *Meiyo* – Honour

Meiyo is sought with a positive attitude in mind, but will only follow with correct behaviour. Success is an honourable goal to strive for.

忠義

Virtue 7: *Chungi* – Loyalty

Chungi is the foundation of all the virtues; without dedication and loyalty to the task at hand and to one another, one cannot hope to achieve the desired outcome.

A Short Guide to Pronouncing Japanese Words

Vowels are pronounced in the following way:
'a' as the 'a' in 'at'
'e' as the 'e' in 'bet'
'i' as the 'i' in 'police
'o' as the 'o' in 'dot'
'u' as the 'u' in 'put'
'ai' as in 'eye'
'ii' as in 'week'
'ō' as in 'go'
'ū' as in 'blue'

Consonants are pronounced in the same way as English:
'g' is hard as in 'get'
'j' is soft as in 'jelly'
'ch' as in 'church'
'z' as in 'zoo'
'ts' as in 'itself'

Each syllable is pronounced separately:
A-ki-ko
Ya-ma-to
Ma-sa-mo-to
Ka-zu-ki

abunai	danger
ama	Japanese pearl divers
arquebus	heavy portable gun, an early rifle
ashigaru	foot soldiers, low-ranking samurai

bakemono-jutsu	ninja 'ghost' technique
bō	wooden fighting staff
bōjutsu	the Art of the Bō
bokken	wooden sword
bonsai	small tree
bushido	the Way of the Warrior – the samurai code
Butokuden	Hall of the Virtues of War
Butsuden	Buddha Hall
cha-no-yu	literally 'tea meeting'
chiburi	to flick blood from the blade
chi sao	sticky hands (or 'sticking hands')
Chō-no-ma	Hall of Butterflies
daimyo	feudal lord
daishō	the pair of swords, *wakizashi* and *katana*, that are the traditional weapons of the samurai
Dim Mak	Death Touch
dojo	training hall
dokujutsu	the Art of Poison
fudoshin	literally 'immovable heart', a spirit of unshakable calm
futon	Japanese bed: flat mattress placed directly on *tatami* flooring, and folded away during the day
Gambatte	Try your best!
Ganjitsu	Japanese New Year festival
gaijin	foreigner, outsider (derogatory term)
geisha	traditional Japanese female entertainers

gi	training uniform
hai	yes
haiku	Japanese short poem
hajime	begin
hakama	traditional Japanese clothing
hamon	the visual pattern on a sword as a result of tempering the blade
Hanami	spring flower-viewing party
hara	'centre of being'
hashi	chopsticks
hatsuhinode	the first sunrise of the year
hibachi	small charcoal brazier made of clay
Hō-oh-no-ma	the Hall of the Hawk
inro	a little case for holding small objects
in-yo	an old samurai prayer meaning darkness and light
irezumi	a form of tattooing
itadakimasu	let's eat
jindou	arrows with their blunt wooden ball heads
kachi	victory
kachi guri	dried chestnuts
kagemusha	a Shadow Warrior
kaginawa	three-pronged grappling hook on a rope
kakegoe	a shout
kakurenbo	Japanese version of hide-and-seek
kama	a sickle-shaped weapon
kami	spirits within objects in the Shinto faith

kamon	family crest
Kampai	a toast, as in 'Cheers!'
Kanabō	large oak club encased in iron or with studs
kanji	the Chinese characters used in the Japanese writing system
kappan	a blood stamp sealing a document to make it binding
kata	a prescribed series of moves in martial arts
katana	long sword
kenjutsu	the Art of the Sword
ki	energy flow or life force (Chinese: *chi* or *qi*)
kiai	literally 'concentrated spirit' – used in martial arts as a shout for focusing energy when executing a technique
kiaijutsu	the Art of the Kiai
kimono	traditional Japanese clothing
kisha	Japanese archery on horseback
kissaki	tip of sword
koan	a Buddhist question designed to stimulate intuition
kukai	a *haiku* contest
kuki-nage	'air' throw
kunoichi	female ninja
Kyosha	a competition archery contest on horseback
kyujutsu	the Art of the Bow
ma-ai	the distance between two opponents

maekuzuke	a short two-line verse to which a *haiku*-style verse is added
manriki–gusari	a chain weapon with two steel weights on the ends
menpō	protective metal mask covering part or all of face
menuki	decorative metal grip under wrapping of sword handle
metsuke	technique of 'looking at a faraway mountain'
mokuso	meditation
momiji gari	maple-leaf viewing
mon	family crest
Mugan Ryū	the 'School of "No Eyes"'
musha shugyo	warrior pilgrimage
naginata	a long pole weapon with a curved blade on the end
ninja	Japanese assassin
ninjatō	ninja sword
ninjutsu	the Art of Stealth
Niten Ichi Ryū	the 'One School of Two Heavens'
niwa	garden
nobori	a long rectangular banner used to identify units within an army
nodaichi	a very large two-handed sword
obi	belt
ofuro	bath
o–goshi	hip throw
omamori	a Buddhist amulet to grant protection

origami	the art of folding paper
rei	call to bow
ri	traditional Japanese unit of distance, approx 2.44 miles
ronin	masterless samurai
Ryōanji	the Temple of the Peaceful Dragon
sado	the Way of Tea
saké	rice wine
sakura	cherry-blossom tree
samurai	Japanese warrior
sashimono	small rectangular personal banner worn by samurai in battle
sasori	scorpion
satori	enlightenment
saya	scabbard
sayonara	goodbye
seiza	sit/kneel
sencha	green tea
senryu	Japanese verse
sensei	teacher
seoi nage	shoulder throw
seppuku	ritual suicide
shaku	a traditional unit of length, approx 30 cm
shinobi shozoku	the clothing of a ninja
Shishi-no-ma	the Hall of Lions
Shodo	the Way of Writing, Japanese calligraphy
shoji	Japanese sliding door
shuko	climbing claws

shuriken	metal throwing stars
sohei	warrior monks
surujin	rope weapon with weights on each end
sushi	raw fish on rice
taijutsu	the Art of the Body (hand-to-hand combat)
Taka-no-ma	the Hall of the Hawk
tanka	a short Japanese poem of around thirty-one syllables
tantō	knife
Taryu-Jiai	inter-school martial arts competition
tatami	floor matting
tessen	a Japanese fan with a reinforced metal spine
tetsu-bishi	small sharp iron spike
tomoe nage	stomach throw
tonfa	hand-held baton weapon
torii	Japanese gateway
uke	training partner who attacks
wakizashi	side-arm short sword
washi	Japanese paper
Yabusame	ritual mounted archery
yakatori	grilled chicken on a stick
yame	stop!
zabuton	cushion
zanshin	a state of total awareness; lit. 'remaining mind'
zazen	meditation
zori	straw sandals

Japanese names usually consist of a family name (surname) followed by a given name, unlike in the Western world where the given name comes before the surname. In feudal Japan, names reflected a person's social status and spiritual beliefs. Also, when addressing someone, *san* is added to that person's surname (or given names in less formal situations) as a sign of courtesy, in the same way that we use Mr or Mrs in English, and for higher-status people *sama* is used. In Japan, *sensei* is usually added after a person's name if they are a teacher, although in the Young Samurai books a traditional English order has been retained. Boys and girls are usually addressed using *kun* and *chan*, respectively.

ACKNOWLEDGEMENTS

This third book in the *Young Samurai* series is about loyalty and sacrifice. The following people have demonstrated immense loyalty to me and many have sacrificed their time, energy and reputation for *Young Samurai*. I would like to thank them all for their hard work and dedication: Charlie Viney, my agent, for being a valiant and courageous warrior always protecting my rights and fighting for my career; Shannon Park, the commanding *daimyo* of editing at Puffin, for the respect she's shown the heart of the story and her sword-like cuts; Wendy Tse for her hawk-like eyes in checking the proof; Louise Heskett, Adele Minchin, Tania Vian-Smith and all the Puffin team for running a successful campaign on the publishing battlefield; Francesca Dow; Pippa Le Quesne; Tessa Girvan at ILA for conquering the world with *Young Samurai*; Akemi Solloway Sensei for her continued support of the *series* (readers, please visit: *www.solloway.org*); Trevor, Paul and Jenny of Authors Abroad for their tireless efforts in managing all my event bookings; David Ansell Sensei of the Shin Ichi Do dojo, an inspiring teacher and a swordsman of great insight and knowledge; Ian, Nikki and Steffi Chapman for spreading the word; Matt, for his enthusiasm; my mum for still being my number-one fan!; my dad, who is the steel behind the sword; and my wife, Sarah, for whom I know this journey has been hard, but the rewards will be lifelong.

Lastly, I offer a bow of respect to all the librarians and teachers who have supported the series (whether you are ninja or samurai!) and all the Young Samurai readers out there — thank you for your loyalty to Jack, Akiko and Yamato. Please keep reading and sending me emails and letters. It makes all the hard work worthwhile. *Arigatō gozaimasu*.

JACK FLETCHER'S ADVENTURE
IS NOW A RACE FOR SURVIVAL

YOUNG SAMURAI
THE RING OF EARTH

COMING
AUGUST 2010

JOIN THE
DOJO
AND
STEEL YOUR NERVES
FOR
GRIPPING **PODCASTS** AND **VIDEOS**
UNBELIEVABLE **MARTIAL ARTS** MOVES
EXTREME **COMPETITIONS**
SWORD-FIGHTING ACTION

AND
MUCH MORE
TO GET YOUR
ADRENALIN
RACING!

Let your training commence at
YOUNGSAMURAI.COM

WANT MORE ACTION? MORE ADVENTURE? MORE ADRENALIN?

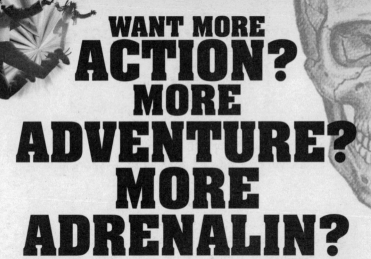

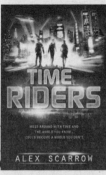

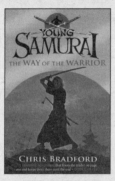

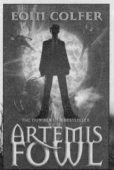

GET INTO PUFFIN'S ADVENTURE BOOKS FOR BOYS

ung Bond, *SilverFin* and Eye Logo are registered trademarks of Danjaq, LLC.
ed under licence by Ian Fleming Publications Limited

It all started with a Scarecrow

Puffin is well over sixty years old.
Sounds ancient, doesn't it? But Puffin has never been
so lively. We're always on the lookout for the next big
idea, which is how it began all those years ago.

Penguin Books was a big idea from the mind of
a man called Allen Lane, who in 1935 invented
the quality paperback and changed the world.
**And from great Penguins, great Puffins grew,
changing the face of children's books forever.**

The first four Puffin Picture Books were hatched in 1940 and the
first Puffin story book featured a man with broomstick arms called
Worzel Gummidge. In 1967 Kaye Webb, Puffin Editor, started the
Puffin Club, promising to **'make children into readers'**.
She kept that promise and over 200,000 children became
devoted Puffineers through their quarterly instalments of
Puffin Post, which is now back for a new generation.

Many years from now, we hope you'll look back and
remember Puffin with a smile. **No matter what your age
or what you're into, there's a Puffin for everyone.**
The possibilities are endless, but one thing is for sure:
whether it's a picture book or a paperback, a sticker book
or a hardback, **if it's got that little Puffin
on it – it's bound to be good.**